FIND ME

CAROL O'CONNELL

WHEELER PUBLISHING
An imprint of Thomson Gale, a part of The Thomson Corporation

THOMSON
GALE™

Detroit • New York • San Francisco • New Haven, Conn. • Waterville, Maine • London

Wheeler Publishing Large Print Hardcover.

The text of this Large Print edition is unabridged.

Other aspects of the book may vary from the original edition.

Set in 16 pt. Plantin.

LIBRARY OF CONGRESS CATALOGING-IN-PUBLICATION DATA

O'Connell, Carol, 1947–
    Find me / by Carol O'Connell.
      p. cm.

    ISBN-13: 978-1-59722-496-3 (hardcover : alk. paper)

    ISBN-10: 1-59722-496-0 (hardcover : alk. paper)

    1. Mallory, Kathleen (Fictitious character) — Fiction. 2. Police — New York (State) — New York — Fiction. 3. Policewomen — Fiction. 4. Large type books. I. Title.

PS3565.C497F56 2007

813'.54—dc22

2007000448

_LP_
O'Connell

Published in 2007 by arrangement with G. P. Putnam's Sons, a member of Penguin Group (USA) Inc.

Printed in the United States of America on permanent paper

10 9 8 7 6 5 4 3 2 1

This book is dedicated to historic Route 66, the Mother Road. One day it will be gone. Pieces of it disappear as I write this line. And when it dies, among its remains will be many tales and memories of the way it never was, and that's all right; for the road is mythic, and myths tend to swell with each telling. From now on, let every tall story begin: *Once upon a time, there was a great highway . . .*

And that part is true.

ACKNOWLEDGMENTS

Only two people in this book are not fictional characters: Fran Houser of the Mid-Point Café in Adrian, Texas; and Joe Villanueva of Clines Corners in New Mexico. Many thanks to them for the history lessons and for permission to write them into my landscape. And thanks to my researcher Dianne Burke for technical support above and beyond. I thank Richard Hughes for musical suggestions and psychological insights. My brother, Bruce, contributed expertise on camping gear that you won't find in stores. He also gave me the recipe for cowboy coffee, and helpful hints like how to set fire to wet logs and kindling. Ed Herland was my Porsche consultant, and I could not have done this without him. Thanks, Ed. And thanks to Patrick O'Connell (no relation) for help with roll bars and airbags, and to his father, Dan, for a guided tour of the Seligman loop of Route

66 in Arizona. And a long overdue thanks to the work of E. W. Mitchell, *The Aetiology of Serial Murder: Towards an Integrated Model* (1997), University of Cambridge, UK. This academic may not appreciate finding his name in a work of fiction, but his excellent paper helped to shape my view of profiling as the dog-and-pony show of junk science. As for The Who, the Eagles, Rolling Stones, Beatles, Bob Dylan, Black Sabbath, Led Zeppelin and all the other musicians, singers and writers of melodies and lyrics — thanks for the road songs.

PROLOGUE

The haunt of Grand Central Station was a small girl with matted hair and dirty clothes. She appeared only in the commuter hours, morning and evening, when the child believed that she could go invisibly among the throng of travelers in crisscrossing foot traffic, as if that incredible face could go anywhere without attracting stares. Concessionaires reached for their phones to call the number on a policeman's card and say, "She's back."

The girl always stood beneath the great arch, pinning her hopes on a tip from a panhandler: Everyone in the world would pass by — so said the smelly old bum — if she could only wait long enough. The child patiently stared into a thousand faces, waiting for a man she had never met. She was certain to know him by his eyes, the same rare color as her own, and he would recognize young Kathy's face as a small copy of her mother's. Her father would be so happy to see her; this belief was unshakable, for she was a little zealot in the faith of the bastard child.

He never came. Months passed by. She never learned.

Toward the close of this day, the child had a tired, hungry look about her. Hands clenched into fists, she raged against the panhandler, whose fairy tale had trapped her here in the long wait.

At the top of rush hour, she spotted a familiar face, but it was the wrong one. The fat detective was seen in thin slices between the bodies of travelers. Though he was on the far side of the mezzanine, Kathy fancied that she could hear him huffing and wheezing as he ran toward her. And she waited.

Crouching.

One second, two seconds, three.

When he came within grabbing distance, the game was on — all that passed for sport in the life of a homeless child. She ran for the grand staircase, shooting past him and making the fat man spin. Sneakers streaking, slapping stone, the little blond bullet in blue jeans gained the stairs, feet flying, only alighting on every third step.

Laughing, *laughing.*

At the top of the stairs, she turned around

to see that the chase was done — and so early this time. Her pursuer had reached the bottom step and could not climb another. The fat man was in some pain and out of breath. One hand went to his chest, as if he could stop a heart attack that way.

The little girl mouthed the words, *Die, old man.*

They locked eyes. His were pleading, hers were hard. And she gave him her famous *Gotcha* smile.

One day, she would become his prisoner — but not today — and Louis Markowitz would become her foster father. Years later and long after they had learned to care for one another, each time Kathy Mallory gave him this smile, he would check his back pocket to see if his wallet was still there.

1

It appeared that the woman had died by her own hand in this Upper West Side apartment. It was less apparent that anyone had ever lived here.

The decor was a cold scheme of sharp corners, hard edges of glass and steel, with extremes of black leather and bare white walls. Though fully furnished, a feeling of emptiness prevailed. And the place had been recently abandoned — unless one counted the stranger, the corpse left behind in Kathy Mallory's front room.

The gunshot to the victim's heart made more sense after reading the handwritten words on a slip of paper that might pass for a suicide note: *Love is the death of me.*

"If only she'd signed the damn thing," said Dr. Slope.

The homicide detective nodded.

Chief Medical Examiner Edward Slope had turned out for this special occasion of sudden death at a cop's address. If not for a personal interest in this case, the remains might have been shipped to his morgue on a city bus for all the doctor cared. A house call was not in his job description; that was the province of an on-call pathologist. But tonight Dr. Slope had departed from protocol and forgotten his socks. And, though he wore a pajama top beneath his suit jacket, he was still the best-dressed man in the room.

By contrast, Detective Sergeant Riker had the rumpled look of one who had gone to bed in his street clothes. His face also had a slept-in effect, creased with the imprint of a wadded cocktail napkin. Drunk or sober, Riker's nature was easygoing, but his hooded eyes gave him a constant air of suspicion. He could not help it, and he could not hide it tonight of all nights. The gunshot victim had been found in his partner's apartment, and now he awaited the official coin toss of homicide or suicide.

Because the medical examiner had known Detective Mallory in her puppy days, the older man was only mildly suspicious, only a *little* sarcastic when he asked, "And where *is* Kathy tonight?"

Riker shrugged this off, as if to say that he had no idea. Untrue. By a trace of credit card activity, he knew that Mallory had filled her gas tank in the states of Pennsylvania and Ohio. But he thought it best not to mention that his young partner was on the run, for the medical examiner had not yet signed off on a cause of death. The detective looked down at the dead woman, who appeared close to his own age of fifty-five. If not for the bullet hole in her chest, Savannah Sirus might be asleep. She looked all in, exhausted by her life.

Dr. Slope knelt beside the corpse. "Well, I can understand why you'd want a second opinion."

Oh, yeah.

And Detective Riker needed this opinion from someone in the tiny circle of people who cared for his young partner, though she did nothing to encourage affection. Both men had been forbidden to call her Kathy since her graduation from the police academy; she so liked that frosty distance of her surname. However, the doctor had found it hard to break a habit formed in Mallory's childhood, and so she was always Kathy to him. Brave man, he even called her that to her face.

Dr. Slope continued his observation of the corpse. "Not the usual way for a woman to kill herself." Women were self-poisoners and wrist slashers. Their suicides were rarely this violent.

"Yeah," said Riker, "but it happens. This looks like a typical vanity shot to me." That much was true; men were inclined to eat their guns, but the ladies seldom messed up their faces with headshots. He saw the victim's chest wound as a small blessing in Mallory's favor.

"There's no evidence that Miss Sirus held the muzzle to her breast," said Dr. Slope, raising a point on the debit side.

Absent was the gunshot residue, the smoky halo of point-blank range, and this had set off alarm bells for the first officer on the scene tonight. This wound more closely resembled a conversational range between victim and shooter. Rather than turn another cop over to Internal Affairs, the West Side detectives had shifted this case to the SoHo precinct where Mallory worked. Riker could still make a case for suicide if the woman had held the gun at arm's length — and that scenario spoke to fear of firearms. Perhaps Savannah Sirus had even closed her eyes before she pulled the trigger.

Or maybe Mallory shot her.

After the corpse had been rolled over, Dr. Slope pulled a thermometer from his black bag. Riker, who was old school, averted his eyes as the medical examiner raised the lady's skirt and pulled her panties down. The detective moved to the couch to wait out the findings on the body temperature.

Alongside the Polaroid shots he had taken of the dead body, a cheap handbag lay on the coffee table. It could only belong to the victim, for this was nothing that his partner would carry. Mallory's taste ran upscale; even her blue jeans were tailored, and squad-room gossip had it that the studs were made of gold. Perverse kid, she did what she could to encourage rumors of illegal income. This was her idea of fun: Catch me if you can.

Hard rain beat down upon a speeding car that was far from home. The small vehicle was deceptive in its styling, for this was not a model rumored to eat up the road, and yet it raced at wild, outlaw speeds.

Nearing the western edge of rainy Ohio, a lone patrolman blinked rapidly to clear his tired eyes, but there was no mistake of blurred vision. His engine was powerful, pushed to the limit on this wet road — and the Volkswagen Beetle was leaving him behind.

Impossible.

His aunt owned a car like that one, and he knew the speedometer topped out at one-forty, though he considered that to be a private joke on the part of the manufacturer.

The convertible's color scheme of silver body and black ragtop was all too popular, and the lack of a visible license plate further complicated the problem of identification. It was a short chase — hardly a race. The other car was not speeding up, nor was there any wobble or weave to signify that the driver was in any way alarmed by the spinning red light and screaming siren. The trooper's radar clocked the VW's cruising speed at a constant one hundred and eighty miles an hour.

Oh, fool!

What was he thinking?

He banged his fist on the dashboard. Damned equipment never worked right. Rain-slick road or dry pavement, that speed was an impossible feat for the little ragtop Beetle. But then, he had never met the driver.

And he never would.

At the subtle rise of road ahead, he could swear that he saw bright streaks of forked lightning under the wheels; the silver car had left the ground, flying, hydroplaning on the water.

The silver Beetle was out of sight when the trooper's car stopped well short of the Ohio state line — beaten. There would be no official report on his patrol car being humiliated by, of all things, a Volkswagen, for this would be akin to reporting alien spacecraft. And so, without a single speeding ticket, the small convertible would run Route 80 through the neighboring state of Indiana and across another border into Illinois. The driver's destination was the Chicago intersection of Adams Street and Michigan Avenue — the eye of the storm.

Behind his back, Riker heard the snap of the doctor's latex gloves. The examination of Savannah Sirus was done.

The detective asked, oh so casually, as if there were not a great deal riding on the answer, "So, Doc, what do I put down for the time of death?"

"Your absolute faith in rectal thermometers is really quite touching," said Dr. Slope. "I don't suppose a helpful neighbor heard the shot while he was looking at his wristwatch?"

The detective looked over one shoulder and smiled at the older man to say, *No such luck.* The neighbors had heard gunfire from this apartment on other occasions, and,

19

good New Yorkers all, they had become selectively deaf to what Mallory was doing in here.

"Well, then," said Slope, "just put down today's date for now. Rigor mortis is always a crapshoot, and I've got too many variables to call a time of death with body temperature. An open window on a cold night — dried sweat stains on her blouse. For all I know, the woman had a raging fever when she died." He circled the couch to stand before the detective. "So what've *you* got?"

Riker upended Savannah Sirus's purse and spilled her possessions across the glass coffee table. There were two clusters of house keys. He recognized a silver fob on the set that would open the door to this apartment. "Looks like the lady was Mallory's houseguest." Another item from the purse was an airplane ticket from Chicago to New York. "I don't think we'll be calling out a crime-scene unit for this one." He was testing the waters here, for the medical examiner had not yet made a pronouncement of suicide.

Dr. Slope turned to face his minions waiting in the hallway beyond the open door. He gave them a curt nod. The two men wheeled a gurney through the front door and set to work on bagging the victim's remains. When they had cleared the room, taking the late Savannah Sirus with them, the doctor sank down on the couch beside Riker. "You think your partner knows what happened here tonight?"

Rather than lie, the detective said, "Well, you tell me." One wave of his right hand included the leftovers of a take-out dinner, an empty wineglass and a saucer full of cigarette butts. "Point taken?"

The medical examiner nodded. He was well acquainted with Mallory's freakish neatness. The young homicide detective would never tolerate anything out of place in her apartment. She was the sort who compulsively straightened picture frames in other people's houses. Ergo, the mess had been made after her departure. Dr. Slope stared at the open window. "Riker? You think our victim originally planned to jump, then changed her mind and shot herself?"

"No." But he understood the other man's reasoning. This was the only open window on a cold spring night — and the screen had been raised. "The woman knew Mallory reasonably well. She's been staying here awhile." He held up the plane ticket. "Got here three weeks ago." He neglected to mention that the ticket was round-trip; Mallory's houseguest had no thoughts of dying in New York City — not on the day she arrived. "Savannah Sirus didn't know much about guns and ammo. Now this is the way I see it. She thought the bullet might pass through her body and mess up a wall. Well, Mallory wouldn't like that, would she?"

The doctor was shaking his head in accord with this.

Riker continued. "So the lady opened that window and pulled up the screen. That's where she was standing when she shot herself. And it looks like she's been planning this for a while." He pointed to the gun on the floor. "You didn't think that was Mallory's, did you?"

"No," said Dr. Slope. "I suppose not."

The weapon on the carpet was a lightweight twenty-two, a lady's gun. Kathy Mallory was no lady; she carried a cannon, a Smith & Wesson .357 with a bigger kick and better stopping, maiming, killing power.

However, Riker knew that this gun on the floor did indeed belong to Mallory. She collected all kinds of firearms, none of them registered, and a twenty-two had its uses. But the matter of gun ownership might interfere with the doctor's finding of suicide.

The detective slouched deep into the leather upholstery as he pondered where his partner was headed tonight. And why had she stopped showing up for work?

Mallory, what did you do with the time — all your crazy days of downtime?

Rising from the black leather couch, Riker forced a yawn, as if he needed to affect a blasé attitude about violent death. In fact, he had been born to it, a true son of New York City. "I'm gonna check out the other rooms."

He passed by the guestroom and caught a glimpse of rumpled sheets and a blanket used by Savannah Sirus. Farther down the hall, another open door gave him a view of Mallory's own bedding. There was not a single wrinkle in the coverlet, as if no one had ever slept there, and this lent credence to a theory that she never slept at all. Mallory the Machine — that was what other cops called her.

Dr. Slope was walking behind him when Riker entered another room of spotless good order, his partner's den, where no dust mote dared to land. Some people had dogs; Mallory kept computers, and they sat in a neat row of three, their Cyclops eyes facing the door, waiting for her to come home. Even her technical manuals were well trained, each one perched on the precise edge of a bookcase shelf. The back wall was lined with cork, and Riker was puzzled by what, at first glance, had passed for striped wallpaper. He turned his head to catch a look of profound shock in the medical examiner's eyes.

And that was puzzling, too.

From ceiling molding to baseboards, the cork wall was covered with sheets of paper, each one filled with columns of figures. Riker guessed that these were telephone numbers by the separation spaces for area codes and prefixes. Though reading glasses rested in his breast pocket, he preferred to squint, and now he noticed that six of the numerals were arranged in random combinations, but one floating sequence of four remained the same in every line. So this was what she had been doing with the time since he had seen her last — apart from pumping bullets into her walls, blowing bugs to kingdom come when she could not find a fly swatter. And, given a dead body in the front room, he suspected her of worse behavior. Thankfully, in some saner moment, she had patched the holes in the plaster.

Dr. Slope's eyes widened as he took in the thousands of numbers on the cork wall. Most had red lines drawn though them, all perfectly straight in machine precision. He moved closer to the wall, the better to see with his bifocals. "Oh, my God. She *drew* these lines with a pen."

And those hand-drawn lines could only indicate telephone numbers that had not panned out for Mallory. The detective gripped the medical examiner's arm and turned the man around to face him. "You've seen this before." Riker's tone slipped into interrogation mode, close to accusation when he said, "You know what this is all about. Talk to me."

The doctor nodded, taking no offense. "I saw something like this a long time ago — on the Markowitzes' old phone bills. As I recall, it was that first month after Kathy came to live with them. So she was eleven years old."

Yeah, sure she was.

Louis Markowitz, a late great cop, and his wife, Helen, had raised the girl as their own, but never would Kathy Mallory talk to them about her origins. She would not even give up her right age. At first, she had insisted on being twelve, and Lou had bargained her down by one year, though she might have been a ten-year-old or a child as young as nine.

The medical examiner stood at the center of the room, wiping the lenses of his bifocals with a handkerchief. "Lou showed me his phone bills, line after line of long-distance calls. Kathy made all of them." The doctor stepped closer to the wall, nodding now. "Yes, it's the same. You see, when she was a child, she was prone to nightmares. Lou thought the bad dreams might've triggered those calls. Sometimes he'd come downstairs late at night and catch her with the telephone. She made hundreds of these calls that first month. This wall reminds me of the Markowitzes' phone bill. In every long-distance telephone number, four of the numerals were always the same, and the others just seemed random. She wouldn't tell Lou anything helpful, but he worked out a good theory. He knew there was someone out there, some connection to her early life, but she could only remember part of a telephone number."

"So Lou called the numbers on his phone bill."

"Yes, all of them. And he found an odd pattern. Every call was made at some obscene hour of the night — so even the men were inclined to remember them. You see, when a man answered, she hung up the phone. But if a woman answered, she'd always say, 'It's Kathy, I'm lost.' "

"That must've driven the women *nuts.*"

"Yes, it touched their soft spots and their

panic buttons." The doctor turned his face to a high-rise window on the dark city. "According to Lou, all of the women begged Kathy to tell them who she was — and where could they *find* her? But the child would just hang up on them. Lou figured that Kathy never got the response she wanted. Those women didn't know who she was. So then she'd dial the next combination of numbers . . . trying to make a connection to someone who would recognize her."

"A woman." Riker fished through his pockets and pulled out a piece of paper given to him by the first officer on the scene. This note listed sketchy vitals of victim identification, including a home telephone for the late Savannah Sirus. One sequence of four numbers matched the ones repeated on the cork wall. "I guess the kid finally made her connection."

Eight hundred miles *away,* another corpse had been found.

Hours after the windows of shops and offices had gone dark, an umbrella was snatched up by a gust of wet wind. Tearing and twirling, it scraped across the broad steps of the Chicago Art Institute. The only watchers were two great cats, standing lions made of bronze and blind to this broken trophy from the battle against horizontal rain. Their green patinas were altered by strikes of lightning and red flashes from the spinning lights of police vehicles. Cars and vans converged upon the construction site at the other side of Michigan Avenue.

Two homicide detectives were soaked through and through. They surrendered, throwing up their hands and then jamming them into coat pockets. Grim and helpless, they watched the heavy rain come down on their forensic evidence and carry it away. There it went, the body fluids, stray hairs and fibers, all flowing off down the gutter. The corpse, washed clean, could tell them nothing beyond the cause of death — extreme cruelty. There had never been a crime scene quite like this one in the history of Chicago, Illinois, nothing as shocking, nothing as sad.

The religious detective made the sign of the cross. The other one closed his eyes.

The dead man at their feet was pointing the way down Adams Street, also known as Route 66, a road of many names. Steinbeck had called it a road of flight.

The rainstorm had abated, but the owner of the gas station had no plans to do any legal business at this late hour. Locked behind the wide door of his garage was one happy crew of gambling men in the grand slam of Chicago crap games, high rollers only, beer flowing, dice clicking and folding money slapping the cement floor.

Big night.

A fortune was in play amid clouds of cigar smoke when the silver Volkswagen's driver, a young woman in need of gas, had come softly rapping at the door. Then she had banged on the heavy metal with both fists and kicked it a few times, calling way too much attention to the activities inside.

Stop the music!

And now he stood beside her under the bright lights of his gas pumps — and the crap game was forgotten.

"Is that what I think it is?" The man gazed lovingly upon her engine. "Oh, yeah." He looked up at her with a wide grin. "Girl, what have you done? A Porsche engine in a Volkswagen Beetle?"

And *how* had she done it?

Even if he had been cold sober, this problem would have given him a headache. It *might* have been possible to modify an old model with the engine in the rear, but this was a new Beetle with front-wheel drive, built for an engine under the *hood*. No kind of engine could work in the damned *trunk.* Yet there it was.

He had to take three paces back to see how this magic trick was worked. The silhouette of the car was slightly off, elongated, but otherwise a perfect job. The girl had fabricated a VW Beetle onto the frame of the 911 Twin Turbo Porsche. Before he stopped to wonder why she had done such a thing, he had already moved onto the problem of the convertible's roof: that tall hump of a ragtop might cut into the speed, but not by much. Now how would this counterfeit body affect the Porsche's performance in cornering?

"Hey, girl? If you take a curve too fast, you'll roll this car. You know that, right?"

Advice and gasoline were all that he could offer her. The tall blonde preferred to work alone. By frosty glare and body language, she had taught him to keep his greasy hands off her immaculate engine.

"You got some time?" he asked. "I could put on a roll bar."

The girl shook her head. No sale. She selected another tool from a lambskin pouch and worked on the mounting for a wiring harness. He guessed there was a rattle that annoyed her. Well, it would never do that again. She made it that tight, stopping just shy of stripping the screws.

"Girl, you might wanna think it over. If not here, then get one somewhere else." It was not her money he was after; he only wanted to keep this youngster alive. She appeared to be the same age as his daughter. "With a roll bar, you'd have a sporting chance to keep your pretty head if the car flips over."

And damned pretty she was with her milk-white skin, her cat's eyes and those long red fingernails. The girl in blue jeans was downright unnatural; real people never looked this good at close quarters. And so he guessed that she was not from his part of the world, but maybe from someplace straight up and past the moon. Hers were the greenest eyes he had ever seen. If asked, he would not be able to describe their color in terms of any living thing. Electric, he would say. Yeah, electric green and bright like a dashboard light — not human at all. And he thought she might be carrying a gun beneath her denim jacket.

His gaze had lingered too long on that bulge where a shoulder holster might be. Her eyes were on him now — so cold. She seemed to be looking at him across the distance between a cat and a mouse, and he knew that this was all the warning she would ever give him. He had his choice of two creatures: she might be a stone killer, and then there was his own kind. "You're a cop, right?" The mechanic pulled a wallet from the pocket of his grimy coveralls, and he did this slowly — no sudden movements to set her off. He showed her the identification of a retired Chicago police officer.

Her face gave away nothing, not her next move, not anything at all. The situation could go sour at any second. If he had guessed wrong about her, he might wind up dead. In his sixtieth year, his reflexes had slowed. But now, as a sign of trust, she ignored him once more and turned back to a perusal of her engine.

He began to breathe again.

"I was on the job for thirty-five years." He faced the bastardized car, and his voice carried just a touch of sarcasm. "Thought I'd seen it all." Still attempting to make conversation, he said, "Nobody would ever figure you for a Volkswagen type. Not your style, girl. It's a car for people my age, burnout rock 'n' rollers who could never get past the sixties. Hell, this should've been *my* car."

The Porsche beneath the fabricated shell explained a lot — on several levels. A true VW convertible was a happy little vehicle with no hard edges, a cartoon of a car, and it got a smile everywhere it went. He took the young blonde's measure again. Cosmetics — like this fake car body hiding a killer engine — could never so neatly disguise what *she* was. And if this young cop believed that she could work undercover, she was dead wrong. But he could think of no other explanation for a civil servant driving a car with an engine that cost the moon and the stars — unless the kid was on the take.

Her dashboard had another modification that never came from the factory. He made another foray to draw her out for a chance at shoptalk, and he meant *cop* shop. "Well, I see you got a police scanner. Me, too."

She studied her engine, forgetting that he was alive.

He tried again. "So . . . you know about the murder on Adams Street? . . . No?" Did silence mean *no* on her planet? "They found the body right in the middle of the damn road. Real piece of work. I heard the cop chatter on my scanner."

"Adams Street and what?"

"Michigan Avenue." He had a gut feeling that she already knew this address, but his guts had lied to him before, and a bullet fired when his back was turned had forced his retirement from the Chicago Police Department.

Casually, as if opining on the weather, the girl said, "And there's something peculiar about the crime scene."

Though she had not asked him a question, he gave her a slow nod to say, *Oh, yeah. This one's about as peculiar as it ever gets.* Aloud, he said, "I bet that's why you turned out tonight. Am I right?" Force of habit from the old days, he would always chain one odd thing to another: this strange young cop, this bastard car with New York plates — this crime. "A serial killer, right? And New York's got an interest?"

Oh, how he missed the Job, his old religion of Copland.

The young blonde packed up her tool pouch and closed the trunk on that fabulous engine. The fuel pump rang its bell — the gas tank was full. She handed him a platinum credit card, giving him second thoughts about her status as underpaid police. She waited in silence for her receipt.

As she was driving off, though he had no hope of being heard, he called after her, "You be careful out there!" His eyes traveled over darkened buildings where innocent people lay sleeping. "And the rest of you stay the hell out of her way," he warned them in a lower voice — in case he had guessed wrong about — what was she called? He looked down at his copy of the credit card receipt and read only one name. "Well, don't that beat all?"

American Express called her Mallory — just Mallory.

The mighty storm front, born in Chicago, had cut a sodden path eastward. It rained on a patch of the Jersey coast, and then, like many another tourist, it crossed the George Washington Bridge, entered New York City — and died.

Only a few drops of water pocked the windshield of a sleek black sedan as it rolled out of a SoHo garage and pulled into the narrow street. The traffic was light, and this was good, because Detective Riker was hardly paying attention to the other cars as he rode out of town.

After another check on Mallory's credit cards, he learned that she had bought a late supper in South Bend, Indiana, still traveling west on Route 80, and leaving no doubt that Chicago was her destination. With one cell-phone call, Riker had activated the anti-theft device installed in her car. And then he had bartered his soul to the Favor Bank to bury the paperwork on her surveillance. Given her straight route and likely point of entry, her LoJack's signal had been picked up when the car crossed the state line into Illinois. And, thanks to a police car tracker in Chicago, Riker knew that his partner had stopped awhile at a gas station in that city — even before she had used her credit card to pay for fuel. Though she was definitely in flight, he took some comfort in her use of traceable credit instead of cash. And she knowingly drove a car equipped with a Lo-Jack device; this alone spoke well for the theory that she had not murdered Savannah Sirus.

And everything else argued against innocence.

In his request for covert assistance from Chicago, the New York detective had traded on his reputation as a shabby dresser with a low bank balance; these hallmarks of a dead-honest cop made his badge shine in the dark. There were even rookies in the state of Illinois who had heard of Riker. And he planned to destroy the best part of himself — for Mallory's sake.

He stopped for a red light and closed his eyes. More frightening than the corpse in Mallory's front room was the wall of telephone numbers in her den. If nightmares had triggered her childhood calls, then Riker had to wonder, *Kid, what are your dreams like now?*

2

The car's engine idled as Mallory pulled an old letter from her knapsack. This was only ceremony; the pale blue ink was illegible by street lamp, and the discolored paper was falling apart at the folds. The opening line, committed to memory, began with green lions — and there they were. The matched pair of statues flanked the broad steps of the Chicago Art Institute on Michigan Avenue, and they pointed the way down Adams Street.

The letter went on to say, *"There are travelers who recognize this intersection of commerce, high art and green lions as the beginning of the Mother Road, though its original starting point was elsewhere. Historically a shifting highway, now it's vanishing, reduced to a patchwork of interrupted pavement scattered through pieces of eight states, all that remains of a fine romance with the journey and the automobile."*

Mallory was not of the romantic ilk. The night was wet and cold, and she was disinclined to wax poetic on the American car culture.

Angling the headlights into the darkness, she anticipated police barricades, but these wooden sawhorses bore the name of a Chicago contractor. The crime scene was also a construction site, and this was one detail that was not picked up on her police scanner. Her high beams lit up concrete segments of an old water main stacked beside earthmoving equipment. The late hour and a recent storm had cleared the area of witnesses — not that she cared. She killed the engine and left her car to push one of the barricades aside, and now she walked toward the bulky machines that might hide more obstructions.

Wooden planks spanned two of the traffic lanes, and an orange sign warned her of a large hole beneath the boards, but all that interested Mallory was a large sheet of crumpled blue plastic nudged along the ground by the wind. At each corner was a crude tear where the thin material had been ripped loose. She easily found the former moorings of this blown-down canopy; bits of twine were still tied around lampposts and signs. Other tarps, ones belonging to the contractor, were made of light canvas and sized to cover machines. The workmen would have needed no cover; they would have been gone before the late-night storm; road repair might carry on in the dark — but not in the rain. And this flimsy material was not something a crime-scene van would carry. It could serve only one purpose here — a temporary cover for a killer who wanted privacy from high windows and the elevated train that bisected Adams Street.

The killer had brought his own tarp to the party, and the crime-scene unit had failed to confiscate this evidence, mistaking it for construction debris.

Mallory pulled out her cell phone and placed a call to Chicago PD. Failing to introduce herself, she demanded the name of the detective who owned this homicide.

"Kronewald?"

Well, that conjured up a familiar face. She could picture the old man turning a heart-attack shade of red when he found out what the CSU team had left behind — *plastic,* a fingerprint technician's wet dream. "Tell him to collect the blue tarp. It belongs to the killer, not the contractor."

The desk sergeant was asking for her name as she ended the call. Mallory, never inclined to waste words, was busy just now.

One more barricade to go, and then she must be on her way before Detective Kronewald turned up to find a New York cop on his little patch of turf.

The blue plastic was on the move again, and she picked up a piece of concrete to weight it down. The wind had carried it clear of the rough boards that patched the contractor's hole, exposing yellow tape laid down to form the crude shape of a body. And this made her smile.

The Chalk Fairy strikes again.

In large towns and small ones, every now and then, a homicide team would arrive at an otherwise pristine crime scene and find this outline drawn with a piece of chalk or a crayon borrowed from a child. An angry detective would then demand to know which helpful idiot had committed this travesty, and guilty-looking young rookies in uniform would flap their arms and fly away with cries of "I dunno. It wasn't me."

It was a mystery.

Tonight, Mallory could easily guess the Chalk Fairy's secret identity. It could only be the scared young cop who had given up bizarre details of this crime on an all-too-public radio frequency — forgetting everything taught at the police academy. Oddly enough, he had remembered the one thing he should never do, a lesson of television cop shows. Instead of chalk for his outline of the victim, he had used crime-scene tape, tacking it down with construction-site nails when it failed to adhere to wet wood. Thus, with every good intention, the first officer on the scene tonight had butchered the evidence of other nails used by a murderer to stake a human body to the ground.

Damn Chalk Fairy.

She should be leaving now. How much time had passed since her chat with the desk sergeant? A police cruiser could only be minutes away. Instead of heading for her car, she pulled out a penlight and trained the beam on the killer's nail holes, the ones inside the taped outline, where the victim's wrists and ankles had been pinned to the boards. Scattered at her feet were nails like the ones used to make the wooden road patch. When she dropped one into a hole, it was smaller than the opening.

This killer's murder kit had duplicated on-site materials. Obviously a cautious one, maybe he was also a long-range planner, and his plan may have begun long before the city of Chicago decided to rip up this street. So he had packed his kit with bulky plastic, heavy iron nails — and bones. How that rookie cop must have freaked to see those bones attached to a fleshed-out corpse. Now the Chicago police had a double homicide, old bones and fresh kill, one corpse short of the body count needed to call this a serial killing, yet Mallory had no trouble making that call with only the evidence laid out before her.

She stared at the taped outline that described the arrangement of the body, an invitation to a game. It had been laid out for show with one arm extended, pointing down the road to say *Follow me.*

A distant siren was screaming, coming closer, and yet Mallory did not hurry. When one more barricade was moved aside, she did not run — she walked back to the car, settled in behind the wheel and started up the engine. The siren was louder, almost on top of her. After depressing a button on the face of the speedometer, her trip monitor went down to zeros.

And now it begins.

The car rolled through the crime scene, continuing west on Adams Street for a while, nearly overshooting the turn for Ogden — just as the letter had predicted. Mallory carried no maps, only a route created from words that were written before she was born. Dropping down, southwest through Cicero, she searched for the next landmark. According to the letter, *"He's so big, you can't possibly miss him."* Yet there was no sign of a giant folk hero holding a large hotdog. She retraced long stretches of Ogden on both sides of Lombard Avenue, where the fiberglass statue belonged, but it was no longer there. Her next landmark was far from here, way past the town of Joliet. She was heading toward a road by that same name and an open field that might not be there anymore. An entire town could have grown over the old baseball diamond since the first yellowed letter was written to say, *"One day you won't be able to get here from there. This is a time as much as a place, and even the stars might be gone. That's the problem with progress. Can't see stars by city lights."*

Detective Sergeant Riker had Route 80 to himself except for the occasional freight truck. His destination was a gas station where Mallory had last used her credit card, and it was eight hundred miles from New York City.

Flying to Chicago had never been an option, though, given his errand tonight, he might have overcome a secret terror of airplanes. However, at the other end of a flight or a train ride, the car rental companies always expected to see a valid driver's license before they would trust him with their wheels. Years back, when faced with a choice between drinking and driving, he had given up his car. In Riker's experience, rehabilitation just sucked all the charm out of life.

Tonight he drove a Mercedes-Benz that belonged to a friend, and the gas pedal was pressed close to the floor. This fine automobile was not a model that he could ever afford or even live up to — not him — not a cop in a cut-rate suit, a man in need of a new pair of shoes and a shave. If he got stopped for speeding on this road, Riker knew he could only be taken for a car thief. A portable siren sat on the dashboard, and he was prepared to slap it on the roof at the first sight of a police cruiser, but since he had not yet crossed New Jersey, he could reasonably expect all the state troopers to be napping at the side of the road until sunrise.

If he could only keep up this speed — nearly three times the legal limit — he would close the gap between himself and Mallory by late morning. Considering the car that his partner was driving these days, that was doable. He knew her lead in miles, but what about time? The doorman at Mallory's New York apartment building had not been able to recall the exact hour of her departure, but then Frank was paid lavish tips to be vague about her comings and goings.

The detective wore a headset for his cell phone, needing one hand free to slug back coffee from a thermos while he spoke to another cop in Illinois. His caller was the man who had picked up the LoJack signal from Mallory's car and tracked her from the safe distance of a mile or two. No shadowing detail could be more covert, less detectable — just the thing for tailing the ultimate paranoid personality. The Illinois cop was bringing Riker up to date on Mallory's travels.

"She drove through a crime scene?"

"Yeah, but no harm done," said the man in Chicago. "The rain did a lot of damage before she got there. Homicide didn't even bother to post a guard."

Riker was well into Pennsylvania when he heard about the number of times that Mallory had traveled up and down the same stretch of road in Cicero.

And the cop from Chicago said, "I think she's lost."

Riker thought so, too, but not in terms of geography. And now he listened to a litany of all the places she had gone since then. Oh, Joliet — now that was a memory and a half. He had not traveled south of Chicago since his teenage days, yet these towns that Mallory had passed through or close to, from Elwood to Gardner, had names that sounded like old friends. And then her car stopped on a desolate section of road.

The Illinois cop also pulled over to maintain a covert distance. "I know that area. No houses out there. Couple of abandoned buildings. You want me to get closer — see if she ditched the vehicle?"

"No, don't go *near* that car."

The cop at the other end of this call had no solid information on the driver, and he could only guess that the vehicle was stolen. By agreement prior to a hefty withdrawal from the Favor Bank, Riker had not provided any details. But now the man in Illinois asked the first hard question, and his voice was more formal — more guarded. "Are you making a request to treat her as armed and dangerous?"

Riker hesitated. Well, Mallory never went anywhere without her gun, and every wounded creature was dangerous; this one was damaged to the core. But all he said to the Illinois tracker was, "Don't get within a mile of that car."

"Okay, I'll just sit tight till she moves."

"Thanks." When Riker terminated the call, dawn was still a long ways off, but he was already framing excuses for not showing up on the job come morning. He was uncomfortable with the idea of lying to his lieutenant or any other cop.

And yet it had been easy to spin a yarn for a civilian who was also a friend, a fake excuse to explain an urgent need for this fabulous automobile. Maybe that falsehood had come so easily because he had always known that Charles Butler would not believe him. And, since Charles was the quintessential gentleman, it was not in his nature to nail a friend for a lie badly told. The man had only intuited one truth from Riker, and that was desperation — a good enough reason to hand over the keys of a wildly expensive vehicle to a driver who was unlicensed and uninsured, a man whose hands shook when he needed a drink. Riker needed one now. He gripped the wheel tightly.

How would he explain his absence to Lieutenant Coffey? Well, he could say it was a family thing and say no more than that.

Was Mallory family?

He had loved her late foster father, a hell of a cop. He loved the old man still, and he missed him every day. And Riker had always been a strong presence during Mallory's kiddy days, back when he was still allowed to call her Kathy. He had watched her grow up, though, strictly speaking, the little sociopath had never been a *real* child. He thought of her as the daughter he never had — thank God — the one that people feared in the lottery of parenthood, and, in all the world, there was no one he loved better.

So, yeah, it was a family thing.

His thoughts turned back to his partner's choice for a new car. The old one had never suited her, but Mallory had held the blind-sided idea that a plain tan sedan would help her to blend in with her surroundings, as if she ever could. No, that kid belonged in a hot Corvette, a car with some flash; that would have been his choice for her. But she had bought a Volkswagen — still traveling in disguise.

With no signpost, only a triple-story bird-house as a marker, Mallory turned onto an unpaved side road and parked her car. Here, where the old ballfield should be, was a slab of concrete and a warehouse with a large for-sale sign painted on its doors. By flash-light, she opened the letter and reread a pas-sage describing paths worn into the grass to form the baseball diamond and the night games played by the glow of lanterns and the headlights of cars: *"We knocked those balls right up to the stars. The crowd roared, the bleachers shook, and the beer flowed all night long."*

All gone now. This was the right place, but the wrong time.

The rains had never reached this part of the state, and the air smelled like dust. Following the next instruction, she lowered the convertible's black ragtop. A cold wind ruffled the paper in her hand as she scanned a disappointing sky with only a few bright points of light, far short of the *"million, billion"* that the letter had promised. The landmarks were gone, and even the stars had been lost, not that she would miss them. Before tonight, she had never thought to look for them.

All of the letters contained notations on the weather, the route and musical directions for the road. At the Bronx autobody shop, where her car's modifications had been done, the owner had suggested a CD player, but the letter writer had only played cassettes, and that was all Mallory had wanted. However, the world had changed, and the cassette she loaded now was wired up to an iPod that could sing ten thousand songs. The tune she selected followed the letter's suggestion for music that worked well with starlight.

Her eyes closed for a moment, and then another. The velvet-soft voice of Nat King Cole was all around her, a blanket of surrounding sound, and singing her to sleep with a stellar rendition of "Nature Boy."

"— a very strange, enchanted boy —"

The car tracker in Illinois assured Riker that the Volkswagen had not moved. Evidently, Mallory had pulled off the road to catch some sleep.

Bonus. Breathing room.

He was near the edge of Pennsylvania with only two more states to cross before he entered Illinois. Easing up on the gas pedal, he lit a cigarette. Riker did his best thinking while smoking and coughing; it relaxed him.

The detective returned to the problem of the gunshot victim back in New York City. He was dead certain that Savannah Sirus had decided to take her life *after* meeting his young partner. One dark picture in his mind was of Mallory teaching her houseguest how to use the gun — so the woman would not bungle the job of self-murder. This bothered him for the next forty miles. Finally, he made peace with the possibility

50

that a violently ruptured heart was Savannah's own idea — maybe a metaphor. Perhaps the note left behind was true and the lady had died of love. Riker had suffered the same ailment once or twice, and this was something he could believe in — if only the note had been signed. Maybe Savannah had been too tired to write anymore, so tired of her life. She was always Savannah to him now. He was on a first-name basis with Mallory's dead houseguest.

The victim's personal effects were in the trunk of the car, and he had hopes of gleaning more from what had been left behind. But his primary mission was to get to Mallory before she cracked up in her mind or in her car.

Deep in reverie and losing track of time, Riker had driven across the Pennsylvania border and into Ohio before his cell phone beeped with another message from the Illinois tracker: Mallory's car was on the move again.

The detective drove faster, pushing the speedometer's needle toward the outside limit, and a sleeping bug beneath the gas pedal died horribly.

A packet of letters, tied with ribbon, slipped from the passenger seat to the floor mat.

Mallory stopped the car to retrieve them, handling them gently, for they had been worn to torn creases during all the years when Savannah Sirus had owned them and read them every day. Mallory knew so many lines by heart and now recalled the description of *"— awesome heaven and a constellation of stars that hung like notes to a road song."* She lifted her face to the sky for the last time that night and saw only a few pinpoints of light arranged with a lack of symmetry. There were no more instructions to follow until sunrise.

She had older guidelines than these, directions handed down by another man, her foster father. Louis Markowitz had given her rules for a life in Copland: *Thou shalt protect the sheep; thou shalt not spend a bullet unwisely and get them killed in the process.*

Nothing about stars.

However, the old man had loved rock 'n' roll, and these letters shared his taste for songs by the Rolling Stones and The Who. She played them for miles and miles. Sometimes an old tune would coincide with favorites from Lou Markowitz's collection of albums that dated back to the days of vinyl records. And when this happened, that old man rode with her for a stretch of highway the length of a song.

She needed food and sleep.

Tomorrow she would try again to grasp the new rules that Peyton Hale had laid down in his letters. The author, once a California boy, had grown to manhood. Homeward bound, he had retraced his old route, laying down tracks with an odd sense of direction. She had failed in her attempt to follow the illogical instruction for how to look at the road ahead by stopping to look up at the sky.

Click.

The undeveloped photograph came out of the mouth of the camera. The image was slow to emerge inside the square Polaroid format. Now a woman could be seen inside the brightly lit restaurant. Her hair was black, her clothes were red. Still as death, she sat there — in the photograph.

The actual woman was in constant motion, head turning, as if she could have heard the camera clicking out here in the parking lot. Framed once more in the viewfinder, she appeared to be posing for the next shot, frozen in a startled moment. But then she moved again, looking at the other customers, no doubt wondering if one of them was the source of her fears tonight.

Wrong.

And now she must sense that the danger was in the parking lot — good girl — for she picked up her red handbag and moved to another table far from the window.

The photographer started up his vehicle and drove out of the lot to park on a dark side street.

Mallory steered into the bright lights of Dixie Truckers Home. Two large commercial rigs, big as houses, were topping off their gas tanks at the diesel pumps. She counted ten trucks in the lot. There was only one car, a red sedan with out-of-state plates, though it was four o'clock in the morning and well past the tourist hours. With her knapsack slung over one shoulder, Mallory entered the restaurant and ordered coffee from the man behind the cash register. Then she moved on to the self-service islands with wells of food under warming lights.

A tray in hand, she shoveled robotically, hardly noticing what was heaping on the plate, yet she knew every detail of the room and its occupants seated in islands of ones and twos. The patrons were outnumbered by empty tables — ten men to match the big rigs in the lot and one fidgeting woman, feet tapping, eyes traveling everywhere, probably jazzed on too much coffee. This tourist could only belong to the small red car. Everything about the woman was a different shade of red: the semi-new shoes, baggy pants and a faded sweatshirt that draped her lumpy body like a tent. However, her hair was the black shade of a drugstore dye job and obviously styled in a bathroom mirror.

Mallory carried her tray to the most remote table, aware that all the truck drivers were smiling her way. Their conversations had stopped, and now they stripped her naked with their eyes. They were so fearless in their sense of entitlement — as if they were ticket holders to a strolling peep show. Oh, if eyes could only whoop and holler. She set her knapsack on the table, then removed her denim jacket and draped it over the back of a chair.

"Oh, *Lord,*" said a passing waitress.

Sans jacket, Mallory displayed a shoulder holster and a .357 Smith & Wesson revolver. With the tight unison of chorus girls, the men turned their faces downward, as if finding their plates infinitely more fascinating.

Problem solved.

Only the waitress seemed to take the gun in stride, shaking her head, as if the lethal weapon might be some minor violation of a dress-code rule. The tourist in red was smiling broadly, raising her fist high in some yesterday symbol of solidarity and sisterhood.

Yeah, right.

Mallory pulled a small notebook from her back pocket and opened it to the page of landmarks. She checked off the green lions of Chicago and drew a line through the missing Cicero statue called Tall Paul. Another line was drawn through the lost ballfield. She checked off a second giant called the Gemini Man, a statue in a space suit, and made one more check for Funks Grove. The list of sights for Illinois was almost done. Only one roadside attraction remained unchecked and that was the Queen of the Road.

"Hi, my name is April." The tourist in red was hovering over the table and waiting out that polite interval where Mallory would offer her own name in exchange, but seconds dragged by and the woman's existence had yet to be acknowledged. More timid now, she said, "April Waylon from Oklahoma. May I join you?"

Mallory looked up with a frosty glare that said no, April should not even think of sitting at this table.

And the woman sat down. "I wondered if

you were traveling east or west." After another long silence, intrepid April pressed on. "If you were traveling east, you might have passed my friends going the other way — on Route 66 — a large group of cars all traveling together. You see, I missed the big meeting in Chicago."

Mallory looked up.

"That's where the maps were handed out," said the tourist, "and I've been trying to play catch-up with the caravan. Well, by now, of course they're at the campsite, but I don't know how to find them. I had numbers to call. They were stored on my cell phone, but the battery died, and then I —"

"Get off this road and take the interstate," said Mallory, who did not intend to listen to this woman's entire life story. "All the public campgrounds are marked by signs."

"Oh, not ours. It's on private land somewhere on this old road. I don't know what to do. I can't go back out there. Tonight I got frightened — really, *really* scared — and I couldn't even tell you why. That sounds silly, doesn't it?"

A man in coveralls walked up to the table, wiping his hands on a greasy rag, and he spoke to the woman from Oklahoma. "Your car's been ready for a while now."

"Oh, I'm so sorry," said April Waylon. "I

just lost track of time. So the tire's all right?"

"No, ma'am, it's not," said the man who smelled of gasoline. "No holes, but you got a busted air valve. That's why it went flat. So I changed the tire. But if this ever happens again, you just stay put and wait for a tow truck."

"I was out in the middle of nowhere, and my cell phone wouldn't work."

"Well, that tire was flat as could be when you pulled in here. Now driving it that way — that's just hell on the wheel and the front-end alignment."

Mallory's remote little table for one was turning into a convention center. A portly waitress had deposited a cup of coffee by her tray, and now the woman stayed to read the list of landmarks in her notebook.

When the man in the coveralls had departed, Mallory made another attempt to get rid of April Waylon. She pointed to a departing trucker. "Follow that man to the interstate and get a room for the night. You'll have better luck finding your friends in the daylight."

"I'm afraid. I can't explain it. I just —"

"Ask the trucker to keep an eye on your car. You'll be fine." But now Mallory noticed that the woman's open handbag had been left at the center table. Either this tourist hailed from some crime-free little town or she lacked common sense.

"But you're a police officer, aren't you?" April Waylon was suddenly hopeful. "And you're traveling west. I can see that now — by your list. It starts in Chicago." She touched the page. "I remember those green lions. So I could follow *you.*"

"No, you can't."

"Tall Paul's out of order," said the iron-haired waitress, her eyes still on the list of roadside attractions.

And Mallory said, "What?"

"Tall Paul," said the waitress. "Statue of a man holding a big hot dog," she added — *slowly* — in case her customer was only half bright. "Well, he's in the wrong place on your list. He belongs between Funks Grove and the queen."

"No," said Mallory, insisting on this. "Tall Paul was supposed to be up north in Cicero."

"Not *anymore.*" The waitress wagged one gnarly finger at the young detective. "I was answering fool questions about this road before you learned to drive, missy, and I should know where that damn statue is. A few years back, it was bought up from an outfit in Cicero and hauled down to Arch Street in Atlanta. That's the next town over.

Now you take a left out of the parking lot and head toward the railroad tracks, but don't cross 'em. You'll see a sign for —"

Mallory was not listening. She was rising from the table, dropping a fifty-dollar bill by the tray — many times the cost of her meal — and then, though her food and coffee were untouched, she headed for the door with some urgency to chase down a statue.

Upon entering Atlanta, Illinois, Mallory had no trouble finding Arch Street; the town was that small. The car lights shone on a fiber-glass man, who did indeed carry a big hot dog, and he was tall. *Tall as a building,* said the letter, *Tall as a tree. Tall Paul.* So the statue had not been lost, only misplaced.

The author of the letter seemed partial to things on a grand scale, but Mallory could not understand the man's passion for this road. So far, she had formed a one-word impression of Illinois — *flat* — with the occasional bump. By flashlight, she reread a few of the letters, wondering what she was missing here. She looked up at the statue.

So *this* was Peyton Hale's idea of spectacle?

Headlights appeared in her rearview mirror, and a car pulled up behind the convertible, blinding her with a ricochet of high beams. She heard the other vehicle's door open and close. When the tourist from Dixie Truckers Home came rapping on the window, the woman found herself staring into the muzzle of Mallory's revolver. April Waylon opened her mouth wide to scream, but all that came out was a squeak, and her arms waved about like the wings of a demented bird.

After watching this for a few moments, Mallory got out of the car, saying, *ordering*, "Calm *down.* Now!" And the tourist froze, hardly calm, but not quite so annoying anymore. "What are you doing out here? I told you to take the interstate."

"There's a car following me. As I got closer to Atlanta, it dropped behind. Its lights went out, but they didn't turn away. You know what I mean?" With one flat hand, April tried to demonstrate how a car might look if it was veering off the road. "Well, it wasn't like that. The headlights just shut *off.* And my cell phone still won't work. I tried the car charger, but that wouldn't — Oh, my!"

Mallory grabbed the cell phone from the woman's hand and opened the battery bay. She had expected to see corrosion or a botched connection. Now she held up the phone so April could plainly see the compartment where the battery should be. It was empty. "That's why your phone won't work."

"But that's impossible. I used the phone when it was still light outside. I made a dinner reservation." April Waylon prattled on. "It was a nice little restaurant. You must have passed it. It was just outside of —"

"While you were having dinner, somebody lifted the cell phone from your purse and stole the battery." Given this woman's carelessness with her handbag, that would have been simple enough. However, the average thief would not risk returning the useless phone.

"Maybe it was *him!* The one who's following me. He's still back there. You have to believe me. I'm *not* hysterical. I'm not making this up."

Mallory did believe her. A disabled cell phone worked well with the disabled air valve on April Waylon's flat tire. "Get in my car."

The woman meekly did as she was told.

The detective walked back to the red sedan. She opened the hood wide and left it that way. Next, she took the purse from the dashboard and locked the car, leaving the headlights on. Returning to her own car and her passenger, she tossed a red wallet in

April's lap, then hurled the red purse into the middle of the road.

"Oh, my handbag. It's got all my maps and —" Here, April wisely closed her mouth and faced forward — quietly.

Mallory started up the car and drove off, keeping one eye on the mirror image of the road behind her. "If I don't catch your stalker, you should go back to Oklahoma when it gets light."

"I can't do that."

Interesting.

Mallory had assessed April Waylon as a silly woman, easily frightened and quick to panic. Yet, here she was, traveling in the dark, working through her fear. "What's so important about this trip of yours?"

"I'm looking for my daughter, my baby. She was only six years old when she was taken."

Mallory watched her rearview mirror. No one was following. She slowed and rolled onto the shoulder of the road, then stopped awhile, minding the passing minutes, waiting until the time was right. "How old is your daughter now?"

"Nearly sixteen."

They sat in silence for a while, and then Mallory moved on, going slowly.

April Waylon's hands folded, fingers tightly

interlaced. "You won't say it, but you think I'm ridiculous. All this time — ten years. You think she's dead. You *know* she is. . . . And I'm a fool. . . . And you're right. But I need to find my child and bring her home. All over the world, children come home every day . . . home from school." She bowed her head. "It was my fault. The school bus stopped right by the house, but I should've been with her . . . till the bus came. I never saw her again. I used to take it for granted — all those little homecomings. She was only six years old. So you see, don't you, why I can't leave her out there?" April turned to the passenger window, watching the nightscape rolling by. "I have to go out and find her." Her voice became very matter-of-fact. "This is what mothers do."

Mallory made a sharp turn and then another. And now she had doubled back onto Arch Street. She cut the headlights and the engine to coast silently through the darkness. Up ahead, another car was parked behind the red sedan, and a man with a flashlight was looking in the windows of April's car. The red purse was in his hand. Mallory opened the car door soundlessly and made her way down the street on foot. The man was so preoccupied, he never heard her coming up behind him — until that moment when she wrenched his right arm behind his back and pressed her gun into his neck.

And he yelled, "Knock it off, I'm a cop!"

But Mallory made the pain of the wrenched arm an ongoing thing until the man produced a badge, and even then she was not quite done with him. She looked at the wallet spread on the hood of the red car and read the ID alongside his detective's shield. This Chicago cop was way beyond his city limit, two hundred miles out of town.

"I know why *I* was coasting in the dark," she said. "Now tell me why you cut your lights before you got here."

"I don't know what you're talking about. I *never* cut my lights. I'm on a car-theft task force. I've been tracking a stolen car all night. I lost the LoJack signal on this road."

It was a bad lie. She knew he was not trailing any car thief to a chopshop, not out here in the boonies. And he would not be worried about a high-speed pursuit at this time of night — no reason to follow from any distance. She believed he was on a surveillance detail, but it had nothing to do with a stolen car. "Where's your backup? Where's your vehicle recovery team?"

The Chicago cop was smiling now, and that was a lie, too, because it came with sweat trickling down his face on a cool night. He thought that she was going to kill him. He believed this with all his heart, but the smile never faltered, and she gave him points for that.

"I'm guessing you're a cop," he said, tossing this off as a joke.

Mallory was not amused.

"Hey," he said, "if this is your car, I'm sorry. It's not the one I was tracking. I saw the hood up and a purse in the road. I figured somebody was in trouble here."

She released his arm and holstered her weapon.

He stood up straight and rolled back his shoulders, acting the part of a man who had not just wet his pants. "You *are* a cop, right?"

She lifted his wallet from the hood of the car. "You know I don't buy your story, *right?*"

"Yeah." His eyes were on her gun, though it rested in the holster, and he still wore a smile, as if it had somehow gotten stuck to his face and could not be undone.

She glanced at her own car down the road and waved to the passenger, signaling April Waylon to come out and join them. Turning back to the cop from Chicago, she said, "I've got a little job for you. If you didn't lie about cutting your lights, then that woman has a stalker. So you're going to play babysitter until she hooks up with her friends." Mallory made a show of reading the ID card in the man's open wallet before handing it to him. "And now that I know where to find you, I can look you up . . . if anything happens to her. Got a problem with that?"

"Oh, hell no," he said, "no problem at all." He was smiling naturally now, just so happy to be alive.

Click.

The noise of the camera was hidden beneath the roar of a car's engine.

From this distance and deep in shadow, the shot would be dicey with no flash. The only illumination came from the streetlamp and the headlights of the red sedan. And the fast acceleration of the VW convertible had been unexpected. The image developing now was a blur of gold hair and silver metal. In many ways, it was a most telling portrait of the young blonde. By definition, enigmas lacked clarity.

Detective Riker had crossed into Indiana,

one state away from Illinois, when he responded to the beep of his cell phone.

The surveillance cop from Chicago said, "She made me, Riker. I swear I don't know how she did it. This never happened before, not to me."

Riker kept a tactful silence. This would not have happened if the Chicago cop had kept a mile between his vehicle and the Volkswagen, but then he listened to the tale of the lady tourist and the stalker, and now he understood how Mallory had caught her tracker. The other man was not done talking, but Riker had ceased to listen. His mind was elsewhere. No believer in coincidence, he tried to force the connection of a New York suicide to a crime scene in Chicago and a stalker in downstate Illinois. It hurt his head.

The other man's long story ended with the tagline, "Sorry."

"Well, she's good at spotting shadows," said Riker. The girl could even see shadows that were not there. "It's a gift." And this was true. Mallory had turned a heightened sense of paranoia into an art form. "But thanks for hanging in there all night. I owe you bigtime."

"That's good, Riker. 'Cause when I get back, I can't tell my boss that I screwed up.

So I'm gonna tell him that you called off the surveillance. That's okay by you?"

"For sure. I'll back you up."

"Thanks. Did I tell you she stuck a gun in my neck?"

"Oh, shit."

"I'm guessing she's no car thief — maybe a cop? Maybe the registered owner of that car — Detective Mallory?" When there was no response from Riker, the Chicago man said, "She doesn't strike me as the type to drive a Volkswagen."

Mallory was searching for an on-ramp to Interstate 55, a well-traveled highway with signs for twenty-four-hour fuel stops. The landscape of this old access road was the dark gray of early morning long before sunrise.

An on-ramp was no longer needed. She saw the lights of a gas station up ahead, and that was strange. Another driver might have felt lucky to find one open at this preternatural hour; Mallory was only suspicious. It was a small station with only one pump, and she wondered how it survived on local traffic. There was no garage for auto repairs, and the nearby interstate highway would eat up the commuter trade for gasoline. There was no reason to open for business before the full light of day, and yet a sleepy boy in coveralls was dozing beside the gas pump when she pulled into the lot.

An old man stepped out of the small wooden building. Rubbing sleep from his eyes, he hitched up his pants as he walked toward her. Mallory waved him off and put the pump's nozzle into her gas tank. The old man shrugged to tell her fine by him — less work, and what did he care if she wanted to pump her own gas? He held up one gnarly finger as he named his terms of "Cash and carry. I don't take no damn credit cards." When she failed to answer him, even by a nod, he stepped up to the car. "You know you're damn lucky I got any gas at all. Those damn tourists took most all of it yesterday."

The young boy was circling the convertible, eyes full of love for it, but giving Mallory a wide berth, sensing trouble if he came closer — if he should actually *touch* her car. Finally, he came to rest a short distance away, asking, "Are you hunting somebody on this road?"

Mallory was rarely taken by surprise, and now it must show on her face.

Encouraged by her reaction, the boy took one step closer, politely asking, "You got a picture to show us?" Failing to get an answer, he took her for a foreigner, and his hands described a square in the air, as if this might communicate a photograph.

"What?"

"A picture!" said the old man, frustrated now that the boy beside him had exhausted his vocabulary in the spoken word and sign language. He jerked one thumb back toward the field on the far side of his gas station. "All those people who camped here last night was carrying damn pictures."

She hung the nozzle on the pump and crossed the lot to round the small building and look out over the field beyond the gas station. They must have been very neat campers. There was no debris left behind, only charred circles from campfires and the tire marks of many different vehicles. When she returned to the gas pump, the old man was still muttering.

"Like I'd remember every customer who stopped for gas in the past twenty years." One hand rested a moment on the boy's shoulder. "And my grandson here, damned if those fools didn't ask *him* to have a look, too. Posters and pictures and itty bitty locket photos — just every damn thing."

"But the ones I saw looked like they was just kids." The boy shyly edged closer to Mallory. "So . . . if you've got a picture —"

71

"I don't." She had no photographs, only letters. And she did not believe that the old man would remember another Volkswagen driver who had come this way before she was born, even though that driver had one standout feature.

Mallory listened to the old man grumble about making change for her large bill, and then she drove on down the road. In the rearview mirror, she could see the boy running after her car, waving both hands, and she heard him yell out, "I hope you find him!"

It was unnerving that this child should know her business. She brought one fist down on the dashboard with the force of a hammer.

Pain brought focus.

She glanced at the knapsack, where she had stashed the letters. They would provide her with the structure she needed to get through this day. Mallory could see no farther into the future.

More cars were trickling onto Route 80. Rush hour was dawning on the state of Indiana, and Chicago was still hours away. But Riker was in no hurry now, and he never reached for the portable siren that would scare these civilians out of his lane.

He no longer needed the LoJack tracker to tell him which way Mallory was going. The world's best technology could not predict where she would go next, but suddenly *he* could. He knew every route she would drive, every town she would pass through. There would be lots of catch-up time ahead, for she was traveling down a very old road, a slow road. He remembered it well.

South of Waggoner, Illinois, if not for the spotlights, she would have driven past the queen. Mallory had expected something larger, given the letter writer's love of spectacle on the scale of fiberglass giants. This white marble statue was merely life-size and maybe smaller. She pulled off the road to park on a small patch of concrete in front of the shrine to the Virgin Mary, also known as Queen of the Road and Our Lady of the Highways. The nearby farmhouse showed no sign of life.

She was no closer to understanding the point of traveling from one odd thing to another. Perhaps she had read too much importance into sightseeing. One clue was in the rule forbidding the use of cameras, lest she *"— fall into the trap of looking at stale minutes of a time that passed you by. Life won't pose for pictures."* However, Illinois was still flat, and this statue provided small relief from the landscape. Disappointed again, she returned to the car and the road.

The sun was rising at her back, and she was playing recommended music for sunrise, Brandenburg Concerto no. 3. The author of the letters had described it as *"—sunlit music with acrobatic notes of many colors, airborne tunes that lift you up out of your seat."*

Failing to be uplifted, Mallory went on to the next song for a new day. She put the car in gear and sped down the road with the Rolling Stones screaming lyrics at the recommended volume of the second letter: *"If it won't deafen a cat, it's not loud enough."*

She found the letter writer's choice of tunes lacked any logic or style. This was not the playlist of an orderly brain that made distinctions between classical and rock, pop and jazz. The man's disorganized mind was irritating. Yet she drove his road and played his songs.

Her car slowed down behind a long line of more law-abiding vehicles. From force of habit, she crawled up on the bumper of the last car, forgetting momentarily that Volkswagens did not inspire fear in the driving public. As the route curved and wound, she waited until the road led her into a straightaway. Switching into the lane for oncoming traffic, she traveled from lawful miles per hour to one-fifty in seconds, passing a Lincoln that trailed a Winnebago following a truck-bed camper and cars pulling small, roly-poly trailers, sedans with roof racks piled high with bedrolls and tent poles, and more cars packed up to the windows with suitcases and duffel bags. It was a caravan of travelers bound together by the close spacing of one vehicle invisibly tethered to the next.

April Waylon's friends?

This must be the band of neat tourists who had camped last night in the field by the gas station, leaving nothing behind but their ashes and impressions of tire treads.

A moment later, the caravan disappeared from Mallory's rearview mirror. She was intoxicated with speed, flying across an open road. Car and woman had merged. Her heartbeat was in sync with the racing performance of a perfect engine, for she had become a new kind of creature, one who had legs that rolled with smooth grace in the weave of changing lanes and taking curves. Half an hour down the road, when at last she thought of food, she thought of it as fuel and pulled into the parking lot of a diner.

The countryside around this southwest area of Illinois was blighted and parched. The trees around the lot were specked with dead leaves that had died in their buds, and the grass of a neighboring field had turned brown. The only other car in the parking lot was an old green Ford sedan that carried out-of-state plates and streaks left by rainwater cutting through road dust, and the back end was attracting flies.

Lots of them.

The black insects buzzed and clustered along the edges of the closed trunk, mad for a way to get inside. She looked up to scan the wide windows that lined the diner. The only occupant was a stout young woman wearing a white uniform and running a rag across a Formica countertop. The waitress went on to polish the fixtures of the coffee machines and even the metal brackets for glass shelves holding muffins and pies. Mallory approved of all things neat and clean, and now she knew that the waitress's car was the old Volvo parked on the dead grass off to one side of the diner. That car had been recently washed, and a pine-tree air freshener hung from the rear-view mirror above the plastic Jesus on the dashboard. Mallory guessed that the woman parked outside the spacious lot because she took great pride in her old Volvo; she would not care to see it dented by some drunken driver seeking sobriety in a pot of her coffee.

Swatting at flies, Mallory turned back to the dirty green Ford. It had one new tire, probably the spare. She bent down to look through the driver's-side window. Old regimens died hard, though it had been months since she had last plied her trade as a homicide detective. There was an auto-club card on the console, and a cell phone was plugged into the ignition charger. A flashlight lay on the floor mat, its lens and bulb broken. So the driver's cell phone was not working. He had stopped to change his own tire — and then something else had gone wrong.

As she entered the diner, she saw an old-fashioned radio on a shelf behind the counter. The tinny voice of a weatherman was predicting another week of drought for the surrounding countryside. The rain-streaked Ford had surely come out of last night's Chicago storm.

As the sole customer of the morning, she had her choice of counter stools and tables, but she selected the booth by the window, the better to watch the frustrated flies still trying to break into the Ford's trunk. Ap-

77

proaching the booth was the smiling wait-ress with a round sign pinned to her ample chest to say: *Hello, my name is Sally!* This cheerful stranger had come to the booth armed with a coffee mug because, "The first one's always on the house. And what else can I get for you, hon?"

Mallory ordered two eggs over easy, the same breakfast she had every day of her life. Then she pointed at the green sedan on the other side of the window. "Where's the driver?"

"Don't know, hon. That car was there, all by its lonesome, when I opened up this morning. The owner's probably down the road scaring up some gas. That's my guess."

It was doubtful that the driver would leave his cell phone behind as an invitation to break into his car. "How long would it take to walk to a gas station?"

"No more'n twenty minutes. . . . Oh, I see." Sally lifted her face to look at the clock on the wall. "He really should've been back by now. Well, I guess he'll be along soon. Not that I begrudge him the parking space." The woman waited for her customer to acknowledge this little joke in view of an overlarge lot with only two parked cars. Apparently a smile was not forthcoming. Undaunted, Sally continued. "My daddy was the counterman back in the heydays before they opened the new interstate. Well, not so new anymore, but I-55 gets all the traffic now."

Mallory already knew the history of this diner. She looked out over the parking lot, seeing it the way it was when the California boy had first come this way, when the road had been called the Main Street of America. But the waitress would not remember the boy who had stopped here in a Volkswagen convertible. And, like Mallory, this woman had not even been born in time for the later trip, when the VW driver had returned as a man in his middle twenties.

"That lot was full all day and all night," said Sally. "Cars and trucks. And did you see the cabins out back? They used to be full of tourists, all of 'em. Folks from all over came through here. Now, *that* was a time."

As Mallory lingered over her breakfast, she learned that Sally held the keys to the tourist cabins. She handed the waitress her credit card to rent a bed for a few hours of sleep.

So tired.

Yet she sat awhile longer in the booth by the window. Two other diners arrived in separate cars, half an hour apart. Both men were obviously locals, for Sally had their orders on the counter before the steel and glass door had swung open. After finishing their coffee — and pie for one, a doughnut for the other — the two men departed at their separate times. An hour had passed.

The green sedan and its horde of flies remained.

There were more flies now, so many that their angry buzzing penetrated the window glass. Back in New York City, Chief Medical Examiner Edward Slope had always referred to these insects and their maggot broods as God's little undertakers.

3

Mallory wondered if murder was a low priority in this part of Illinois. Twenty minutes had passed between her phone call and the appearance of a patrol car in the diner's parking lot. The young state trooper who emerged from the vehicle was close to her own age, though the small nose, almost pug, belonged to a boy years younger. She guessed that he had played football in high school. He carried himself with the confidence of an athlete who has won a few games and fancies that he did that single-handed. Worse yet, he was the moseying type. She marveled that he could drag out the simple maneuver of leaving his car and donning his hat for the long walk of six steps to the diner.

A key to one of the tourist cabins was in her hand, and she planned to make short work of this business so she could get some sleep.

The door swung open, and the trooper nodded to the waitress. "Hey, Sally." He approached the booth by the window and, with the fine deduction of a hick cop, addressed the only customer as "Miss Mallory?"

"Just Mallory," she said.

After introducing himself as Gary Hoffman, "Just Gary, if you like," he settled into the other side of the booth, removing his hat and smiling. "Would've been here sooner if I'd known how pretty you are." When this attempt at charm fell flat, his smile became foolish. He opened a notebook and fished through his pockets to find a pen. "So you want to report a suspicious vehicle." He looked out the window with a view of the green sedan and the silver convertible. "I'm guessing that old Ford's not yours. I got you pegged as a Volkswagen girl."

If the trooper had seen the brief smile that crossed her face, he would not have taken it for any happy expression.

"I want you to pop the Ford's trunk," said Mallory.

He gave her a kind but condescending smile, as if he were playing Officer Friendly to a kindergarten class. "Well, now, you see . . . here in Illinois . . . there's a reason why we don't usually do things like that."

Mallory squeezed the cabin key until the metal dug into her hand. She was badly in need of sleep, and she was not going to wait around all day for him to finish his sentences. "Last night, back in Chicago, the cops found an unidentified murder victim — and it's missing a body part."

"The way I heard it —"

"The corpse was laid out like a damn road sign pointing this way."

"Ma'am, Chicago is hundreds of miles —"

"I *know* that. I *drove* it. That's why my car has the same water streaks as the Ford." She nodded toward the window on the parking lot. "Out there, you've got an abandoned vehicle that was rained on in Chicago last night. This part of the state hasn't seen rain for a month. Did you notice the flies all over the back end of the Ford?"

"Oh, flies," he said, waving off the one that had flown in the door with him. "I've seen that before." And by that, he meant for her to know that he had seen it *all* — every damn thing. "You're not from around here, are you?"

She wondered what might have given that away — her accent? Or was it the New York plate on her car, the one parked right under his nose?

"Now what we've got here," said the trooper, perhaps pausing to catch his breath — so many words to get out and all in one day, "well, it's probably a deer carcass in the trunk . . . and that's no reason to break into a man's car."

"A *deer.*" Mallory stared at the green sedan, as if reading the trooper's entire future on the hood of that car: He would never open his eyes to any observation but his own; he would never rise higher in rank; and he would be taken by surprise on the day he was fired. She planned to alter his future, but not from any act of kindness on her part. Cutting this man at the knees would open his eyes very fast — and then she could get some sleep.

"No dents in the front end," she said. "He didn't hit a large animal with his car. So you have to figure he was hunting, right? Now, assuming our *hunter* could fit a full-grown deer into the Ford's trunk — and he can't — you don't think they have enough deer back in Colorado, where his *license plate* was issued? Maybe they've got a shortage? And what's the deer population in Chicago — where his car got rained on last night?"

The trooper grinned, having thought of a solution for this little problem, too. He opened his mouth to speak, but Mallory was faster, saying, "I favor blowflies over cadaver dogs for finding stray body parts. You've got jurisdiction and probable cause. So pop the damn trunk." And then, when he showed no signs of moving, she added, "It's a good career move."

Grinning, he shook his head, as if she had just told him a fine joke. Then he glanced at the row of pies on the shelf behind the counter, maybe planning to stop awhile for breakfast.

But Mallory did not shoot him.

Though she had hoped to avoid this, she laid down the gold badge, an emblem of New York's Finest. "Don't fool with me. Just do it."

The Mercedes-Benz was at a standstill, and Detective Riker waited for an overturned truck to be cleared from the road up ahead. After bumming a cigarette from the driver in the car behind him, he stretched his legs as he sorted through the entries in his notebook. He knew that Mallory had traveled across four states in the fairly straight line of Route 80. That had ended when she stopped for gas in Chicago. Thereafter, she had traveled on back roads separated by stretches of driving on I-55, where that highway had displaced an older one. At first, it had seemed like aimless meandering — just a girl on the road and maybe any road would do. Or the kid might be lost and, true to herself, incapable of asking for direction.

The last pass of her credit card had paid for a meal and a room rental a mile outside a tiny town near the southwest border of Illinois. He knew it for a small town because he recognized it. He also recalled other places she had passed through from night into morning. Riker had a loving memory of that old road in its glory days when he was in his teens, and he could still recite the names of every little burg where a girl had kissed him and bedded him or decked him. This was the Mother Road, the old decommissioned Route 66, still traveled by middle-aged pilgrims seeking vestiges of better times and memories of the way they never were.

He knew young Kathy Mallory did not belong on that road, not as a tourist.

She was hunting.

Mallory opened the window on the parking lot to let in the roar of flies, but the state trooper still did not get it. Sally, however, received a clear message, and she was out the door with a can of insect spray in hand.

86

While the waitress did battle with the cloud of flies, the trooper *slowly* moseyed out to the parking lot, slid behind the wheel of his cruiser and drove off laughing.

On the way out of the diner, Mallory pulled a metal hanger from the clothes rack and reconfigured the wire to form a straight shaft with a hook. After relieving Sally of her can of insecticide, Mallory jammed the wire between the window glass and the car body to work the lock. Upon opening the door, she reached in and found the lever for the trunk release. She was not up to dealing with the operatic drama of a civilian unaccustomed to gore after breakfast, and so she sent Sally away. And now, standing upon ground layered with dead insects and many that still squirmed, the detective had her first look inside the trunk. The most intrepid flies had found their way in, having survived the waitress's game attempt at genocide.

After pulling out her cell phone and checking the stored list of numbers, she placed a call to a Chicago homicide detective who was owed a few favors by NYPD. On the other end of the line, a gruff male voice said, "Kronewald!" followed by a slightly menacing *"What!"* This was not a question; it was an order to state her business or get the hell off his damn phone.

"It's Mallory from NYPD."

"No shit!" This was said with sudden good cheer. "How the hell are you, kid? And how's that partner of yours — Riker?"

Not one for small talk, she said, "I popped the trunk of a car and found a man's hand. It's cut off at the wrist."

"Well, damn! That works real nice with a mutilated corpse right here in Chicago." Then he told her what had been left in place of the man's stolen hand, and, in typical Kronewald fashion, he added nothing that she had not already learned from her police scanner last night when a rookie cop had run amuck on an open radio.

Always holding out.

And now she gave him the name of another tourist with car trouble and a dead phone — just like the Ford that carried the dead man's hand.

The Mercedes was on the move again, but only doing civilian time through the last few miles of Indiana. Where were all these people going so early in the damn morning? It was a rare day when Riker ever made it into work before nine. Responding to the beep of his cell phone, he heard a familiar voice out of Chicago.

"Hey, you bastard, it's Kronewald. Your

partner turned off her damn cell phone."

"Yeah, she does that a lot," said Riker. "What can I do for you?"

"You guys have done enough for one morning. Mallory wanted a guard on the green Ford so she could get some sleep. Tell her we're sending the same trooper back there. His barracks commander thinks the humiliation might do the boy some good."

Riker listened to the details of an incomplete corpse found at the start of old Route 66 and not far from where Mallory had refueled her car. That Chicago gas station was becoming more interesting all the time. The rest of the body, according to Kronewald, had turned up in downstate Illinois — with Mallory. And how did the mutilation of a Chicago corpse tie in with a gunshot victim on the floor of his partner's New York apartment? Mentioning Savannah Sirus might be dangerous.

"Did Mallory give you the name of a woman who might figure into this?"

"Yeah, she even told us where to start looking," said Kronewald, "and thanks. Only took three phone calls to find April Waylon's motel."

Four hours had passed before Mallory awakened in the tourist cabin. There was no need to look at the alarm clock on the table; she possessed an interior timepiece that never failed her. However, she did carry a hand-me-down pocket watch for show. The heirloom had belonged to Louis Markowitz, and the back of it bore the engraved names of four generations of police: his grandfather, his father, himself and, last, his foster child, the single name *Mallory.* Shamelessly, she had pulled it out many a time as a reminder to others of favors owed to that old man, favors she had inherited. And sometimes she opened it in the squad room when she felt most alienated from her coworkers, the fifteen elite homicide detectives of Special Crimes Unit, men who had loved Lou Markowitz with all their hearts and loved her not at all. And now, though her freakish brain kept better time, though no one was watching and there was no advantage to be had, she opened the pocket watch and stared at the antique face for a moment — though she would never admit to a need for comfort or any understanding of sentiment. Mallory had no idea why she did this, and she did it all the time.

After a splash of cold water on her face, she turned the key in the cabin's lock and headed for the diner, where she expected all the paperwork to be ready for her so that she could sign off on the chain of evidence. That done, she planned to sit down to a cup of Sally's good coffee, all she needed to get back on the road. Her next landmark was across the state line in Missouri.

She found Trooper Gary Hoffman in the parking lot. He was sitting on the hood of his cruiser and swatting flies. The waitress, Sally, had been forbidden to use any more insecticide on the green Ford.

The rest of the lot was crowded with vehicles from the caravan she had passed on the road. She recognized a round trailer hitched up to a car and one of the larger mobile homes. The caravan had swelled in numbers while she was sleeping. The paved lot had space for thirty cars but it could not hold them all, and some were crowded into the neighboring field, where a few dogs were barking from rolled-down windows and others strained at leashes tied to grillework and door handles. The diner would not have seen this much business in the quarter century since Interstate 55 had supplanted the old road.

April Waylon's red sedan was nowhere in sight. Kronewald's people must have tracked the woman down before she could get back on the road.

Inside the diner, there were no empty

tables or stools and not much hope of fast service, either. Frazzled Sally was pulling sodas from the cooler when three customers invaded her territory behind the counter. The waitress did not struggle when the women captured her by each arm and led her to a table. With the gentlest hands and smiling all the while, they forced her to sit down and relax. Other people had quickly formed an assembly line of waving butter knives coating bread, more hands slapping down meat, and sharper knives at work thin-slicing tomatoes and blocks of cheese. Two men at the end of the line acted as sandwich wrappers and bag stuffers, and they called out the menu prices to a woman who noted the cost of the food as they packaged it up for the road.

At the center of the room, the waitress was studying posters and photographs laid out on a table for her inspection. The shake of her head said, no, she could not remember having seen any of these faces. And more pictures were laid out before her.

"Take your time," said a caravan woman, raising her voice to be heard above the babble of twenty conversations.

Over and over again, Sally said, "Sorry, no. Sorry, not that one, either."

An elderly man in the far corner booth

succeeded in catching Mallory's eye. He gave her a nod that was both a greeting and a recognition, though they had never met. Since April Waylon had not yet caught up with her friends, Mallory laid the blame on Sally. Apparently, the waitress had been very chatty while her only lodger had been napping in a tourist cabin.

Did all of these people know that she was a cop?

Heads were turning all around the room, smiles and more nods. Every table held a stack of posters for missing children. These people would be in the habit of meeting and greeting the police everywhere they went. At least Sally had not been able to tell them what was in the trunk of the green Ford.

Mallory remained by the door to study the old man in the back booth. He was a standout in this company. Though these people were a jumble of sizes and shapes, races and generations, no one else approached his advanced age. His hair was a mass of white curly tufts and his wrinkles were deep. Also, though the room was crowded, he had a table to himself. Some of the caravan people had formed a short line, stopping by his booth, one by one, to speak with him, then moving on and finally leaving the old man alone again with his collection of spread maps. He was more than their navigator; he was their leader.

The old man's suit jacket was a loose fit, as if he had come through a long illness, and she guessed by the cut and the cost of the material that he was not poor. His face was gaunt, and this made his sunken dark eyes seem larger. Smiling, he stood up and gestured to a seat in his booth, inviting her to join him, or he might be pointing to the plate of doughnuts on his table — every civilian's idea of cop bait.

Why not? She was hungry.

She sat down at his table and started to work on the doughnuts before he had a chance to introduce himself as "Paul Magritte. And you could only be Mallory. Is that your first name or your last? The waitress didn't —"

"Just Mallory." A group of three people moved to one side, and now she had a view of two dark-haired, blue-eyed children sitting together. A facial resemblance made them sister and brother. Though the little girl was five or six years old, the boy, closer to the age of ten, was feeding her ice cream from a bowl, as if she were too young to wield a spoon. "Those kids should be in school," said Mallory, always on the lookout for leverage in every confrontation, friendly or hostile.

"I hope you don't plan to turn them in," said the old man. "I think, just now, they're better off with their father. He's traveling with them."

That admonition was Mallory's first warning sign; she had a radar for the psychiatric trade and distrusted all of its practitioners as a species. This profession would explain his suit of good threads and his polyester followers. Now she made him the owner of the only luxury car in the parking lot, for all doctors were rich, and, judging by the rest of the customers, this one lived off the poor.

She glanced at the table where the caravan's only children were seated. They had been joined by a man with the same dark hair and light eyes. He had a well-muscled build and a face that had taken too many blows. By the one ear gone to cauliflower, she took him for a boxer. It was odd to see this hulk of a man so tender with the little girl; he stroked her hair and spoke to her in soft, lilting tones. Another patron, a nervous little man with a tray piled too high with food, accidentally jostled the girl's chair. The child abandoned her ice cream to rock back and forth. Arms tightly wrapped around her body to keep herself safe, she hummed the same four notes over and over.

The girl was insane, and this was more evidence against the old man who led this group. Paul Magritte was definitely a shrinker of heads, analyst of dreams and secrets — a damn witch doctor.

After wrapping one protective arm around his sister, the little boy glared at the detective, suspicious of any pair of eyes that might fall upon the smaller child, the crazy one. The boy was that rare individual who could win a staring contest with Mallory. She was the first to look away.

"So — no mother. She's the one they're looking for?"

"No," said Paul Magritte. "The missing are mostly youngsters like little Dodie there. A few teenagers like Ariel Finn. She's Dodie's sister. I'm sorry, I thought you were aware of the situation. The state trooper hasn't been very communicative." The corners of his mouth tipped up even in serious moments, and his somber brown eyes seemed to be forever apologizing. "Our waitress said you carried a badge, but you're not here to talk to us about the missing children?"

Mallory tapped the window glass to point out the green sedan in the parking lot, but she never took her eyes off Paul Magritte. "Ever see that car before? The Ford with the Colorado plate?"

He was too quick to snap his head toward the window glass; he stared at the car for too long, and now he had become fascinated by the flies gathered around the trunk. Perhaps he even understood what the insects wanted — and yet he smiled. "No, I don't recognize it."

Shrinks so rarely gave anything away without a warrant.

"Then I don't need to talk to you." Mallory picked up a doughnut and rose from the table, as if she planned to eat it elsewhere, not wanting his company anymore. Paul Magritte raised one veined hand in a gesture to stop her from leaving him.

She knew he would.

"What!" she said, as Kronewald would say it — implying that the old man should spit it out now, or leave her be.

"I know a man from Colorado. He was supposed to join our caravan yesterday, but he never showed up at the meeting place."

"Which was where?"

He only hesitated for a moment, for it was hardly privileged information. "In Chicago." He reached into his shirt pocket and pulled out a plastic pen imprinted with a hotel logo and address. "This place."

"I need your friend's name and address."

She sensed a stall in the making. *No time to think, old man.* "Give me his name — *now*."

"Gerald Linden. He's from Denver. I have a phone number," he said, fumbling with the zippered pockets of a nylon knapsack. "I'm afraid I never knew his street address. We communicated by e-mail. Did something happen to him?" Paul Magritte's concern was the genuine article.

She knew the Ford was registered to Gerald C. Linden of Denver, Colorado. However, because Mallory was in the business of getting information and not giving it out, she said, "We're done."

This time, Magritte wore a smile of relief to see her rise from his table, and she understood his logic: He believed that she would have stayed to ask more questions if this car, which so interested the police, had belonged to the man he knew.

But Mallory had other reasons for leaving a frail old man in peace: Chicago homicide detectives might appreciate her collecting information for them, but *not* conducting their interviews. Kronewald's squad could track down the old man and his troop of parents later on. These people would move slowly, stopping everywhere with their posters and photographs of missing children. They would not get far into Missouri before nightfall, and she knew where they were going. They were following old Route 66, and one glance at the maps laid out on the table told her where they would camp come nightfall.

The caravan people were filing out of the diner, arms laden with brown paper bags, and some were carrying coolers freshly stocked with ice and sodas. Mallory discarded her half-eaten doughnut and went behind the counter to check the inventory. She was pleasantly surprised to find the makings for cheeseburgers among the ruins of Sally's stock.

The waitress remained in her chair at the center table, and she was softly crying. The old man, last to leave, offered her words of comfort before he joined the others outside.

A few minutes later, Mallory was flipping burgers and listening to the day's news on the radio. The lead story was not a grisly homicide in Chicago, but a sudden change in weather patterns and a forecast of rain.

Most of the vehicles had cleared the parking lot, and Sally was still seated in the same chair. She took a deep breath as she ran a wet rag around the tabletop, slowly gearing up to the job of assessing the damage to her larder. Two of the caravan women returned to the diner and set to work taping posters to all the windows, and they would not leave before the counter and every table, chair and stool had been wiped clean, not before they had shaken Sally's hand and blessed her for her kindness.

Finally the door closed behind them.

Peace. Quiet.

The waitress sat back in her chair, dumbfounded as she took in the whole expanse of papered windows — her freshly cleaned windows — looking from one gang of lost children to the next. More tears rolled down her face.

Mallory carried two plates with cheeseburgers to Sally's table and sat down to share a meal. "Don't worry about the posters. I'll help you take them down."

The waitress was appropriately shocked, but only for a moment. "Can we *do* that?"

"Sure."

Absolved of all guilt, Sally bit into her cheeseburger with gusto.

Gerald C. Linden's severed hand was only a few yards from where Mallory ate her lunch and listened to the news station on the radio. Chicago Homicide and the Illinois State Police had done a good job of containment — no press leaks. Apart from police, no one knew what had been attached to the corpse on that city crossroad last night. The caravan parents could have no idea — for their faces had all been so hopeful.

4

Lieutenant Coffey looked out his office window as the first tourist of the season was strafed with droppings from a low-flying pigeon, and now it was official: Springtime had come to New York City. On the street below, those happy pedestrians who had not been defecated upon were shrugging their arms out of sweaters and jackets and lifting their faces to the warmth of the sun at high noon. The sky was a brilliant blue, and it was a foul day in Special Crimes Unit. At the age of thirty-six, Jack Coffey was considered young for a command position, yet his mind was on his pension.

He pictured it circling a toilet bowl.

All morning long, he had done a frantic tap dance on the telephone, spinning lies and dodging questions, trying to give a good impression of a man in charge, though he had no idea why one of his detectives had traveled to Illinois. But now he was more at ease with the paperwork for Mallory's erstwhile houseguest, Savannah Sirus, and the official finding of suicide. If Detective Mallory had committed murder, she would not be reporting abandoned cars and found body parts to the local cops along her escape route.

The lieutenant's second window was a sheet of glass spanning the upper half of one wall. It gave him a view of Police Commissioner Beale on the way to the stairs at the other end of the squad room. Men with guns were rising from their desks as the skinny old man passed by them. It was a rare day when the top cop visited the lower echelons, and he had come without his entourage — no witnesses. There had been no appointment, not even a warning telephone call, and there would be no record of the meeting just concluded. Commissioner Beale was planning to put the screws to the FBI — old grudges died hard — and he needed Mallory to do it.

The commissioner had assumed that Detective Mallory was on vacation in Illinois. If the old man ever thought to check, he would find no paperwork for any sanctioned leave time. She had been clocked in this morning as a cop on active duty. And, apparently, she *was* on the job today. She was just working for the wrong police department in a different city far from home. So, if the boys from Internal Affairs should drop by for a chat with her commanding officer, Jack Coffey could say, "Hey, the kid got confused."

By a thousand miles.

Oh, *yeah,* that would work.

Given the chance, he would make the same mistake again. The Job had damaged his detective and made her unfit for duty — and the Job owed her something. His only other option had been to officially relieve her of duty, but Kathy Mallory could never have passed the psych evaluation necessary to get back her badge and gun.

Other cops had covered for her, and Riker had done more than most, working insane hours and getting results for two, himself and his missing partner. And now Commissioner Beale wanted to loan Mallory out to Chicago. Well, that would legalize her presence in the state of Illinois, but first the lieutenant would have to assess the damage to Mallory. And how was he going to do that from the distance of four states?

And where was her partner today?

Riker's desk still had a deserted look about it, all tidied up by the cleaning staff and absent the usual mess. And the detective's cell phone had been busy all morning, but at least the man had called in. Jack Coffey looked down at a slip of paper in his hand, a message jotted down by a civilian police aide during a busy hour. Only three words, and what the hell did they mean? Was Riker planning to be a day late or just another hour?

He picked up the phone for one last try, and his tardy detective responded with, "Yeah, boss, how's it going?"

"Riker, where the hell are you?"

"In traffic. Didn't you get my message?"

"Oh, yeah. I'm looking at it now. But it's a little on the cryptic side." He held up the note and read the three words aloud. "*'A family thing.'* Just a wild guess, Riker — does this mean your partner's still crazy? I know that's a relative term with Mallory, but do the best you can."

"She's gonna be fine, boss, just fine."

Gonna be? Oh, *shit!*

Was Riker in the dark or did he know what she was up to right now? Hardly expecting a straight answer, Coffey approached the problem sideways. "So you see a lot of your partner these days?"

"Well, boss, it's funny you should ask. I'm on my way to see her right now."

"No, Riker, I don't think so. You're just

late for work. Mallory's a thousand miles away in southwest Illinois."

"Okay, you got me. *I lied.*" A surprised Riker negotiated the Illinois traffic. As he listened, he learned that even the police commissioner had a fix on Mallory's location, and now his lieutenant was ordering him to take a plane to Chicago and do damage control. "Yeah, right, boss. I'll get there as fast as I can. . . . No, no problem. I can do the travel vouchers when I get back." The Mercedes glided onto the exit ramp that would land him close to a Chicago gas station.

His lieutenant was still talking, and Riker only listened, never interrupting, as if this might be the first time he had heard the story of Gerald C. Linden's disembodied right hand. More details were added to what little Kronewald had already told him. According to Jack Coffey, civilians, a battalion of them, were on the road in downstate Illinois, all hunting for their missing children. Though this did not appear to work well with the Chicago murder of a grown man, Riker suspected that Mallory had tied them together. The late-breaking news was a turf war between Chicago Homicide and the FBI.

"They wanna snatch a body from Kronewald? . . . Okay, but I'm gonna need Charles Butler on this one." Riker made a right turn as he listened to his lieutenant's arguments against hiring an outsider: the strain on the budget and the overkill factor of using a psychologist with more than one Ph.D.; plus, Jack Coffey knew for a fact that Charles Butler flew only first class.

"I think I can get him to kick in the airfare." Riker pulled up in front of the gas station where Mallory had used her credit card last night. And now he lost the threads to what his lieutenant was saying. The detective was focused on a tired soul in the greasy clothes of a mechanic. The man was unlocking a metal gate that protected the door of a garage bay. This was the way a workingman should look at the end of a shift, not at the beginning. And what kind of gas station blew off the commuter traffic to open this late in the day?

On the cell phone, Jack Coffey was saying that the Chicago Police Department was crawling with shrinks, and one of them would be just as useful — and free of charge to NYPD.

"Just a few problems," said Riker. "One — department shrinks always suck, and two — Mallory knows that. The kid won't work with 'em. But she likes Charles Butler, and her old man liked him, too. . . . No, I think Commissioner Beale's gonna go for it." He knew it would take a few minutes for his lieutenant to appreciate this scheme, but it was going to happen. The boss knew Charles Butler as a man who could keep his mouth shut if Mallory proved unfit for duty — and she was. Sending in his own psychologist would keep the Illinois shrinks at a safe distance from one very messed-up young cop.

"Boss? Think it over. Get back to me, okay?" Riker folded his cell phone into his pocket as he watched the mechanic raise the garage door to expose a large party of men inside. Their ties were undone, and suit jackets were slung over their arms as they shook hands all around. And now the suits came outside, wincing and blinking into the sunlight. Riker could see tools racked on the back wall, but no oil stains on the cement, just the debris of liquor bottles, cigarette and cigar butts, what any cop might expect to find after a marathon crap game. This was not a gas station, not a repair shop — it was a damn casino.

Oh, this was going to be way too easy.

Riker left the car at the curb and stood in the small parking lot in front of the open garage. Hands in his pockets, like he had all the time in the world, he watched the gamblers, and they watched him. Everything about Riker said *cop.* Though his nature was laid-back, his stance had the easy confidence of a man who carried a gun everywhere he went. He never even had to show the badge. The gamblers scattered in all directions. The only one with nowhere to go was their host in the greasy coveralls.

Mallory stared out the window on the diner's parking lot, where State Trooper Hoffman sat on the fender of his car. He cradled a collection of cigarette butts and sundry trash that had probably blown in from the road during the night. Apparently his crime-scene training had been incomplete. Everything picked up off the ground had gone into a single garbage sack instead of separate evidence bags with helpful notes to say where he had found each object. What he had was next to useless, but at least he had collected his finds before the caravan's arrival. They were indeed a neat crowd. They had cleaned up after themselves, and evidence might have been lost if Hoffman had not gotten to it first.

An hour had passed since her last phone call to Chicago, but she had not yet given this trooper the news that, up north, a war was being waged in Copland — and that the FBI was en route to this diner with a plan to take his garbage bag away from him.

Back in Chicago, Detective Kronewald was fighting to hold onto his case, and he had made it clear to Mallory that he was counting on her.

Tough luck, old man.

In her mind, the debt that NYPD owed to the Chicago detective had been paid in full.

She looked up to the ceiling, listening to the sound of aircraft hovering over the diner. Outside, the whirling rotors of the helicopter were creating a windstorm in the parking lot, and the garbage bag was blown from the trooper's arms. He ran across the lot, chasing his precious evidence and his hat. Mallory looked up to see the FBI marking on the descending helicopter, surprised that any field agent would direct a landing so close to the green Ford. Why would they dust up a crime scene for a grand entrance to impress a lone state trooper? This told her that the war over the Chicago corpse was not yet won.

Detective Riker held *out* the wallet at the arm's length of a man too vain to wear reading glasses in public. He handed it back to the garage mechanic, who was now identified as a former Chicago policeman with thirty-five years on the Job. All the leverage of illicit gambling was gone. Retired or not, there was etiquette to be observed, good manners learned at police cotillion: No cop wanted to know that another one was breaking the law. Any conversation between them would be a waltz around the giant turd; you could smell it but never speak its name.

The two men had yet to exchange a single word when Riker said, "The pretty blonde with the green eyes and the silver Beetle — you filled up her gas tank."

"Last night," said the mechanic, who was even more economical with words. He pointed west. "She went thataway toward Adams and Michigan."

Riker smiled. Cowboy directions, such as *thataway,* so seldom included cross streets. "So she *told* you where she was going?" Not likely. He watched the older man retreat to the garage and return with two cold cans of beer.

Ah, Chicago hospitality.

The mechanic popped the tab on his beer can, then took a long draught and wiped his face with the least greasy sleeve. "She didn't say much, but cops don't show up to dish out information, do they? And her car had New York plates. So how big *is* this case?"

"What made you think she wasn't just passing through?"

"I asked her if she turned out for the murder on Michigan and Adams. That's when she said there was something peculiar about the body." He tapped his head, then frowned. "Or maybe she asked me about it."

"She pumped you for information?"

"Nope. The girl never said another word — like she didn't care. But I saw the police scanner in her car. Same frequency as mine. Now, I don't shoot craps myself. I leave that to my customers. So, all night long, I listened to the cop chatter on the air. When your friend Mallory mentioned the body, I figured she just wanted to know how much that rookie cop spilled out over the radio before they shut him down."

"And how much did this kid spill?"

"A lot. He was the first cop on the scene, and, like I said, he sounded young. Had to be a rookie. I know he was scared shitless when he saw what was laid out on that road. You could hear it in his voice. Stupid kid. Instead of just calling in a code — well, I guess there isn't a code to cover a thing like that — he was babbling about the crime scene. Didn't get real specific about the damage to the man — some carving on the face was all I heard — two lines and a circle. Something like that. I was pretty wasted last night. Anyway, the corpse was a full-grown man, fresh kill, but this rookie on the radio went *on* and *on* about the little bones."

"Little bones," said Riker.

"Baby bones," said the mechanic. "That's what the rookie called them."

Mallory kept her seat by the window, preferring to watch the action from a comfortable distance. Outside in the parking lot, the state trooper was facing off against a federal agent, the only man in a suit and tie. The pilot of the helicopter had wisely remained inside the aircraft. A small gallery of FBI civilian employees watched from the sidelines; these four men wore jackets identifying them as crime-scene technicians.

The fed's thinning red hair was cut short, and his scalp was even more sunburned than his face — lots of hours spent out of doors on this case. His arms were waving, sometimes pointing to the cruiser, and no doubt telling the young officer to get his ass on the road. But Trooper Hoffman was making a stand. He had been through a hard morning of humiliation and degradation — compliments of herself — all for that damned green Ford, and he was *not* going to give it away to the FBI.

The trooper dropped his guard and turned to look at his own vehicle. The cruiser's radio was calling him, and he ran toward it. Pulling the door open, he reached inside to press a receiver to one ear so he could listen to his communication in private.

No need for Mallory to hear the spoken words.

The trooper banged one fist on the roof of the car, and that said it all. The war between cops and feds had been lost in Chicago. Hoffman put on a stoic face, carried his garbage bag to the FBI agent and attempted a graceful surrender of evidence.

The redheaded fed, in Mallory's opinion, was not so graceful. He was going off on the younger man, and this was not normal FBI behavior, not after winning a major battle over turf rights. These two should be kissing and making up by now. She left the comfort of the booth to stand in the open doorway of the diner and only drew the attention of the four technicians.

The federal agent was facing the trooper and shaking his head at the sorry garbage bag that was being held out to him. It continued to hang in the air between them.

"Thank you," said the frustrated FBI man. "Thank you for this worthless bag of crap that wouldn't stand up as court evidence if it had the killer's name and address on every item. Did you sleep through *all* your classes on crime-scene protocols?"

Mallory came up behind the agent so quietly that she made the man jump when she spoke to the trooper. "Never mind him," she said, indicating the FBI man with a dismissive wave of one hand. "Give your bag to the crime-scene techs." Still ignoring the agent, she turned to the oldest technician, the one she had picked for the senior man on the forensics team. Pointing to the bag, she said, "That's what the helicopter would've blown away — if the trooper hadn't policed the area before you landed." When the senior tech smiled, she said, "I thought you'd appreciate that. You didn't want to land in the parking lot, did you?" And now she turned to the FBI agent. "That would've been your idea, right?"

The fed had no response, nor did he find it necessary to ask for Mallory's identification. Her denim jacket had been discarded on the steps of the diner, and he was looking at the cannon parked in her shoulder holster. The gun and a state trooper who was obviously under her command — this was all that was needed to make her the highest-ranking police officer on the scene.

Trooper Hoffman quietly made his transfer of evidence, signing the paperwork and accepting the receipt for his garbage bag. Then it was a surprise to see him hand over a thick packet of photographs taken with an instant camera. She had underestimated him. The boy had been very busy during her morning nap in the tourist cabin. And she even approved of him holding out on her.

"I shot every square inch of the lot on a grid," said the trooper. "On the backs, you'll find the location where I found every item in the bag." He pointed to an area on the top photograph. "That dollar bill is mine. I put it there to give some scale for the tire track."

Mallory smiled. Early this morning, after her first failed meeting with this trooper, she had borrowed Sally's old Polaroid camera to make her own record of the tire tread on the dusty pavement before it could blow away. Her shot was clearer, but, in many ways, his was better. And the second photograph would remain in her knapsack.

"I know that tire tread was there at sunrise," said the trooper. "That's when the waitress opened the diner. She didn't see any vehicles parked in that same spot before I got here. The tread mark was real close to the green Ford."

All four of the technicians showed great interest in this picture.

And the FBI agent kept his silence.

Wise choice.

The trooper signed receipts for the photographs, then handed the technicians another surprise, a diagram of the parking lot and every item found. Hoffman had even marked it by compass points.

The senior technician nodded his approval. "Nice job, son — especially if it goes to court. Made by the first officer on the scene." Alongside this diagram, he held up the trooper's best photograph and openly admired it. "Doesn't get much better than this."

And that was all that was needed to make the FBI agent look like a complete fool, but Mallory had one last touch. "Don't forget the marks you found on the Ford's bumper."

They had not been on speaking terms for the past hour, and it took a moment for the trooper to understand that her find now belonged to him — a present. "Chain marks," he said. "Looks like the Ford might've been towed into this lot by the other car."

The FBI agent stepped forward to break

up this festival of love between his people — traitors — and the local cop. "Thanks for your help, kid. We can take it from here."

The trooper stood his ground, all but digging his heels into the asphalt.

"Hey," said the fed, "we're gonna dust the car for prints, maybe cut out some upholstery. We are *not* going to load the whole fucking car into that helicopter. So you can hit the road, okay? I'll give you a call when we're done. You can have it towed anyplace you like. Fair enough?"

"No, sir," said Hoffman. "My captain told me to stay. And he wants an inventory of everything you take with you." He looked to Mallory for backup.

She sighed. It might be hours instead of minutes before she got back on the road. But now she realized that Chicago Homicide had not surrendered gracefully — not at all. She had already guessed that Kronewald had a bigger stake in this than one dead body found in his hometown.

"Back off," said Mallory. Every pair of eyes was on her as she spoke to the FBI agent. "The trooper stays, and that's not negotiable. You're outnumbered here. So play nice."

"Well, math isn't my strong point," said the fed. He turned his smile on the crime-scene technicians. They did not smile back. "I count —"

"They're civilians — no weapons," said Mallory. "I misspoke. I should've said you were outgunned." Turning to the technicians, she said to them, *ordered* them, "Wait by the helicopter."

The four men turned around and walked toward the far side of the lot until the startled fed found his voice and yelled, "Just *stop* right there!" He turned to Mallory, his voice strained but calmer when he said, "I need to see your badge. I like to know who I'm dealing with."

The detective pulled a black wallet from the pocket of her jeans, opened it and held up her gold shield, as if it were a talisman for warding off fools. Cops were dirt to this man, and she knew that, but the fed already had his little smile in place for settling minor turf wars with local cops ranking higher than a trooper. He leaned down for a closer look at her badge and ID card so that he could use her name in a sentence and win her heart — she knew this drill too well.

"A *New York* detective?" He held up his own badge and the card that identified him as Special Agent Bradley Cadwaller of the Federal Bureau of Investigation. "Mine

119

trumps yours, Detective Mallory."

"Not in the real world," she said. "You're from the Freak Squad, right?" This was the only scenario that would resolve the odd problem of a middle-aged FBI agent who made rookie errors. Before he could confirm or deny that he was with the Behavioral Science Unit, she rolled over the first words out of his mouth. "They don't let you out much, do they? No, your people just want to look at *photographs* of the crime scene." She waved one hand at the green Ford. "Nothing like the real thing. Too bad you've forgotten every crime-scene protocol. I can't believe you landed that damn helicopter in the parking lot. And don't ever forget that Hoffman saved your ass before you could blow the evidence away."

The crime-scene technicians were smiling again. They were enjoying this — a lot. She wondered how long they had been riding with this man. It took a while to break down the tight chain of FBI command, even among the civilian employees. They must have been traveling with him for longer than the time it took to snatch one body part — maybe months. Kronewald might find that useful.

She turned away from the agent and called out to his technicians, "You can come back now." One of the techs gave her a mock salute as he stepped forward with the others. The federal agent was speechless for all the passing seconds it took to understand that he was not in charge anymore.

When the senior technician stood beside her, Mallory issued her last orders of the day. "The trooper will observe and take notes. Make sure you give him a complete inventory of everything you take." With that, she returned to the diner, knowing that the FBI agent would follow her inside.

A folded newspaper hit the gas station's door with the crack of distant gunfire, and the drive-by artist pedaled away to make deliveries to other doors. The mechanic opened his copy of the *Chicago Tribune* and shook his head. "Amazing. It never made the papers."

"Yeah, yeah," said Riker. "Amazing. I need to know how much you figured out."

"So you're on damage control, right?"

"That's my job today." And that was no lie. "So . . . baby bones."

"Yeah, well, the dispatcher says to the rookie, 'You found a baby, too?' And the kid tells her no, just some real small bones, a kid's hand. And that's when the dispatcher shut him down." The mechanic grinned.

"Don't take much to make a connection with the federal body snatchers."

"The feds took everything?"

"You mean last night's murder? How would I know?"

"You know how this works," said Riker. "I ask the questions and you talk."

"Well, I'm talking about the old cases — cold cases — those missing kids. The damn grave-robbing FBI made off with their bones. I know there's real hard feelings between the cops and the feds around here, and it's been going on for a long time."

Without thanks, the FBI agent accepted coffee from the waitress, then cut short her cheerful speech on how the first cup was always free. He waved Sally off to the other side of the diner, then fiddled with the knot in his tie and turned a smile on Mallory. "Call me Brad."

She preferred the man's surname, Cadwaller. It vaguely reminded her of a species of fish.

"I'll call you Kathy," he said.

"You'll call me Mallory," she said, correcting him, "or Detective."

"Is this a feminist thing, the use of —"

"It's a cop thing," she said. "More like a superstition. If a fed gets close enough to your case to use your first name, it's considered bad luck." She did not hate all feds. There were New York agents, a few, who would not be shot on sight if she found them at one of her crime scenes. It was the Freak Squad that offended her most, and this man was certainly a profiler, a witch doctor without the credential of a Ph.D. "Now tell me who's in charge of your operation."

"I am." Agent Cadwaller polished a spoon with his napkin, the better to see his reflection in the stainless steel, and now he smoothed back his hair. "I'm in charge."

Mallory thought otherwise, and she took him for a poseur. The FBI would never let the Behavioral Science Unit run an investigation. Cadwaller's people were an embarrassment best kept in the basement. It was surprising that they had allowed this man in the outside world long enough to alienate an entire forensics team. But she had already guessed that the case was large, and field agents would be spread thin.

"And you're a New York cop," he said. "So we know this isn't *your* case."

Mallory was annoyed by this statement of the obvious, and he would have to pay for that as well as other sins: his smirk, his arrogance, his lies. "Cadwaller, you know how many bodies we're talking about?" Detective Kronewald had not mentioned more bodies. Cagey old bastard, he had given her nothing to work with beyond the skeletal hand left in place of the one that was cut away from Linden's body. But now she could make more sense of a frantic rookie's ramblings on the police scanner last night — the lines and the circle carved into the dead man's flesh. "The serial killer who murdered Gerald Linden was a —"

"Hold it," he said. "No one's calling the Linden murder as a serial."

"Really? Well, let me clear that up for you. I know you'll never be allowed near that body. But maybe you'll get to look at the *photographs.*"

His smile was smug, and he took some satisfaction in saying, "I've seen the body."

"Good. Then you saw the number carved into Linden's face." She was bluffing with only the description of two lines and a circle on the dead man's forehead, but now Cadwaller's eyes were rounding, and she knew he had never seen that corpse.

"It was a large number." Mallory leaned back and regarded him through half-closed eyes, as if this subject might be boring to her. "The first cop on the scene took one look at that body and figured it for a serial killing," she lied. "He was fresh out of the academy, and twenty Chicago detectives agreed with him. But you're not sure yet? And they put you in charge?"

Cadwaller's professional smile was showing some wear, and it was obvious that he was hearing about the number for the first time. He slugged back his coffee and studied her face for a moment before he spoke. "So New York has an interest in this case?"

"The victims come from everywhere." This was more guesswork based on Gerald Linden's Colorado plates, but she was onto something here. The agent's eyes darted to the menu, as if his next tactic might be posted alongside Sally's special of the day.

"So, yeah," she said. "New York has an interest. Now give me the name of the SAC on this case."

"Mallory, all you need to know is that the FBI has officially taken over."

"And now I *know* you don't get out much. That idea only works on paper." She planned her next bluff with the link between the caravan parents, the old highway they traveled — and the FBI man's sunburn. "You've been on the road awhile. You're working Route 66 — that's eight states." Right again. The proof was in this man's startled eyes. "Lots of cops to deal with along the way." She turned to the window on the parking lot, pleased to see the trooper only nodding while the technicians did the talking. All the boy had to do from now on was listen to their gripes and sympathize. Mallory cared nothing about the forensic inventory — only the job complaints, one working stiff to another.

The federal agent was having a quiet time-out, probably regrouping for another round with her and maybe trying to remember some useful line from an old psychology class. But, no — the man was rising from the table, ready to end this now.

Mallory broke the silence only to keep him inside the diner and away from his crew. "Can I assume the FBI will protect the caravan?"

The agent slowly settled back into the booth.

Nodding toward the green Ford beyond the window glass, she said, "Gerald Linden was one of the parents, but you already knew that, right?"

Cadwaller winced. Apparently the caravan was a connection he wished she had not made. He could only stare at her, unwilling to confirm or deny anymore.

"The caravan's in Missouri by now," said Mallory. "Since this is *your* case —" Yeah, *right.* "I guess you'll be asking Missouri troopers to guard those people. Before you try that, you might want to clean up the mess you made here in Illinois." She turned back to the window. "I suggest you suck up to that state cop before you leave."

Detective Riker held the cell phone to his ear as he walked back to the Mercedes. "Yeah, boss. What's the word?" He listened for a moment. "Oh, sure. I'll touch base with Kronewald. . . . Yeah, as soon I get there." In fact he had already set up that meeting. "I got Charles Butler? Great. . . . No, that's okay. I'll talk to him. . . . No problem. He'll be in Chicago today."

Riker opened the car door and spoke to his sleepy passenger, a man fifteen years his junior, who stood six-four in stocking feet — when he could stand. The passenger had awakened as they were crossing Indiana, but he was still groggy, and now it was all he could do to push strands of curly brown hair away from his eyes.

"Hey, Charles, you're gonna get paid for this little vacation."

"Vacation. . . . Yes." Charles Butler nodded, then stared into a bag of cheeseburgers with a look of wonder, as if it might contain moon rocks instead of greasy food. But the man always looked that way; it was his eyes — small blue irises floating in the center of heavy-lidded hen's eggs. Charles went everywhere with that same look of surprise, the aftermath of a popped balloon. Adding to the comedy that was his face, the hooked nose was of eagle-beak proportions. However, from the neck down, this forty-year-old man might pass for a rumpled model from a magazine ad for Savile Row tweed and Oxford linen.

Riker took the bag of burgers away from his friend. "Never mind that. I'm gonna get you some *real* food." He put the car in gear and rolled westward. "You can't start a road trip like this one without a good meal."

Charles Butler had been slow to wake, slower to grasp the fact that Riker had taken him eight hundred miles from his home, and now he said, "*Another* . . . road trip?"

The state trooper entered the diner and approached the booth that Mallory shared with the FBI agent. Hoffman hesitated, probably sensing that the atmosphere had been poisoned. As he came forward, he looked back over one shoulder to make sure that the waitress was out of earshot.

"What's up, kid?" asked Agent Cadwaller.

Trooper Hoffman spoke only to Mallory.

"I got the inventory. Those guys are ready to leave. They just have to pack up a tire."

"A tire?" The fed slapped his hand on the table, perhaps with the idea that this would call the younger man's attention back to himself. It did not.

The trooper was facing Mallory when he said, "It's the flat tire from the trunk."

By wince and moan, the fed implied that his own men were idiots. He looked up at the trooper. "I want photographs and evidence bags. That's it! Go back out there and tell them we're not taking the damn tire on the helicopter."

The trooper would not even look at the man. Mallory was his higher power in this room, and her next words to Agent Cadwaller were heavily laced with acid. "Does Hoffman impress you as the handmaid type?"

Eventually, the FBI man realized that he was his own messenger boy today, and he left the diner. The trooper waited until the door had closed on Cadwaller, and then sat down on the other side of the booth. "The techs seem to think that flat tire might be important."

"And they're right. Did they open up the cell phone they found in the car?"

"No, ma'am. It didn't work, and they were

in a big hurry. They told me Cadwaller never gives them time to do the job right. So they just bagged the phone."

"And what does that tell you?"

He did not answer right away, but gave it some thought. Over the course of one morning, she had taught him, by punishing sarcasm, to use his head. He held up both hands to say that he could not come up with any brilliant answer for her. "All I know is this. They've been riding with this guy for a long time, and they hate his guts. Oh, and they do all the digging. Agent Cadwaller just stands around and asks if they can't dig any faster. I don't know what that was about. I just listened. They're digging up bodies, aren't they?"

Mallory nodded. "So they've all been on the same case for months." It would take at least that much wear before the techs would gripe to anyone outside the FBI. "And they do the digging. That means they're beating local cops to the bodies. Write that down."

Obligingly enough, now that they had a common enemy, he was quick to do as he was told. He took out a small pad of lined paper and scribbled his notes. Done with this chore, he looked up, his pencil hovering, waiting for her next order. But Mallory was watching the action outside in the parking lot.

Something about Cadwaller bothered her, nagged at her. "You need a background check on that agent." Before the trooper could ask why, she said, "The FBI never gives a crime-scene unit to the Freak Squad. You might see a profiler along as an observer, but that's rare. You know why?" She pointed to the redheaded man in the suit. "Not one of those bastards ever solved a case. Field agents do that. The profilers sit in the cellar and look at pictures. Now write this down. And when you turn in your report, remember that this is what *you* came up with. All the bodies they're digging up are buried on Route 66."

He looked up at her. "And how did I figure that out?"

"The caravan parents, the posters of missing kids." Beside her in the booth was a stack of flyers that she had helped the waitress take down from the windows. She laid them out on the table. "Our victim, Gerald Linden, was supposed to join those people back in Chicago. Detective Kronewald already knows about the caravan connection. I phoned it in. And maybe he's figured out the rest, but he'll like your report." And she would be free to get back on the road.

"Kronewald?" The trooper put down his pencil. "No, you meant my captain."

Mallory shook her head. "You'll be filing a written report in Chicago tonight. I'll clear it with your captain."

While the trooper worked over his notes with much erasing, Mallory turned back to her view of the parking lot. The fed was reaming out the technicians as he stood over the bag containing the disputed flat tire. The senior forensics man had a defeated body language; he ripped off his latex gloves, tired and angry and beyond caring anymore. This told Mallory that the tire would be left behind, and the victim's cell phone would not be opened for examination anytime soon. Telephone company records would be the source for Gerald C. Linden's last phone call, and she doubted that it would have anything to do with the case.

Agent Cadwaller's arms were in motion, and she could hear him hollering words guaranteed to drive the techs crazy. "Hurry up! Get a move on, people! Lift those feet!" One by one, the remaining bags were hauled across the parking lot and loaded onboard the chopper, all but the bag containing the tire.

Mallory wrote a telephone number on one

of the posters of missing children, then passed the whole stack of them across the table. "That number is Kronewald's direct line. Tell him the feds didn't know about the victim's missing cell-phone battery. So he's got a sporting chance to find it first." In answer to the trooper's unspoken question, she said, "The man was trying to charge his cell-phone battery before he died. That's why he didn't call for help when the tire went flat. After I popped the trunk, I opened up his phone — no battery. Tell Kronewald the tire was sabotaged at the last place Linden stopped to eat."

"Or get gas?"

"No, too open," she said. "A restaurant parking lot full of cars would leave the killer less exposed. When you talk to Detective Kronewald, you're going to suggest —" She held up one finger in the air to stress this word. "*Suggest* that Kronewald does a credit-card trace to find that restaurant. He'll want to get somebody out there to search the parking lot for the discarded battery. It might have fingerprints. He would've done that anyway, but he'll like that touch. I know this man. And he'll like you, too. Tell him you're driving all the way to Chicago to bring him a flat tire. The crime lab should find a tool mark on the air valve."

He just stared at her in lieu of asking any more questions.

"The killer loosened the tire's air valve," she said. "Then he replaced the cap. He needed to disable the car, but he wanted it to stop down the road and away from witnesses. So the victim pulls over with a flat tire and checks it out with that little flashlight. He's on a dark road, no lampposts. He can't find any holes in his tire. Probably figures the problem is wear. The other three tires looked due for a change. And he couldn't see much with that little flashlight of his. You've got the size of the broken bulb on your inventory?"

"Yes, ma'am. It's a small one."

"Close enough."

"But won't Detective Kronewald have to turn all of this over to the FBI?"

"He will — a piece at a time — every screwup Cadwaller made today, and Kronewald's going to love every minute of it. Then he'll probably solve the case for the feds. He's a good detective." She picked up her knapsack and rose from the table. "I'm out of here."

"Wait, ma'am. Please? One more question? Why didn't the killer just steal Mr. Linden's cell phone?"

"Good question," said Mallory — with no

sarcasm. "It helps if you know the murder weapon's not a gun. It's a sharp object. Kronewald wouldn't like it if he knew I told you that."

The trooper shook his head to say he would never betray her.

The lesson went on. "The killer went to a lot of trouble to remove that battery, and that was risky. He probably borrowed the phone from Linden, then told him it wasn't working. That's why Linden had it plugged into the car charger. He thought the battery was dead."

"What about the tire? Why didn't he just slash it? Or a puncture — a small hole for a slow leak. Why risk being seen fooling with that air valve?"

Mallory waited for the trooper to answer his own question. He had a good brain, and he must learn to use it.

The trooper nodded his understanding. "The killer wanted everything to look normal when Mr. Linden stopped on that road. If the phone was stolen — if the tire was slashed —"

Mallory was nodding, prompting him. "And don't forget the caravan connection. The victim was on his way to join them. Gerald Linden already had murder on his

mind. If he was suspicious, maybe scared
—"

"The killer wouldn't have gotten close
enough to do him in — not without a fight."

"That's right." Mallory was making her
escape as she spoke — almost free. "So
Linden's out on a dark road with a flat tire,
a weak flashlight and a dead cell phone. And
suddenly — a dream come true."

"Along comes a Good Samaritan — to kill
him."

"Now you've got it." Her eye was on the
clock; her hand was on the door. "And it
was a familiar face. This was the man who
borrowed his cell phone. Linden walked
right up to his killer and shook the man's
hand."

"Wait." The trooper was rising from the
booth as Mallory was backing out of the
diner. "Where can I reach you?"

"You can't."

The door closed on the New York detective,
and the trooper settled back into the booth
to gather up his notes and posters. He
looked out the window in time to see the
silver convertible when it was only *aiming* at
the road. A second later, a fly had found
him. In the time it took to swat an insect,
Mallory was gone. He could see over a fairly

136

long stretch of open country, but he could not see her car. She had just traveled from zero miles per hour to *gone.*

This vanishing act was the only event of the day that did not have a clear explanation — considering the vehicle that she was driving — and it would color his permanent memory of her. Over the years to come, whenever he told his best story of old Route 66, he would not make Mallory any taller than she was, and even the size of her gun would remain the same. Nothing would need to be exaggerated.

Hours and miles west of the Illinois diner, one vehicle changed lanes to glide up alongside another, and now the encroaching driver was close enough to the Finns' old Chevy to see the silhouette of a little girl in the back seat.

The six-year-old had been facing the other side of the family car when she turned suddenly to peer through her own window, as if she had felt a breath on the back of her neck. The watcher's car dropped further behind and blended into the line of the caravan. Dodie Finn turned toward the front seat and a reassuring sight, the back of her father's head. She rocked and hummed.

Her brother, Peter, rifled the glove compartment, then reached over his seat to pass her a stick of gum, asking, "Everything okay, Dodie?"

Inside she was screaming; outside she was smiling, unwrapping her gum.

"Seat belt," said their father.

Peter obediently pulled back and disappeared with the click of the belt fastener.

Dodie hummed her little song; it quieted her heart, this same refrain, over and over — all that she could remember. She raised one small hand to rub the back of her neck, still sensing a touch of something nasty.

5

Charles Butler was wide awake, a great improvement over yesterday, when he had returned to New York from Europe after being marooned in one airport after another, missing planes for security searches and suffering massive sleep deprivation. Late this morning, he had awakened in the passenger seat of his Mercedes, wondering whither he was bound and what had possessed him to give the car keys to Riker, a man with no driver's license. Try as he might, Charles could not remember any conversation from the previous night, and thus he had traveled through the morning in the silent fog of the jet-lagged brain.

However, this afternoon he was rather enjoying himself, seated in this bright and lively restaurant. He was in the excellent company of two homicide detectives, who, between bites of steak and potato salad, discussed the bloody details of a recent murder.

So cheerful.

Detective Kronewald bore a slight resemblance to the late Louis Markowitz, particularly when the heavyset man gathered his hound-dog jowls into a brilliant smile. Riker seemed to like this Chicago policeman, and the oft-used phrase "you bastard" was apparently a term of endearment.

"Okay," said Riker, "I'll tell you why Mallory turned you down cold. It's the way you dole out information." He leaned closer to the Chicago detective. "You think the kid doesn't know you held out on her? She's a better cop than I am, and fifteen minutes after I hit town, *I* found out about the other bodies."

Riker paused a beat to accept the paperwork that would attach him and his absent partner to Chicago Homicide. "If you don't give us everything, then I can't talk Mallory into working this case." He unfolded an Illinois map and laid it out on the table. "Now, if it's not too much trouble — you bastard — just mark the places where the feds dug up the kids' bodies."

When Kronewald hesitated, Riker put a pen in the man's hand, saying, "Mallory's as good as they come, and you know that. By now, I promise you — these gravesites are all you got left to give away."

"No, there's more," said their host, for this meal was compliments of the city. "I got it all with me."

Riker made a rolling motion with his hand. "Let's have it before my hair turns white."

"I got the background check on Paul Magritte." Apparently Detective Kronewald assumed that this name would be meaningful to his luncheon guests.

Charles leaned forward to beg a question from the stout policeman. "Sorry, but I'm rather late coming into the details on this matter." Indeed, he had only recently discovered that Riker and Mallory were working on a case. "Who is Mr. Magritte?" While awaiting a response from Kronewald, he saw relief and thanks on Riker's face. And what was that about?

Kronewald responded with the hint, "Magritte's leading that civilian parade."

No help. What parade?

Charles turned to Riker for clarity. However, the New York detective was apparently clueless on the subject of parades and unwilling to expose his ignorance.

After crossing the state line, Mallory lowered her visor to reach for a tattered old brochure of the Missouri caverns, but it was gone. She checked her knapsack and the glove compartment. Could she have thrown it away by mistake? No, that was not possible. Even in the privacy of her own mind, she was slow to admit to mistakes. She checked under the seats and in the back, and a search of the trunk proved fruitless. After ransacking her duffel bag, she emptied out the contents of her knapsack and checked each buckled and zippered compartment twice. She could *not* have thrown it away. Her next theory revolved around a light-fingered member of the caravan. Had she forgotten to lock her car?

Yes, that was it.

No, that would not work. Nothing else was missing from her car, and she was the only person on earth who would see any value in a torn and faded brochure with a few notes that matched the handwriting on Peyton Hale's letters. She searched the car again, every hidy-hole and crevice where her hand would fit, and finally forced herself to stop. Where had her mind gone? And the time? She was running out of time.

Enough.

As Mallory put the car in motion, she decided that the wind had taken the brochure while the convertible's top was down.

Yes, blame it on the wind.

Kronewald handed a sheaf of papers to his fellow detective. "This is background material. If Mallory's right, all the people in that caravan met on the Internet. Paul Magritte runs online therapy groups for the parents of missing and murdered children, but we can't break into his website."

"Wait," said Riker, a man whose credulity had been overstretched of late. "You're telling me Mallory couldn't hack her way into a simple —"

"She's not traveling with a computer," said Kronewald. "I thought you knew that. Don't you guys ever talk? Does that kid *ever* answer her cell phone?"

Charles Butler and Detective Riker exchanged glances of perfect communion, both of them sharing the same thought: How could Mallory have become unplugged from her computers — and why? Riker seemed even more disturbed by this radical change in his partner, for he had often voiced the theory that Mallory was not simply in love with high technology, but actually required batteries in order to walk and talk.

"Now I got techs that can get me into the website," said Kronewald, "but not the private chat rooms, not without a warrant. Mallory was right about that, too. The old guy's a bona fide shrink. His site's protected by doctor-patient confidentiality. And while we're on the subject of shrinks." He turned a charming smile of apology on Charles. "Pardon the expression, Dr. Butler."

"Call me Charles." No one ever called him doctor, though his business card had a boxcar line of initials that stood for the degrees of a fully accredited and somewhat overqualified psychologist.

Kronewald leaned down to search a bulky briefcase on the floor by his chair. While the Chicago man's attention was thus diverted, Riker donned his reading glasses — in public — a rare departure from his only vanity. The detective scanned the background information on Magritte, mad to catch up with his missing details. Each finished sheet was handed to Charles, a speed reader who only needed a fraction of the time to cover every line of text, and now he learned that a sorry troop of parents were driving the roads of Illinois in search of lost children. How many of their youngsters were dead and carted away by the FBI as skeletal bones in body bags? And how might this tie in with the murder of a full-grown man?

Oh. On the next sheet, the victim, Gerald C. Linden, was mentioned as a member of numerous Internet groups for parents of missing children. His own child, a little girl, had been taken by "a person or persons unknown."

"I could use a second opinion on this killer." Kronewald, frustrated in the search through his papers, lifted the heavy briefcase from the floor and emptied out the file holders on top of the map. He turned to Riker, whose spectacles had vanished in a quick sleight-of-hand. "I just got off the phone with a state trooper. He's bringing me the flat tire."

Charles and Riker both smiled and nodded, as if a flat tire might be a perfectly normal thing to drop into the conversation. It made more sense when the Chicago detective had finished laying out Mallory's theory on the murder of Mr. Linden.

"So now," said Kronewald, "we got a slew of new questions. I'll tell you what the department psychologist told my squad. He says this insane detail work — stealing a phone battery and sabatoging that air valve — he says that indicates a compulsive personality, a control freak. Everything has to be just right."

The portly detective plucked one folder

from the pile and opened a preliminary report on the Linden autopsy. "Our shrink saw this and decided that the perp had to be a small man to make the fatal cut to the throat. The medical examiner agrees that Linden was looking down when his throat was slashed. So — the whole picture? We're looking for a short detail freak. And he's probably a very tidy serial killer, not a hair out of place. He's between twenty and thirty-five years old, and he does this for kicks — a thrill killer. Our shrink also says the guy's territorial. Now I'm hoping that last part's solid, 'cause the feds got no right to move in on my case if it doesn't cross state lines. Tell me what you think, Charles."

While he waited for a response, Kronewald cleared the paperwork off of Riker's map so he could mark the requested locations where bones of children had been stolen by the FBI. His pencil stopped in the middle of one of his X's as he looked up to prompt his civilian guest. "So . . . you think our guy's right about everything?"

"No," said Charles.

"Well, good, 'cause I never trusted that shit-for-brains twerp." The man sat back in his chair, his smile exuding a charm so at odds with his language and his manner. "What can you tell me?"

"Very little."

"An honest man," said Kronewald in an aside to Riker. He turned back to beam at Charles, the new center of his universe. "Okay, gimme what you got."

"I can't tell you if your killer is short or tall, only that Mallory's theory agrees with the autopsy. Her Good Samaritan — if that's what we're calling him — he was probably holding the flashlight while Mr. Linden changed that flat tire. Then the killer simply leaned down and slashed the victim's throat. So you see, the angle of the blade won't help you with the killer's height. Linden was most likely looking down at the tire — not a short murderer. And you shouldn't limit yourself to an age range, either. That's an FBI cliché."

Riker leaned forward. "But we can all agree that the killer is male."

"Not necessarily," said Charles. "You decide. I'll tell you what argues for a woman. It's a certain physical timidity in the act of murder. Hence all the trouble with the cell-phone battery and the tire valve — to eliminate all the warning signs on a desolate road late at night. And Linden would be less suspicious of a woman, wouldn't he? The detail work only shows a concern that the murder should go smoothly. She wants to avoid combat with her victim — a man. Apart from the murder itself, there's a great deal of exposure and risk taking. Consider the marks from the tow chain — traveling with the victim's car in tow and a severed hand in the trunk. But there was no risk at all in the act of killing Mr. Linden. That was remarkably well thought out, and women are more detail oriented than men."

"Charles, I just can't buy a woman doing this," said Riker.

"Because the victims are children? Let's say Mr. Linden was the first adult victim. A child can be coerced by guile and easily managed with minimum strength. A full-grown man is a whole new problem — for a woman. Hence the careful planning of Linden's murder in contrast to the more risky behaviors — transporting the body and laying it out in such a public place. I see a cockiness that comes from experience and confidence."

Kronewald seemed skeptical. "You think the next victim will be another adult?"

"Since Mr. Linden was the father of a missing child — probably a murdered child — the killer may have changed his focus to the parents."

"And that ties back to Dr. Magritte's

caravan," said Riker.

The Chicago detective pretended not to hear this, perhaps because the caravan had already traveled into the next state, a moveable feast for a serial killer, and Kronewald was being left behind. He resumed his chore of marking out gravesites between Chicago and the southwest border.

"I have one more disagreement with your department psychologist." Charles hardly needed to consult his own map, the one Riker had marked for him in red to show all the different names for the same old chopped-up highway and all the towns it passed through. "Linden's killer wasn't out for thrills. He just needed another body to decorate his road."

"His . . . road," said Kronewald. The detective lifted his pencil from the map.

Riker leaned over to see what had been drawn. "Oh, shit. Five graves on that route, and you're not even done yet, are you? Don't even think about spinning me a lie. How many bodies so far?"

Kronewald looked down at his map. "I swear there's only five confirmed gravesites we can link to the feds' team of body snatchers." He looked down at his map again. Reluctantly, his pencil moved on to draw more X's. And now there were ten.

"These three here." He tapped the map with one finger. "These are places where an FBI helicopter was reported landing. Evidence of digging, but no confirmation on whether or not the feds stole a body."

"And the last two?" Riker leaned closer. "Come on! *Give!*"

"Fifteen years ago, a pack of kids found a grave here." Kronewald tapped the map location with his pencil. "They thought a pile of rocks just looked too neat — like somebody was hiding something. So they started digging." His pencil moved to another gravesite. "And this one was found when a phone pole was relocated. That was about ten years ago."

Riker closed his eyes in the manner of a man who has seen enough for one day. "I'll ask once. I know about the lines and the circle carved on Linden's face. And I know you were never gonna share that, okay? So don't bullshit me. Just tell me this. Do the lines and the circle look like a number? A hundred and one? A hundred and ten?"

Before the other detective could answer, Charles said, "My guess would be a hundred and one killings. It works nicely with a sudden drastic change in victim profiles — children to adults. Am I correct?"

Kronewald nodded.

"Well, then," said Charles. "It appears that your department psychologist was right about the territorial aspect. Unfortunately, this killer's territory ranges for another two thousand miles beyond Illinois. He's fixated on Route 66."

Eyes wide open now, Riker leaned close to Kronewald, as if to whisper in the man's ear, and then he yelled, "But you already *knew* that!"

Mallory had traveled thirty miles into the state of Missouri to arrive in time for the last tour of the caverns, but it had been disappointing so far. Trailing behind a small group of German tourists on a trek of more than three hundred feet below ground, she listened to the tour guide's spiel on points of interest: three species of bats never seen and a river of blind cave fish that were also unseen because they shied away from the light — even though they were blind. Now and then, the guide would pause to turn on a switch so lights could dramatically illuminate stalactites and stalagmites.

Mallory endured all of this.

If she could only believe in the man who had written the letters, the best was yet to come, and he had promised, "— *the payoff will be Miss Smith.*"

Onward and upward they walked single-file on a gentle incline to the finale, touted as the world's largest cave formation. "Seventy feet high," said the guide, "and sixty feet wide. *Millions* of years old."

Following the Germans, Mallory climbed some fifty-odd steps to arrive in another cave. This one was outfitted with rows of chairs facing into the dark. When the small audience was seated, the guide turned on the lights to stun them with a formation of stalactites that draped in the shape of an immense theater curtain. The rock bed below it resembled a stage with the hollow of an alcove where a narrator might stand.

Now she understood the poetry that had accompanied this landmark in the letters, lines from Rilke: *"And you wait, are awaiting the one thing / that will infinitely increase your life / the powerful, the uncommon, the awakening of stones."* Mallory stared at this fantastic formation like any other theater-goer who had every right to expect the ancient curtain to part, the rock to open wide. Anticipation alone was exquisite — almost magic.

The guide was reciting a history that involved a large-chested diva of the nineteen fifties, the late Kate Smith, and now he had Mallory's attention again, for Miss Smith was the promised payoff.

"On with the show," said the guide as he pressed a button on a console. A woman's booming voice sang, *"God bless America —"* at a startling volume. The lights flashed red, white and blue, and, for the finale, a gigantic American flag was projected onto the natural wonder of the stone curtain.

The German tourists were tactfully, *quietly* shocked by this marriage of staggering beauty and kitsch. The guide was crestfallen, perhaps expecting applause for the dead diva, the flag and the disco lights. Those who knew Mallory and swore she had no sense of humor would never have looked to her as the source of the giggling. It bubbled up out of her mouth, and, unaccustomed to any spontaneous outburst of happiness, she was helpless to stop it. Her on/off switch for the giggles had been lost when her mother died. She laughed — she roared. The rest of the party, fearing hysteria, hovered around her but could do nothing with her.

Mallory recalled another line of the letter, the one that had lured her in here; and now she recognized it as the punch line to this joke on a grand scale: *"The Midwest is a very scary place."*

The FBI rendezvous point was near another

gravesite, and the special agent in charge could observe the diggers from the window of his room.

Dale Berman was a man of ordinary features and below average height, yet he knew that most of his associates would describe him as handsome in the way that professionally charming people can seem more attractive than they truly are — taller and wittier, too. For the past six months, he had joked about spending his retirement years writing a book on Route 66, a tourist guide on how to survive in these motels. Whether the accommodations were deluxe or as shabby as this one, he always slept on the side of the bed that was opposite the telephone, for near that phone-side pillow, the last ten thousand guests had planted their rear ends while calling home.

Special Agent Berman would soon be taking early retirement, and his wife, playful old girl, was counting off the calendar dates by carving wide notches into their front door so he could not fail to have his paperwork in order when the great day came.

He squinted as he leaned closer to the window, watching his team of gravediggers racing the light of day, brushing away the dirt and sifting it for clues to a skeleton's identity. In response to a knock at his door, he called out, "It's open!" He turned to face his last appointment of the day. The man entering the room was the senior forensics technician from the Illinois digs. That sector of the investigation had always been a battle-ground.

The state of Missouri was less like a war zone due to more covert body snatching. Agents and civilian employees had been gathering here for hours. He planned to address his troops en masse tomorrow. He would deliver an uplifting line of bull, impressions of progress in the hunt for a serial killer also known by a song title, "Mack the Knife."

Dale Berman's favorite rendition of that fine old standard was sung by Bobby Darin, and it conjured up Las Vegas nights, smoky rooms and the clink of ice in a glass of booze. It was the only murder song he knew. Once, the boxer's child had been able to hum more of it for him. But these days, Dodie Finn only had a few notes left in her crazy little brain. He had recently issued memos to the agents who traveled with him and to those flung out along Route 66: Anyone caught singing that song, humming or whistling that song, would be dismissed or shot at the discretion of the SAC, the special agent in charge — himself.

The phone was ringing in his pocket. He responded while waving his guest to a chair and a waiting glass of rye. He held up a bottle. "Your favorite brand, right?"

After listening to his caller, Berman sighed and tossed the cell phone on the bed. Turning to face the civilian forensics man, he feigned a smile. "The Illinois situation just keeps getting better and better. Could I have any more shit on my plate today, Eddie? I don't think so."

The forensics man, Eddie Hobart, held a sheaf of papers in one hand and a half-empty glass in the other. He was clearly waiting for his reprimand and probably wondering why it was taking so long. "I guess you've seen Agent Cadwaller's report already."

"No, Eddie, can't say I have. The paperwork caught fire while the man was still holding it in his hand." Dale Berman clicked his butane lighter and lit a cigarette. "He's rewriting it now."

Brad Cadwaller's new report would not lay blame on any member of the forensics team. No one in Dale Berman's command ever made mistakes — not on paper.

How could Riker possibly sleep through the noise of the portable siren perched on the roof of the Mercedes?

Charles Butler quite enjoyed the racket — so invigorating — and most of all he loved the sensation of speed. Following Riker's instructions, he had taken the interstate highway, the quicker to close the gap between themselves and Mallory. Ninety miles an hour was his personal best lawbreaking in this evening traffic, and he hoped that his passenger, upon awakening, would not be too disappointed in their progress.

His eyes strayed to the sleeping rider. Should he awaken Riker to tell him that something was not quite right? No, he lacked the heart to disturb this man who had driven eight hundred miles in one mad flight. Still, the problem of time and distance would not go away. The dashboard was littered with Riker's notes on Mallory's gasoline purchases between New York and Chicago. If the detective had not been bone tired at the outset of this journey, he would have worked it out for himself with only the times listed at every stop. A Volkswagen could not have covered that distance so quickly. Even the Mercedes could not do it.

Might she be driving a different type of car?

Charles's mind was full of maps and distances. When Mallory had suggested an onboard navigation computer for this car, his eidetic memory had enabled him to recite a virtual atlas of roads for her. She had grudgingly admitted that he *was* an onboard navigator. As a quasi-Luddite, he had relished that rare win in his ongoing battle against all things computerized and sanitized. He missed those arguments. He missed Mallory.

So he argued with her in absentia.

How could you outstrip the performance of a superior automobile?

No explanation would work with hard logic and geography, time and space.

Oh, fool, I.

The mechanical paradox linked him back to another odd thing: Mallory was totally immersed in high technology, and yet she was traveling without a computer. Perhaps she had exchanged the love of one machine for another. Had she tinkered with her car? Over the years of their friendship, he had never known her to take an interest in automotive engineering. Well, what was an automobile anymore but a mass of computer chips that ate gasoline? Ah, but no amount of tinkering would change the fact that, in comparison to his own car, her Volkswagen had a smaller, relatively low-performance engine.

Or not.

He wondered if it was possible to blend a Beetle with a race car?

Twenty-five years after the letters were written, it was nearing the end of another blue-sky day, and a low-riding sun shone warm and bright. Mallory barreled down the Mother Road playing vintage rock 'n' roll. Twenty miles later, the sky was clouding over, and she was searching for the next landmark along this stretch of road.

It was the right day in May, the right hour, but decades late.

The letter had described a line of trees, and there was none. She stared at the stark acreage and a row of thick stumps. Only the cement foundation of the old country store remained. And there were no brilliant colors in the sky, not today. The sun was just a patch of lighter gray on the overcast horizon line, a sign that the regional drought would soon end.

However, this stop had not been a complete waste of time. Music selections in the letters made more sense to her now. The current song, an upbeat tune, was all wrong for a sky that promised rain. She flicked one finger around the wheel of her iPod until the car stereo played a ballad to match the cloudy day of another letter, and now Bob Dylan sang to her:

"— and you better start swimming or you'll sink like a stone —"

With the push of a button, the convertible's black ragtop rose to give her cover, and Mallory latched it but left the windows open. She unfolded a letter, taking great care lest it fall apart with one more reading. She was seeking the description of the way the world used to be at this time of day, that time of life.

"— the present now will later be past —"

A hit-and-run gust of wind stole her letter, ripped it from her hand and escaped through the passenger window. She left the car at a dead run to chase the airborne sheet of paper across the open land, teased by the rise and fall of it as she ran toward it. Her angry eyes turned upward, as if to pin the blame on a Sunday-school God, Whom she had abandoned when she was six, going on seven, the year her mother died.

But she would not believe in such beings anymore. Kathy Mallory was a child of high technology and cold logic. Her nemesis of the moment was only the wind that carried her letter away, farther now and faster. Done with anger, on came panic — a novel emotion for a woman who carried a very large gun, someone who lacked a normal, healthy sense of fear. She was afraid of nothing until she heard the rumble of thunder. A storm was coming. As the letter rose higher and higher in the air, she was afraid it would be lost or wrecked by rain. And now her race was run against time.

The first drops fell. More panic. And then her anger returned in a twisted form of faith that her old enemy was truly up there, hiding from her, *stealing* from her again.

That Great Bastard in the sky, Mother Killer.

"God damn it!" she yelled into the wind, hands balling into fists, just six years old again, going on seven, and maddened by events beyond a child's control. "Give it *back!*"

In that moment, the letter hovered in the air, motionless, levitating there, as birds do when they fly against the wind. Slowly, it drifted to earth. She ran toward it, heart a banging, as if this bit of paper meant more to her than life.

The laptop was open, and Special Agent Dale Berman scanned recent communiqués from Chicago. Staring at the photographs, he moved his head slowly from side to side. He had only finished half of Eddie Hobart's field report, but everything was clear. At last he understood how the team of snatch-and-run gravediggers had wound up in a confrontation with a state trooper in the borderlands of Illinois.

"I liked the trooper," said Eddie Hobart, draining his third shot of rye. "Nice kid."

The FBI man nodded absently and poured himself another drink. The computer screen was showing him a picture that had been forwarded compliments of Chicago's Detective Kronewald. It was a magnified image of an air valve on Gerald C. Linden's flat tire. "I know you didn't miss this tool mark."

"Yeah, I did," said Hobart. "No time to check it out at the scene, and Cadwaller ordered us to leave the tire behind. He said the helicopter was over the weight limit."

"And was it?"

"No. We had some soil samples and the body bags from three more graves. Little bones don't weigh much. But the pilot only takes orders from ranking agents." The civilian nodded toward the field report in Berman's lap. "Officially, I'm taking the hit for everything. I should've left Cadwaller behind and loaded the tire instead." Hobart was watching the computer screen when it flipped to the second photograph of a

162

fingerprint on a phone battery. "I missed that, too."

"The cops found it in a restaurant dumpster north of Chicago. That's where the victim stopped for his last meal, and it was way off your route, Eddie."

"No, that was *my* screwup. I didn't even know the battery was missing from Linden's cell phone. Never got a chance to open it. And I'm not sure I would've gotten around to it, even if I'd had the time to do my job right."

"Well, somebody opened it."

"Could've been the trooper or that New York cop, Mallory." Hobart leaned closer to the screen. "Is the print any good?"

Agent Berman shook his head as he read the companion text. "Kronewald says it's a smudged partial. No clear ridges. It's not even useful for ruling a suspect out."

"Well, it's enough to make me feel like an idiot."

"Don't beat yourself up, Eddie. You're just burnt out on this case." Dale Berman refreshed the civilian's drink — the anesthetic. "Too many little bodies."

And then there was the problem of close confinement with an abrasive fool. Cadwaller had gone to a lot of trouble to insinuate himself into this investigation. To minimize the damage, Dale Berman had personally assigned the man to grave-robbing detail. More skillful agents had been sent off to deal with the Chicago cops. Bloody as that fight had been, Cadwaller had managed to make a bigger mess with the Illinois State Police.

And the tale was not over yet. It went on, blow by blow, as the sky grew darker. Ice cubes clinked in their glasses, and Special Agent Berman listened to his bedtime story of a tall blonde from New York City, the cop who had run the show at the Illinois diner. In the telling, Eddie Hobart appointed himself president of the Detective Mallory fan club.

Berman nodded and smiled. "She's Lou Markowitz's kid."

"No shit!"

"You've heard of him? 'Course you have. Well, I knew her old man when I was with the New York Bureau. My team worked a big case with NYPD's Special Crimes Unit, and we made a made a mess of it. *I* did. All my fault. Well, Markowitz exploded. He cleaned all the feds out of the cophouse, tossed us on the curb with the rest of the day's trash. Then his homicide squad wrapped the case in less than four hours. It was humiliating . . . and instructive. I had major respect for that old bastard. And I liked him . . . even while he was booting my ass out the door." He stared at his glass. "You know . . . there are times when you hear that someone's died . . . a man you worked with. And you say, 'Aw, too bad.' You really mean it, but then you go on with your golf game and never miss a stroke. Lou Markowitz's death stopped a lot of people cold. Every agent in the New York Bureau turned out for his funeral. And there were others. They came from everywhere when the old man died." He lifted his glass in a toast. "Hell of a cop."

"And Mallory?"

"She's a pisser. I noticed that Cadwaller isn't even limping, no bullets to the knee-caps. Lou's kid must've been having an off day."

The storm had ended, and no rain had reached this patch of road. The moon was rising.

Mallory turned off the music and her headlights, not wanting to announce herself as the car approached the glow of campfires and lanterns. She cut the engine and coasted into the lot of a convenience store. Its windows were dark, and there was a for-sale sign in the window. Her car rolled to a stop on the far side of the wood-frame building, keeping to the shadows and out of the moonlight. Most of the caravan vehicles were parked together off to one side. She left the car and rounded the store for a look at the encampment. Groups of people were gathered around small fires and cookstoves, and there were more of them now. Paul Magritte's party had grown by a score of travelers since leaving Illinois.

A woman stood in the lighted doorway of a Winnebago. She was handing out camping supplies to a small group of people in an orderly line, and Mallory took them for newcomers. One man was presented with a shiny new hatchet. It was small, but just the thing for chopping the hand off a homicide victim.

The caravan had not been here long. She could see pup tents and larger ones being raised on the perimeter of this caravan city. Some of these people were very poor; there were bedrolls laid out under loose canvas that had been slung over cars and moored to trees.

Where was the protection detail? She should not have been able to come this close to the campsite unchallenged.

The headlights of a new arrival were pulling into a gravel road that bordered the field, but this was no FBI vehicle. She could make out the star of a sheriff's logo painted on the door. And she knew that the driver had not come to protect these people. She could read his angry face when he stepped out of the car. He reached down to uproot the stake of a no-trespassing sign. The sheriff was on a mission to run the campers off this land, down that road and well out of his jurisdiction. He would only need to hold up the sign — all the authority necessary to send them on their way.

Evidently, Paul Magritte had also come to this same conclusion. The old man had spotted the official car, and he hurried his steps to head off the sheriff before the lawman could advance more than a few yards. The wind was with Mallory, and she could hear the conversation from her hiding place.

"Good evening, sir." Magritte held up a piece of paper. "This is the owner's consent to use the land. I made the arrangements a while back, as you can see by the date."

The sheriff lowered the no-trespassing sign, as if it were a gun that he had only half-decided on firing. He leaned it against one leg, freeing both hands to take a proffered flashlight and the paper from the old man. He read the letter of permission, then raised his suspicious eyes to say, "There's still the problem of sanitation." He looked out over the caravan city. "I don't see no outhouse, no Port-O-Potties." He waved the paper, saying, "This don't mean —"

"All taken care of," said Magritte. "The owner's son is on the way with a key to that building." He pointed to the abandoned store, and Mallory withdrew to deeper shadow. "We'll have the use of the restroom inside. The owner wanted cash, so it's just a matter of passing the hat to pay his son. And we have mobile homes with toilet facilities."

Other campers had noticed the sheriff's cruiser, and they came running, waving their posters of children's faces, all speaking at once. Louder voices in the babble were more distinct, asking if he had any news of Christie, who was sixteen on her last birthday; had he heard of Marsha, only six years old when she was taken; and the rest of the names rolled on and over one another.

The sheriff backed away from them, looking guilty, as if he had killed all their babies single-handed. He was addressing the dirt when he muttered something too low for Mallory to clearly hear. It might have been a prayer or a curse, for God was in the wording. And now he fled to his cruiser and fired up the engine. Wheels spinning, gravel flying, then back on hard pavement again, his roof rack of lights died off down the road.

He had escaped.

Mallory returned to her car. Her headlights were dark as she rolled quietly out of the lot to pursue the sheriff's cruiser down a moonlit road. The night was bright and he might have seen her if he had once looked back, but he never did. And this was another sign of guilt in Mallory's eyes. She followed him into a town, where he parked his car in front of a municipal building with several doors, and one had a sign for the sheriff's office. She was still his silent shadow as she followed him inside. The man never heard her footsteps, but he caught a look of surprise from the deputy at the reception desk. The sheriff turned to see her standing behind him, and it spooked him.

Good.

Holding up her gold shield and police ID, she said, "My name is Mallory."

She thought the man was going to cry.

"Oh, Christ." His voice was hoarse. "Mallory? Well, if that ain't enough to make you believe in signs and omens and God Almighty." He only glanced at her police ID. Turning away from her, he held up one hand, beckoning her to follow him through a door to a private office, where he pointed to a chair. "Have a seat. I got a feeling this might take a while."

6

Mallory settled into an old armchair that was entirely too comfortable, not her idea of office décor. The rug of many colors had probably been braided early in the last century, and a telephone with extension buttons was all that she could date to modern times.

She had a shortlist of blunt questions and demands for the man seated behind the carved wooden desk, but this Missouri sheriff was part of a cop's lifeline that extended from coast to coast. Instead of asking why he had run from the caravan parents, she said, "Tell me what you didn't tell Magritte."

"Probably nothing the old man didn't already know," said Sheriff Banner. "Eighteen months ago, we found the remains of a little kid, and she wasn't one of ours. I figured that's why all those folks turned out tonight."

"How old was the girl?"

"Oh, she could've been tall for five or small for seven. Can't be a hundred percent sure of the sex, either. Female was just the coroner's best guess. So when the town picked a name for the gravestone, we wanted something that worked for a boy or a girl."

"Then the body was decomposed." She could not ask if it was buried or missing a hand. That would be like an invitation to a round of give-and-take. "You didn't find it in plain sight."

"Hell, no. She was buried and *way* past decomposed. Probably been in the ground for years. Never would've found her at all, but this old fart from California, he took it into his head to build himself a retirement house on Route 66. Said his best memories were on that old road. So a contractor's crew found the body — the skeleton. Idiots. They didn't have the sense to leave it be and call the cops. They brought what was left of that child into town in a sack — a sack of bones."

"Anything unusual about the bones?"

"Nothing to tell us how she died — if that's what you're asking. When the bones were all laid out, we couldn't account for one of her hands. My men were all over that construction site looking for it. Never did

172

turn up."

"Any chips on the wrist bones you had?"

It took a moment for the import to settle in, and he did not like this ugly picture she had planted in his mind. "No tool marks — it wasn't chopped off. Could be predators got at the body before burial, but there were no teeth marks, either."

Mallory preferred her own theory of a killer revisiting the grave after the child had gone to bones. "Did you ever ask the feds for help?"

"Bastards. They turned me down. Said she was probably a runaway. Did you know there's ninety thousand runaway kids on the road in any given minute of a day? I guess they thought that little tidbit might be helpful, 'cause that's all I ever got from them. Not their kind of case, they said. Then, about four months back, the feds went out to the cemetery and dug her up. Pissed *everybody* off. They wouldn't tell us *nothin'*. I don't think there's more'n two or three people in this town that didn't chip in for the burial and the stone." He slumped forward, as if the weight of this day had bowed his back. "I hope you can tell me something useful — before all those folks come knocking on my door tomorrow, maybe thinking that little girl was one of their own."

That was not going to happen. There were rules about giving up details of another detective's case, and this one belonged to Kronewald. However, this sheriff could catch a crumb or two if he was quick, and she thought he might be. "Did you ever get any flyers from other police departments — something similar?"

"Not really." The man straightened his back a little. He had caught the drift of a serial killer in those words — and now they had a game. "Got a fax from Kansas awhile back. But that was about a teenager or a woman on the young side. And the Kansas victim was laid out in the middle of the road. No decomposition at all. One hand was missing. That was the only thing that matched up." He sat back in his chair and waited for her to toss him another piece of an old puzzle. By all appearances, he was a patient man.

There was no point in asking if the Kansas police had found a child's hand bones left in place of the missing adult hand; it was a detail that would have been withheld from the Missouri sheriff. And neither would Chicago Homicide want this known. "Did the fax mention anything odd left behind at the scene? Maybe the cops in Kansas had a few questions?"

"All I know is what I told you." He waited her out for a few seconds, and now he nodded, understanding that no more information was coming his way. "Well, I expect you'll be meeting up with the feds. There's a whole pack of 'em about twenty miles down the road. If you talk to those bastards, I'd appreciate if you'd tell 'em we'd like to get the kid's remains back for reburial . . . if they can't find her own people. Whenever I ask, all I get are damn form letters."

Mallory stared at the bulletin board on the wall behind the man's desk. It was a jumble of paperwork, duty rosters, letters and posters. Dead center was the snapshot of a gravestone, a grand affair of carved filigree and angels, but no dates of birth or death. So many flowers, heaps of them covered the ground.

Curiosity renewed, the sheriff followed the track of her startled eyes to this photograph. "Oh God, you didn't know." Pushpins went flying as he ripped it from the corkboard, and an apology was in his voice when he said, "I thought you came on her account. I'm so sorry." He handed her the photograph. "That's the kid's grave. We used that picture on the flyers. Like I said, we needed a name that would work as well for a boy or a girl. Now, that shot's a little blurry. The line you can't read — that one just says 'Someone's child.' "

But all the stone-carved text that she could make out was the largest lettering that spelled *Mallory* — just Mallory.

Near the southwest edge of Illinois, Detective Riker ordered a late supper at the roadside diner where, earlier in the day, a severed hand had been found in the trunk of a car. Their waitress, Sally, was recounting Mallory's skill in flipping burgers and how the young cop had helped her to take down all the posters of missing children.

"It was enough to break your heart," she said, "all those little kids."

Riker carried his coffee cup back to the booth, where his traveling companion was poring over the contents of Savannah Sirus's handbag.

"Sorry," said Charles Butler. "If you're looking for some connection between a suicide and serial murderer, it's not in this purse."

"Naw, that would've been too easy." Riker looked out the window at the local remains of Route 66. "But I know that suicide has something to do with Mallory being on this road. I don't believe in coincidence. She's hunting. And there's gotta be a connection to Kronewald's case. You know what's really got me worried? She drove her car right through another cop's crime scene. Now that's *rude*."

"But hardly a solid connection."

"Mallory lives for cases like this one. And it's not like she's got a life outside of the Job anymore." Riker ducked his head in apology for raising a hurtful point.

Once, Kathy Mallory had been a regular fixture in Charles Butler's life. This man had entered her small social orbit via the backdoor of friendship with Louis Markowitz. Lou, that crafty old man, had ruthlessly woven Charles into a safety net created for Mallory — so she would not be alone when he died. Lou had not been able to count on his foster child to make friends on her own. She would not know how.

But the introduction to Lou's pretty daughter had come with a terrible cost. And sometimes Riker wondered if Charles's one-sided love affair had also been part of the old man's plan. No — call it faith — Lou's cracked idea that Mallory could one day grow a human heart that could beat and love back.

He wanted to ask what she had done to drive this man away. Instead, Riker stared at the dead woman's handbag on the table. "A woman dies in Mallory's apartment, and the kid disappears the same day. At least there's a solid connection there."

"But you said it didn't happen in that order. You told me that Mallory left town before —" And here Charles Butler faltered. He picked up Savannah's round-trip airline ticket, proof of the woman's belief in life after New York City. His expression abruptly changed to a gentleman's equivalent of the *"Oh, shit"* response. "You think Mallory helped her over the edge? You think she pushed this woman into suicidal ideation . . . and then left town, *knowing* what would happen? Did the gun belong to Savannah Sirus?"

This was not really a volley of questions; it was a mind-reading act.

"Charles, sometimes you're even stranger than Mallory."

The empty store that bordered the caravan's campsite stood open, and the long line had dwindled to a few men and women holding toiletry kits and towels, waiting for their turn at the restroom inside. The owner's son had been patient while the hat was passed. Paul Magritte counted the dollar bills, the tens and fives as he laid them in the teenager's hand.

"Oh, yes," the older man assured him, "we'll leave the restroom spotless." He was walking away from this transaction when he heard a familiar voice.

"Stop right there, old man."

He turned around to see Mallory coming up behind him with a slow stalking gait. Where had she come from? Strange girl — so stealthy. None of the dogs had barked.

Her voice had changed, no rising notes; it was almost mechanical, and this was more unsettling than malice when she said, "You forgot to mention some critical details of your little road trip."

She was no taller than he was, no more than five feet ten. When she had closed the distance between them, their reflections in the dark glass of the store window showed two people of equal height. And yet he had the unshakable feeling that he was looking up at her. The old man wondered how she worked this trick upon him. He watched two other people exiting the small building. In passing, these larger men also appeared to be looking upward when they glanced her way.

Child, thy name is Paradox.

Yet a common cliché was the first thing that came to mind, for here before him was the living illustration of someone larger than life; her sense of presence did not recognize the boundaries of her body. Her eyes were cold, and so was her stance, arms folded against him. The girl's face was set with grim suspicion, and this was merely what she allowed him to see. At their previous meeting, that lovely face had been an impenetrable mask, and he had been able to discern nothing from it. Now he realized that Mallory was putting him on notice: she knew that he could tell her more, and, before they parted company — he would.

Though he saw every individual as a unique creature in the world, some of Detective Mallory's qualities sounded familiar warning bells. He could sense the tight control that checked her desire for expedient mayhem; she dwelt forever in that moment before the taut string snaps. He knew how truly dangerous she was — and she gave him hope.

"We'll want some privacy." Paul Magritte smiled and waved in the direction of his car on the other side of the campground. "I'll tell you what I can."

Oh, no, Mallory corrected him, but only with her eyes and the subtle inclination of her head. Silently she said to him, *You're going to tell me every damn thing you know.*

Charles was behind the wheel again and crossing the state line into Missouri.

"We caught a break," said Riker, returning the cell phone to his shirt pocket. "Mallory checked in with Kronewald. She turned up an old grave down the road. Another hundred miles and we can close the gap."

"If she stays put," said Charles.

"And if she doesn't, we can outrun her."

Miles ago, Riker had resolved his friend's conundrum of time and distance relative to Volkswagens. He had blamed the computers that processed Mallory's credit-card purchases of fuel between New York and Chicago. "A computer glitch. You can't trust those damn machines."

Charles seemed unconvinced, though he was usually the first in line to damn technology. But he did not pursue the problem. Instead, he picked up threads to another disagreement begun over dinner. "About that wall of telephone numbers in her apartment. I don't think Mallory isolated herself to make all those calls. What if she made her connection to Savannah Sirus *before* she stopped showing up for work? That might've triggered the isolation — that first contact."

Riker's resistance to this idea was slow to wane. Miles down the road, he waved one hand to say *maybe.* The detective's own theory was that the Job had derailed his young partner, or, more precisely, her work on a homicide squad had finished what was begun when she was only a wildly damaged child.

"Chicken and the egg," said Charles. "Which came first, missing work or making phone calls? You could find out, couldn't you? Check with the telephone company? Just ask them for the date when Mallory first called Savannah's number. That wouldn't have to go through NYPD, would it?"

"Okay." Riker pulled out his phone, and his attitude made it clear that he was only humoring Charles. After identifying himself for the New York operator, the detective seemed almost bored as he waited for the records on Mallory's home telephone. And then his expression changed. He thanked the operator, ended the call and closed his eyes. "Mallory made a lot of calls to Savannah. But her first contact was months ago — just before she started missing days from work. How did you know?"

"Everyone has a hobby," said Charles. "Mallory's is just a bit outside the norm —

she makes phone calls. You said she was doing that as a child. I rather doubt that she ever gave it up. She's compulsive that way. She had to work through all her numbers until she had a resolution. Given the numerals in a long-distance number, minus the four that she started with — oh, and then you have changed area codes and new ones. So, factoring in all the possible combinations, well, I doubt that she'd run out of telephone numbers anytime soon. That reinforced my theory of the calls as an ongoing thing — maybe a binge activity. Any sort of stress could set it off. Over the years, she's probably tried many more numbers than the ones you saw on her wall."

Riker lifted one hand like a traffic cop — stop — too much information. He liked his facts in small fragments that covered no more than a line in his notebook.

Mercifully, Charles cut to the summary. "She had a houseguest for three weeks, but what did Mallory do with the rest of her time? Do you know when she bought the new car?"

"A few months ago."

"After the first telephone call to Miss Sirus. That's when Mallory started laying plans for a road trip. Savannah's hometown of Chicago was a likely destination long before Gerald Linden died. Detective Kronewald's crime scene was simply in Mallory's way when she passed through town. Adams and Michigan is the official starting point for Route 66."

"Okay, you're right," said Riker, rubbing his eyes, wondering what else he had missed for lack of sleep. And now he had a headache — and a heartache. He reached into the liquor store sack, his idea of a first-aid kit, and pulled out a cold beer to kill the pain.

Following Paul Magritte, Mallory walked between hot coals in cookstoves and bright flames of burning wood. She heard the humming, the same four notes, over and over, and turned to see the two children huddled on the blanket before an open campfire. Mallory hunkered down beside them, her eyes on the little girl when she asked, "What's that song?"

The boy moved closer to his sister, and the hum was muffled as he enfolded her in his thin arms and held her close to his breast. Mallory turned her focus to him — interview subject number two. "What's the name of that song?"

"My kids don't talk to strangers," said a voice from behind her.

The detective rose to a stand and turned around to see the father. He was staring at his son and not liking that wary look in the child's eyes.

Paul Magritte made the formal introduction to Joe Finn and his children, Peter and Dodie.

Mallory looked down at the girl as she spoke to the father. "Those four notes that Dodie hums — you know the song?"

"No, lady, I got a tin ear. I only know she hums when she's uneasy." And it was clear that he laid the blame for this on Mallory.

His face bore fight scars from cuts to the eyes and jaw, but, by stance alone — legs apart, fists at his sides — she knew she had made the right call back at the diner. Boxing was Joe Finn's trade, and he had taken a lot of punishment to feed his family. What might he do to protect them? Angry now, he moved between Mallory and his children, wordlessly telling her to go.

Mallory lingered a moment longer, for this man must understand that she did not take orders from civilians. Lessons learned from Markowitz, a lifer in Copland: *Better to take a beating, Kathy. Don't ever embarrass the Job.* And now, in her own time, she moved on.

■ ■ ■ ■

Charles Butler scanned the road ahead for signs of gas and lodging. "So we can definitely rule out the idea that she was just badly in need of a vacation."

"Yeah," said Riker. "This is definitely not about Mallory joyriding into springtime. She's hunting solo, and she's coming apart." He counted up some of the early warnings for Charles — but not the worst of them. "One day, the little punctuality freak was late for work."

And that had been the beginning of her slow good-bye. There had been a string of days when she had come in late — if she came in at all. And then she had ceased to answer phone calls, e-mails and knocks at the door. The squad's commander, Lieutenant Coffey, had put it down to burnout. Other detectives in the squad had ceased to call her Mallory the Machine, for this was something human that they could connect with — lost time and down time, lying awake in the night with the shakes and odd thoughts that could not be driven off except by booze or pills or by eating the gun, muzzle to the mouth, top of the head blown off, so quick — all gone. Drowning cops were never pressured; they were watched over, and that had been Riker's job from the distance of the curb outside her building. By long tradition, burnout cops were clocked in and out so that docked paychecks would not pile on more anxiety.

Sometimes they came back. Sometimes they died.

"Take that exit," said Riker. The overpass ahead would give him the high ground he wanted. As the Mercedes climbed the ramp, he lit a cigarette and rolled down a window. "You know what drives most people nuts?" And now the detective had to smile. *Well, yeah.* The man in the driver's seat *would* know that. Psychology was Charles Butler's stock and trade. But, what a gentleman, he kept his silence.

"It's all the things that just aren't fair." Riker shot a burnt match out the window. "Mallory's early life was one long bad trick on a little kid." He squinted into the darkness, as if he could see her as a child out there, cadging loose change from whores and eating out of garbage cans. "I think the kid's on a mission. She's counting up all the cheats, the stolen things, lost things. That's what drives people crazy. Imagine the life she could've had — if her mother had lived. Funny thing is, I don't think that other life would've measured up."

"How can you say that?" Charles made a hard right turn at the top of the overpass. "If her mother hadn't died, she wouldn't have ended up homeless and lost."

"Lost? Never," said Riker. "The kid was a born survivor. But let's say you're right. In another life, she gets all the perks — two real-live parents, a dog and a swing set in the yard. You think she would've turned out better? I don't. Lou and Helen had her tested when they took her in."

"Louis told me." Charles pulled up to a gas pump and turned off the engine. "Her gift was mathematics."

"Yeah, a math whiz." Riker stepped out of the car in a futile attempt to pay for the gas, but Charles already had his credit card in the slot. "So she was always meant to be a computer witch. No change there. And she'd still be real pretty. If you saw her on the street, you'd stare long and hard. But then you'd move on. Most every guy would, and you know why."

Charles watched changing figures on the gas pump. He nodded. He knew. How many men could believe they had a shot with her? Hobbled by that matchless face, she would have been just as unapproachable as she was today.

Riker smiled at the frog-eyed, eagle-beaked man who loved Kathy Mallory. "You think she would've turned out more human, Charles? The kind of girl who could see her reflection in mirrors? Well, maybe she'd be a vain little snot, and you wouldn't waste six minutes having a beer with her."

Oh, this was heresy in Charles Butler's universe, where Mallory stood at the exact center, and all else revolved around her. "No," said Mallory's apologist. "She would've had a real childhood instead of all those feral years. It would've made all the difference in how —"

"A lot of her talent came from those years on the street," said Riker. "Your alternate Mallory wouldn't be able to open pick-proof locks. So she might let you call her Kathy, but she wouldn't have the makings of an even better cop than her old man — and I mean back when Lou was in his prime." And now he played to the other man's senses. "Oh, and the way she walks. You can see it all coming at you, the badge and the gun and all that power. If she'd gotten that other life, she'd be ordinary — or worse." The detective exhaled a cloud of smoke. "Not the kid that Lou and Helen raised, the one who fascinates you — not *my* Kathy."

Riker dropped his cigarette butt on the ground and crushed it with his shoe. "I wouldn't change a minute of her history . . . not one screwed-up brain cell in her head . . . nothing. You look at her and see all that potential. And me? I only wish I could make her see what a great kid she is." And maybe she *was* a sociopath with the eyes of a stone killer, but Riker had never expected perfection from those near and dear.

Dr. Paul Magritte led Mallory to a Lincoln Town Car. He held the back door open so that she could enter first, but this was not to be. Of course not, and he smiled at his error; she would hardly trust a stranger at her back. Trust was not in her stars, her style or her pathology.

He entered first. When she closed the door for privacy, he braced himself.

"Your missing camper," she said. "Gerald Linden? He's dead. His body was found at the beginning of the road."

The doctor closed his eyes. "It can't be connected. The FBI has been finding bodies along Route 66 for more than a year now, but they're all children."

"And you know this *how?*"

"The Internet. I ran several online therapy groups for parents of missing children."

190

"And murdered children," said Mallory. "You left that part out."

"Yes," he said, "forgive me." Oh, what a foolish idea that was. Forgiveness would be anathema to the likes of her. "I have five therapy groups, twenty-eight patients all told."

"I counted forty-two people when you stopped at the diner in Illinois." Detective Mallory said this as if she had caught him in a lie. She turned to the window and the rows of parked cars to one side of the field. "How many more people have joined up since then? Twenty? More than that?"

"Parents have been joining us all along the road. Obviously, not all of them are my patients. The rest came from other Internet connections. A year ago, the FBI located the graves of a few children and told the parents where the remains had been found. The fathers of two of those children were in one of my therapy sessions. Now that got my attention, two children, both buried near roads. Odd behavior for a murderer — to risk being seen burying a victim. Most bodies are found in remote areas with more concealment and less —"

Oh, he could see she was losing patience with him. He was telling her things that she already knew, and he should not make that mistake again; that much was clear as she leaned toward him — just a touch of menace to train him properly.

A quick learner, he continued. "The graves were on different roads, but an acquaintance told me that they were both segments of old Route 66. He's something of an expert on this road. And he has a gift for seeing connections and patterns. When he explained the odds of this happening to —"

"What's his name?"

When he hesitated, she leaned in close — too close — saying, "Now we've established that *'acquaintance'* and *'gift'* are code words for *'patient'* and *'crazy.'* "

Paul Magritte chastised himself and vowed to choose his words more carefully. "I contacted psychologists with other Internet groups. I found more parents of murdered children with roadside graves. Some of the bodies turned up years ago — all Route 66 burials, all little girls, aged five to seven."

"You knew you were dealing with a serial killer." This was an accusation.

He nodded. "According to my sources, the FBI hasn't contacted any parents in the past ten months, but rumor has it that they're still digging up the remains of children on this road. One grave was found not three miles from here."

"Why would you bring all these people into a serial killer's territory?"

"Adults won't fit his pattern."

"Gerald Linden." Detective Mallory wielded this name as a hammer.

"You can't connect that to —"

"Can't I? You're a shrink. You know the victim profile can change at any minute in a murderer's day. So don't even try to hide behind that. Now back to my question. Why would you put all these people in danger?"

"The parents were suffering too publicly. I wanted to get them off the Internet."

"So you *know* he's in one of the therapy groups," said Mallory, "probably all of them. You had to know he was fixated on the parents."

Though all her traps for him were laid with words, he envisioned Mallory digging a deep pit and covering it over with twigs and branches. "I'm not so talented," he said. "I never foresaw a prolific child killer making the jump to murdering adults. But I could see the danger of the Internet. What an opportunity for someone who feeds off the pain of others."

"You're holding out on me. You've had contact with this freak." She leaned closer to drive this point home. "You just diagnosed him."

He turned to his windshield and the lights of the caravan city. Mallory's hand was on his arm, and her grip was tight. No escape.

"Gerald Linden was part of your core group," she said, "the people you met up with in Chicago."

"Yes." He watched the Finn children as they walked by, hand in hand. Dodie had been announced by her humming. Those four notes were almost a mantra to him.

Mallory's eyes were also on Dodie Finn. "You have to get these people off the road before the next one dies."

"They can't go home. If the killer could find Gerald Linden before he ever joined the caravan — well, you see what that means." He looked out over his flock, mindful of the humming child. She was always in his thoughts — his sights. "The killer knows their names and addresses."

"Not all of them." Mallory lost interest in Dodie Finn and turned her eyes back to him. "He knew Linden's movements, where the man lived, what kind of car he drove. He would've learned all of that when he stalked Linden's daughter. The killer only knows the parents of his victims. And so do you."

Dodie's humming had stopped.

He looked around nervously, searching every window of his car. Ah, there they were. Peter and Dodie had wandered back to their own campfire, where their father still struggled to set up their tent. Paul Magritte's interest in the Finn children was not lost on Mallory. She looked at him as if she had caught him in some obscene act. Did she take him for a child killer, or did she only share a suspicion about that insane little girl?

"Back in Illinois," she said, "you told me Joe Finn had a missing daughter. How old was she?"

"A teenager. I really can't say more than that." But did he have to? She was nodding, adding this to her store of evidence against him. And now she turned back to look at that little family only yards away. Her interest should have waned with the information that Ariel Finn had not been a child. But no, her focus on the Finns was keener now.

Canny Mallory.

She pointed toward Joe Finn and his children. "So you're not worried about them?"

As she searched his face for telltale furrows and maybe tics, he found her method of extrapolating information was something akin to vampirism. She had bled him until she was satisfied, and now he was almost certain that young Dodie's secret belonged to Mallory.

"Tell me about April Waylon," she said. "I know that woman was invited to the meeting in Chicago. When were you planning to tell me that she was missing?"

"Oh, but she's here. April arrived an hour ago." He observed a slight fault line in Mallory's façade, a look of surprise, fleeting — gone now.

"Make a shortlist," she said. "All the parents who make likely targets. Then get them off the road and off the killer's radar."

"By sending them back home? If the killer is targeting parents, they're safer here. What chance would they have isolated in their own houses? You think they'd ever see it coming?"

"*It*," said Mallory. "You mean the killer, don't you? Interesting word for a shrink to use. But then you know him better than I do."

He shook his head, and the line of the detective's mouth dipped on one side to tell him that denial was wasted on her. And just when he thought the inquisition was about to begin in earnest, she opened the door of the car, preparing to leave him.

"The sheriff will be back in a little while,"

she said, one hand resting on the chrome door handle. "He's arranging a guard of deputies to get you through the night. The locals have a personal interest in this case." She stepped out of the car. "So maybe you'll tell Sheriff Banner what you wouldn't tell me." The door slammed in anger.

He thought that she had vanished, but then her face appeared in the open window, startling him.

"Something else to think about," she said. "What if it was the road trip that made him decide to kill one of the parents? If you'd left them on the Internet, he might've been satisfied with that — feeding on all their misery . . . but then you cut off his food supply."

After so neatly slaying Paul Magritte with words, she wiped her hands together, seeming to shed his problems along the ground as she left him behind. And yet he was still hopeful as he watched her walk away. In this new century, he had regained his faith in gods and monsters — and she was both.

7

The caravan was twenty miles behind her when she found the motel. This was the place Sheriff Banner had named as a federal rendezvous point.

The silver convertible rolled into the parking lot, and Mallory counted up the FBI jackets on people standing by their vehicles, twelve of them. This was not a typical task force. Every face was newly minted, unlined. And where were their mentors? These fledgling agents should be partnered up with senior feds. The youngest of them hurried to block her path before she could drive into the last remaining space.

And Mallory did not run over him.

This was to be expected of kiddy agents — they ran in front of moving cars.

"The motel's full up, ma'am." The young man pointed toward the access road. "If you get on I-44, it'll take you to a —"

Mallory flashed her gold shield, but not

long enough for him to read the city of issue by the poor light of the motel's neon sign. "Who's in charge of this operation?"

The young man hesitated too long.

"The SAC, the special agent in charge," said Mallory, as if she needed to spell out the initials. "Give me a name." She made this demand with all the authority of a woman who carried a bigger gun. She left her car to stand toe-to-toe with the rookie agent. "You don't want to waste my time while people are dying. And I know you've got orders to play nice with cops. So give me a name."

"Special Agent Dale Berman."

Bad news — the worst. Why did it have to be Berman? But now she understood this playgroup of unseasoned agents without their mandated babysitters. When did Dale Berman ever pay attention to protocols? She supposed one or two rookies would have to die before someone in Washington realized that the wrong man was in charge.

"Where is he?"

"You just missed him." The agent pointed to a field where a helicopter was spinning its rotors in a small cloud of dust as it lifted into the air. "Agent Berman's destination is more than a hundred miles away, but he'll be back tonight. If you can't wait, we can raise him on the radio."

Mallory got back into her car, wondering what the air speed of the helicopter might be. A landing site on Route 66 was predictable, but the aircraft would not be hampered by traffic and winding roads. She would have to move back onto the interstate to catch it — and maybe even beat it. Her engine was a perfect machine, and FBI equipment was crap.

"Detective, you don't want to drive that distance for nothing." The young fed had to raise his voice, for she was revving the engine to drown him out as he yelled, "Agent Berman will probably just turn around and —"

He was talking to the air. Mallory was gone.

Riker blew smoke from the passenger window as the Mercedes pulled up to a field lit by campfires and the smaller flames of propane bottles. Spinning cherry lights flashed from the roof racks of cruisers parked out on the road, and officers in uniform patrolled the perimeter on foot.

"So that's the caravan. Definitely worth a look." Riker had gotten only a few steps from the car when he held up his badge for the inspection of a man with a deputy's star, who now turned his attention to Charles Butler.

"He's with me," said Riker. "Maybe you met my partner tonight, Detective Mallory?"

"Never heard of her, sir. I just got here." The deputy pointed across the hood of his cruiser to an older man a few yards away. "You want to talk to Sheriff Banner. He's in charge."

Riker clipped his badge to the breast pocket of his suit before he approached the sheriff. The two men shook hands and moved in tandem toward a more secluded spot, talking cop to cop as they walked.

Charles looked out over the campsite. Some tents were no more than lean-tos. Others were dome-shaped and lit from within like glowing igloos. Small groups of men and women huddled by firelight and lantern. It was an end-of-the-world scenario peopled with survivors of an apocalypse, and he supposed that, given their loss, this was more than metaphor.

As he walked through the caravan city, dogs barked and then were hushed by their owners, and now he heard a small voice humming. It was a surprise to see two school-age children in this company. The little boy appeared to be on sentry duty, standing over the body of a prone man asleep by the fire. The child was so alert in his stance, so serious in his mission. He moved to one side, giving Charles a better view of the girl, the source of the music, albeit a limited repertoire of one refrain. She sat upon a blanket and rocked back and forth as she hummed, sometimes looking up as sparks flew out of the flaming wood-pile. He took this as a startle response and nothing more. The child was not really among them. Her mind had gone elsewhere.

The boy stared at him with distrustful eyes that were far too old for a youngster who could be no more than ten. Charles smiled, and the boy was instantly amused.

Of course he was.

Though a height of six feet, four inches could be intimidating, Charles now presented himself as a hapless, harmless fool, and he knew it. Not his fault — it was all in the genes. He had been born with this great hook of a nose and bulbous eyes with a permanent aspect of surprise, and every time he smiled, he took on the look of a recent escapee from clown school.

He donned his travel-worn suit jacket and straightened his tie as he approached the children. Hunkering down beside their campfire, he spoke softly so as not to wake the sleeping man. "Hello, I'm looking for Dr. Magritte," he said, pronouncing it *Mah-greet* and even screwing up his mouth for a funny French r. He presented his wallet identification to the little boy and won the child's heart with this adult transaction. "I'm a doctor, too."

"Dr. Magritte," said the boy with uncertainty.

"Yes, Paul Magritte."

"Oh, Dr. *Paul*." The boy pointed toward the other side of the encampment. "You can see him from here. He's the old man, the only one with white hair." Cupping both hands around his mouth, the boy told him that Dr. Paul's last name was pronounced *Mahgrit*. He whispered this with great good manners so that the visitor would not be embarrassed in front of nearby campers.

Ah, then Magritte was not a Frenchman, but a fellow countryman, whose citizenship dated back so many generations that his forbearers had ceased to resist the American mangling of the family name. Charles turned to the far campfire and saw one head of curly white hair in a group of other people standing and seated, all facing the old man with rapt attention.

So this was their shepherd.

■ ■ ■ ■

The helicopter was hovering up ahead, preparing to land. Mallory had matched time with it all along the road, even outstripping its air speed to make up for the extra distance while the chopper flew in a beeline. Her car pulled over to the side of the road near a yellow van with an electric-company logo. The curtains strung up on poles advertised a crime scene disguised as a repair underway by a crew of utility workers. The use of the FBI helicopter was over the top in blowing the local cover story, and now she knew this was one body that Dale Berman needed to see — or steal — in a hurry.

The detective stepped out of her car and was immediately met by a man in his early twenties and a woman twice that age. Though neither of them wore FBI field jackets, they could only be feds. Mallory held up her gold shield for the senior agent. Back in New York, this badge was her crime-scene passport, and she was accustomed to people moving aside for her. But these two had obvious plans to annoy her. They were still blocking her way.

Standoff.

"Sorry, I didn't get a good look at your ID," said the younger agent.

It was the older one, the woman, who took the badge when it was shown a second time. After shining a flashlight on the wallet, she returned it, saying, "You're a long way from New York, Detective."

Mallory put all the weight of a gun in her voice. "And you thought I might be lost, maybe stopping to ask for directions?" Could she communicate any more clearly that she took these two for minions? "I'm here to see your boss, Dale Berman."

"Special Agent Berman isn't in this sector, Detective. And now I'll have to ask you to wait in your car."

Pointing at the helicopter settling to the ground, Mallory said, "That's Berman. His business is urgent, and he'll be leaving soon." Gesturing toward the lighted curtains and the fake utility crew, she said, "Right after he takes a look at the kid's grave. Now, is there anything else I can tell you about what's going on at your own crime scene? No? Then back off."

Neither of them made a move to stop her as she circled round them and crossed the open ground to the helicopter. Feds had standing orders never to lay one hand on a cop. And there was good reason for that:

The police were not hampered by any such protocol. So, failing in a block, the tackle was not an option, and the two agents could only follow her — closely.

It was Riker's turn to meet the Finn children, Dodie and Peter. He agreed with the sheriff's theory, one arrived at after the Missouri lawman had placed a phone call to Kronewald in Chicago: It was no coincidence that a damaged youngster was traveling with this group.

Her bodyguard, a boy of ten, lurched forward as Riker reached out to gently touch the little girl's dark brown hair. The detective smiled at the older child, saying, "It's okay, Peter. I would never hurt your sister." He tapped the badge clipped to the pocket of his suit jacket, but this only added to the boy's alarm.

Curious.

Now the father was awake — and angry. A police badge should be a magnet for everybody in this group, a source of news, good or bad, and one more cop to look at their posters. But Joe Finn clearly wanted him dead.

"Get away from my kids." The big man was rising from the ground, muscles tensing, two fists ready. "You freaks have done enough damage."

The man had gone from deep sleep to full alert in an instant. He had seen the flash of a badge but not clearly. Did they share a common enemy? The word "freaks" was a good clue.

Riker's choices were few. He could not ask the sheriff for backup, not without losing face. So he could have his jaw broken by a younger man in better shape — and then there was reverse diplomacy. "I'm a *cop*, not FBI. If that's what you thought — well, I'm insulted."

This seemed to mollify Joe Finn. Fists relaxing, he rammed his hands into his pockets, thus putting away his only weapons.

And the only apology was extended to the little boy. "Sorry, kid," said Riker. "I won't bother your sister again." The detective moved away from the campfire in company with the sheriff, a man much like himself; Sheriff Banner would also connect every odd thing with another. They watched the little family from a distance.

"So — you think I'm right?"

"Yeah," said Riker. "Too bad. If that little girl saw something, she's useless as a witness." But she would make good bait for a child killer, and he looked around for evidence of this idea. Somewhere in this group, he should find at least two moles; FBI agents on this kind of undercover assignment would work in pairs, though many of these parents were solo. He turned to the sheriff for his best guess. "You've talked to most of the campers?"

"Oh, yeah, all of 'em, and I've looked at their posters. One's a solid match for the little girl in our cemetery." He pulled a folded paper from his pocket and clicked on his flashlight for the detective's benefit. "See this line about the horseshoe key chain? It's got engraving on the back. We found that in the dirt where the girl was buried. The FBI had to know whose child she was, but they never told the parents. Ain't that cold?" His eyes were fixed on a couple who sat on campstools, drinking coffee in that companionable silence of husband and wife. "And now I have to tell them their kid is dead. Sometimes I hate my job."

"Tell them in the morning," said Riker. "I'll be here if you want backup." In truth, he would rather face a loaded gun than the parents of a murdered child. And now he had to wonder what had gone through Mallory's mind when she visited the sheriff's office — when she saw the picture of the gravestone with her own name chiseled into the marble. What had that done to her? How close to the edge was she?

Catching up to her in the night might be a bad idea.

Yeah, daylight was best.

He wanted her to see him coming, slow and easy, smiling just like old times. Then she might be less inclined to shoot him, and this was not entirely a little joke he told himself.

The detective was distracted by the arrival of a newcomer in a pickup truck. A bearded man leaned out the driver's window to open his wallet for a deputy, and then he parked among the other civilian vehicles. When the tall, skinny driver emerged, he was leading a large black dog on a leash made of heavy chain, and the other dogs were spooked. None of them barked to challenge this animal.

The dog was better fed than his master, a tall, thin man with long matted hair, one gold tooth and one tooth missing. His cracked-leather boots were rundown at the heels; his eyes were the color of dust, and he carried the ripe smell of clothing that had not been laundered in days and days.

However, Charles Butler's first impression of him was not one of poverty, but of disregard for appearances and a loss of appetite for food and creature comforts. Among the parents of the caravan, there were others in this same sorry state. This man only breathed because he must; his body made him do it. But all the acts that were voluntary — these went by the board.

The tall stranger stood before Paul Magritte's campfire, extending his hand and introducing himself as "Jill's dad — from Austin, Texas."

Dr. Magritte smiled warmly as he stood up and shook hands, apparently recognizing this man by the mention of his child. "Of course, how are you?" He turned to Charles. "Jill's Dad — that's Mr. Hastings' Internet name."

Charles's attention shifted to the Texan's canine companion; its fur was thick and black. Possibly a cousin to a malamute? No, that was wrong. He had attended many New York dog shows and possessed eidetic memory, but he could not recall a breed quite this strange. However, though he had never had a pet of his own, he always got on well with domestic animals, and now he reached out to stroke the beast's head.

His hand froze in midair.

He was suddenly the sole focus of the dog's attention; it fixed him with pale blue alien eyes, detached from all emotion —

chilling. And Charles's last thought was that this was *not* a dog.

"It's a wolf, right?" Riker materialized at the campfire and quickly pulled Charles's hand back before it could be bitten off.

Thank you, thank you.

"Mostly wolf," said Jill's Dad, "maybe one quarter mutt."

The sheriff stepped into the firelight, one hand resting on his holstered sidearm. "Lock him up in your truck. If I see that animal out tonight, I'll shoot him dead."

Jill's Dad nodded. Man and wolf walked away.

Riker watched the departing animal for a moment. Then he slapped Charles on the back. "It's got weird eyes, huh? Real cold. Remind you of anybody we know?"

Dr. Magritte was first to respond to this, albeit silently with a look of surprise.

And now the detective turned to the old man and gave him a slow grin. "So you had a little talk with Mallory. Was that fun?"

Detective Mallory squared off against Special Agent Berman, and there was no other way for him to read her showdown pose. All that remained was the question of whether she intended to draw on him or deck him. As he recalled, she liked her old grudges; she kept them for years.

Agent Cadwaller had been dismissed, but kept looking back over his shoulder as he walked away. Dale Berman waved one hand to move this man along a little faster. The escorts remained, sensing hostility. Hostile was Mallory's other name. And now he faced the young cop from New York City, admitting to her that she had guessed right about his moles, the two agents embedded in the caravan. "But that's all the manpower I can spare."

"Two agents on Dodie Finn? That doesn't work for me," said Mallory. "You need more guns riding point and rear."

He could try denial. No — bad idea. This cop was not fishing or bluffing. She knew things about the humming child. "Okay, Mallory. I'm spread thin, but I could send maybe two more warm bodies for the protection detail."

"You're not protecting anybody," she said. "You're stringing a little girl out as bait. Either you send a real security detail or I organize state troopers for the next two thousand miles. Then I call out the media."

He shook his head. "I know you won't do that. It's just what this freak wants."

"You think I care? It's more pairs of eyes on those people. Less chance of another one getting killed. Other parents are joining up with that caravan all the time. That should make it easier to work in new agents. I'll tell the old man to back up their cover stories."

"All right. Done," said Dale Berman. "I'll have agents riding point and rear." He held up both hands in surrender. "See? I'm perfectly happy to be extorted. Anything else you want? My wallet?" He turned his eyes to his audience, Agents Allen and Nahlman.

Mallory took a step closer, saying, "One more thing."

He never saw it coming. One moment he was smiling, and then he was bent over with the explosion of pain from his crotch. Mallory had smashed his testicles with a lightning kick. Agent Berman never saw the second shot, either. Her kneecap connected to his jaw and sent him sprawling backward. He was on the ground and tasting blood on the tooth that had split his lip.

Agent Barry Allen was only reacting with wide eyes, but this youngster was new to the job. Agent Nahlman had no such excuse; she was a veteran with eighteen years of experience. And yet there was ample time for Dale Berman to prop himself on one crooked arm and look up at Mallory, yelling, "Are you *nuts!*" Now — *finally* — his agents were stepping forward — a bit late in his view — when he held up one hand to stop them. Teeth clenched, he said to them, "Just walk away."

They did as they were told.

When his people were out of earshot, he was still on the ground at Mallory's feet. Standing up to her was important enough to work through a world of pain, and he did. Gaining his feet, he dusted off his suit jacket. "I guess your old man had good reason to take a shot at me, but what did I ever do to *you?*"

Mallory gave him half a smile and a look of utter satisfaction that only payback can bring. She turned away from him and walked toward the road with a casual stride, as if decking a federal agent might be an everyday thing with her.

Riker lay beside his duffel bag on the lumpy motel mattress. He was too tired to hunt for his toothbrush.

Charles Butler sat tailor fashion on the other bed. He was examining the contents of Savannah Sirus's purse and a suitcase recently pulled from the trunk of the car. Riker's own Polaroids of the dead woman were lined up in a neat row. This was all the physical evidence for the psychological autopsy of a suicide victim. And while the psychologist sorted these items, he spoke to the detective from some other compartment of his giant brain where he dealt with the more current problem. "Kronewald's very tight with his information. You're sure that Mallory knows the name of the FBI agent in charge?"

"Maybe not," said Riker, "but he's not the reason she's on this road. Dale Berman is one coincidence I can buy. He was always ambitious. No surprise he'd worm his way into a major case." Riker pinned his hopes on coincidence, for Mallory was not in any shape to settle old scores with that fed. Her foster father was dead and in the ground, beyond all pain and regret, so what would be the point of going after Dale? He had no desire to talk about this anymore — any reminder of that FBI agent depressed him. "So what can you tell me about the little girl from the caravan?"

"Dodie? She belongs in a hospital." After gathering up all of Savannah Sirus's clothing, Charles returned it to the suitcase. Then he laid out the remaining items on different squares of the bedspread pattern, patiently working on a suicide while discussing serial murder with his friend. "Dodie's missing sister won't fit the victim profile.

Ariel Finn was a teenager." He looked up at the detective on the next bed. "But you knew that, didn't you? Of course. Sorry. The sheriff told you, right? Yet you're still interested in that little family."

Charles began to move the items around, departing from his patchwork grid to create orderly piles. Savannah's lipstick was paired with a checkbook, and a folded envelope shared a patchwork square with a black-and-white snapshot. "So you're wondering if Dodie Finn might've been the real target. Maybe her sister Ariel got in the way." And, in answer to a question that Riker had just thought of, Charles said, "If Dodie saw her sister's murder, that would be consistent with her present condition. But I can't tell you that's what happened. I can't work magic."

"Right." The detective continued to watch his friend's methodical sorting process. Savannah Sirus's postmortem photos, all but one, were cast aside. The groupings of her personal effects made no sense to him. A driver's license now kept company with the round-trip plane ticket.

"This woman wasn't suicidal before she met Mallory." Charles picked up the plastic card. "Just look at her in this license photograph."

Rolling on his side, Riker squinted at this picture the size of a postage stamp.

"This driver's license is more interesting," said Charles, "if you know it was renewed ten days before Miss Sirus arrived in New York. In this picture, her hair is styled. You see? She's well groomed — eye makeup, rouge and lipstick."

"The works." Riker nodded, pretending that he could actually make out these details on the tiny photograph. There was no need to see it clearly. Charles had just described the war paint worn by a middle-aged woman who had a life worth living — until she stepped off a plane in New York City. It was easier to read the larger, more recent photograph in Charles's other hand. This was the close-up of a dead woman with lank, dirty hair, and no makeup at all. "Mallory did all that damage in just three weeks?"

"Tell me you don't believe that Mallory deliberately drove this woman to kill herself."

"Naw, of course not," said Riker. First he would have to know what Savannah had done to deserve it.

Charles held up a checkbook. "Miss Sirus was planning another sort of trip when she was interrupted."

"I saw that," said Riker. "The check entry

217

for a cruise line."

"This woman wanted to see the world. Thirty thousand dollars would buy stops in a great many ports. The check is recent, and this sort of trip would be booked and paid for months in advance. A woman with suicidal ideation wouldn't be able to plan that far ahead. She wouldn't see any future at all. And, apparently, Miss Sirus — I should say Dr. Sirus — had no money worries." Charles held up a business card. "She was a dermatologist. Judging by her other checkbook entries, she was very successful. Mallory's mother was a doctor, too."

"But not so successful," said Riker. Mallory's natural mother had been a general practitioner in a tiny town. "Cassandra was probably paid in dead chickens and sacks of potatoes."

"But there's more," said Charles. "Savannah's from Chicago. Did you know that Mallory's mother interned at a Chicago hospital?"

Yawning, Riker said, "No, I didn't. The brat never tells me anything."

"But you knew Cassandra was originally from Louisiana." Charles held up the driver's license to bring his point home. "And Savannah is a southern name."

Riker grinned. He had met New York

hookers from Harlem to the Battery who called themselves Savannah.

Charles Butler wore such a patient smile, waiting for the tired detective to put it all together, not wanting to commit a rudeness by stating the obvious thing.

"All those phone calls would make sense," said Riker, grudgingly, "if Savannah knew Mallory's mother in her younger days." He was thinking of a child's trademark line on the telephone in the late-night hours: *It's Kathy — I'm lost.* All those years ago, had she been trying to find an old friend of the family? Why then, after this happy little reunion, would Savannah Sirus kill herself in Mallory's apartment? And what was the link to Route 66 and a child killer? He so longed to bang his head against the wall. In his experience, that actually helped.

"Can you find out if Miss Sirus ever lived in Louisiana?"

"No, Charles, I can't put that name through cop channels — not till I know what happened back in New York. Somebody might get the idea that it wasn't a suicide. So what else have you got?"

"I found a letter in the suitcase."

"No way." The detective had searched the luggage himself. Ah, but he had been sleeping in catnaps for days. So he had missed something else — maybe a lot of things.

"It was in the lining," said Charles by way of apology for contradicting a friend.

"Read it to me."

"It's short," said Charles. "Mallory dated it months ago. She writes, 'I want the rest of my letters. I want all of them.' "

"What? Mallory isn't the letter-writing type. She e-mails."

"Maybe Savannah doesn't have a computer," said Charles, the sworn enemy of technology. "Now consider all the times that Mallory called this woman. Miss Sirus may have stopped answering the phone. Then think about the days that Mallory missed from work — I mean, before she stopped showing up altogether. Maybe she turned up at Miss Sirus's door in Chicago. Maybe the door was never opened to her. Hence this letter from Mallory. The postman always gets through." Charles handed him a small black-and-white photograph. "This was also in the lining."

Riker squinted at the small portrait of a long-haired boy. Reluctantly he pulled out his reading glasses and donned them. Now he could make out the youngster's T-shirt design as an old album cover from another era. "Early Rolling Stones. The kid had taste."

"I found that snapshot in here with Mallory's letter." He held up a large manila envelope. It was folded twice in order to fit inside the torn suitcase lining. "This is big enough to hold quite a lot of letters."

The detective nodded. "Yeah, I guess that makes sense." Letters were all that Mallory had asked for, and it was unlikely that her houseguest would travel to New York empty-handed.

Charles made a show of opening the envelope, turning it upside down and shaking it to demonstrate its emptiness. "Apparently all the letters were surrendered to Mallory. Yet, her houseguest found it necessary to tear the lining in her suitcase — just to hide that photograph. I'm guessing Miss Sirus never went anywhere without it."

What was this? Witchcraft?

Riker rolled on his side, the better to study the picture by the dim bulb of the bedside lamp. "How the hell would you know that, Charles?"

"Oh, there's a lot more you can extrapolate from that photograph. Perhaps if you looked at it in a brighter light?"

These were the last words that Riker heard before falling into a deep sleep.

8

Past the small sleeping town of Galena, Kansas, Mallory departed from a street marked by signs as Historic Route 66. She turned right to travel down a narrow road that cut through countryside and crop fields. Watching her trip monitor, she counted off the miles to her next turn: ten, eleven, almost there. Over the distance of green flatlands, she could see the silhouette of the autobody shop, a garage described as *"— the size and shape of an airplane hangar."* And the letter went on to tell her that this place did a round-the-clock business with three full-time crews, and *"— old Ray was always up before dawn."*

She turned onto a long dirt driveway, then stopped to select Led Zeppelin music to orchestrate her entrance. Moving forward again, she played it at top volume. "Black Dog" was reported to be Ray Adler's secret theme song. Mallory roared into the lot, revved her engine and honked her horn to add to the noise of the band. The song was switched off and the visor lowered to hide her face. She sat very still in the shadows of the car, her back to the rising sun.

A man in his fifties came to the door of the garage and stood there squinting into the morning light. And now came the look of recognition — the song and the car. He was running across the lot, grinning and yelling, "You old son of a bitch, is that you?" The man's eyes were still half blinded by sunrise. "I knew you'd come back." He all but ripped off the driver's side door in his haste to open it. He bent down to look at her face, and now he wore an expression of dumbfounded surprise. Though he had expected to see someone else behind the wheel, his smile spread wider.

"Even better," he said, standing back a pace to stare at her. "You're Peyton's kid, all right. You got his weird green eyes. Not another pair like 'em. And you got your mama's pretty face. But this ain't your daddy's car. Well, damn. Let's see what you got, girl." He started toward the front where the engine ought to be on this recent model, and then he stopped, saying, "No, don't tell me." He turned around and headed for the trunk, and she obligingly pulled the release lever to open it for him.

"Oh, damn, that's beautiful!"

She left the car to stand beside him as he admired the Porsche engine.

"You outdid old Peyton, girl. His Porsche was old when he bought it, and that was before you were born. What a damn wreck that car was. Not a bit of the body that wasn't dented or crushed. He got it for a dollar and a promise not to sue the drunk who totaled his Volkswagen. Happened back down the road not twenty miles. God, how Peyton loved that old VW. That would've been the Bug's tenth run down Route 66. Well, your dad was determined to finish the trip the way he started out. When he pulled in here, he was driving the Porsche and towing the Bug. But we couldn't splice 'em together. And I wasn't about to waste all the best parts of that sports car. So you can see, can't you — just using the Porsche's engine was out. Now Peyton once put a V-8 in another Bug. But that's another story. So we used the old car's convertible top — all we could salvage — and we put it on a prefab shell a lot like this one here. Big as a Beetle, and maybe a little longer. Same paint job, too. Now, silver to go with that black ragtop, that was my idea. Back then, there wasn't another car like it on the road."

Mallory already knew the history of the other car, but never lost patience with this man's retelling of the story. She had yet to say a word, and Ray Adler was only now realizing this. His face turned beet red.

"I talk too much. My wife, rest her soul, used to tell me that all the time. Never give folks a chance to get a word in." He smiled at her, not able to get enough of her green eyes, the eyes of Peyton Hale. "So tell me, how's your dad and his pretty bride?"

"I never met the man," said Mallory. "My mother died when I was six, and she was never married."

Riker tried to ignore the knocking on his motel room door, but the early morning caller was persistent. The shower was running in the bathroom; no help was coming from Charles Butler. The detective dragged his legs to the edge of the bed. The drapes were flimsy, and the room was entirely too bright. He put on his sunglasses to answer the door.

Standing in the awful sunlight of a cloudless new day was the young desk clerk he had met last night. The boy handed him a bag imprinted with the name of a local restaurant. "Mr. Butler already paid for it, sir. The tip's covered, too."

Evidently, Charles had finally broken the language barrier and explained the concept of room service to the staff of this backwater motel. And the tip must have been huge. The boy's grin was that wide, that friendly. Riker slammed the door.

Too much sun.

The paper bag yielded coffee to start his heart and pastries for a sugar rush. He lit a cigarette, and his life was complete — all the drugs necessary to begin the day.

Eyes all the way open now, he noticed the small black-and-white photograph of a young man in a rock 'n' roll T-shirt. It was propped up against the alarm clock so he would not fail to see it. This was the picture once hidden in the lining of Savannah's suitcase. On the back of it was a date that made the boy close to Savannah's age when this snapshot was taken. Riker flipped it over to stare at the faded portrait of a damn good-looking youngster in his twenties. Long, fair hair grazed the shoulders, and the face had the makings of rock-star style: a touch of wit to the eyes and the hint of a wild side in his smile. The image was worn in the center with traces of pink lipstick, and he guessed that Savannah had kissed it too often. That spoke to the absence of her lover. So the lady had lost this man. The affair had ended and the photo was all she had left.

Or maybe not.

Riker looked up to see his friend in a bathrobe. He held up the photograph of the boy. "The letters Mallory wanted — the kid meant old love letters, right?"

"That would be my guess," said Charles Butler. "It's the sort of correspondence that Miss Sirus was most likely to keep for all these years." He nodded at the snapshot in Riker's hand. "You saw the date on the back? The relationship probably ended when Savannah Sirus was as young as that boy."

Riker set down the photograph. "This doesn't tell me why Mallory would want that woman's old love letters."

Charles, the quintessential gentleman, kept silent, showing great confidence that the detective would work this out in another minute.

And Riker did. Everything was clear, for Mallory's short note to Savannah had demanded the letters, as if she had a right to them. The kid had wanted *her* letters. "They were written by Mallory's father."

"Seems logical, doesn't it? But more important," said Charles, "the love letters were written to a woman who was *not* Mallory's mother."

That would explain a lot, given the compulsive way that Mallory had always kept track of every transgression, real and imagined. "So Mallory's father abandoned her mother to run off with Savannah Sirus." One more cheat, another old score to settle. And now, in Riker's own personal autopsy of suspicious suicide, he had motive.

Mallory, what did you do to that woman?

"The first time I met your dad, he was a sixteen-year-old car thief out of California," said Ray of Ray's Autobody Shop. "Didn't even have a driver's license." Mallory's host sat down at a long wooden table stained with rings from a thousand coffee cups. "Well, not a car thief — I'm exaggerating. I'm sure he owned that old Volkswagen — even if he wasn't legally old enough to drive it. But he tried to steal the parts he needed to keep it running."

Mallory looked around the kitchen, aching to put it in order. This was the mess of a man who lived alone, though finger paintings and photographs of young grandchildren were stuck to the refrigerator with cartoon magnets. The washing machine in the corner was merely a repository for dirty laundry that even this impossibly grimy man

228

would no longer wear. Here and there, she could make out the layer of years when his wife was still living. Signs of her were in the rosebud pattern of the curtains. The teacups were ornate. Judging by the pile of dishes in the sink, he used the good china every day — because it reminded him of his wife. She looked at the worn pattern on her spoon — real silver, and silverware was a traditional wedding gift. The kitchen called up memories of her foster father's house in the years following the death of Helen, the woman who had raised her from the age of ten.

Ray Adler poured hot coffee into her cup, then set a carton of milk on the table alongside a five-pound bag of sugar with another silver spoon sticking out of the tear in the top. "Now the last time Peyton came through, he was heading the other way, back to the West Coast, and it was ten years later. He had two college degrees and he was working on a third. That was a predictable outcome. Peyton was one smart kid."

Mallory drank her coffee black and listened to the story of Ray's father catching the young thief in the act of stealing engine parts by dead of night. This might have been her own story, but Lou Markowitz had caught her robbing a Jaguar when she was a child — a more precocious thief than Peyton Hale.

"My father didn't turn him in," said Ray. "Dad didn't want to mess up a kid's whole life for thirty dollars' worth of parts. So he made Peyton work for what he stole. Well, it was like going back to school for my dad — and me, too. That boy could make a busted carburetor rise again from the dead and bark at the moon. In other words — the boy had a way with cars. All that summer, old junkers rolled into the garage, and they rolled out again the next best thing to new. It was magic. Our local trade doubled, and we even pulled in folks from Missouri. That's when Peyton got Dad going on the autobody work, prefabs, real strange modifications. That got us business from four states. These days, I build race cars, too. I get work from as far away as Oregon. Oh, your father was so smart. The back seat of his car was just chock full of old paperbacks, real thick ones. Instead of a salary, Dad gave him a cut on the trade that summer. So when Peyton got back on the road again, he had a stake."

"And he went back to school."

"Yeah, he did. But he'd come back here every summer, work some to make his tuition, then drive on to California and back. Last time through, he was writing a history of Route 66. He wanted to get it all down on paper before it disappeared. But it was more than history. He was building a whole new philosophy around the car. Philosophy, that was his major in school. Odd thing is — it suited him. If you'd only known him, you'd see that clear as I do."

Ray left the room for a minute or two and returned with a wooden box. "These are things that got left behind on his last road trip." He opened it with a key and a trace of reverence, as if it contained religious artifacts. Gently he picked up a photograph. "This is him and your mother. You look just like Cass. That could be you standing there. But I don't know the lady on his other arm."

Mallory did.

Savannah Sirus's young face was turned toward Peyton Hale who, like her mother, Cassandra, was smiling for the camera. Was this a picture of a crime in progress, maybe taken on the day when Savannah began to lay her plans?

The two men wore more casual clothing this morning. Of course, Charles Butler's blue jeans and denim shirt were matched by the same dye lot, custom-tailored and more costly than the entire contents of the detective's closet back home. However, Riker felt great affection and loyalty for his own flannel shirt and authentically faded jeans that fit in all the right places. Years of wear had made them baggy and threadbare at the knees — good driving jeans. He was at the wheel and on the way to the sheriff's office as they rehashed last night's conversation. "No, I've got no idea what her father's name is. I never thought of anyone but Lou Markowitz as her dad. You think Mallory's hunting her real father down for payback?"

"Payback," said Charles. "For what? Think about it. She's only now looking for this absentee father? I'd let go of the vengeance idea."

Riker knew that Mallory had been born out of wedlock, and now he could lay the blame for that on Savannah, the other woman. Charles was probably right. In all likelihood, father and daughter had never met by reason of mutual disinterest. Yet he still worked on a revenge theory. "Let's say Cassandra was pregnant with Mallory when this guy took off and abandoned her. You don't think that would piss the kid off?"

"Without knowing the circumstances, I couldn't say. Now what about this FBI agent, Dale Berman? What exactly did *he* do to Mallory?"

"Oh, *Dale* doesn't even know." There were

a hell of a lot of cops who could enlighten the man, but they no longer spoke to Special Agent Berman.

"It wouldn't be a small thing," said Charles, "not if you think Mallory still carries a grudge."

"Are you kidding me?" Riker rolled to a stop and cut the engine a block away from the sheriff's office. "Did you ever hear her call Lou Markowitz by his first name? No, you never did. In her kiddy days, she called him Hey Cop. Years later, after she'd warmed up to Lou, his name was Hey Markowitz. She loved that old man, I know she did. But right up to the end, the kid was still packing grudges from her days as a runt street thief. Lou was always the cop who caught her. She *never* forgets, *never* forgives."

"But surely Dale Berman factors into —"

Riker waved off any further discussion of the FBI man's offenses. This was a subject that always made him sad. He restarted the car and glanced at the dashboard clock as he eased back on the road. "Mallory should be in Oklahoma by now."

"You mean Kansas. That's the next state on Route 66."

"The Kansas segment is real small," said Riker. "You blink, you miss it." When he finally chased Mallory down, he would have to deal with payback for his own black mark in her personal account books. It would only have taken her six seconds to make a connection between himself and the Chicago LoJack tracker. She would vote him the cop most likely to activate her antitheft device and spy on her. And this time her paranoia would nicely mesh with reality. Only one telling question remained: Did she know Savannah Sirus was dead?

He had to see her eyes when he gave her the news.

And now he thought of another question. He did not want to pry into this personal area, but he had no choice. Everything that might contribute to Mallory's current malady was also the detective's personal business. "Hey, Charles? Is the kid holding a grudge against *you*?"

"No, why would she?" The man faced the windshield not wanting to meet his friend's eyes, and he wore the slight blush of a lie — a small one, most likely a lie of omission. Poor Charles had a give-away face that could not hide a falsehood or a good hand in a game of cards.

The Mercedes slowed to a crawl when the sheriff's office was in sight. Riker was not willing to end this conversation just yet.

"I'm guessing you two had a fight. Mallory holes up in her apartment for months, and you go off to Europe. What am I supposed to think? So what happened?"

"I asked her to marry me." Charles pointed to the windshield. "Oh, look. A reception committee."

Startled, Riker almost hit a deputy as he turned the wheel to enter the municipal lot. Another man in uniform flagged down the Mercedes and waved them into a parking space.

Charles rolled down the passenger window and asked, "We're not late, are we?"

"No, sir," said the deputy. "Things just got off to an early start. The FBI agents didn't want to wait." He ushered them inside the building and down the hall to a small conference room and a meeting in progress.

Sheriff Banner made the introductions, gesturing first to the old man. "You've met Dr. Magritte." He turned to face two strangers on the other side of the room. "But not these folks."

Riker had expected to see a young couple from the caravan, the two people he had picked out for embedded FBI moles, but these were new faces. He ignored the younger agent, who had just started shaving

235

last week, and he stared at the woman.

No one would call her pretty, but she was appealing. He would guess her age at forty by the strands of silver mixed in with the brown, but the short haircut gave her a youthful tomboy look. And a man could get lost in those tranquil gray eyes. The sun had popped out a few freckles on her nose, and she had a slight overbite; these were Riker's other favorite qualities in a woman. The lady was dressed from a catalogue for campers. There was even a Swiss Army knife clipped to her belt. Riker wondered where she carried her gun; it was that well hidden.

The light-haired man beside her was attired from the same mail-order box, but he was much younger, a recent graduate of the FBI academy with the requisite well-scrubbed, earnest face — no wrinkles, no experience.

"Agents Christine Nahlman and Barry Allen," said the sheriff. "They'll be traveling undercover with the caravan. Dr. Magritte's cooperating with the FBI."

"So that makes four of you," said Riker, nodding to the woman. In this count, he was including the two campers he believed to be FBI moles. Agent Nahlman's silence was slightly frosty, neatly confirming this theory.

"This is for you." Sheriff Banner reached across the conference table to hand a folded paper to Riker. "It's a message from their boss, the agent in charge. He called this morning to make their arrangements."

Riker opened the sheet of paper and read Dale Berman's simple question, "What's eating Mallory?" This was followed by the FBI man's coveted cell-phone number, one that even Dale's wife would not have.

Trouble.

The detective waved this note as he faced the two federal agents. "So you guys met my partner? Detective Mallory?"

Oh, yes, they had — no doubt about it. And, in the strained exchange of glances between them, he could see that theirs had not been a happy experience. Riker smiled. "The kid makes a hell of a first impression, doesn't she?" And by that, he meant permanent damage. "So how's old Dale? Haven't seen the guy in a while. No recent bullet holes, no broken bones?"

"She kicked him in the balls." Agent Barry Allen's voice had a trace of awe.

"That's my baby." Riker said this with pride — and relief. Dale Berman's punishment could have been so much worse.

After looking over the FBI-approved route map, he listened to their plans to make

Oklahoma by nightfall and agreed that it was doable on the interstate, where they could get up some speed. Then he sided with Dr. Magritte after hearing the old man's concerns about the proposed hotel.

"The doc's right. They should camp on this private land." Riker held up the map marked with a prearranged site. "It's isolated, easier to keep all the sheep together. You don't wanna move these people indoors tonight, not even if it rains. No walls between them and you."

Nahlman, the older, seasoned field agent, was nodding in agreement, but her younger partner asked, "Why?"

"Well," said Riker, always patient with kids, "you wanna be able to hear the screams."

"Your dad only stayed two weeks that last visit," said Ray Adler. "Just time enough to rebuild the wrecked Porsche."

Mallory was hardly listening anymore. She stared at the photograph of her father, taken when he was her own age. His blond hair was tied back, and his smile was slightly crooked and winning. "Handsome and wild," her mother once said on that rare occasion when she was willing to talk about him with her six-year-old daughter. The photograph had one other detail, a pair of wire-rimmed spectacles tucked into the breast pocket of his shirt. "He wore glasses."

"Well, he *owned* glasses." Ray laid down an earlier photograph of himself and Peyton Hale as teenage boys. "Your dad's only sixteen in this one. See the eyeglasses in his pocket? Never once caught him wearing them. Men can be as vain as women — sometimes more so."

Ray wore his own spectacles as he sorted through the papers in the box. "Your dad wrote me from time to time. Always got a Christmas card. After he came through that last time, I got a few postcards from the road, then nothing." Sitting well back in his chair, he pushed his glasses to the top of his head. "Nothing in all this time." Ray heaved a sigh, then looked down at the floor for a moment of silence. "I love Peyton Hale. And I wouldn't say that about another man in this world." He turned his sad eyes to Mallory. "If you meet your father on the road, you give him my regards. If he's dead, then lie to me. I don't ever want to hear that."

He pushed the box toward her. "That's all yours now. Old notebooks, more pictures and such. You might want some quiet time to look it over." He rose from the table. "And now, if you'll excuse me, I've gotta check on my crew. I've got them working on a roll bar for that car of yours."

"I don't *want* a roll bar."

"But you're gonna get one. If you flip that thing, you'll die."

Having already seen a gravestone with her name on it, Mallory did not offer further protest. When Ray had quit the house, she opened one of Peyton Hale's notebooks and read the opening lines. *"In the beginning, there was the wheel. Then along came the fire of the internal combustion engine. The car was born. And away we go. It's a romance that has no end."*

Next she picked up the photograph of her parents posed with Savannah Sirus. After ripping the latter — the interloper — from the picture, Mallory dropped the torn piece into an ashtray and looked around for matches to burn it. Throwing Savannah into the garbage can was not enough. Only total destruction would do.

The two parents from the caravan had arrived. They were excited and hopeful. Anticipation was everything to them. These two still abided in that fantasy world where little girls never died, where a lost child could still be found innocently wandering in the woods, perhaps a little dirty after all

240

this time — years of time — but no worse for wear, no harm done — not dead, not murdered. The mother and father were looking into the corners of the room, leaning a bit to see around the long table and chairs. Charles Butler winced. They thought they were here to pick up their living daughter and take her home.

The Missouri sheriff held up a keychain fob in the shape of a horseshoe. The mother seized it, ripped it from the plastic bag and kissed it. And then the sheriff told her that the fob had been found with the remains of her child.

"Your little girl was laid to rest in local ground. She was among good people, and her grave was always tended to. Fresh flowers every —"

The mother collapsed. She would have fallen, but she was caught by the helping hands of her husband and Sheriff Banner. A chair was fetched close to her, and she was lowered into it. The husband stood behind her so she would not see his face contorted in agony, a silent scream of *No!* followed by tears and the quake of crying with no sound.

On the other side of the room, Riker, a veteran of many scenes like this one, kept his voice low when he spoke to Charles.

"There's no good way to tell the parents, but I like to think that quick is better. Less torture."

Dr. Magritte stood apart from the parents and was wisely quiet. It would be a while before these two people were ready for grief counseling. Closure was a term dreamed up by fools. Today the parents' pain would begin in earnest, and their imaginings would send them reeling.

Charles turned to the tall brunette beside him, finding this FBI agent less forbidding as he detected in her eyes a profound sympathy.

"They can't go home again, can they?"

"No," said Agent Nahlman. "There's an escort car on the way. They'll be taken to a safe house till this is over."

"Rather extreme," said Charles. Suspicions were contagious things, and he had picked this one up from Riker: What if Gerald Linden was not the only adult victim? "So you believe there's a real threat to the parents, a permanent change in victim profile."

There would be no response. He knew this when Agent Nahlman raised her chin, a sign of intractable tenacity. She silently recomposed herself, losing that sad, soft quality of the eyes — unreadable now.

Riker leaned toward her. "You guys should get the rest of the parents off this road." The detective might as well be addressing the stone building that housed a giant federal bureaucracy. The FBI agent only stared straight ahead, deaf to this good advice. Riker edged closer to the woman, saying, "But hey, Nahlman, it's only life and death, right?"

That got the field agent's attention. She turned to the detective and gave him an almost imperceptible nod, the single give-away that her opinion of FBI command decisions was only marginally better than his. But she would follow her orders, and that was made clear as the good soldier walked in lockstep with her partner, following Dr. Magritte's lead as the old man guided the parents out of the room.

The sheriff sat down at the table, and his head lolled back, so tired, as if he had run a marathon this morning. "I'll tell you what I got from Dr. Magritte. Their little girl was never an FBI case — not till long after she turned up dead. Right after the kid disappeared, the feds told her mom and dad that she didn't meet their criteria. Can you imagine that? Their kid just didn't make the cut. No agents ever helped with that case." He turned to the window on the sidewalk, where an official car had arrived to take those wounded people away. "I told them to hire a lawyer to deal with the feds. Then they might get the child's body returned for a proper burial." He looked away from the sad little scene being played out on the sidewalk, the crying man, the destroyed woman, who were being folded into the back seat of a car like felons. "I talked to a few more folks while I was out at the campsite this morning. There's one man who joined the caravan yesterday in Illinois. California plates. He's been driving Route 66 from the other direction. Suppose I told you this guy might be seriously crazy?"

"That might describe all of the parents to some degree." Charles was thinking of the one who traveled with a wolf. He took that for a recent relationship, for he had not detected any bond between the man and his — pet. "Grief can work odd changes on people."

"This one's a corker," said the sheriff. "All he wants to talk about is patterns. He can't follow a conversation that doesn't have compass points or map sites. Those two FBI agents just blew him off. Well, crazy or not, he might be worth talking to." He nodded to the deputy standing in the doorway.

"Bring in Mr. Kayhill."

Ray Adler had assured Peyton's daughter that the roll bar would be done real quick, and that was true enough. However, in New York time, two days was too damn slow. She stood at the center of the garage, stunned to find her car in pieces.

When she turned on one heel and left for the house, he walked behind her to cross the yard and explain to her back, "Now if my boys were just real fine mechanics, a job like that would take two weeks. A roll bar's no good unless you marry it up with the frame. But these guys are damn *artists* — I'm talkin' real talent here. So, you can see why two days is fast for a roll bar. There's not another shop in the country that can do it faster — not if you want it done right."

He followed the girl through the back door of his house. More than three hours had passed since he had last seen his kitchen, and now he opened his eyes wide to bulging with a bad case of surprise, believing for a moment that he suffered from early onset of Alzheimer's — that he must have wandered into some stranger's house. Truly, the first word to pop into his head was *insane,* and this was followed by *flat-out crazy.*

Kathy Mallory was standing by the table, her angry eyes cast down as she strung the loops of freshly laundered curtains on a rod. And he could not help but notice that the material was six shades brighter. While she turned her back on him to hang the curtain rod over the window, he looked around the room.

How had she done this in half a morning?

He had forgotten the pattern beneath the dirt on the linoleum, and now the checks of many colors shone through a new wax shine. The mountain of dirty laundry was gone, and the dryer was spinning with a load of wash. His old wooden table had been scrubbed raw, and every last splatter and ring, each memory of past meals was gone. Even the faucet gleamed with maniacal cleaning. Ray guessed that this was payback for her roll bar; he had refused to do money with her. But oh my, this kitchen was insanely tidy.

He sat down at the table and watched her run a rag over a cupboard door handle that could not get any cleaner unless she stripped off the chrome. "Girl, you're a damn cleaning machine. How is it that you're not married yet?"

"Never crossed my mind," she said, setting two cups and saucers on the table.

"But don't you want kids?"

"No." Next she brought him a strange coffeepot without a single fingerprint on it.

"Damn," he said with a bit of wonder. She filled his cup with a brew that smelled better than any he had had since the death of his wife, and he was late to wonder if this might have anything to do with cleaning the pot. When the girl sat down with him, he had to ask, "Why don't you want kids?"

She gave this a moment of thought before saying, "I don't know what they're for."

The two FBI agents had returned to the sheriff's conference room. They stood near the door, perhaps as a reminder that they should be leaving soon, and they planned to take the interview subject with them. Nahlman made a point of staring at her watch.

Charles Butler sat at the long table beside Mr. Kayhill, a member of the caravan, who was also known as the Pattern Man. Kayhill was well below average height, not more than a few inches over five feet, and his physical appearance was best described as a distracted pale white pear with black-rimmed eyeglasses. The little man was also rather clumsy, and this he apologized for while mopping up the coffee spilled across his maps. The nervous disposition and clumsiness could be put down to a bad overdose of caffeine.

Horace Kayhill's record time for driving Route 66, he was proud to say, was three days, fueled on little more than coffee and cola.

Riker's jaw dropped in a sign of naked admiration. "Back in the sixties, I did it in four days, but I was driving drunk on tequila — the good kind with a worm in the bottle."

Sheriff Banner allowed that, in his own teenage days, he had once driven Route 66. And he reckoned that he had done it "— under the influence of something, though I couldn't say what." He had no memory of the entire trip. This story was declared the winner.

Charles, who had never driven the famous road, looked down at the maps as Mr. Kayhill unfolded them and spread them on the table.

The Pattern Man had spent considerably more travel time on his latest expedition, thus accounting for being late to join up with the caravan at the edge of Illinois. He pointed to small crosses drawn to indicate gravesites. "I got some of these from the Internet groups." And he had discovered others by making inquiries among people who lived along his route. "Now, this grave was found ten years ago. The locals say the remains were mummified. In other places, people told me the bodies were just skeletons — and one guy said the bones turned to dust when they took them out of the ground, but that was a shallow grave in a flood zone." He reached across the table to run one finger along the desert area of a California map. "As you can see, these three graves are the same distance apart, roughly twenty miles. Now you might read that as a cluster pattern, but you'd be wrong. I see it as a continuous line, thousands of miles long, at least a hundred graves." He never saw the startled look on Agent Nahlman's face when he said, "The FBI agents can back me up on that."

Charles watched as Nahlman quickly folded her arms and looked up at the ceiling. She did not intend to back this man up on the time of day. Her partner, Agent Allen, pressed his lips in a thin tight line, determined to blow his teeth out rather than confirm or deny. The young man's eyes were fixed on the California map and its little crosses, each one a grave.

"Tell them!" Kayhill stood up suddenly and glared at Agent Barry Allen.

"Easy now," said Sheriff Banner, waving

the little man back to his chair.

Kayhill was calmer now, even dignified when he said — when he *insisted,* "The FBI dug up the center grave." He pointed to the first cross in a row of three. "Now this site here — this one was found by a highway construction crew twenty years ago." His finger moved on to the last of three. "And this one was found nine years ago. They're forty miles apart." He looked up at Agent Allen. "So how could your people dig up that middle ground and find another grave if you didn't see the larger pattern? You knew right where to dig."

The two agents maintained their silence. Frustrated, Kayhill unfolded other maps, and these had arcs drawn over the crosses along the road. "I have other patterns. Would you like to know where these children came from?"

Nahlman moved closer to the table, saying, "No, I think we've seen enough, Mr. Kayhill. It's getting late. Agent Allen and I will drive you back to the caravan."

"No," he said, edging his chair away from her. "I want to explain my data."

"We should be leaving now," said Nahlman, disguising the mild order as a request.

This prompted Riker to ask Horace Kayhill if he wanted another cup of coffee.

Charles picked up one of the maps. Some crosses were drawn in ink. He guessed that the ones done in pencil were projected gravesites, as yet undiscovered. "Isn't this a bit like geographic profiling?"

"Yes!" said the Pattern Man, suddenly elated that someone in this company could appreciate his work. "And it's based on consistent spacing of gravesites. I've been able to pin down fourteen bodies dug up on this road, and that's enough to project numbers for the entire group. Some of my data comes from websites for missing children." He glanced at Agent Nahlman. "One of them is an FBI website." Now he leaned toward Charles, who was clearly his favorite audience. "Think of Route 66 as the killer's home base."

Sheriff Banner handed a slip of paper to Riker. The detective nodded, then turned to the Pattern Man. "So, Horace, maybe our perp drives a mobile home."

"Yes, of course!" Horace Kayhill glowed with goodwill for the detective. "That's very good. So the killer actually lives on this road — the *whole* road."

Charles shifted his chair closer to Riker's at the head of the table, and now he could clearly read the paper in the detective's hand. It was the vehicle registration for Mr.

Kayhill's mobile home.

The little man was exuberant, unfolding all of his maps to cover every inch of table space. "You see these half circles in green ink? The arcs represent the areas of day trips between abductions and graves. If he's as smart as I think he is, then he takes the children from one state and buries them in the next one down the road. Of course, that's based on the only two girls who were ever identified. Police searches for missing children are usually confined to a single state — unless the FBI becomes involved, but they so rarely bother with these children."

Nahlman stiffened, then signaled her partner by sign language to make a phone call, and Agent Allen promptly left the room.

Riker called after him, "Horace likes his coffee with cream and lots of sugar." The detective smiled at Nahlman. She looked at the floor.

And the Pattern Man continued. "Think of him as a shark."

"A shark?" Nahlman drew closer to Kayhill's chair. "How did you come up with that analogy?"

This was not mere curiosity. Charles detected a more authoritarian note in her voice. She was slipping into the interrogation mode, though she forced a smile for Kayhill's benefit, and the little man returned that smile, so happy that she was at last showing interest.

"A shark fits the pattern," said Kayhill. "It has a vast territory, wide and long, and this creature is constantly in motion, always looking for prey." One hand waved low over the spread maps. "These gravesites have no chronological order. So he goes back and forth over the road. And look here." He pointed to long red lines that spanned one of his maps. "This is his outside territory. Now I admit that my data is limited for this particular pattern. Only one fresh corpse was ever found, and that girl was kidnapped within twenty-four hours of finding her grave. So I assume he won't keep a child for more than a day. And he'll always drive the lawful speed limit."

Charles nodded. "The killer wouldn't want to attract attention from the police."

"Yes!" said the happy Pattern Man. "That's how I fixed his geographical limits."

"Good theory," said Riker. "And a mobile home would cover his dig site. Hell, he could dig a grave anywhere on that road in broad daylight. All he'd have to do was let the air out of one tire and leave a jack propped up in plain sight. That would guarantee that no cop's gonna stop to give him a hand." He studied the lines drawn on either side of the map. "So how big is our shark's territory?"

"Well, I've drawn lines to include an area six hundred miles wide, two thousand and four hundred miles long. Amazing, isn't it?" He reached under one of his maps and pulled out a small notebook. "These are more specific calculations on gravesites that haven't been found yet. I used the distance between known graves, then made allowances for populated areas and inaccessible places. There's one segment in Illinois where Route 66 dead-ends into a lake." He handed the notebook to Riker. "It's yours. I think you'll find it helpful."

"You got that right." Riker accepted this gift with a rather disingenuous smile. He lit a cigarette and slumped low in his chair, so relaxed — almost harmless. "Now what about you, Horace? Did you lose a kid?"

"Oh, no. I've never even been married."

"You don't say," said Riker. "So what do you do?"

"My interest is mainly statistics, patterns and such, and — of course — Route 66. I know every website for that road. That's how I found two of Dr. Magritte's people. I met them in a Route 66 chatroom. Other parents, too. They were coming together with common statistics, stories of murdered children recovered along the old road."

Riker exhaled a cloud of smoke and watched it curl upward. "And what do you do for a living, Horace? You didn't say."

"I'm a statistician."

"Of course," said the smiling detective. "What was I thinking?"

A deputy entered the room and laid down a sheet of paper in front of her boss. After a glance, the sheriff handed it to Riker, and Charles read over his friend's shoulder. It was a background check on Horace Kayhill, and it fit all the expectations for a man with his disorder. He was on full disability, unemployed and unemployable. Though the sheet of rough data did not include the nature of his disability, Charles already knew. The man was an obsessive compulsive, which neatly explained all the layers of patterns, one chaining into the other.

Riker studied the map of Missouri, which included sections of neighboring states. One of the penciled crosses was twenty miles from here. The next one was in Kansas. The detective planted one finger on this penciled-in cross for the small Kansas segment of Route 66.

And now Sheriff Banner was also staring at the map, saying, "That's where they found that teenager with the missing hand, but she wasn't in the ground. They found her body laid out on the road — maybe a day after she was killed."

"A teenager? Well, that's wrong," said Mr. Kayhill. "And an unburied corpse won't fit the pattern. The pattern is everything. There's a child's body buried there. You simply haven't found it yet." He leaned toward Riker and tapped his gift, the notebook in the detective's hand. "But you'll find it. You'll find them all."

Ray Adler handed Mallory the keys to his pickup truck so she could finish the Kansas leg of Route 66. "It's just a little bitty corner of the state," he said. "Shouldn't take more than fifteen minutes from Galena to Baxter Springs. It only takes a little longer if you have to get out and push the truck."

She rejoined the old road and returned to Galena, where people on the street waved to her, blind to the driver, seeing only the neon-green truck with the fabulous prefabricated front end of a giant, vintage Jaguar, replete with a silver-cat hood ornament. After a few minutes, she slowed down for a look at the old arch bridge, another landmark from the letters, but all of the graffiti had been painted over, and the structure served no function anymore; traffic crossed a new bridge built alongside it.

That took a minute more of her time.

Mallory followed the road around the inside corner that squared off the Kansas segment. She stopped by a baseball field, but this was no landmark of old. The small stadium had the clean red-and-white look of newly laid bricks and fresh mortar. So Peyton Hale's old ballfield in Illinois had vanished, a new one had appeared here in Kansas — and another minute of her life had been lost.

What caught her attention next, and held it, was the digging equipment down the road. She rolled on, moving slowly, wanting to attract attention — and she did. She cut the engine a few yards away from a utility truck and an unmarked van. The vehicles partially obscured the dig site, and a plastic curtain had been raised to hide most of the hole. The workmen were gathering at the edge of the road and taking an equal interest in Mallory. And so they stared at one another until a police cruiser pulled up behind her. She knew the diggers had called local cops to drive her off.

An officer approached the window of the

pickup truck, saying that old standard line, "Driver's license and registration, please."

Mallory ignored this request and leaned out the window to ask, "Is this where they found the body of Ariel Finn? It was about a year ago. The teenager with a missing hand?"

Predictably, the officer rolled up his eyes, taking her for a crime-scene tourist. He would have dealt with quite a few of them a year ago when the mutilated teenager had made the news in this state. And now he would designate her as ghoulish but harmless. His next words were also predictable. "Miss, forget the license and registration, okay? But I have to ask you to move along now."

"Fine," she said, satisfied that Dale Berman would never know she had been here. "Just tell me where I can find your boss."

Ten minutes later, she pulled up to the curb in front of a police station, where an old man with a badge and blue jeans was sitting on a sidewalk bench. His face was lifted to the sky and washed in sunlight. Smoke from his cigar curled in the air as he turned her way and a smile crossed his face. The man stepped up to her window, grinning, saying, "I suppose you killed ol' Ray. No way he'd let you drive this truck unless you drove it right over his body."

She was opening her wallet to show him her badge and ID. He waved this away. "No need to see your driver's license, miss. Any friend of Ray's is a friend of mine, even if you *did* kill him."

When they had exchanged names and she had tacked the word "detective" onto hers, he guided her to the bench, arguing that it was too nice a day to conduct any business indoors. He asked if a little cigar smoke would bother her. No, it would not. Lou Markowitz had loved his pipes, and she had grown up with the smell of smoke. Sometimes she missed it. She had forgotten to ask Ray Adler if her real father had been a smoker, and suddenly this seemed more important than the latest grave by the side of the road. She closed her hand to push her long red fingernails into the skin. Pain. Focus. She knew there was a reason for finding two bodies — one year apart — in the same location. A moment ago, it had been clear in her mind.

Get a grip.

She loosened her fist before the fingernails could draw blood, a telltale sign that she was not in complete control of herself.

Two bodies in the same location — one found on the road and one in the ground.

259

Yes, she had it now. The lawman beside her knew better than to give this information away — even to another cop. She would have to guess right the first time.

Riker assured Horace Kayhill that the caravan would not leave without him. "They'll be getting off to a late start."

Agent Nahlman glanced at her watch. "It's twelve noon. They'll be at the campsite for another hour."

"But we'll get to Kansas before —"

"No, Mr. Kayhill," said Nahlman. "We're taking a different route. The caravan will bypass Kansas. My partner and I will be leading all of you into Oklahoma on the interstate highway. Now if you'll just come with us?"

Riker and Charles stood on the sidewalk outside of the sheriff's office, watching Kayhill drive off with the FBI agents. And now, finally, they had some privacy, and the time was right. The detective turned to his friend. "So you proposed to Mallory." He splayed his hands, only a little frustrated with the other man's silence. "And that's *it*?"

Charles nodded and stared at his shoes, clearly embarrassed. Evidently, one day this poor man had snapped, cracked and blown his cover as an old friend of the family; he had dared to propose to Mallory, who liked him well enough, but treated him more like the family pet.

And, of course, Charles had been turned down, but that was for the best in Riker's opinion. The detective had always believed that this man would be happier with someone from planet Earth, a nice, normal woman who did not collect guns. And this prospective wife should want children. Charles would make a wonderful father, and Riker could easily see a brood of eagle-beaked, bug-eyed kids in this man's future. But he could not believe in a world with more than one version of Mallory; a gang of little blond clones with her green eyes and inclinations was too great a risk; he could not even be certain that she would remember to feed them.

Riker had lost the heart for this interrogation. Turning to the road and the departing car, he changed the subject. "So tell me what you think of the little guy."

"Kayhill? Obsessive compulsive." Charles was suddenly cheerful again — now that the inquisition was clearly over. "Obviously good cognitive reasoning. But he can't sustain eye contact for more than a few seconds. That might indicate mild autism — that and the maps. He's so totally absorbed in his patterns."

"Some of them seem a little far-fetched," said Riker, "but we'll know more in another few minutes. The sheriff's on the phone to Kansas."

Mallory's knapsack rested on her lap. She sat in a wooden chair beside the police chief's desk. They had taken their conversation indoors so he could check out her reference on the telephone. The chief carried on a guarded conversation with Sheriff Banner, answering most questions with one word. Reassured now, he became more chatty with the Missouri man. "Oh, sure I remember. . . . Yeah, how long ago was that? . . . No, we identified the girl. . . . No, that's what we thought at first. Turns out she was a few years younger than we figured — just sixteen. . . . Well, we landed a flyer in her hometown. . . . Ariel Finn was her name. . . . You don't say. Well, I assumed he identified his daughter. We shipped the body back there."

Eavesdropper Mallory wondered why Joe Finn would be traveling with the parents of missing children when his child had been found. Denial was the easy answer. She could see him staring down at the dead body, refusing to believe that it could be his daughter. A corpse was nothing like a sleeping child. Only hours after death, the features would subtly change, eyes clouding and retracting into their sockets, the skin losing its bloom. Some parents used each alteration as a rationale for denying their own children.

There was another possibility that Mallory liked better: Joe Finn might be planning to meet his daughter's killer on the road and take some satisfaction in a murder of his own.

When the police chief hung up the phone, Mallory said, "You didn't tell Sheriff Banner about the feds digging up the ground just down the road."

"Feds? No, that's just a crew fixing a busted underground cable." He sounded only mildly sarcastic when he added, "And I'm sure you saw the electric company's name on the side of their van." His crinkled eyes and a smile echoed her own thought: *Yeah, right.*

And now it was her turn to be sarcastic. "And you never told the sheriff about the bones that were found in place of Ariel Finn's missing hand."

He only stared at Mallory, saying nothing, no doubt reassessing her. "Either you're a really good cop, or the feds told you way

263

more than they told that Missouri sheriff." He seemed to be giving this puzzle some thought as he lit another cigar. "If you'd come by yesterday, I wouldn't have had any idea what you were talking about. A year ago, Ariel Finn's body was found by two kids on their way to school. One of them has a very suspicious mother. Yesterday afternoon, she ransacked his room, thought he was doing drugs. And he was only eleven on his last birthday. Don't you wonder what the world's coming to? Well, imagine how surprised the mother was to find an old cigar box with bones in it." He stopped here, waiting for Mallory to add something of her own.

She knew just the right words. "Tiny bones — from the hand of a child — not the teenager you found on the road."

He nodded. "Only half of them were in that cigar box. You see, both of the boys wanted souvenirs. Damn kids. The other boy had the rest of the bones, but he'd thrown his half away a long time ago. Said it gave him bad dreams. I expect he still has nightmares about that girl's mutilated body. So that boy's half went out in the garbage with the family chicken bones." And now he made it clear that it was Mallory's turn.

She never missed a beat. "When the boys

found the bones of the hand laid out in the road, which way was it pointing — was it toward the latest grave?"

He smiled to tell her she had gotten it right. "Off the road a bit, I found a pile of rocks just a little too neat to be natural, and there was a hollow in the ground, the way grave dirt settles after a burial. I didn't have to dig very deep before the shovel hit the skull — a very small skull."

Each fact dropped into its logical slot, and, though Ariel Finn had died a year ago, Mallory still believed that it was the killer's recent decision to turn from children to older victims. "Back when you found the other body, the teenage girl, I understand you had a problem pinning down her age. You told the Missouri sheriff she was a teenager or a young woman. So I'm guessing Ariel was tall for sixteen and well developed."

The chief nodded. "Her death doesn't fit too well with a child killer, does it?"

"No, I think he screwed up somehow. Something went wrong. He probably killed Ariel because she could identify him."

And this had also been the chief's theory, for he was nodding as she spoke, and now he said, "So — not one to waste a corpse, this sick bastard used Ariel's body to call attention to the real work — killing a little kid. And he screwed that up, too." He leaned forward. "Should I be looking for any more bodies in my neighborhood?"

"I don't know." She reached for a piece of paper and a pencil. "But I'm sure you've already been over every road around here. You looked for signs of another grave and came up dry." After printing out a telephone number, she pushed the paper back across the desk. "Call this detective in Chicago. Kronewald knows where lots of little bodies were buried. I think he'd like to hear from you."

"Little *bodies?* A serial killer with a preference for kids. So, I'm right. Ariel wasn't meant to die that day." He rolled his chair over to an open filing cabinet, then pulled out a manila folder and tossed it on the desk. "That's Ariel's autopsy report. I'll make you a copy — pictures, too, if you like. That poor girl was stabbed fifty times. Half those wounds were inflicted after she was dead, but that still leaves time for a lot of cold terror. Can you even imagine what went through that girl's mind while she was bleeding to death? . . . And it was all a *mistake.*"

Yes, a mistake. The humming child — crazy little Dodie Finn — had been the

266

intended target. The older sister had simply gotten in the way.

One by one, she examined the many autopsy photographs and counted up the defensive wounds on the hands and the arms. Not a quick kill. Mallory had difficulty achieving pity and seldom tried — what use was it to her? And so it was with something closer to approval that she imagined a teenage girl — terrified and all alone in her battle with a serial killer — fighting to protect her little sister and giving that child a chance to run, to live.

Fierce Ariel.

9

Ray Adler hovered close to the back door. The aroma of roast beef had drawn him in from the yard, but now he was repulsed by the photographs that Peyton's girl had spread across the kitchen table. They put him off his feed, these pictures of death.

"The second crew is working on your car," he said. "It'll be finished tomorrow for sure, but it might be real late at night."

She only nodded, then moved down the length of the table, looking from one photograph to the next.

"I think you'll like the guest room. Your dad used to stay there." His eyes kept straying to her pictures, and now he could not look away. He recognized that patch of road, and it was not every day that a murdered teenager was found in his quiet corner of Kansas. "That's Joe Finn's girl, isn't it?"

"You know him?" She looked up. The spell of the pictures was broken.

"No, never met the man. But I saw his last fight." Ray pulled up a chair and sat down at the table. "It was maybe a year ago in Kansas City. He was overmatched and a little past prime, but that man would not lie down. I think the other guy just got worn out from punching him. That would've been around the time they found his girl's dead body — and not too far from here. That was a sad business."

The position of Ray's chair gave him a view into the next room, and he could see that she had been busy in there. He could smell the cleaning solvents that must have come from the grocery bags she brought back with her — along with the bloody photographs.

The girl checked the roast in the oven, then opened the refrigerator door. He saw all his beer bottles lined up like soldiers on the bottom shelf, and every other bit of space was filled with six colors of fresh vegetables, meats and cheeses. His crew would eat well tonight, but it made him feel bad that the girl believed she had to work for her roll bar. And he could not argue with her. Peyton's daughter was the willful kind, and she carried a gun.

Dale Berman had ordered them to take the

parents onto the interstate, the fastest route to the new rendezvous point — as if speed mattered to him. In Agent Christine Nahlman's view, her supervisor had dragged his feet everywhere he went with this case.

Agent Nahlman drove the point car, and she was the first to witness the desertion as highway patrol cars peeled off and raced away to other destinations, abandoning the caravan. Two undercover agents posing as parents were riding in the last car, but it had been the job of the Missouri State Troopers to ensure that there would be no defection of parents taking the exits back to the old road. And now the escort was gone.

Nahlman turned to her young partner, who was engrossed in his road map — and missing the road. In her role as wet nurse to a rookie, she asked, "Notice anything?"

"Huh?" Agent Allen looked up, and his head swiveled to peer out every window. "What happened to the troopers?" And now he must have realized that this was a stupid question. "I'm on it." He pulled out his cell phone and placed a call to the SAC. "It's Allen, sir. . . . Yes, sir. . . . We were making good time, but now the troopers are gone. . . . Yes, sir, I'll tell her. . . . No, sir. . . . Sorry, I thought you were aware of . . . We're taking them to a campsite on private land.

. . . Yes, sir. I'll pass that along."

"Let me guess," said Nahlman. "He's not happy about the change in plans."

"And there won't be any more state cops. We're supposed to keep them out of this from now on. He didn't know you were going to bypass that hotel back in Springfield. You never cleared that with him? Well, anyway, he reserved more hotel rooms up ahead in Joplin."

"That's not going to happen," said Nahlman.

"You don't think the parents will go for it?"

"Something like that." She had no plans to string these people out down a corridor of hotel rooms like fresh meat in a butcher shop. "Call the moles. They haven't checked in for a while."

Allen called up the number for the embedded agents riding in the last car. Only half a minute into the cell-phone conversation, he said, "Oh, shit." The young agent turned a worried face to his partner. "We lost some of the parents when the troopers left. Two of them took the exit back to Route 66."

Nahlman nodded. "Of course they did. They're looking for their children." She smiled at him, never tiring of paper-training the puppy. "And now we don't have the state troopers to round up the strays."

Allen looked down at his cell phone, regarding it as something that might explode in his hand. "I'm sure Agent Berman had his reasons."

"For screwing us over on backup?" Nahlman's hands tightened on the wheel. It was a mistake to put this youngster on the defensive. He would always defend Dale Berman, a man with a gift for garnering undeserved loyalty. "Don't worry," she said. "I won't ask you to call in for help. We'd never get it."

"What if something happens to one of the strays?"

"That's what sheepdogs are for," said Nahlman. "I knew the trooper escort was all for show. Berman just wanted to keep Sheriff Banner happy. I'm surprised it lasted more than six minutes." And now — back to school for Barry Allen; he was about to learn the value of a backup plan. "I asked that New York cop and his friend to drive the scenic route. When the parents take exits, the moles will feed the plate numbers to Riker. He'll round them up."

"When were you going to tell me?"

"That Dale was going to screw us over with the troopers? Was that something you'd want to hear?" She smiled at him with genuine affection. She knew that Barry Allen would give up his life for her, but she could never count on him.

Mallory and Ray Adler sat on the stoop outside the kitchen door, tipping back cold bottles of beer and listening to rock 'n' roll playing in the garage across the yard. The sunset was not spectacular given a cloudless sky, but Ray supplied the evening entertainment, telling her the story of Joe Finn's last fight.

"I went with my dad — big fight fan. Now, that boxing match was as dirty as it ever gets. My old dad called it close to murder. Joe Finn was about thirty-five years old, and he'd stayed in the game too long — too many blows to the head. Not much speed left. The promoters put up a young kid to fight him. Well, that boy was all cheap shots and no talent. But he was a born killer, and the bookies favored him to win. And Finn? Well, he was no kid, and he had no chance. Just didn't have the juice anymore. Ah, but the moves? Damn. I never saw that kind of grace in a man — even when the blood was in his eyes and he was bouncin' off the ropes. It was almost like a dance. My old dad put a bet on that dancing man, *knowing* he was gonna lose. Dad was Joe Finn's biggest fan. And that night we were ringside for the finish."

Ray Adler made his hand into a fist. "That fighter had the biggest heart God ever gave a man. He was beaten half to death, and he would *not* go down. And *every* time he landed a punch, the crowd roared, even them that bet against him — *on* their feet — screaming, whistling — what a *night.* We watched him go ten rounds of pure punishment, and I think the referee was paid to look the other way. I thought that boxer was gonna die. Cuts filled Finn's eyes with blood, but he stayed on his feet — fighting stone blind. And finally the referee stopped the bout. . . . My father's eyes were full of tears. . . . In all my life, I never saw Dad cry for anyone but Joe Finn."

Click.

The woman in red was framed in the viewfinder as she exited the convenience store where she had paid for her gas and taped her poster to the window. The camera kept her in frame when she opened the door to her red sedan. Here she paused with a little shudder. Her head was turning slowly.

Did she sense a pair of eyes on her?

Yes. She was looking toward the back of the lot and the row of parked cars and trucks. All in a panic, her movements were jerky as she climbed behind the wheel and started her engine. A rear tire was losing air from a recently broken valve, but it had not gone flat, not yet. That would happen miles down the road in a place where there were no houses, no people — no help.

Click.

A runaway camper and sometimes a fool for love, April Waylon knelt on the old road beside her disabled car. She stared at the flat tire with the quiet understanding that she was going to die tonight. The lights of the interstate highway could be seen from here, but no one there would ever hear her scream.

Yet she felt no panic. April was beyond that now.

Though there were no headlights to be seen on old Route 66, not for miles in either direction, she had company tonight. Depression had come back to her like a faithful black dog. It was huge and overwhelming all her fear as it crouched beside her. April's eyes welled up with tears. A little girl was waiting for her somewhere on this road; she would wait forever.

A car was coming.

April turned to look down the road toward

the sound of that distant motor. Twin beams of light were rushing toward her, slowing — crawling. There was time to realize that her lost child was not miles away but only minutes, and a ten-year odyssey was nearly done. She bowed her head and said a sorry prayer.

And she waited.

What had been done to her baby would be done to her, and this would suffice for answers to every question save one — why?

A car door slammed. Footsteps on the road came closer. He stood beside her now, and she looked down to see his shoes — so close.

Any moment.

"Lady, I hope you've got a spare tire," said the detective from New York City.

Riker pulled into the gas station, leading another errant parent from the caravan. After they had pulled up to the pumps, he reminded the man, "Don't leave your car unattended. If you need to use the restroom, ask Charles Butler to watch it for you. Nobody gets near that car but you. Got that?"

The detective was about to slip his credit card into the gas-pump slot when his friend beat him to it. "Hey, Quick Draw," said

Riker, "how's it going with the babysitting detail?"

"A very well-behaved group."

"Good. Unless the moles missed a few license plates, I've got all but one of them."

"While you were gone, I had a chat with April Waylon." Charles nodded toward the woman dressed in red. "She's been telling me about her adventures with Mallory — and a LoJack tracker." He waited a moment, perhaps thinking that Riker might want to fill him in on that little side story — but no, the detective was not so inclined. And Charles continued. "Apart from that, Mrs. Waylon's story is rather similar to what happened to Mr. Linden. The battery was stolen from her cell phone. Oh, and she had a flat tire that night, too. The problem was a —"

"A busted air valve? Jesus. So she survives that, and here she is — going out on her own again. What's it gonna take to scare that woman?" Riker checked his watch. "I got one more town to check. It's gonna be late when we catch up to the caravan." And now he looked up to see April Waylon flagrantly disregarding his order to never leave a vehicle unattended. After pulling a poster from the dashboard of the red sedan, she walked away, leaving the car door hanging open while she taped a picture of her daughter to the gas station window.

Riker sighed. "Why don't I just shoot her? Less work."

Charles was also watching April Waylon. "She's been wearing red for ten years — ever since her daughter disappeared." He handed Riker a much-needed cup of coffee, and the two men leaned back against the Mercedes.

"Everything in her wardrobe is red," said Charles. "It saves her from making decisions in the morning. She used to find that very difficult. That's common among people in profound depression. But lately, April has structure in her days — important work to do. And she doesn't think she'll find her daughter on an interstate highway."

"Okay, I get the point. I'll talk to the feds." Riker crumpled his empty paper cup in one fist. "I've still one missing parent." He slipped behind the wheel of the Mercedes and drove off into the night, leaving his witless little flock to go out in search of the lamb that was lost.

The caravan city had taken shape under Oklahoma skies, and the hour was late.

Agent Christine Nahlman watched the man and his wolf walking across the prairie well beyond the campsite. In terms earlier laid down by Detective Riker, this parent, who called himself Jill's Dad, was allotted only fifteen minutes to exercise the animal, and his time was nearly up.

He had offered to camp by himself down the road, perhaps recognizing his status as a pariah here — though not on account of the wolf. Other parents shied away from him because he carried no pictures of his lost child, and because his eyes had gone dead — and his hopes — all gone.

The agent looked at her watch. His time was up. She waved her flashlight to call him back into the fold.

Most of the campfires were burning low, and some had been extinguished in favor of acetylene heaters inside the tents. The smell of coffee hung in the air. The breeze carried it everywhere. Dr. Magritte was passing out paper cups, holding court with those who had not yet retired. He seemed to give these people comfort, but Agent Nahlman had no faith in his ability to keep them in line.

She watched the man and his wolf approaching the camp. One hand was on her gun; the other held a cell phone, though she was hardly listening to Dale Berman's assessment of the day's damage — the missing parent that Riker had failed to find. He gave her no credit for the backup plan that had snagged four other strays.

"This wouldn't have happened," he said, "if you'd checked all those people into the hotel."

"And if I'd put them up in the hotel, a lot more of them would've bolted, and they'd be scattered all over Route 66." Her cell phone went dead. Sometimes she forgot that self-defense was against the rules. Later he would call her back. Dale Berman was predictable that way. He would pretend that they had never had this conversation — that she had not all but called him a screwup, and he would forgive her for the mistakes she had never made.

When the wolf had been safely locked up in the cab of the pickup truck, Agent Allen joined his partner, saying, "Why not call Animal Control? They'll just take the wolf away."

"This is Riker's idea, and we owe him. So you're on wolf watch tomorrow morning."

He was unenthused.

And now, because every day was a school day for Barry Allen, she added, "Never miss an opportunity to do a favor for a cop. It makes them feel stupid when they butt heads with you."

Nahlman sent her partner off to get some

sleep while she took the first shift of guard duty with one of the moles. She spent the time checking license plates against the list made at the last stop. The caravan had not shrunken by five runaways — it had grown. But only the parents from the last campsite had the map for this place. She suspected that Dr. Magritte could clear up this little mystery, and she waited until he was done with the small band of parents around his campfire.

Twenty minutes later, when she approached the old man, he was quick to look up at her, his face full of fear. He must believe that she was bringing him bad news about the runaway parent code-named by Riker as Lost Lamb.

The FBI agent only wished that all of these people could be scared so easily. "Sir, your caravan is growing by the hour."

"It's all right. I know who the new people are."

"You led them here, didn't you — by phone?"

"Well, yes." Dr. Magritte seemed relieved now, assured that she only wanted to lecture him and that no more of his people had died. "You see, not everyone could make the meeting in Chicago. Some of the parents

are coming in from neighboring states as we
—"

"How many parents?"

"Hundreds."

"What!" Had the old man gone insane? "You can't be serious. They'll choke the roads and —" And now she understood all too well. "That's what you want, isn't it. All the traffic will come to a stop for miles around. . . . It's like sending up a flare."

The old man gave his apt pupil a generous smile. "Excellent metaphor — a distress signal. Do you know what these parents go through just to keep the story of a kidnapped child alive?" He looked out over his sleeping caravan. "They were invisible for so long. You've done a very good job of keeping reporters at bay."

Nahlman nodded, though she could not take the credit for media control. Dale Berman had an idiot savant's genius for manipulating reporters. To give Dale his due, he was brilliant at this game.

"The news media doesn't know we're alive," said Magritte, "but I don't think that will last much longer. As the caravan grows, people will notice. Oh, and your presence here will guarantee media attention. *Finally* the FBI will actually help these people."

"But most of these parents have nothing

to do with this investigation — their children won't fit the victim profile." Her words trailed off to a whisper. Of course the old man was already aware of this, and now she realized that the caravan parents must also know. "So the pattern of bodies on Route 66 — that's only part of it."

"That's right," he said. "The only criteria for this road trip was a missing child."

With stunning clarity, Nahlman saw the real caravan pattern in her list of license plates issued in coastal states, Heartland and Southland states. These parents came from all over the nation as representatives of grief — round eyes and Asian eyes and every shade of skin, carting prayer rugs and crosses and six-pointed stars. How damned democratic. This was America searching for her young; her numbers were legion, and she would not be stopped.

Her cell phone was ringing. The lighted number belonged to Dale Berman, and she let the call go through to voice mail. Agent Nahlman was too tired for another round of this man's favorite game, Big Daddy Knows Best. She only wanted a little peace to listen to the music; some distant radio was playing a golden oldie. It was a car radio, and the song came from the Mercedes. Riker was behind the wheel and rolling across the campground, leading a small parade of five cars. Five! The lost parent was found.

It was early in the dark of morning, and the neon-green pickup truck was driving northwest through Kansas along a patchwork quilt of county roads and state roads far afield of Route 66. Mallory had an appointment with a farmer in a distant town. She would have made better time, but now her car slowed down behind a wide load, a tractorlike vehicle with mechanical wings jutting out into the next lane — no hope of passing here. She had only two and a half hours to get to the Finn homestead at the hour when a school bus had arrived one year ago, the hour when Ariel had been kidnapped from her home and killed.

It would be impossible to keep this appointment if the young detective drove the legal speed limit of a serial killer who wanted no traffic tickets. She was going to be late, and yet she did nothing to hurry the tractor that blocked her way, no horn blowing, no tailgating.

Mallory had lost her edge.

She was actually listening to the words of a familiar song played by a local radio station.

"— *some fine things have been laid upon*

your table —"

This tune was not on Peyton Hale's song list, nor did she remember it from her foster care days when Lou Markowitz had taught her how to dance to rock 'n' roll.

"— but you only want the ones that you can't get —"

It was a cut from an Eagles album that Riker had given her when she was eleven years old. At the time, he had told her it was more than just a gift of music — he had found her a theme song called "Desperado." She had played this ballad a thousand times — and then put the album away when she was twelve.

"— your pain and your hunger, they're driving you home —"

Riker thought that Agent Nahlman lacked Mallory's talent for scaring people.

The fed's tone of voice was too civilized as she addressed the mothers and fathers of lost children, saying, "You can't leave the safety of the group and go out on your own. You all know about Gerald Linden. Well, here's something you don't know. He wasn't the only murdered parent."

This was news to Riker and he wondered if Kronewald was aware of it.

"Another dead parent," said Nahlman,

"was found in California. And one in Arizona. The crime scenes were identical to Mr. Linden's. A lot of you knew both of these people. You belonged to the same Internet groups. We have a serial killer focused on this caravan."

Nahlman's partner, Agent Allen, committed the sin of smiling when he stepped forward to hand out the route plans for the day. Next, he made the mistake of good manners, saying, "I know you don't want to travel on the interstate, but *please* don't take the highway exits."

"Or you'll die," said Nahlman, doing damage control with more force. "If you leave the group, he'll pick you off, one by one." Now she demanded their patience, for they would be getting off to a late start this morning.

And that was fine with Riker. He stretched out in a reclining seat of the Mercedes to catch up on the sleep he never got last night. An hour had passed by the clock on the dashboard, but it seemed that he had just closed his eyes when he was shaken awake.

"Riker," said Charles. "The FBI agents counted noses, and six more parents are gone. They just slipped away."

Mallory approved of Kansas. It was a flat

but orderly state with neat squares of crop fields and straight roads that intersected at true right angles.

She found the long shed easily enough, though it was set back on private land. The broad side facing the road had been leased out to advertise a store in the next town. A gravel driveway led her past the shed and on toward the Finns' empty farmhouse. Its wood was painted a crisp clean white, and the shingled roof had gabled windows. Beyond the house was a barn but no sign of animal life — no life at all. Brown wicker furniture lined the front porch, but this did not save the place from a look of desertion. She imagined the yard the way it had been a year ago. The wide green lawn would have been littered with toys and bicycles, the advertisements that young children lived here.

Mallory had driven halfway to the house when she stopped and looked back to take in the lay of the land. She could only surmise that a serial killer had waited for his victim by that long shed near the road. It would hide him from the people in the house. And no one passing by would take any notice of a vehicle parked on private property. A windbreak of trees would have prevented anyone in the house from seeing his car roll off the road to shelter behind the shed.

How many homes had the killer scouted before he found the layout that would give him the best chance of avoiding detection — and confrontation with an adult?

Mallory drove on to the house. A jeep was parked in the driveway, but the man she had come to meet was on the front porch. He rose from a wicker chair and waved to her with a smile of recognition. No doubt the police chief had found it necessary to explain to this man why a New York detective was driving a bright green pickup truck with a Jaguar hood ornament.

After showing him her badge, she endured that getting-to-know-you dance that everyone in these parts was so fond of. They talked as they walked back toward the shed by the road, and she learned that Myles White had taken early retirement from his job as an investigator for the county sheriff's office. His father was no longer able to run the family farm and someone had to take charge of it. Before reaching the road, she knew the names of his four children, none of whom showed any interest in farming, and Mr. White knew nothing about her beyond what he had read on her ID card. However, something in her eyes had given this former lawman a clue that they were done with this quaint custom.

She was a busy woman.

And so he began his murder story at the end. "We had Ariel's body in the local mortuary for a solid week, but Joe refused to make the identification. Said it couldn't be his daughter. How could Ariel be dead? No, she was only lost, he said. Well, the neighbors buried her in the church cemetery down the road. The headstone's blank. They figure one day Joe will come to his senses, and then they can get on with the engraving. We're very patient people around here."

As they neared the edge of the road, he spoke of the day when Ariel was last seen alive. "Joe's a widower. A neighbor woman stayed with the kids when their father was on the road. But that morning little Peter woke up with a cold, and Mrs. Henry drove back to her own place to get him some cough medicine. So it was just the three kids in the house, Ariel, Peter and Dodie."

"Where was Joe Finn that morning?"

"He was in a Kansas City hospital. His last fight tore him up real bad. When I gave him the news, his eyes were so swollen he couldn't see. But he just had to get home to his children. Well, he damn sure couldn't drive, but he would've walked all the way home if I hadn't given him a ride."

"So the three kids were in the house," she said, prompting him, only wanting him to get on with it.

"Ariel was trying to get the little one — that's Dodie — ready for school. Peter was in his bedroom, but Dodie had a set of lungs on her, and he could hear his little sister badgering Ariel to finish making up her lunch box or she'd be late and the bus would leave without her." He pointed to the edge of the driveway. "That's where the school bus stopped."

"Did they all take the same bus?"

"No, Dodie missed the cutoff date for first grade, and she was real disappointed, so Joe sprung for a year of charter school. Peter went to a public school a lot closer to the house. His bus came by about forty minutes later. But, like I said, the boy was sick that day."

"And Ariel?"

"Oh, no bus for her. She was a smart one. Graduated from high school when she was just fifteen. She had a scholarship to an eastern college, but that got put off a year. Joe thought she was just too young to leave home."

"You know this family pretty well."

"I've known Joe Finn all his life." Myles

White stopped at the end of the driveway. "I see where you're going with the business of the buses. You think the killer staked out the house for a while — learned everybody's habits. Some might figure that he just drove by that day and saw Dodie out here all by herself. Now, I'm with you. I think he was waiting for her."

"So you knew the real target was Dodie."

"Oh, yeah — and I'm gettin' to that." He turned back to look at the house. "So Peter was up in his bedroom when he heard Ariel yelling at Dodie to wait for her lunch box, and it was real loud like she was calling across the yard. Then Peter heard the screen door slam and figured she'd gone after Dodie." Myles White looked down at the ground near the corner of the shed. "This is where Ariel dropped the lunch box." He walked toward the midpoint of the shed on the side that faced the road. "And this is where I found Ariel's blood, but not her body. The ground was drenched with it. I knew she had to be dead."

Mallory nodded. The killer's vehicle would have concealed the act of murder from any traffic on this road. "I guess Dodie wasn't much help with the investigation."

"Oh, sure she was. She told me the color of the van and gave me the first three numbers on the license plate. It turned up abandoned in Oklahoma, just the other side of the state line. But that was months later. The owner never reported it stolen. It was an old junker, and he didn't think it was even worth a phone call to the police."

"Did the feds help you find that van?"

"They didn't help with squat. Months went by, and they never answered a letter or returned a phone call. Then one day they turned up to interview Dodie. Well, Joe told them to go straight to hell. I think I would've felt the same in his place. Then the feds sicced Child Welfare on him, and he lost the kids for a while. Peter went into foster care and the feds made off with Dodie. Called it protective custody of a material witness."

"So that's when they realized that Dodie was the target, not her sister."

"But I *told* them that the day Ariel was taken."

"Then they didn't care until they could link her to a bigger case." And now Mallory had to wonder if another one-handed corpse had turned up on Route 66 in those intervening months. That would've sent up the red flag for Ariel's murder. Maybe Gerald Linden wasn't the first parent to die.

"Feds." Myles White spat out this word.

"It took me weeks to clear up the bogus charges and get those kids back for Joe. Dodie wasn't the same when she came home again. She was real quiet — and that was never her nature."

"Any idea what happened while she was in custody?"

"No way to know," said Myles White. "Just a theory. I think they gave her the idea that Ariel's death was her fault. It's not true. Her sister never had a chance that day. I figure he went after her because he didn't want to leave any witnesses. And Ariel never screamed — all that time when he was stabbing her." The man looked up at the sky. "I know you've seen the autopsy photos. You know how long it took for her to die? All those wounds."

"I'll tell you why she didn't scream," said Mallory. "She was protecting the kids. She didn't want Peter to come outside, and she bought Dodie some time to run. And you're wrong about one thing. Ariel did have a chance to save herself that day. Ariel could've run, too, but she stayed to fight."

Myles White slowly moved his head from side to side. This did not square with his notions about tender young girls. "You're saying —"

"I'll show you," said Mallory, who was not

inclined to say things twice. She opened her knapsack and pulled out the autopsy photographs. "Look here." She pointed to the reddened knuckles of Ariel Finn's right hand. "She tried to deck him. So Ariel made the first strike. She only had one chance to land that punch. After that, she would've been warding off the knife blade, fighting for her life."

"Oh, God." His fingers trembled as he held the photograph. "I've looked at these pictures a hundred times."

But this quiet farming community was not a murder capital, and this man had only seen what he had expected to see — the defensive wounds of a helpless girl. He had not understood the lesser damage to Ariel's right hand — wounds of a fighter — just like her father.

They walked back to the house in silence.

Riker ended his day in the same place where it had begun. Back from the road and a new search for strays, he could hardly keep his eyes open. All this time had been wasted. He was no closer to Mallory, and one of the caravan strays had eluded him.

Nahlman shared half her sandwich and poured more coffee into their cups. "Enough. You're done. I told them what the risks were. Why don't they listen?"

"I was watching their faces this morning — while you were reaming them out. They were looking around, counting heads and figuring the odds. It was like they were playing some backward kind of lottery."

Agent Allen joined them. A cell phone was pressed to one ear as he spoke with his boss and relayed apologies to Riker. "Agent Berman's sorry he can't supply any backup, but he's really spread thin."

Riker ripped the cell phone from the younger man's hand and relayed a string of obscenities to Dale Berman that concluded with the words "shit for brains." He ended the call by sailing the cell phone far across the Oklahoma grasslands.

Mallory stood in the open doorway of Ray Adler's autobody shop, the keys to his truck in one hand. Her own vehicle was no longer in many pieces, but it still needed work.

"We'll be done tonight," Ray promised, "or tomorrow morning for sure."

She returned to the house and fired up the vacuum cleaner for an assault on the last bastion of dust, the basement. Around midnight she was almost done labeling the cardboard boxes with lists of junk that Ray never used but could not part with. There was no way to play the cassettes or the vinyl records. The man's stereo only accepted CDs. Among this useless collection, she had found a box with Peyton Hale's name on it. It was filled with music, and she wondered which of these songs had been his personal favorite. None of the letters had been able to tell her.

At one in the morning, showered and ready for bed, the detective placed a call to Chicago. This chore had been saved for last in hopes of waking Kronewald from a sound sleep. She had some new issues with this man, and every little bit of payback counted.

The groggy Chicago detective answered his home phone, saying, "This better be good."

"It's Mallory. Find out if any other adult bodies turned up on Route 66 — or maybe you *already* know."

"Two of 'em," said Kronewald, perhaps not realizing that he had just confessed to holding out on her. "One was found on the road in California and one in Arizona. And here's the kicker. That number carved on Linden's face? They've all got that, and I mean the exact same number, a hundred and one."

Ariel Finn had no numbers carved into her flesh, but Mallory let this slide.

"Weird, huh?" Kronewald was more awake now. "He doesn't count the grownups when he tallies up his kills."

"So you've been holding out on me — *again.*"

"Naw. Riker phoned that in hours ago. Don't you guys ever talk?" He endured her silence for three seconds, the outside limit of his patience. "Got anything else?"

"Do you have a current list of Dr. Magritte's campers — the ones with kids who fit the profile?"

"Yeah."

"Find out if they live in rural areas, no close neighbors. I think I know how the perp shops for the little girls. He follows the school bus. That gives him a chance to scout out the kids and the property, too."

"Okay, so our perp might be a stalker. Thanks, kid. I'll get on it. Where are you now?"

"Still in Kansas. This perp is comfortable with car theft. He was probably driving a stolen car when he killed Linden. It's all about the road. He lives to drive. Long distances don't faze him."

"Okay, I'll start with stolen car reports for the —"

"No," said Mallory. "There may not be a police report. You're looking for *abandoned* cars, old junkers with nothing as fancy as a car alarm or a LoJack. Maybe you'll get lucky with forensics."

"Did you give any of this to Riker?"

Mallory ended the call without the formality of saying good-bye. Maybe tomorrow she would run Riker down, perhaps literally.

Click.

The photograph was expelled from the camera, and it took some time to develop. The blood from the victim's slashed throat was bright red as it flowed onto the Oklahoma road.

A less inspired photographer might have discarded this picture and taken another, for it was slightly blurred by motion. The victim was still twitching — still alive.

10

The beeping cell phone startled Riker, but he was slow to open his eyes. The detective had no memory of crawling off to sleep last night, and now it was day. He awakened in the front seat of the Mercedes. Fortunately, Charles Butler was driving.

Riker pulled out his cell phone and said, "Yeah?" And now, with no pity, he listened to Kronewald's own story of interrupted sleep in Chicago. "Where'd she call you from? . . . So our perp's a car thief. . . . Yeah, thanks." He tossed the cell phone into the back seat, where it would not trouble him anymore. "Mallory's in Kansas. Now where am I?"

"You're approaching a travel plaza."

Riker patted down his shirt pockets and he found a crumpled pack of cigarettes. "I guess this is weird for you, huh? I mean chasing Mallory." He was still seeking a way back into the story of Charles's last meeting with her, the one that had ended with a proposal of marriage.

"Well, I don't think she expects to see me again."

"So I'm guessing she didn't let you down easy." After a few miles of silence, Riker tried again. "Did she at least say good-bye?"

Charles steered the Mercedes onto the exit road for the travel plaza. "That night after dinner, I walked Mallory home, and she kissed me." He pointed to his left cheek to indicate that this had not been a moment of passion. "Later — a month later — when she wouldn't return phone messages or answer the door, I realized that the kiss — *that* was good-bye." Charles pulled into the large parking lot. "Lunchtime."

This place was also a rendezvous point for the FBI. Riker's first giveaway clue was the slew of government cars and the rentals favored by feds in the parking lot. He checked out the young people near these vehicles, almost standing at attention. There were no agency logos in sight, though their clothing approached a kind of uniform in the similarity of blue jeans, hiking boots and navy blue jackets that were missing only the initials of the Bureau. The colors of their T-shirts varied, but the detective gave them no points for this lame attempt at disguise.

"Mallory's not in Kansas anymore," said Charles Butler.

Riker turned his head to the other window in time to see Mallory glide across the parking lot with the top down on her silver convertible. And he could not speak nor even move. This was the culmination of night-into-day worries and tension. Finally, the road-weary detective managed to stumble from the Mercedes, and then he treated everyone in the lot to an explosion of involuntary emotion.

Mallory was on foot and heading for the door of the restaurant when she recognized that loud, laughing voice. She turned to face Riker. He walked unsteadily, approaching her Volkswagen Beetle and pointing at the roll bar. The other hand was holding his side where the laughter had caused him a stitch of pain. An impartial observer might have likened the man's outburst to hysteria, for he could not stop himself. He was so happy, he was in tears.

Later, he would put his mistake down to lost sleep, but now he committed the worst error on Mallory's scorecard of crimes against her — derision. He pointed to her convertible and said, maybe a bit too loud, "A *roll bar* on a *VW?*" When laughter subsided long enough to speak again, Riker said, "I've seen it all. I can die now."

Mallory glared at him, perhaps with an idea for arranging this early demise.

He yelled, "Hey, kid! You planning to *race* this car?" His best line spent, he was truly helpless, leaning against the side of her Volkswagen for support. He was enjoying himself so much that he thought he might fall down.

In icy calmness, the control freak turned her back on him with not even a word of hello after all this time when they had not seen one another.

Charles Butler appeared at his side, saying, "Uh, that might've been over the top. I'll just explain to her that you were tired and overwrought."

"Oh, come *on*." Riker slapped the roll bar, saying, "*This* is funny."

"I have another theory." Charles was watching the wide window of the restaurant. "Wait — she's going into the ladies' room." He pointed toward her car. "Can we take a look under the hood?"

"If that car's got an alarm — and I promise you it does — Mallory won't even bother to step outside. She'll just shoot you through that plate-glass window, and then she'll order a cheeseburger."

In a test of this theory, with one pull on

the handle, the car door opened quietly for Charles.

"Bad sign," said Riker. "Normally, the kid's too paranoid to leave a car unlocked." And now she had walked away from an open convertible. He leaned inside to search for the hood release and found it. He noticed that the dashboard was oddly absent Mallory's usual road show of technology toys. There were no built-in computers, no global navigator, only a police scanner, but who, besides his anti-tech traveling companion, did not own one of those?

Charles Butler lifted the convertible's hood, and then his face went blank.

The detective moved toward the front of the car, figuring that his friend was simply clueless about engines. Had Charles expected to find a herd of horses under there — or something equally obvious that would explain the need for a roll bar? Riker looked down at the engine compartment.

What the hell?

Under the hood, where the engine should be on every recent model of this car, there was only a duffel bag.

Impossible.

"Well, that settles it," said Riker. "The kid's just getting *way* too spooky."

Charles turned to the restaurant's window,

and then he quickly closed the hood. Inside the building, the door to the ladies' room was opening. The two men edged away from Mallory's car, and Riker was showing more respect for this vehicle.

Mallory sat down at the only vacant table by the window. She reached into her knapsack and retrieved the small notebook of roadside attractions, and a checkmark was placed next to Mickey Mantle Boulevard in Commerce, Oklahoma. She also checked off the blue whale found in the town of Catoosa.

Done with this daily chore, she looked up to glare at the middle-aged man seated near her table, for he had already taken notice of Mallory, who missed nothing, eyes lowered or shut. Caught in the act of staring at her, the little man's head ducked low, and he resumed a study of his maps, not an odd preoccupation for a traveler at a road stop. However, the hand holding his coffee cup trembled, spilling hot liquid into a tote bag on the floor, where the rest of his map collection was turning soggy and brown. She remembered him from the diner back in Illinois, a customer too twitchy to go ignored.

It was the map spread on the table that made him truly interesting. The state of

Oklahoma was overlaid with multicolored lines and arcs — and a small cross drawn with green ink. Other more temporary markers were made with a pencil and evenly spaced along this state's segment of Route 66.

"We call him the Pattern Man," said Riker. "That's his Internet moniker." Unacknowledged, her partner pulled up a chair and sat down beside her. Charles Butler remained standing, awaiting an invitation. She nodded to him in lieu of hello, for he had not laughed at her car. And now they were three.

"The little guy's name is Horace Kayhill." Riker nodded toward the neighboring table.

Charles explained the map collector's peculiar bent with patterns, but Mallory paid no attention. She was focused on Dodie Finn, who sat with her brother at the center of the room. Their father stood in line at the counter, holding a tray and ordering food for his family. The little girl was silent, but she had begun to rock — a prelude to the humming.

Riker lifted a leather case from his lap and set it on the table in front of Mallory. "I brought this all the way from Chicago. It's a present from Kronewald. He said you left your computer at home." In a voice reserved for coaxing small children to eat their vegetables, he said, "This one's probably loaded with all your favorite goodies." When she would not even look at him or the gift, he shrugged and left the table to fetch them all a round of coffee and burgers.

Mallory unzipped the case and looked down at the laptop computer. It was a recent model, but she doubted that it would have the software she was accustomed to. She expected no illegal lock-pick programs, nothing useful for unlawful entries in cyberspace. However, she had everything necessary to wake up her slumbering computers back in New York City.

"There's a sign in the window," said Charles. "There should be a computer access around here somewhere. Oh." He watched her unravel a wire, plug it into an outlet by the napkin holder, and then power up the computer.

Bonus.

The FBI icon on the screen gave up Detective Kronewald's password. But first — a little improvisation. The keys began to click, and a thousand miles away in New York, a computer came to life in her apartment. It yawned in hums and whirs, and then it fed her lock picks and pry bars and her coveted store of stolen passwords. She cut the remote computer loose and entered the Federal Bureau of Investigation, leaving no footprints behind. She passed beyond the Internet holding pen where police inquiries were stalled, and now she jumped three links toward her goal of a secured site. This was, more accurately, the Bureau's antiquated idea of security. She was inside the vaulted files, free to pillage and plunder whatever she liked. Mallory took no great pride in this, for defeating the FBI's outdated system was a rite of passage for small children all over America.

She looked up from her screen to smile at Charles Butler. He would need some occupation to discourage him from being helpful. "You see that couple at the corner table," she said, "the man and woman with red and green baseball caps? They're with the caravan."

"Yes, I've met them."

"Watch them for a while. Tell me what you think." Her fingers flew across the keys, doing a little dance of codes and passwords, evading watchdog alarms and red flags to gain access to an enemy file. Ah, and now the door lay open, and Dale Berman was stripped naked on her screen. Scrolling down his biographical data, she found the report on the New York fiasco with Markowitz, followed by Berman's reprimand and promotion. That last entry angered her but came as no surprise. Once it had been Dale's lot to clean up the messes of other agents. He would be too dangerous to fire or demote. Working backward, she found a psychology degree from his younger days. And now she hunted for his job application process, though she had never believed the myth of the foolproof FBI applicant investigation.

With a light touch on Charles's arm, Mallory called his attention away from the assignment to study the couple in the corner of the room. "Is it true that most people who study psychology have a few screws loose?"

He stared at her for a moment, probably wondering if she was alluding to himself. "Well, a lot of people who work in the field had some early exposure to the mental health process. But that could be any sort of therapy."

Close enough.

She closed Dale Berman's file. "So . . . the couple at the corner table?"

"Well, they wear wedding rings, but they're not married," he said. "They never have been. I'd say their relationship is relatively new. You can tell by the body language. He's in pursuit, flirting with her. She's looking around, hoping that no one hears what he's saying to her. This is a game they've played before. It's the conversational equivalent of stroking. She's in retreat from him, but she actually likes the attention. See? Repressing a smile. If not for the setting, I'd characterize this as an office romance, one of those relationships that springs from propinquity, perhaps the time they've spent together on the caravan." He turned to Mallory. "They're the FBI moles. That's the way Riker introduced them to me. Oh, sorry, was that the short answer you wanted?"

Mallory smiled at this hand-me-down friend of her foster father's. And to show him how much she had missed his company, she had not interrupted his diatribe once, nor made the usual hand signals to speed it up. "I only want to know who they're watching."

"Well, it's not the little girl." He seemed pleased with her flash of surprise. "And that's odd because that was Riker's guess. No, their only interest, apart from themselves, is Dr. Magritte."

Mallory glanced at the Finns' table as Dodie began to hum. "Always the same four notes."

"*Eight* notes," said Charles, the man with perfect pitch. "There's a slightly different nuance that begins the next bar." One finger went up, as if pointing to the notes passing by. "And there — a minor pause following the eighth note — and she begins again. Hear it now? It's an old standard." Charles whistled the string of eight notes with a more upbeat inflection.

Riker returned to the table with a tray of cheeseburgers, coffee mugs — and the lyrics. " *'Oh the shark, babe . . . has such teeth, dear . . .'* " And now he added more notes to Dodie's limited refrain, singing, " *'and he shows them . . . pearly white —'* "

He stopped abruptly, and Mallory followed the track of her partner's eyes to a dark-haired woman seated nearby with a younger man. Riker had a keen appreciation for the ladies in their forties — and every other age bracket. The brunette stared at him — spellbound.

"Damn, I'm good," he said as he bowed to this woman. "And now my favorite line. *'Scarlet billows . . . start to spread.'* "

Though the civilian diners took little notice of Riker, Mallory watched other faces turning to stare at the singing detective. It was easy to identify them as FBI agents, and they were not a happy group.

Where was Dodie?

One tiny castoff shoe lay near the Finns' table. Mallory caught sight of the boy standing at the magazine rack, leafing through a comic book. And now she had located his little sister. One shoe off and one shoe on, the little girl had crawled beneath the table. Dodie was not humming anymore, but folding like a flower when night comes, drawing her knees into her chest, head bowing. The toes of one bare foot curled tight.

Charles Butler was also watching the child, and his face was grave when he said, "Riker, don't sing anymore."

"Everybody's a critic," said the detective, now aware of the agents all around the room who also wanted him to stop.

Dale Berman was standing frozen by the door, and Mallory made an easy guess that he had heard Riker's rendition of "Mack the Knife." Her partner had also noticed Berman and looked down at the floor, not wanting even eye contact with this fed, their common enemy. With this change of perspective, Riker could see the little girl beneath the table.

"Dodie!" yelled young Peter Finn, suddenly noticing that his sister was gone from her chair. His eyes went everywhere, crazed to find her.

"It's okay, kid!" Riker called out to the boy. "I got her." He reached under the table to take Dodie's hand, and she began to scream. He drew back, wounded, for he was a man who loved children. "What did I do? The other night, she was fine with me."

"Let me guess," said Dale Berman, drawing closer to the New York detective. "You weren't wearing that red shirt." The FBI man hunkered down by the table and smiled at the rolled-up ball of a little girl. "Hello, Dodie. Remember me? It's been a while, hasn't it?"

Her screaming stopped. She did not reach out to him, but neither did she protest when he took her small hand and led her out of hiding.

Riker stared at Berman. "And she hasn't seen you for a long time? The kid's good with faces?"

"No, it's probably my suit," said the agent, openly appraising the detective's flannel shirt and faded jeans and finding them wanting. "Dodie spent a long time with people in suits. She's very compliant with —"

"Interrogation?" Riker, brows knit together. "A kid?"

Berman ignored this. He only smiled down at the little girl beside him, and Dodie stared straight ahead, blind and deaf to everyone. "Anyway, Riker, it's nothing personal — just the way you're dressed — the red shirt."

Riker marched outside and crossed the parking lot to Charles Butler's Mercedes. Mallory watched him pull his bag from the trunk and rifle its contents, probably searching for his least rumpled shirt of another color — so a little girl would not be afraid of him anymore. Her partner was a sucker for children, and this child had freckles, his other weakness.

Charles leaned toward Mallory. "You know that man lied to Riker. It wasn't the color of the shirt — it was the song."

Yes, Mallory knew that.

Her eyes were on Joe Finn. The boxer was slow to cross the room. There was great deliberation in each step, and she knew he was trying to bring his temper under control and only succeeding in part. His fists remained at his sides, but his eyes were full of hate when he finally stood before Dale Berman, a poor specimen compared to the prizefighter.

Joe Finn's voice was oddly soft, almost soothing, and he spoke with the singsong meter of reading his daughter a fairy tale. "Back away from my kid or lose all your damn teeth. Those are the only two choices you get."

Mallory approved of the boxer, the enemy of her enemy.

Riker returned to the restaurant with another shirt in hand and found himself on speaking terms with Mallory again. He made a mental note — no more car jokes.

"You won't need that," she said, taking the shirt away from him and draping it over the back of his chair. With a little backup nodding from Charles Butler, Mallory assured him that Dodie Finn would not care if he changed his clothes. "Trust me, the kid's out of it. She wouldn't know if you were wearing a red shirt or a dress." She angled the laptop computer so that he could see the screen and a recently purloined FBI file. The code name the feds had selected for this serial killer was Mack the Knife.

"Aw, what've I done to that kid?" Well, he had sung the words to her scary little tune, and then, as bogeymen will do, he had reached out for her. "And Dale's little story about the red shirt?"

"Misdirection," said Charles. "The key to every good magic trick. If you thought it was the shirt, you'd never look at the song."

Mallory turned to the door as a redheaded

man, tall and reedy in a dark suit, entered the restaurant. "Riker, we've got trouble." She nodded toward the new arrival with the crew-cut red hair. "That one's a witch doctor."

"Agent Cadwaller?" Riker smiled and held up his cell phone. "Kronewald called. Said to tell you he checks out. You were right. Cadwaller's last posting was the Freak Squad."

"You mean the Behavioral Science Unit?" Charles turned to look at the red-haired man. "But they're not Ph.D.'s. I thought your criteria for a witch doctor was an accredited —"

"You're right," said Mallory, cutting Charles off as she usually did when his longer and more predictable sentences tried her patience. "Cadwaller's just a screwup. That's probably why they shipped him off to Dale's field office."

Riker watched as the man spoke with Dale Berman, who pointed him toward the Finns' table. As Cadwaller approached the small family, Joe Finn was rising from his chair and all too clear about his intent to knock the agent back into the parking lot — via a broken window — if the man took one more step toward the children.

Caring nothing about losing face in a

room full of feds and cops, Cadwaller wore a placating smile and raised one hand to beg a pardon as — *he* — *backed* — *up.* Nothing more was needed to classify him: this was a man who rarely, if ever, went into the field. By Bureau regulation, every fed was required to carry a weapon, but this one had the look of a man unaccustomed to walking around with a gun. Or maybe, at the start of this day, the agent had left his sidearm on his motel-room dresser — along with his testicles. A moment ago, Cadwaller had seemed an ordinary man, maybe a little on the pale side, and now Riker found him vaguely creepy, soft and unsexed.

Ten-year-old Peter Finn watched the red-headed man withdraw to a safe distance from his father, and then the man handed a paper to Agent Berman. Now both of them were looking at Dodie. The last time Peter had witnessed this scene, he and his sister had been taken away and not allowed to see their father. It had been so easy for FBI agents to goad Dad into the last fight, the one that left two children screaming for their daddy as the Child Welfare people took them away.

He knew what would happen next, and so did his father. Dad was watching all of this play out and shaking his head slowly to say, *No, not again.* The big man turned to his young son with a halfhearted smile, a failed reassurance that things would be different this time.

Peter was looking elsewhere for a champion that the FBI could not arrest for fighting back. His eyes passed over Riker, for that man was just too cozy with the lady FBI agent. He settled on the tall blonde, the pretty woman he had first seen in the diner back down the road in Illinois. She had also come to the Missouri campsite to talk with Dr. Paul. Peter remembered being afraid of her then. What had Dr. Paul called her?

Mallory.

And she carried a gun.

Agent Berman was crossing the room toward Dodie. Peter knew he would have to be quick, and he was. Rising fast, the boy ran to the pretty woman's table, saying breathless, "You're a cop, right?"

Without looking up from her computer screen, she said, "I thought you didn't talk to strangers."

"Well, I'm talking now, okay? I need help. I think they're going to take my sister away."

"You mean protective custody?" asked Riker. "That might be for the best, kid."

"No!" Peter pounded the table, his eyes fixed on Mallory. "They don't care about me and Dad. It's Dodie they want. The last time they took her, she was worse when she came back. She wouldn't even talk anymore."

And *now* Mallory looked up. "What did Dodie tell you — back when she was talking?"

"Please, there's no time. You have to stop him." The boy pointed to the man he knew as Special Agent Berman.

Too late.

Peter's father pushed Agent Berman away when the man reached out to touch Dodie. And now the FBI man was closing in on her again, one eye on Dad. A moment later, the agent lay sprawled on the floor, bleeding from his lip — and *smiling.*

Mallory was rising from the table with Detective Riker. She said to Peter in passing. "We'll talk later. Deal?"

"It's too late." Peter stared at the bloodied FBI man on the floor. Pain could only be moments away. The family would all be taken off in separate directions — just like the last time. The boy had tears in his voice, crying, "Not again. We can't go through this again." He was looking up at Mallory's face, her strange green eyes — no mercy.

Agents slowly converged on the boxer from all quarters of the room, trying to appear natural and normal as they skirted the tables of civilian patrons. Joe Finn saw them coming. He did not care. He would take them on, one by one, or in twos and threes. That much was clear by his stance and his closed fists, and Mallory liked this man better and better.

Dale Berman was rising to support himself on one elbow, but wisely staying close to the floor and out of immediate danger.

Only the people from the caravan remained in their seats, and their conversations were ending as each one in turn saw the fallen man and then noticed the encroaching circle of men and women, their holstered guns exposed for quick access.

The two New York detectives moved in quickly to flank the boxer. This brought the group of FBI agents to a standstill; their course of action was less clear now, and all of them lowered their eyes to the prone Dale Berman. They were stalled and awaiting his orders.

Mallory leaned close to Joe Finn, saying, "The bastard on the floor belongs to me. Stay out of my business and sit down. That's a direct order from a cop. *Don't* fool with me."

The boxer nodded his understanding of a prior claim, and he seemed to have no problem with her authority. This was not about his manhood; this was all about his children. Slowly he settled into his chair.

Riker held up his gold shield, and Mallory drew her denim jacket to one side, displaying the gun in her shoulder holster. Better than a badge, this act screamed *cop war* to every fed as she revolved slowly, making eye contact with agents all around the room. The feds were not backing down, but neither would they advance, and their own weapons were no longer on view to the gaping civilians. There would be no gunplay today, not with so many sheep in the house, and not ever with cops.

Mallory's voice only carried as far as the floor when she said, "Berman, call them off *before* you get up. If I deck you, the troops won't forget that."

He smiled. "You think that's worse than kicking me in the balls in front of —"

"Much worse," she said, looking down at him with no expression. Her voice was a harsh whisper, and, to the surrounding agents, this must look like a normal conversation. "When you're picking yourself up off the floor? When you're just a little off balance? That's when I take my best shot. Closed fist. They'll talk about that for a *long* time. And I won't pull my punch . . . like the boxer did."

"Say, Dale." Riker spoke softly when he hunkered down, smiling for appearance's sake, as if he might be consoling the fallen man. "Your front teeth — those are caps, right? Cost much?"

"Don't interfere," said Berman. "And that goes for your partner, too. Assault charges —"

"Provoked assault," said Riker, ever so politely correcting the agent.

"I'm bleeding."

"And you had that split lip when you walked in the door," said Riker. "So you cheated. You saw the punch coming. Hell, you *asked* for it — and then you rolled with it. More like a tap, I'd say. Just dumb luck that Finn reopened the cut on your lip. And I wonder where *that* came from."

In unison, both men looked up at Mallory.

Berman spoke to her in a low voice, possibly believing that she was listening to him. "You've got three seconds to stand down, Detective."

"Count real slow," said Riker. "You giving

orders to Mallory — that's a good one —
for a man who's still walks funny. You
thought her shot to balls was bad?" Riker
raised his voice to laugh, and this had a
calming effect on the surrounding agents;
the tension level in the room was dropping.
"Don't fool with my partner. She'll bite
your head off. I've seen her kill six pigeons
that way." Riker reached out and ruffled
Dale Berman's hair to assure him that this
was just a small joke, and then he leaned in
close and whispered, "I have no control over
her."

Magic words.

The man on the floor was a true believer.
"All right. Enough." Berman called out to
the surrounding agents. "Everybody settle
down. Back to your tables. Now!"

"And no penalty for Joe Finn," said Mallory.

"No deal," said the agent as he regained
his feet. "Finn's a prizefighter. He knows
the law. His fists are —"

"Considered weapons," said Riker. "Yeah,
yeah." Before Dale Berman could say any
more, the detective jumped up the stakes by
humming the opening bars to "Mack the
Knife."

"Okay," said Berman, magnanimously,

"no charges."

Special Agent Dale Berman gave Mallory a wide berth in passing the table where she was deep in conversation with the boxer's boy. Still holding an ice cube on his split lip, the FBI man sat down with Charles Butler and Riker. He laid an official fax communiqué in front of the detective.

"I just want to clear up one little thing," said Berman, tapping the fax. "The sheriff back in Missouri requested protective custody for the Finns."

"And that would be us," said Riker, not bothering to even glance at the fax. "Me and Mallory, we're the protection now. And let's clear up another little thing. You should pray that Joe Finn doesn't talk to a lawyer. Provoked assault, abuse of power — oh, and that time you snatched his kid."

"In your dreams, Riker."

The detective glanced at the far table where his partner was discussing murder with a child. "Little Peter makes great witness material, doesn't he? I'm betting that kid can cry at the drop of a dime, and that might come in handy. Now a charge of kidnapping Dodie — that won't stick in court, but it might get some airtime on the evening news — prime time. And that would be a damn shame. Up to now, you've been real good at squashing media interest. So play nice with the boxer. Your balls belong to him now."

Riker crossed the room to deposit a laptop computer on Mallory's table. And now the detective's tall friend, Charles Butler, was left alone to make conversation, faltering for words and finally saying, "So you're in charge here."

Agent Berman smiled in faint appreciation for Butler's dry punch line. His smile became more affable when the detective returned to the table. "Riker, I got Kronewald's presents from Mallory. If you're curious about the tool mark on the air valve and the fingerprint —"

"Not good enough for matches," said Riker. "I know."

"So you and your partner plan to give us a hand on this one?"

"Cooperation? Not your style," said Riker. "You'd rather cut cops at the knees."

"Hey," said Berman, "that business with Kronewald in Chicago — that wasn't my call," he lied. "I wasn't even there." That part was true. He gave Riker his very best good ol' boy smile and lightly slapped the table with the flat of his hand. "So, we do a little deal? Share and share alike?"

"Just like old times?" asked Riker. "With Lou Markowitz?"

"What? You're still pissed off about *that?* Mallory, too? Okay, I held out on Markowitz. But that was years ago, and it's not like somebody died."

Riker's response was instant and strong, every muscle tensing. The detective wanted to hit him; that much was very clear. Instead, Riker rose and left the table, and this time he did not plan to return, but slouched into a distant chair with an air of permanent repose.

Agent Berman turned to Charles Butler. "You know what that's about?"

"The old business with Louis Markowitz? Sorry, I don't have any facts to work with. However, given Riker's reaction, I'd say it's obvious that someone *did* die."

Dale Berman's luck with Mallory was no better. He waited until the little boy left her table, then pulled up the chair next to hers. "We could help each other on this one."

Too clearly, he understood the look in her eyes that said, *Yeah, right.*

"I have legal authorization to take Dodie Finn into custody." And now, lest she misunderstand and send a knee toward his privates, he held up one hand in surrender.

"That's not a threat. I won't, okay? See, I'm just trying to —"

"This is the new and improved FBI?" She continued to stare at her laptop screen. "So now you can disappear a little girl? How did you do it the last time? Did you fob her off as a terrorist? Oh, wait, I forgot. The feds don't have to give reasons anymore."

Berman had a comeback for that, but he was interrupted when a large woman settled into the chair beside Mallory's and introduced herself as Margaret Hardy, widow of Jerold Hardy, and mother to young Melissa Hardy, who had gone missing when she was six years old.

"I think about her every day." Mrs. Hardy opened her purse and pulled out a fistful of snapshots that pictured a little girl in different costumes and poses. Apparently six-year-old Melissa was a born performer, mugging for the camera in her ballet dress and her Halloween costume. "And this shot was taken at her school play. That's her in the carrot suit. She likes carrots and peas — just the colors, not the taste — and she plays the piano. I thought you should know that . . . something . . . personal." Mrs. Hardy wore a constant smile, but she seemed always on the verge of tears.

Mallory was on best behavior with this

civilian. She looked at each photograph and asked polite questions about the place where Melissa had lived. "Any close neighbors? Did your daughter take a bus to school?"

Even before these questions were answered, Dale Berman knew that the lost Melissa Hardy fit the victim profile — and now Mallory knew it, too.

As the FBI man's gut knotted up, he had to wonder what else this New York cop had worked out on her own. When Mrs. Hardy had left the table, and Mallory was once more absorbed in her computer, Berman edged his chair closer to hers, saying, "Back to the subject of Dodie Finn. I didn't want to —" He forgot what he had intended to say, for she finally looked up to acknowledge him, and he wished that she had not.

What cold eyes you have.

The young detective leaned toward him — too close. She was robbing him of personal space, and each of her words had equal weight, as if a metronome could speak. "If you touch that little girl one more time, I will mess you up so bad."

She turned back to her computer screen. He was now dead to her, and it did not matter whether he left her table or not. There would be no discussion of the good old days or his last assignment in New York. Years had passed since then. How could she hold a grudge? The case had been delayed on his account, but that kidnapped child had been found alive. He decided that Charles Butler must be wrong. No one could have died because of what he had done to Lou Markowitz. Yet the idea would remain with him all through the day.

Riker and Charles took turns shooting covert glances at Mallory, who sat alone on the other side of the room. The caravan parents were also staring at her. Apparently a kick-ass cop had more cachet in this room than ten feds. But none of the parents were quite as brave as Mrs. Hardy. They preferred to admire the young detective from afar.

"I think I'd feel better," said Riker, "if there was some connection between Savannah Sirus and this serial killer. It's a pain in the tail working two cases at the same time."

"Surely Mallory's not a suspect in Miss Sirus's death."

The detective shook his head. "No, Charles. Suicide was Dr. Slope's official call. The kid's got no trouble with the law. But the details are gonna get out, and every cop in town will have a problem with that case. And then there's her little vanishing act —

all the days she missed from work. Now, thanks to an out-of-town serial killer, I can put out a rumor that the kid was working this case all that time. But I need a solid reason for Savannah's suicide — something other cops can believe in . . . or they might not wanna work with her anymore."

Charles turned toward Mallory's table. "She seems all right to me."

Riker's face brightened like a proud parent. "And look. She's playing with the computer. I think that worried me the most — the kid traveling without one. And that low-tech Volkswagen. Remember her old car? It had equipment that only another computer could recognize."

He could see that Charles was about to raise a point about the empty engine compartment, but he cut the man off, saying, "Hold it. Now, just put the invisible engine to one side. Did you get a look at her dashboard? Nothing you wouldn't find on a regular car, right?"

"I don't have a police scanner in *my* car."

"You wouldn't even have a car if you could get around on a horse. But Mallory? Going low-tech is just strange." The detective sat well back in his chair and smiled. "But now she's wired up to a computer again — just like her old self. Yeah, that's a

329

good sign — a real good sign."

Rising from her chair without a word or gesture of good-bye, she quit the restaurant, got into her car and drove out of the parking lot in no particular hurry. Riker stared at the laptop, its screen still glowing on the table. She had abandoned it — a very un-Mallory-like thing to do. He closed his tired eyes. "I take it all back."

A small hand tugged on Riker's sleeve, and he looked up to see Peter Finn. The boy had panic in his eyes.

"Where is she going?"

"Don't worry," said Riker. "She won't be gone long."

Did he believe that?

Well, so much depended on the way that Lou Markowitz had raised his foster child, and how much of the old man's rulebook remained with her. Riker recalled one of Lou's key commandments: *Thou shalt not abandon the sheep . . . or the lamb.*

According to Kronewald, there was another child's grave up ahead. Mallory pulled over to the side of the road, switched on her scanner and listened to the chatter for a moment, then said, "You're right."

"What," said the Chicago detective on the other end of the cell-phone connection, "you couldn't take my word for it?"

"How did they find the grave?"

"They didn't," said Kronewald. "I did — with a little help from you and Riker. And thanks for the FBI files, but they didn't have any of Nahlman's reports. So I call in my own guy, and he —"

"Why would you expect to find reports from Agent Nahlman?"

"She's a geographic profiler. You didn't know? I checked her out. A real hotshot — as good as it gets."

This made no sense. Mallory prided herself on being a very thorough thief; she overlooked nothing. A geographic profiler's work would have been the bedrock of a case like this one. How could that data be missing from the purloined files?

"Anyway," said Kronewald, "I fed the data to my guy, all the known grave locations. He gave me the same twenty-mile spread that Riker got from the Pattern Man. Now, eighteen years ago in Oklahoma, about twenty miles from where you are now, a drunk hit a dog on the road."

"I'm going to hang up on you now."

"Hold on, kid, I'm getting to the good part. Well, this guy's a dog lover. He's out in the middle of nowhere, and he decides to bury this dog. So he pulls out his silly little camp shovel, and, before he digs the hole, he looks around for some stones to put over the body. He doesn't want wild animals to eat the dead mutt. Now remember, this guy's real drunk, and he's just determined to do this right. Well, he finds a pile of rocks, and the dirt underneath is real loose. The ground's been turned over. Less work, right?"

"So he dug a grave for a dog and found a dead child."

"Right. A fresh kill with one wound — the kid's throat was cut. Now the Oklahoma cops can't find the old files on that kid, but they say there was no molestation."

"They lost the files?"

"Hell no. Those cops had a visit from Dale Berman's crew nine months ago, and the feds probably walked off with everything they had on the case. So I asked them to check for another rock pile down the road."

Finally — an answer to a simple question. Mallory abruptly ended the call.

After a search of the iPod menu, she selected Led Zeppelin's "Stairway to Heaven." Following this music recommendation, Peyton Hale wrote, *"If you only follow the Buddha's road, you can only go where the Buddha goes . . . only know what he knows. But all our questions are personal.*

Why am I here, where did I come from, where am I going?"

The letter was put aside. Her cell phone was beeping again, probably Kronewald, and she responded with a testy, "What now?"

"I know what you did," said a familiar voice. "Have you gone psycho?"

"You can't blame all your screwups on cops." She wondered if Dale Berman was recording this call in some lame attempt to document her footprints in the FBI computers.

"No, don't bullshit me," said Berman. "I'm talking about the database — all the case details. Now Kronewald's got everything. And he's got cops calling him from seven states. Containment is shot to hell. That's your work, isn't it?" There was a moment of silence, as if he actually expected an admission of guilt, and then he said, "Tell me you didn't call out the media."

Her thumbnail rested on the button that would end this call.

"Just one more question, Mallory. This perp we're looking for — is he another psychopath with spooky green eyes? Does insanity run in your family?"

Agent Christine Nahlman sat at Riker's

table, comparing notes on parents missing from the caravan. "We raised the Wolfman on his CB radio," she said. "He lost a muffler on the road a few miles back."

"Jill's Dad," said Riker, correcting her. He liked this Internet name and loathed the monster-movie tag that the feds had pinned on that sorry man. "I had Kronewald run a background check. His daughter's name is Gillian on the birth certificate, Gillian Hastings."

Nahlman's eyebrows were slightly raised, and her lower lip tucked under her teeth, the only tells that the more formal name of this child was familiar. So preoccupied was she with this little surprise that Riker caught her nodding in unconscious agreement when he blamed the feds for making a mess of the last leg of the trip.

"It's way out of control," said the unshaven detective, "and it's gonna get worse if you try to keep these people on the interstate."

She shook her head. "I've got no choice. The old highway couldn't handle all of them, not without one bottleneck after another. There's a public campground only a few hours down the road. Dale wants them all together in one place while it's still daylight."

"So he can count noses? Like that matters anymore. His moles couldn't even keep track of how many people we lost today. No offense. I lost count myself. All these people wanna be on the old road. Let's get them back on it. Speed isn't everything."

"I can't do that." Nahlman rose from the table.

She agreed with him; he knew she did, but the agent would not say a word against her boss, the prince of pricks. Instead, she said, "The best solution would be to catch this guy and catch him quick."

Riker took her arm to stop her from leaving him. "Dale's idea of speed is reckless. Don't let him get you killed. If you're in a bad place —" He took out his pen and scribbled across a semi-soggy napkin, then handed it to her. "That's my cell. Call me. I'll come get you."

She put the napkin in her jacket pocket, then wiped the smile off her face before she turned around to rejoin the other agents.

He looked out the window on the parking lot. Dr. Magritte and Charles were still trying the reasonable approach with Dale Berman, but the agent only gave them his political smile, a cue that he was not even listening. In another hour, all of these people would be back on the road — the wrong road. How many more parents would they lose today?

The detective looked down at the open laptop that Mallory had abandoned — again. The screen came to life at the touch of the mouse pad, and it was good that she had left it running. Normally, it took him an hour to find the power button on a strange computer, but that was with a hangover. Today he was merely in with-drawal, and the solution for that problem was in hand. Riker popped the cap off his beer bottle, lit up a cigarette and remem-bered to say grace. He blessed the state of Oklahoma for not going completely nuts on the issue of second-hand smoke. God love these people — they even put ashtrays on the tables.

An icon on the laptop screen had his name on it. *Thank you, Mallory.* Now he would not have to rely on that ten-year-old boy for technical support. He watched Peter Finn take his little sister by the hand and lead her to the window. Both children faced the direction that Mallory had taken, as if expecting her to reappear at any moment.

Riker rested one finger on the mouse pad and moved the little arrow to his icon. One click and the computer's screen changed to a simple menu. Mallory had created a number of options for him: F★★★.doc was Riker's idea of overly polite obscenity, but it was Mallory's old code for *feds,* which meant the same obscene thing in her lexicon as well. He knew that all her FBI data was stolen goods — finest kind. It was the next item on her menu that troubled him. The media was subdivided into links for every news blog and marginally more legitimate press with websites. Last was a personal note, and he opened that one first.

Riker, by the time you read this, Mack the Knife will be in the Chicago PD data bank, and cops all along this road will report to Kronewald. He'll be calling you soon. You may also hear the sound of helicopters. That will be the media. The more eyes on the sheep the better. Good hunting.

Her letter was disappearing even as he reread it, words breaking up before his eyes. The other documents remained, but he knew every trace of her would be gone from this computer.

Good hunting?

What the hell? She would never abandon the caravan parents to the likes of Berman. No, she had to come back. If she did not, then what was he supposed to tell that little boy? As if the child had read his mind, Peter Finn turned his face to Riker's, and the detective died a little.

His cell phone was ringing.

He answered it, and, even before Krone-wald could give him the details called in by an Oklahoma trooper, Riker knew that one of the stray parents had been murdered. He was watching the sudden activity in the parking lot. All the portable sirens were coming out as agents burned rubber, their cars ripping back down the road to a fresh kill site.

And Kronewald had an additional piece of news, another child's grave found by the road, but in the opposite direction — the way Mallory had gone.

The Mamas and the Papas sang — *"California dreaming . . . on such a winter's day"* — as Mallory drove slowly past the digging men. Pulling up in front of a crime-scene van, she parked on the shoulder of the road.

A police officer walked up to the car. Not bothering to check her ID, he gallantly opened the door for her, saying, "You'd be the cop from New York City. A Chicago detective — Kronewald was his name — he said you might be by for a look." He shook her hand as they exchanged names: Henry-J.-Budrow-but-most-people-call-me-Bud and Mallory — just Mallory.

He pushed a police barrier out of their way, and they left the road to walk side by side to the edge of a small grave. A man and a much younger woman had their backs bent over this hole in the ground, and they used soft brushes to remove a layer of dirt from a small skull that had yet to lose its baby teeth.

Now Mallory was told that these civilians were on loan from the anthropology department of a university, and then her guide in uniform asked, "So who's running this show? Chicago PD or the FBI?"

"It's Detective Kronewald's case," said Mallory. "He's your liaison with the feds." Loosely translated, the old man was gleefully parceling out information to humiliate the Bureau.

The officer stared at her knapsack. "Your cell phone is ringing."

"It does that," she said, but made no move to answer it.

He grinned. "Mine has the same problem every six minutes. I wish they'd never invented the damn things." The officer watched the anthropologist and his student as the pair slowly uncovered the rest of the skeletonized child. He turned back to Mallory. "You know there's a much fresher corpse back down the road about twenty miles. That one's an adult, but Kronewald says it's connected."

She nodded, giving him nothing useful, as she looked into the open grave. "You should find something to help with identification — something small that a kid would carry."

"Already found it." He led her over to the police van. The back door hung open, and what he wanted was within easy reach. "This what you're looking for?" He held up a bag with paperwork attached.

Through the clear plastic, she could see a small identification bracelet. "I can't make out the engraving."

"The metal's corroded, but her little dress is still holding up. Can you believe that?"

Yes, she could. This was the upside of poverty. Cheap polyester and simulated leather would last forever in the ground.

He reached farther into the van and pulled out a charcoal rubbing. "The professor made this from the bracelet so we could make out the words."

The tiny bracelet identified six-year-old Melissa as a diabetic.

At a more recent crime scene twenty miles down the road, Dale Berman wondered aloud, "What does he do with their hands?" He looked down at the corpse of a middle-aged woman.

The dead body was laid out on the shoulder of the old highway. Her right hand had been chopped off at the wrist. Agent Nahlman noted that this mutilation was postmortem. The pool of blood had spilled from the wound to the throat. The rest of the pattern was also holding up. Tiny bones had been positioned near the stump, and so it was a child's skeletal hand that pointed toward another roadside grave. State troopers with shovels owned this crime scene, and they were waiting on their own people to finish the job of uncovering the smaller of the two victims found early this morning.

Kronewald had been a bit late to share this information with the FBI.

The federal contingent was forced to watch the exhumation from behind a police barricade. Dale Berman leaned toward one of the young agents, saying to this man, "Get a picture of the woman's face. Fax it back to the moles at the restaurant. They might recognize her."

"I can identify her," said Nahlman. "She's one of the parents who joined the caravan in Missouri."

"Why in hell would she leave the group?" He asked this so innocently, as if Nahlman had not apprised him of the problem with the strays and the need for backup. He was still waiting for her explanation.

Of course.

He would want witnesses to *her* incompetence, her failure as the senior agent to keep the caravan together. Nahlman's head lolled back. She was looking up from the abyss, that black hole for agents with down-spiraling careers, and she could see Dale waving good-bye to her as she fell from grace.

"Nahlman, I don't blame you for this." His hand was on her shoulder, marking her with all but a Judas kiss, blaming her in front of all these people. He came off well before this audience, so generous with his forgiveness. And the little bastard knew he could depend upon on her not to defend herself.

"Well, we won't lose any more of them," said Berman. "I'm personally taking charge of the caravan. If we keep them moving on the interstate, it'll be safer."

"No," said Nahlman. "It's only faster. I explained why —" Her words trailed off. What was the point of trying anymore?

If he was annoyed by her contradiction, it did not show. He was wearing the smile of a charming boy, almost an invitation to skip school today. But she was immune to professional charm. Nahlman looked down at the dead woman, not listening to the company line any longer, as Dale babbled on about the importance of carrying out command decisions.

Agent Allen was running toward them, cell phone in hand. "The parents are getting ready to leave the restaurant." When he stopped in front of them, he was out of breath but posture perfect, and Nahlman half expected him to salute his hero. "They're going to —"

"I told them to stay put till we got back," said Dale Berman, as if this mass disobedience of civilians were still inexplicable to him. "How many of them are leaving?"

"All of them, sir."

"On whose authority?"

"That detective from New York, Riker."

Dr. Paul Magritte stood in the parking lot, placidly handing out area maps and the simple guidelines for picking up after themselves. Only yards away, an insurrection was going on with his approval and his blessing.

Detective Riker sat on the fender of the Mercedes-Benz, alternately sipping beer and shouting instructions to the people gathered all around him.

A young man who had passed himself off

as a grieving parent now identified himself as a federal agent. He used his FBI credentials, waving his open wallet as he vied for the policeman's attention, shouting, "You can't do this!"

"I'm doing it," said Riker. To the crowd around the car, he yelled, "Everybody top off the gas tank whether you think you need to or not! No stops till we get to the campsite! And from now on, keep more distance between the cars. Faster traffic can leapfrog the slower vehicles. We don't want to turn the interstate into one long parking lot. At the next campsite, you will meet and greet the ladies and gentlemen of the press for your coast-to-coast publicity."

A chorus of cheers rose up from every quarter.

"So," Riker continued, "nobody goes off on their own. I don't wanna see any cars taking exits back to the old road. Anyone who does that loses a shot at national TV coverage. Is everybody clear on this?"

"Yes!" was the rousing comeback from the crowd.

"Good. We take the interstate all the way to the exit on your maps. Just follow this car." He slapped the Mercedes' fender. "Remember — no side trips! Pee in the car if you have to, but nobody stops."

There were nods all around the parking lot as people headed toward their vehicles, and Riker took his place in the passenger seat of the Mercedes. "Okay, Charles, let's get in position. You're the lead car."

Charles Butler started the engine and proceeded to the front of the lot. Other cars were falling in behind him. "I wonder how many people we've already lost."

"Don't think about that anymore."

After Officer Budrow had introduced her as Kronewald's cop on the scene, Mallory hunkered down beside the anthropology professor, a man ten years her senior. He was dusting arm bones still partially embedded in the dirt. His student, a teenage girl, ran a soft brush over the tiny shoes.

"Any marks from a weapon?"

"Not yet — nothing obvious," said the professor. "I'll know more when we get the bones back to the lab."

The detective had heard this old song before back in New York City.

"Shallow grave," said the cop called Bud. "The killer didn't waste much time with the digging."

Mallory stared at the little dress on the skeleton. The dark brown stains began at the neck and spread down to the small shoes. "That's blood."

"It *could* be." The teenage assistant wore a condescending smile, for she had just promoted herself to the wise woman of science. "We have to test the stains before —"

"I don't," said Mallory. "That's blood from a wound to the throat." The detective moved a piece of the dress — the school dress — away from the skeleton's neck. "Stop what you're doing and clean these bones."

The teenager leaned over the skeleton, brush at the ready, when the professor stayed her hand, saying, "No, Sandra. I think she means me." And now the man bent over the exposed bones, and the student went back to cleaning the shoes.

Officer Budrow turned to the New York detective as his new source of expertise. "You think the freak did anything to Melissa before he killed her?"

Mallory recalled the reports of bodies found along this road. "There was a slashed throat on one fresh corpse and a few of the mummified bodies."

The anthropology professor kept his eyes on his work when he said, "The mummified bodies won't help you establish a pattern. Tearing of the skin around the neck is common — no matter what the cause of death."

346

"No nicks on the spinal column," chimed in the assistant, almost gleeful as she leaned in for a closer look. "No signs of a knife wound."

The anthropologist shook his head as he worked his brush over the small neck. "I wouldn't expect to see any nicks, not unless the murderer tried to decapitate this child."

"So it wasn't a deep wound." Mallory looked up at Officer Budrow. "And now we know it wasn't a rage killing. He just wanted her dead. All the blood stains come from one wound to the neck."

"Well," said Officer Budrow, "I guess there's only so much you can tell from the bones. Any way to know if there was anything sexual? That's what I was wondering. The parents will ask. They always do."

"Well," said the student, "science can't help you there. Without flesh and fluids —"

"Melissa wasn't molested," said Mallory. Gerald Linden's death had been planned out for minimum physical contact with the victim, and this theme was also playing out with the children. "Pedophiles usually strangle the kids."

Before Mallory could finish this thought, the student took over, saying to Officer Budrow, "So you see, the key is the hyoid bone."

"No, Sandra, it's not," said the soft-spoken anthropology professor.

This man seemed tired, and so Mallory took over his student's training. She planned to teach this girl not to interrupt one more time. "The hyoid bone wouldn't fuse until Melissa was in her twenties." The detective pointed to the remains of the child in the hole. "But she was only six years old. Melissa died too young. If she was strangled, the hyoid would only flex — it wouldn't break." And now for the lesson of simple observation. "Look at the blood pattern on her dress — it flows down to the shoes. That tells you Melissa was standing when he hurt her. So she wasn't fatally injured yet — not when he cut her. And killers so seldom strangle little girls *after* slashing their throats."

The student had lost her annoying smile and turned sullen — and learned nothing.

"So that's settled," said Officer Budrow. "The perp favors a knife."

"And that's odd for this kind of murder," said Mallory. "I don't think he likes to touch the victims — not while they're still alive." The detective looked down the road the way she had come. "That other crime scene you mentioned — the one with the fresh corpse. Did they find another grave near the victim's body?"

"Yeah," said Budrow, "a state trooper found a woman's corpse on the road. It was left out in plain sight. One hand was chopped off and . . ."

"A woman," said Mallory. "What was her name?"

When she was told that the victim was April Waylon, the detective wanted to hunt that dead woman down and kill her all over again.

11

The caravan vehicles followed Riker's instructions, via waving arms and hand signals, to form a tight configuration around the campsite. This was inspiration from a childhood of cowboy movies: always pull the wagons into a circle. The detective smiled as FBI agents arrived en masse to find parking spaces on the fringe, their cars exiled from the little city.

Supplies were disgorged from one of the mobile homes, but these were automotive: cans of oil, transmission fluid, plugs and points and patch kits for threadbare tires. One of the parents, a mechanic, traveled from one old clunker to another like a doctor making hospital rounds. He listened to odd pings and grinds and other engine noises that only he could decode. On the Internet, he was known as Lostmyalice, but the other parents called him Miracle Man.

Come twilight, Riker and Charles accepted the hospitality of Dr. Magritte, who prepared rib eye steaks from the freezer of a larder on wheels that doled out similar fare to other campers. And now they learned that three of the mobile homes were leased by the doctor and driven by parents who had no vehicles of their own. The old man was a good cook. He favored a grill set over an open fire, and he had actually paid good money for it.

"But the best grills," in the detective's opinion, "are those little fold-out pieces you steal from shopping carts."

Throughout this tasty meal, Riker was working, albeit casually. He chewed his meat and sipped his coffee while noting every new face — there were many — and watching for signs of trouble. He found them. "Doc, your people are scared. Check out the weapons." With one moving finger, he pointed out pup tents and lean-tos where deer rifles and a few shotguns had been propped up in plain view. "I always knew about the guns, but yesterday they were kept out of sight. Tonight they're on display."

"It makes them feel more secure," said Dr. Magritte. "And the FBI agents haven't objected."

"And you know why," said Riker. "Except for Nahlman, all the agents here are kids.

351

You noticed that, right?"

Paul Magritte opened a cooler to win back Riker's goodwill with a cold bottle of beer. The old man smiled. The detective did not. But he took the beer.

"And then there's the problem of the handguns," said Riker.

This startled Magritte, and he looked around him, squinting to see the distant campfires.

"You'll never see them," said Riker, "but they're here, tucked away in tents and bedrolls — like bombs waiting to go off." The detective stood up to take his leave of Charles and the doctor. He thanked the man for his dinner and said, in parting, "Don't go walking after dark. This is a very scary place."

The detective glanced at his watch. It was time to walk the wolf.

George Hastings, alias Jill's Dad, led the animal on a chain, and Riker followed them outside the circle of vehicles. None of the camp dogs barked when the wolf was out and about, for every mutt loved its own life; they quieted down and cowered on their bellies, hoping death would walk past them tonight. Man and beast walked a straight line into the dark landscape, and Riker sat down on the ground with his flashlight, a gun and a six-pack of beer. Stone sober he was not a great shot, but, if he had to kill a charging animal, a little alcohol might steady his hand, and four or five spent bullets should hit some vital organ. He had trained Jill's Dad not to stray beyond the flashlight beam. Riker only took his eyes off the wolf one time to look up at a sky unspoiled by the lights of the caravan city. The evening stars were popping out, one by one, when he heard the first helicopter.

It was about time. He had wondered when the media planned to show up.

Nahlman came to keep him company on wolf watch. She held a clipboard with a list of vehicle registrations as she sat down beside him. "So far I've only found one fake name." The agent highlighted a page with her penlight as one finger traced the lines, then stopped. "This one, Darwinia Solho." She looked up from her list and caught him in the act of being unsurprised. "You knew."

"Yeah, it always had the sound of a made-up name." He placed a bottle of beer in her free hand. "But we're not hunting for a woman. No offense, Nahlman. Personally, I think women are better at murder." His eyes were on the sky, reading the call letters of a major television network on the bottom of the helicopter. "Hey, prime-time news."

"Damn reporters," said Nahlman. "Our people have the rest of the media bottled up down the road."

Oh, Christ.

"You have to let 'em through," said Riker. "Reporters are only manageable when you're throwing them bones. If you make them dig — and I mean really earn their money — then you lose control."

"It's not my decision."

"It could be," he said, planting a hint at disaffection from the ranks. "Let's say we give them easy rules. No parent leaves the circle without an escort, and only the parents get back inside. You see how simple this can be when Dale's not running the show? And now I need you to call down the road and get those reporters turned loose."

"I haven't got the —"

"Do you see Dale Berman anywhere? No, he's holed up in a motel while you and your partner sleep on the dirt. You'll never find him when you need him. That makes you the senior agent in command. So just tell the kids down the road to let those reporters come through the lines — or mama will spank."

Oh, *big* mistake.

Obviously, the NYPD's diversity training had been utterly wasted on him. He watched her mouth dip on one side just before she turned her face away from him. Riker looked down at his empty bottle, but he could not put the blame there. That was the problem of being a hard-core alcoholic: He could down so many drinks while talking and walking a sober line.

Riker tried again, one hand on her shoulder. "Hey, sorry, but I need this favor." He pointed into the heart of the campsite. "It's for them. It's so hard for these parents to get five seconds on some backwater news show. This is their only shot at national coverage. And tomorrow, you know they'll all stay with the caravan. No more dead strays — if we let the reporters join the parade."

The FBI agent was relenting; he could see it in the slump of her shoulders.

"Dale might go along with it," she said, "if you were the one who asked him. I think he respects you. God knows why. And I know you've got his cell-phone number."

"Not me. I haven't had *that* much beer." Riker pulled another bottle from his six-pack. "I figure a pretty woman has a better shot."

Whoa!

Nahlman stood up way too fast, and now her hands were riding on her hips. Showdown! What's a boy to do? He was too drunk to win a fair fight with a woman, but not drunk enough to stomach one more conversation with Dale Berman.

"I'll drink faster," said Riker.

Agent Christine Nahlman made the decision to bypass her boss, and it was not the second bottle of Riker's beer that had won her over. She wanted no more dead parents on her watch.

The floodgates down the road were opened, the reporters turned loose, and now the circus had come to town. The news crews arrived at the outskirts of the caravan circle, carrying pole lights and cameras, juggling microphones and makeup kits. The parents were overjoyed, holding up their posters and lining up for interviews, but not Jill's Dad, though his wolf was safely locked up for the night. Another oddly camera-shy parent was Darwinia Sohlo, or whatever her real name was. Joe Finn was not in line, either, but that was no surprise to Nahlman.

While waiting a turn at the reporters, Mrs. Hardy and two other parents could be heard comparing notes on how many seconds their tragedies had received on the local news back home, how many lines of type in their town papers and how many flyers they had tacked up to telephone poles in an average month.

Searching for lost children was very hard work.

Finally, it was Mrs. Hardy's chance to face the camera and tell America, "My Melissa plays piano." She held up the photograph of a six-year-old child. "This little girl," she would have them know, "has the brightest blue eyes, the sunniest smile. And she plays the piano. Oh, I'm sorry. Did I already tell you that? I'm such a fool."

After dinner, Peter Finn watched his father work the poles, the canvas and the ropes. Practice should have made this job easier, but it just got harder and harder all the time. Almost done, the big man used the back end of a hatchet to drive the stakes into the ground, each one the mooring for a tent line.

A year ago, this man had been the monster in the dark, a creature who came late at night to sit beside young Peter's bed. Some nights, his father's face had been beaten into unrecognizable shapes. Blood had seeped through the bandages applied at ringside by the cut man, another monster in the boy's cast of characters from the boxing world.

When Ariel was taken from them, the boxing days were ended, and this man had inexplicably become the Tooth Fairy who paid out coins for baby teeth, the cook and housemaid and packer of school lunches. The boxer was not much good at all these jobs that Ariel had done so effortlessly and fine. Over time, as Peter had watched his father struggle with each small improvement in folding laundry, the boy had cried with overwhelming sorrow and love.

Joe Finn drove the last stake into the ground. All the ropes were taut, and the poles were straight. Oh, but now the big man discovered that he had laid the tent floor on a bed of rock. After pulling up every stake — silently with no complaint — collapsing the canvas and bringing down the poles, the boxer began again.

Young Peter bowed his head. The tears flowed freely.

Riker was alone on nightwatch, unless one counted unseasoned FBI agents. He did not.

Interviews had ended hours ago, and most of the reporters had retired to a town down the road. A few of the jackals still haunted the perimeter of the caravan city, probably hoping for fresh blood, or maybe the sound bite of a scream in the night. Cooking smells haunted Riker with every breeze, though all the campfires were burning low, embers only. The site was better lit tonight. He had appropriated stationary power packs and pole lights from departing television crews. More illumination came from the traveling flashlights of patrolling FBI agents. Apart from the tinny music of a few radios and small conversations in twos and threes, all was quiet.

And along came Mallory.

Riker never heard the sound of her engine or the slam of a car door. She was simply there when he turned around and already passing him by. A knapsack was slung over one shoulder. She carried it everywhere these days, and he wondered if this was where she kept the letters that had once belonged to the late Savannah Sirus.

Mallory walked toward the campfire of Mrs. Hardy, and now he knew whose little girl had been found in the grave down the road.

And the mother sensed it.

Mrs. Hardy sat on a blanket spread before a dying fire. She forced a smile for the approaching detective, perhaps believing that escape was still possible. But no — Mallory's stride had the resolve of a train wreck in the making — this was going to happen. And now the older woman patiently waited for the younger one to come and destroy her with words. The detective sat down on the blanket, and the ritual began: the slow shake of the mother's head — disbelief — no, not her child — some mistake. And when it was finally understood that denial was wasted on Mallory, the mother collapsed against the young cop's breast. Mrs. Hardy cried for a long time. None of the other parents approached her, as if the death of a child might be a contagious thing. And Mallory did not desert her.

Turning his sad eyes away from Mrs. Hardy's campfire, Joe Finn doused his own embers with a pail of water. Then he leaned down to kiss the brow of his sleeping son. Sleep was his only chance, for Peter had arrived at that heartbreak age when he would not hold his father's hand in public anymore — a big boy now. One day a gangly teenager would take Peter's place, a sullen moody version who would not even speak to his father, and that time would come all too soon. He kissed his child again, so greedy to love this boy while love was still allowed.

He laid Peter down in the tent alongside sleeping Dodie. Fixing his eyes on his youngest girl, he stared hard, willing her damaged mind to heal. Settling for keeping her safe, he unrolled his sleeping bag in front of the tent so that his body would bar the way to his children.

Irony was not in the boxer's store of words, but he had the sense of it in every twinge of pain from old fight wounds. He had endured so many blows and spent too much time away from home, and he had done this to buy a fine future for his children. But now he used his savings to go in search of the child that was lost because he had not been there to protect her.

Ariel, my Ariel.

His late wife had drawn from Jewish roots to give their firstborn child that name. In Hebrew, it meant Lioness of God.

"How much can you stand to hear?" Mallory held the crying woman in her arms.

"I want the rest of it. *All* of it." Mrs. Hardy's reply was a struggle, a gurgle of words. "I have to know."

The FBI agent standing behind them finally made her presence known to the crying mother. Mallory had been aware of Nahlman from the start, listening to the shift of feet, a clue of reticence to come any closer to raw emotion.

Agent Nahlman knelt down on the blanket beside Mrs. Hardy. "I read the old police report. They found blood on the ground at the bus stop. So that's where Melissa died."

"Then he didn't — he never —"

"No," said Nahlman, "she wasn't molested. We never found a child with signs of more than one wound — the fatal wound. That's how I know she died where they found her blood on the road."

Mrs. Hardy nodded, for this was confirmation of what Mallory had already told her.

"It was a quick death," said Nahlman. "I don't think Melissa ever saw the knife. There wasn't even time to be afraid. It happened that fast. Shock was setting in. Melissa was losing consciousness."

"Like going to sleep?" Mrs. Hardy pulled back from Mallory the better to see the young cop's eyes, wanting reassurance that this was true.

Mallory only stared at the FBI agent and marveled that any mother could be taken in by that fairy tale.

"Yes," said Nahlman, stumbling for a beat in time, "just like going to sleep . . . no fear." Having done her good deed for the night, the agent stood up, turned her back on them and walked away.

Mallory was not a believer in kind lies to grieving parents. She had a clear picture of a little girl with a pounding heart, watching, wild with fear, as the blood flowed from her slashed throat to run like a river down her dress and splatter her shoes. And she could even see the terror in Melissa's eyes as she was dying.

All through the night, Mallory stayed to cradle Mrs. Hardy, lightly rocking her, patiently waiting for this woman to work through the lies. It was hard to fool a mother for very long; and Mallory should know, for she had two of them: Cassandra, who had borne her, and Helen, who had fostered her. Mothers knew things. They were spooky and wondrous that way.

On toward morning, Melissa's mother cried fresh tears and said, "She must have been so frightened."

"Yes, she was." Mallory held a bottle of water to Mrs. Hardy's lips, forcing the woman to drink. "I'll tell you one true thing." And now she drew upon her own life for the right words to say. "When kids are really scared, they always yell for their mothers."

"But my Melissa —"

"No," said Mallory, "she couldn't yell — her throat was cut. But I know she tried.

And that's how I know Melissa was thinking about you when she died."

The driver's-side door of the Mercedes hung open. Riker had one foot on the ground and one hand on his gun. The sun was rising, and he donned his sunglasses to keep watch on the man who walked beside the wolf. This camper had more names than most: In Riker's notebook, he was the George Hastings who matched up with the owner registration of a pickup truck. On Dr. Magritte's growing list of parents, he was known only by his Internet moniker. And the young FBI agents had code-named him Wolfman, a mistake in Riker's opinion. This parent was not a mean or quick-tempered sort. He seemed like a very patient man, and this was what worried the detective.

Jill's Dad led the wolf close to the Mercedes and lifted one hand to show his wrist-watch, acknowledging Riker's rule of only fifteen minutes for exercise. And now he moved on to his pickup truck, where the animal was locked up in the cab as promised.

Riker holstered his gun, but he continued to watch the pair for a while. The man did not appear to have any love for the wolf —

and the wolf loved no one. This animal was no pet, nor had it been brought along for security; it never barked. And the man? He carried no posters of his missing daughter and cared nothing for reporters. He had even less use for the FBI.

What listless, lifeless eyes. Yet Jill's Dad was quick to spot each newcomer and just as quickly disappointed every time. This man was definitely waiting for someone, a person he would know on sight.

Riker knew he should kill the wolf, shoot it right now. Ah, but then Jill's Dad might buy a gun, and the detective did not want to shoot this man.

Done with his wake-up coffee, he lit a cigarette and tossed the match on the ground. When had he last seen a car equipped with an ashtray or a cigarette lighter? Now there was only a hole for car chargers. He plugged in a portable television set confiscated from a news van. The screen was only eight or nine inches on the diagonal and called for much squinting, but the volume was clear. He listened to a replay of last night's interview with Melissa Hardy's mother. And now the anchorwoman gave her national audience the updated report that six-year-old Melissa no longer played the piano. She was dead.

Riker left the Mercedes to greet a state trooper's car as it parked near the circle of caravan vehicles. Two civilians emerged from the back seat, and they were introduced to him as the Hardys from the Oregon branch of the family. Some woman named Mallory had called and asked them to come for their cousin. They had taken the very next plane.

And how many Hardys had Mallory called before she found someone to come for Melissa's mother and take her safely home? This argued well for the existence of a human heart — but it was also police procedure, and so Riker still had no proof in the young cop's favor.

At this moment, he was watching his partner drive off again, and so was the boy beside him. But Peter Finn did not seem alarmed this time. Her return last night was proof that Riker had not lied to him, and Mallory had not abandoned him — not yet.

The detective and the boy stood side by side as the silver car disappeared down the road. Riker rested one hand on Peter's shoulder, saying, "Let me guess, kid. You're wondering if Mallory's eyes glow in the dark." He took a drag on his cigarette and exhaled the words with the smoke. "Yes . . .

they do."

The sun was half risen, and Mallory was running late for this appointment with the road. After rolling the car onto the shoulder and cutting the engine, she opened another letter that had been penned long ago when Peyton Hale last passed through Oklahoma. She read his instructions for how to watch a sunrise by looking at the roadside instead. The land was waking, going from gray to green, silence to gentle noises and birdsong.

But the morning was spoiled. The bottom of this letter was marred by a smudge of lipstick that could only belong to Savannah Sirus, and now this flaw was fixed with the scratch of one long red fingernail. All gone.

Not quite.

The image of this woman remained: Savannah on her knees, mascara running — the weeping had lasted for days; Savannah reaching for the letters — a little moment of horror — they were *Mallory's* letters now; Savannah's hand grasping air.

Mallory did not recall closing her eyes, but an hour had passed before she awakened. She wanted to check off this last stop, but could not find her gold pen, an old birthday gift from Charles Butler.

A pencil would do.

Back on the road again, she recalled placing the pen on a napkin at the restaurant. She had missed the napkin when she reached out to use it, and she had forgotten all about her favorite pen. How was that possible? She carried it everywhere. Mallory put this bit of carelessness down to lack of sleep.

Not a natural-born camper, not a nature lover, the New York detective checked into a motel. The cell phone was turned off, and the shower turned on to fill the bathroom with steam. When the last of the road dust was gone down the drain, she was ready for a few hours of sleep, all she needed, but sleep would not come. She emptied her knapsack on the bedspread, but the lost pen was not there. Ariel's autopsy photographs mingled with pictures of a man with green eyes. The image that hurt her most was the one of Peyton and Cassandra. The questions posed in yesterday's letter ran round her brain in an endless chant: *Where do we come from? Why are we here? And where are we going?*

She had no idea.

And now these mysteries resolved themselves into one: *Why did I have to be born?*

Riker ended his cell-phone call to the

undercover agents riding at the rear of the caravan, and turned to the man at the wheel. "It's working, Charles. The moles haven't spotted any cars taking the exits. Who knew reporters would come in handy?"

On the downside, the moles had counted ten more parents joining up with this parade. The caravan had swelled to a hundred and fifty vehicles, yet they moved along the interstate at a good clip. By some miracle, only one old junker had broken down, and that one was now being towed by a Winnebago.

"This is it," said Riker. "Take Exit 108."

The exit ramp led them uphill to the Cherokee Restaurant, another travel plaza. When they pulled into the parking lot, the news crews were already there, unloading sound equipment, lights and cameras.

While Charles parked the car, Riker's eyes were trained on a sign for homemade pies, and he gripped the door handle as soon as the car stopped. But his friend remained behind the wheel and showed no signs of moving.

"Problem?" asked Riker. "Hey, just spit it out."

"About Mallory," said Charles. "When were you planning to tell me the rest of it? There has to be more to this than her not showing up for work. You're so confident that she's coming apart. You don't think you can trust me with all of it?"

"No, it's not that." Riker released his grip on the door handle. He rolled down the window and lit a cigarette. This was going to take some time. "Her doorman, Frank, called me one night. He said there were shots fired in Mallory's apartment. So I asked him if he'd thought of calling 911. Well, Frank didn't say a word. Finally, he tells me he talked to Mallory on the house phone. She told him somebody left a window open . . . and she had to kill a few flies. Now the kid's a real big tipper. So Frank wouldn't turn her in if she shot four tenants right in front of him. He calls me instead. I go over there. Mallory opens the door, but just a crack. I had to muscle my way in. She goes for her gun. She aims it at the wall. I look — I see a fly — I hear a bang. And now there's a hole in the wall where the fly used to be. She's good. I don't know a single cop who could've made that shot."

Charles closed his eyes. "When did this happen?"

"Two weeks ago."

"When Savannah was there."

"But I didn't know that," said Riker. "I swear — I never saw one sign of her in that apartment."

"The poor woman was hiding," said Charles. "So Mallory was —"

"Torturing her houseguest? Probably." Riker blew smoke out the window and considered the odds that this story would ever be told in a competency hearing. He knew that Charles Butler would lie for Mallory in a heartbeat — if he only could. Unfortunately, the man's face gave away too much, and his blush prevented him from ever pulling off a lie to save her.

"You didn't take her gun away?"

"Naw. This wasn't her regular gun. It was a small-caliber revolver, and Mallory was only picking off flies on the street-side walls — a double row of solid brick. A twenty-two caliber's got no penetration."

"A twenty-two penetrated Miss Sirus's heart," said Charles — just a reminder.

"I did tell the kid that they'd lock her up in Bellevue for sure if she didn't keep the noise down."

"A short hospital stay for observation might've been the best thing."

"I couldn't do that to her," said Riker. "She'd never be a cop again, not after a turn in Bellevue. And I've done worse when I was drunk. Now Mallory's problem is she does these things when she's sober. Anyway, there was no more gunfire after that."

"Until Savannah Sirus died," said Charles — another reminder. "Any ideas about what might've set off the fly-shooting incident?"

"Just what Mallory told the doorman. Somebody opened a window and let in some bugs."

"Well, I think we can guess who that was," said Charles. "In order to let the flies in, you'd have to open a screen as well as a window. That might've been Miss Sirus's first attempt at suicide — interrupted by Mallory, who then proceeded to teach her houseguest not to let in any more flies."

"Good theory," said Riker, biting back the sarcasm. "I like it." He tossed his cigarette out the window. "So Mallory's just doing this woman a good turn — preventing Savannah's suicide by scaring the crap out of her."

"Here's another thought," said Charles. "Maybe it was Miss Sirus who tortured Mallory."

Special Agent Dale Berman led Riker and Dr. Magritte away from the Cherokee Restaurant, past the statue of a giant Indian and down a narrow curving road and a chain-link pen with a small herd of buffalo.

"Ah, bison burgers on the hoof." The

detective was hungry and willing to eat wildflowers if this damn tour did not end very soon.

Dale was pointing out the amenities as they entered the public campground at the bottom of the road. "The managers are great people. They opened the facilities to the caravan free of charge."

On the other side of the paved lot, Riker saw Agent Nahlman riding herd on campers who formed a neat line outside a small building. The parents were holding towels and toiletries, waiting for their first hot shower in days.

Dr. Magritte was less than enthusiastic as he looked over the marked slots that accommodated motor homes and cars. "There's not enough room to hold all of us."

"But there is," said Dale Berman, pointing toward the restaurant at the top of the road. "The parking lot up there is huge. It'll take the overflow. And now, over there —" He was looking into the trees beyond the lot. "Six cabins. So," he rubbed his hands together, "everything we need — food, lodging. And the reporters like the idea of a permanent base."

"Spoken like a true PR man." Riker turned to Dr. Magritte. "Public relations was Dale's job a few years back. He's not thinking this through. That's a bad habit with him."

"The restaurant has elevation," said Berman. "We can see anyone approaching the caravan."

"And that might work," said Riker, "if we were expecting an Indian raid. You think you'll recognize this freak when you see him coming?"

"You won't," said Dr. Magritte, raising his voice for the first time. Obviously regretting these words, the old man edged away from them and pretended interest in the bison pen.

The detective marched back up the hill. He was hungry, and a banner hanging outside of the restaurant had caught his eye and promised him homemade pies.

Dale Berman called after him. "We'll stay the night. See how it goes."

"No we won't," said Riker. He was hoping for blueberry pie, but he would settle for apple, and he planned to cross the state line into Texas before nightfall.

At the top of the road, he headed across the parking lot to the restaurant. A noise close by made him stop. His hand was on his gun as he turned to the passenger window of George Hastings' pickup truck.

Thump.

The wolf's head hit the window. How many tries would it take before the glass broke? And now the animal drew back, eyes fixed on Riker, seeing him all of a piece, a single piece of meat. The detective's hands were wet with sweat and clammy. Adrenaline iced his veins, and his heartbeat was jacked up to a faster rhythm. It was a lot like falling in love.

Thump.

The animal slammed his head into the glass again, but the window held.

Riker wondered if the man had stopped feeding the wolf yet.

Dale Berman accompanied Dr. Magritte back up the road to the parking lot. The FBI man drove away, and the doctor remained to watch his watchers. Back in Chicago, these two undercover agents had introduced themselves as the grieving parents of a missing child, but he had never found the couple credible. Neither had Riker, who alternately referred to them as the moles, or the mole people, and sometimes as Mr. and Mrs. Mole, though they were certainly unmarried.

It did not require his degrees in psychology to spot the early warning signs of love and lust, but theirs had not begun until that first night under the stars and a few hundred miles from Chicago. The moles' mutual involvement had deepened every day since then. Now they were so taken with one another, feverish in their glances. They had even worked out a little language of their own — hand signals, nods, winks and blinks. The rest of the world did not exist for them, and Paul Magritte found it easy to slip away.

He walked back down the sloping road, past the bison pen and into the woods of pine trees, seeking solitude for his ritual.

Charles had completed his assignment to nail down a table with an ashtray for the smoking detective. Hardly a problem. It was the nonsmoking section that had the least seating. A teenager in a red T-shirt took his order and left him. He was content to sit alone.

After months of licking wounds in the solitude of European hotel rooms, he felt a sense of awakening to the sounds of clinking glassware and people talking all at once — so many voices — proof of life after Mallory. How he had missed her. And now he was chasing after her — again. However, he was resigned to this: Following her was a pleasure; catching up to her was pain. Yet he watched the windows on the parking lot, waiting for a glimpse of her car. At least there was no residual awkwardness on her part. He should have known that she would forget his proposal of marriage the day after he had uttered those foolish words. He died every time he saw her, and he could not wait to see her again.

He was distracted from his vigil at the window when a floorshow passed near his table. A middle-aged woman was being photographed each time she paused to strike a pose with one of the parents. A young man in the entourage handed Charles a flyer. According to the text, the woman was a "celebrated criminal profiler." Apparently, she was interrupting a national book tour for a photo opportunity with the caravan.

Charles was presented with his own copy of her latest book. Agent Cadwaller dropped it on the table as he pulled up a chair. The garish dust jacket was splashed with the blood of printer's ink, and another version of the lady's credentials was printed in large type. "A forensic psychiatrist?"

"That's what she calls herself." Agent Cadwaller smoothed back his hair, using a butter knife for his mirror.

Charles turned the book over and read

the biography on the back, noting the third-rate medical school and the woman's home state. It was lamentable that there were places where the most incompetent M.D. could hang out a shingle and call herself a psychiatrist.

A young man introduced himself as the author's personal assistant, and he made a lackluster defense to the agent's overheard remark. "She *is* a forensic psychiatrist. Accredited and board certified." He presented Cadwaller with a handout sheet. "See for yourself."

"Already saw it," said the FBI agent, waving the sheet away with one hand. "She was accredited by a board of clowns, the group with the lowest standards. So, it might be legal, but that doesn't make it right."

Charles was also familiar with this board. It took a more in-depth course of study to become an accredited plumber. And now the author was advancing on other parents. He leaned toward the FBI profiler. "Uh, don't you think this is a bad idea, given the subject of her book — serial killers?"

"I tried to stop it," said Cadwaller, using his knife blade reflection to straighten the knot of his tie. "The reporters are running the show today. They want a few sound bites from the author, something colorful and bloody. And Berman won't do anything to piss them off."

Charles was appalled. The reporters were snapping photographs while the faux psychiatrist hugged a stunned parent against the man's will. "What else do you know about her?"

"She's a hired gun for defense lawyers. If your client's a murdering rapist and he needs a bad-potty-training defense, she's your girl." The agent held up the flyer and pointed to a line of type. "Now this is a lie. She never worked on a police investigation. Her books profile the perps after they're caught and jailed. And even then she screws it up."

When the author and her followers moved in a straight line for the Finn family, Charles stood up, knocking over his chair in his haste to cross the room and plant himself in her path, saying, "You don't need your picture taken with those children."

With the air of royalty confronted with a filthy commoner, the author only glanced at her liaison to the masses, a young man, who pranced up to Charles and puffed out his little bird's chest. "Are you a cop?" He folded his puny arms. "I didn't think so."

"I'm a cop," said Riker, moseying into the fray. He only had to touch the smaller man's chest with one light finger to deflate it. "Take it outside, pal."

The dinning room quickly became an author-free zone, and three men sat down to lunch.

Cadwaller looked around, saying, "I thought Dr. Magritte was going to join us."

Riker turned a disinterested eye to the parking lot window. "I left him with Dale, down by the bison pens. He'll be along. I don't think the old man can take much more of your boss's idiot ideas about security."

Cadwaller smiled, obviously enjoying this slam on the special agent in charge. Charles found that odd, but just now his attention was focused on the agent's hands as the man unconsciously aligned the salt shaker with the pepper shaker.

Mallory would have done that if she had been here.

Dr. Paul Magritte had found a quiet place with the cover of shrubs and trees, and he was deep into his daily ritual.

Unwinding time was a habit with him, and he did it with ease, as if merely fiddling the hands of a clock. Call it penance — undoing the onslaught of hours, days and decades, until all but one of the dead were unkilled. Next came the reconstruction of an afternoon, one detail by another.

He closed his eyes the better to see.

The old Egram place perched close to the highway that ran far beyond Illinois, and some called it the Main Street of America. The lines of the house were not true; the porch sagged and its posts leaned forward, fair warning to every visitor who ventured into the yard. His view was partially blocked by a truck parked in the driveway. The householder's trade was boldly but badly lettered on one broad side: Short Hauls and Long Ones — not a profitable business.

The police had never expected a ransom note.

He pictured the Egrams' oldest child standing outside on the lawn. The younger one was dead and in the ground that day.

Paul Magritte opened his eyes. His hand closed tightly upon a small velvet pouch, the repository of tiny bones, one hand only, the hand of Mary Egram, five years old. She had been the first to die.

12

Yes! Blueberry pie. Riker sank his fork into the warm flaky crust.

Charles Butler had finished eating a civilian's idea of food: meat, vegetables, and no sugar. Who could live on that? And now he was using a cell phone and losing his war against modern technology. "I have a new theory on the killer," he said to Detective Kronewald. "I think this man —"

"Or woman," Riker interjected.

Charles covered the phone for a moment to say, "No, I'm off that now." He lowered his hand and resumed his conversation with the Chicago detective. He had to repeat himself. Apparently Kronewald had also reminded him of that earlier theory. "Yes, I know," said Charles, "but I've just learned that he kills the children where he finds them. It would make more sense to scoop them up and take them to a covert location. He doesn't want to handle them while they're alive, but dead bodies are no problem. You see, what I took for timidity in regard to physical contact with his adult victim — Oh, I see. . . . Yes. . . . Well, thank you."

Handing the cell phone back to Riker, he said, "It seems that Mallory's already thought of the phobia angle."

The detective smiled. "She's good, isn't she? Crazy or not, she's a hell of a cop."

"Sorry," said Charles. "I'm sure Mallory never doubted that the killer was male."

"Probably not. So our boy is phobic. When I told you about my little problem with airplanes, you said that phobia was treatable."

"Oh, yes. I could suggest a —"

"And this serial killer? *His* phobia?"

"Is it treatable? Well, it might have been possible with early treatment. Perhaps a course of drug therapy and psychiatric counseling."

"Suppose he did get treatment. Maybe this slaughter fest is backsliding. Say he met up with the right doctor in his younger days. You think he could've fathered a child?" Riker had only to watch the man's eyes to see the connections being made at light's speed. This poor bastard had just realized that question was about Cassandra's child

— Mallory. And now the detective knew that his scenario was possible. It was all there in Charles Butler's sorry eyes.

Riker's attention shifted to one of the parents, a woman who was shying away from the cameras, using her long hair as a veil to hide her face. It was odd behavior for this group. And now a cameraman was walking toward her, pointing his lens at her, and this was every caravan parent's golden moment.

She left her table and headed for the rest-room — to hide?

The detective opened his notebook to jot a few lines on his shortlist, where he had crossed out Darwinia Solho's name and replaced it with another, the one she had been born with. He added a star, his personal method for ranking murder suspects. He looked up as Dale Berman entered the dining room in company with the redheaded profiler. "So, Charles, now that you've had a little chat with Cadwaller, what do you think of the guy?"

"I'm not sure." Charles smiled, so happy with this change of topic. "For someone from Behavioral Sciences, that man is surprisingly ignorant."

Jill's Dad walked by. The bowl of water in his hands was no doubt meant for the wolf, but Riker thought this lethargic man was suddenly in too much of a hurry, and the detective left his pie unfinished to walk outside. Agent Nahlman was standing by her car. He only had to lift one finger to tell her that something was up, and she nodded to him as he crossed the lot to the pickup truck.

The bowl of water lay spilled on the ground by the front tire. Jill's Dad had opened the passenger door and pulled the wolf out of the cab by its chain. For the first time, the man's face registered emotion — guilty surprise — when he turned to see Riker standing by the front end of the truck, his gun drawn and aimed at the animal.

"We had a deal," said the detective. "No unsupervised exercise for the pooch."

"It won't happen again."

"Let's take a walk." Riker stooped low to pick up the empty bowl. He stared at the wolf. "He's probably thirsty. I saw a water fountain down that road."

The wolf led the way downhill toward the bison pens, and Riker walked behind Jill's Dad, hoping to get this over quickly. It was best to do it now. All the answers to his questions were not worth the likely cost. The greatest risk was killing the wolf in the presence of the man. "It's just past that pen," said Riker, knowing that there was no water fountain.

It should have been predictable that the wolf would want to stop awhile at the chain-link fence that penned the bison. The cold blue eyes were riveted to a small calf. Twenty larger animals abandoned the baby buffalo in their sudden rush to take the sun on the other side of their enclosure. Only the wolf loved the calf. His jaws hung open, panting with love for it, mad to get at it, rising on hind legs, as if he could rip down the metal fence with his front paws. Jill's Dad pulled on the wolf's chain to drag him down and away. The animal choked, resisting. And now — so fast — he turned on his master. Teeth bared, he crouched, and then he lunged.

Riker fired once. Two shots rang out. The wolf lay dead.

"Sorry, pal," said the detective, though he knew he could take credit only for the shot to the breast. The bullet that had taken out one blue eye was the one that felled the wolf. Riker turned to see Agent Nahlman, his appointed backup, holstering her gun. Beyond her, he saw a gang of agents on the run, guns out and ready, and Dale Berman was leading them — from the rear.

Riker put his gun away and raised both

hands, yelling, "Settle down. The animal went a little nuts. That's all that happened." No reporters had turned out yet, and he wondered if gunfire could be heard above the sound of jackals noshing in the buffet room at the top of the road.

Dale Berman stepped to the front of the pack, pushing his people aside, as if they were suddenly in his way and not acting as human shields. He glared at Nahlman and then pointed at the tall thin man with the startled eyes. "Tell me you didn't shoot this poor man's dog."

Riker shouted, "She saved his *life!*" And why did this good news seem to disappoint the FBI man?

Turning on his heel, Dale led the posse back up the hill to the restaurant. In that same moment, Jill's Dad slumped to the ground in a pile of skinny sticks bent at the elbows and knees. "He didn't even know who I was."

Nahlman knelt down beside him. "I didn't recognize you, either, Mr. Hastings. The last time we met, you didn't have that beard. I think you wore a suit and tie that day."

"It was a brand-new suit," said the man Nahlman knew as George Hastings. "I bought it for the funeral." His eyes welled up with tears, and his head moved slowly from side to side. "It wasn't *fair*. I had all my paperwork in order." He reached into his pants pocket and brought out his wallet. Opening it, he produced a folded piece of paper and handed it to Riker. "That's the permit to bring Jill's body home on the plane. We bought the plot and the coffin, my wife and me. The stone was ordered. The funeral was all arranged. But that bastard wouldn't let Jill go. My wife's still waiting for me to bring our baby home." He turned to Nahlman. "You people are driving us crazy."

Riker could guess the rest of the story. Apparently young Jill Hastings had been buried twice. After digging up her body, the feds had interred her under the avalanche of a giant bureaucracy. The detective leaned down to reach inside the other man's jacket and found the source of the suspicious bulge — not a gun — a plastic catsup bottle. But it smelled like bacon. He squeezed, aiming the nozzle at the ground. "Bacon grease?"

He had to admire George Hastings' ingenuity, though the plan was full of flaws, entirely too risky and seriously insane. Spattering a federal agent with bacon grease was only a crime in dry cleaners' circles, but sudden death by starving wolf was an original attention getter. Or maybe the man had never intended to escape the penalty. Riker could see that the father of Jill Hastings was only minutes away from a full confession, and plotting to assassinate a federal agent was worth five years in prison.

"Hey, Nahlman? You don't want to hear any more of this," he said, as if she had better things to do with her time — as if she did not know what was coming next.

Her head inclined a bare inch to acknowledge her part in an upcoming crime, a conspiracy of silence. The agent walked back up the hill alone.

Riker stared at the dead wolf's one blue eye. "It was a beautiful plan. If you kept your mouth shut, at worst, you'd have to pay a fine." He nudged the animal with one foot. "No dog tags." He spoke softly now, going gently with this man. "The target was Dale Berman, right?"

Jill's Dad nodded. "I'd like to break this to my wife — if that's all right — before you arrest me."

"Naw." The detective waved this idea away with one hand. "Stupid me, I forgot to read you your rights." He hunkered down because he needed to see this man's eyes. "So here's the deal, George. You forget about Dale Berman, and I'll find your daughter's body. I'll send Jill home."

An hour later, the wolf — the evidence — was buried among the tall pines. Riker locked up the pickup truck, slapped the fender of a state trooper's car, and sent George Hastings into protective custody for the duration of this hunt for a serial killer. Much as he liked Jill's Dad, the detective did not trust crazy people to keep their promises.

The caravan was getting underway. He slid into the passenger seat of the Mercedes, and Charles Butler leaned over to ask, "When do you plan to tell Mallory about Savannah Sirus's suicide?"

"It never seems like the right time," said Riker. "This morning, I told her April Waylon was dead. She already knew, and she wasn't taking it well. I think she blames me, and she's right. April wandered off on my watch."

"I believe in the car," wrote Peyton Hale. *"Break it down to all the parts and lay them on the floor of a garage. Let's say that no one has ever seen a car all put together. So what would people make of these separate pieces? There's some who'd latch onto the battery; it's familiar, and they know it can power their electric lights. The battery people are not even*

close to the idea of an automobile; they've seen the light, and they're in the dark. Others would pick up the tires and run them downhill — and lose them that way. They only see a tire's potential to go somewhere without them. The fenders and the hood, all the exterior metal belongs to the unbelievers; they can see how these parts fit together for a fact, and all they ever see is a shell. Useless, they say.

"Blessed are they who can see the whole car because they're looking at the road ahead instead of all this crap on the floor of the garage."

Mallory put the letter back in her knapsack, too distracted to read any more. She started up the car and pulled back onto the old road, Route 66.

The late April Waylon had come to ride in her car for a while. The dead woman was missing one hand, yet she seemed cheerful. "It's a bright day," said April's corpse. "You should be wearing your sunglasses, dear."

Ah, but Mallory had lost her dark glasses. She had laid them down on the motel reception desk alongside her car keys while checking out this morning. That was the last time she remembered seeing them, and now they were lost. And her mind — lost.

Dead April prattled on as they drove down

the road.

Click.

The Volkswagen convertible was far away now, reduced to a small silver dot in the dark eye of a camera. The photographer held a pair of aviator sunglasses with gold rims. A tongue flicked in and out, as if it were possible to taste Mallory by licking the lenses. The sunglasses were folded away in the glove compartment to join the young detective's stolen cavern brochure, a pen and a napkin that she had once used. A long-range plan was forming, piece by piece of her.

Mallory entered the state of Texas miles and hours ahead of the caravan. Stopping in the small town of Shamrock, she made her duty call to the U-Drop Inn, but it was too early in the day to find this landmark saloon open for business. She only stayed long enough to make a checkmark on her list of things to see. She had greater hopes for the next stop.

She traveled westward toward the map coordinates for a patch of dirt, then pulled off the road and stopped the car on a flat Texas prairie *"— with a vista that went to the end of the world."* She stepped out and walked toward the horizon line. Every sign of life on earth was behind her and out of sight.

And she waited.

"There is only one way to see America," wrote Peyton Hale. *"An airplane or a train won't do. You have to feel the earth underfoot. You must be alone and in danger of losing your way. Oh, the sheer size of this country can send a man to his knees. This prairie, this great expanse of open space has that power. It's the overwhelming sense of emptiness you feel. Only a few steps away from the road and you're lost — and then you're changed."*

Without once falling to her knees and unchanged in any way, Mallory returned to the car, where she opened her notebook and crossed off one more disappointment.

Not his fault.

For her, the sense of emptiness was the familiar thing.

After driving only a few miles, she summoned up a passenger. Sometimes there were so many ghosts in the car that Mallory could not breathe. This time the murder victim was forced to ride in the back seat. Mallory could not quite let go of April Waylon, but, dead or alive, the woman was annoying.

The recently killed mother caught her eye in the rearview mirror and smiled. Dead

April leaned forward to say, "It wasn't your fault, you know. I mean — my murder. You can't be expected to save the same people *over* and *over* again." In Mallory's mind, a door suddenly appeared in the back seat of a two-door convertible. It flew open, and April was pushed out of the car.

Her foster mother, Helen Markowitz, was resurrected to ride in the front seat. Mallory had restored the soft roundness that had been lost to cancer years ago.

Gentle Helen, never leave me.

"Oh, Kathy, just look at this mess." The dead woman was staring at the empty soda cans and wadded-up credit-card receipts that littered the floor mat. There was no derision in Helen's tone. She had been the kindest of people — and the neatest. Everything Mallory knew about cleaning solvents and dust mites she had learned from this extraordinary housekeeper, and then she had taken it to great extremes, never tolerating one thing out of place and not one spot of dirt, not one —

"Something's gone wrong," said Helen, frowning at the discarded paper cups. "This is not like you, Kathy." Tactfully, the late Helen Markowitz said nothing about the dust on the dashboard, but Mallory noticed it and silently inventoried other signs of trouble: a chipped fingernail, a windshield covered with bugs, and a lying mirror that showed her eyes full of tears. But her face was dry. Maybe these were her father's green eyes — *his* tears.

At the last stop in Oklahoma, when all the people had been fed and the reporters, too, Riker went over the same instructions for parents who had recently joined up. The ranks of the caravan had swelled to fill every bit of the lot. "Pump your own gas. Don't leave your car unattended anywhere on this road."

The FBI and local police had managed to contain the detail of victim mutilation, the chopped-off right hands, but the press had acquired the news and names of the murdered caravan parents. And now Dr. Magritte was allowed to convene the campers in a minute of silent prayer for those who had lost their lives on Route 66. The prayer group was hardly a tableau of statues in silent reverence. They were antsy, feet shifting, anxious to be gone — and *smiling.*

Riker understood. One of their number had died yesterday, but they were still alive. Civilians and their television ideas of murder — they believed that everything would be all right if they only followed the good camper's guidelines for traversing a road of sudden death.

"It might be a mistake to give them rules." Charles Butler was obviously in the mind-reading mode as he sipped coffee from a paper cup. "Makes it all a bit too innocent — like a school field trip."

"I'd like to clear them all off the road." Riker shrugged. "But I can't do that without an act of Congress. The feds want the parents here."

"As bait?"

"Yeah, but even if I spelled that out for these people, they still wouldn't leave. Every time somebody dies, they think they're getting a little closer to finding their kids. And they're right about that. Cold, huh?"

Mallory barreled down the road with the volume turned up sky high, and a group called The Who sang, *"Won't get fooled again."*

Was this the one?

Back in New York City, she had asked, "What was my father's favorite song?"

"There were so many," Savannah had said, unwilling to admit that she did not know.

And thereafter, Mallory had played a waiting game until one truth emerged and then another. Her enemy had weakened more each day.

Savannah Sirus was one dead woman who would never come for a ride in this car.

She — would — not — *dare.*

Mallory rejoined the old road and entered a small Texas town. This was the home of Peyton Hale's beloved Avalon Theater, a going concern when his letter was written. It was closed now. The movie posters had all come down, and the doors were padlocked. The glass of the ticket booth was cracked, and a nearby sign proclaimed this place as a landmark. The silver convertible was the only car on the street. Every parking space was hers for the taking. She had seen other ghost towns along the way, but there were people living in this one. A few of the storefronts were not empty, and one was a town museum that still posted hours.

A diehard town.

She crossed the old theater off her list with no sense of letdown this time. She had come to understand this kind of landmark, *"— like a bookmark for a memory."*

Down the road, she found the old Phillips 66 gas station, a tiny house of brick that had been restored for appearance only; it no longer pumped gas. Beyond that was a likely patch of road to bury a body, and troopers were hard at work digging it up. Kronewald's pattern for the children's graves was holding up in the state of Texas.

She passed the diggers by. The young detective had had enough of the dead today, both the people and the places. Her car had been emptied of ghosts, and she was done with death. She rejoined the section of newer highway that had displaced the old Route 66 and put on some speed. The music was faster now, more frantic.

"Rock 'n' roll was the end of boyhood," wrote Peyton Hale. *"The music was wired into my skull, and my toes tapped to rhythms that only I could hear. Dogs were not so quick to come to me just for the pleasure of licking my hand. And the fathers of girls could see me coming from a long ways off. Oh, and the girls, they found me dangerous, and didn't I love that? My salad days, my outlaw days. The road and the music — just sixteen. And now that I'm an old man of twenty-five, my road is disappearing as I write, as I ride."*

Mallory took the next ramp that would turn her car east. She was heading back toward the grave-digging troopers, though she could not say why. Her debt to Kronewald was surely paid in full. Perhaps it was because April Waylon had come back for another ride, eyes popped wide and searching every bit of road, still so determined to find a lost child.

It might be this one.

The caravan was crossing from Oklahoma into Texas when Riker reached out and turned off the fire and brimstone of a radio evangelist. "Okay, that's enough local color. Could you talk to Joe Finn when we stop for the night?"

"No point," said Charles Butler. "He won't leave the road. Mr. Finn is really no different from the other parents."

"Oh, he's different all right." And Riker had had his fill of wild cards. "Finn's daughter's is buried in a Kansas cemetery, and he has to know that's her body. I'm not buying into this denial crap. I've been through this before. It doesn't last a year — usually just a few minutes. The parents shake their heads at you like you're crazy. How can their kid be dead? 'No, you made a mistake, you stupid cop.' And then they cry. Now this guy, he wouldn't even look at the corpse. I think Joe Finn wants payback. Probably figures he can find this freak before we do."

"No, he wouldn't bring two children on a mission like that."

"You're right. That's nuts." The detective

turned to the passenger window and nursed a theory that fathers of murdered children were not very stable people.

Ten miles of Texas prairie rolled by before Charles broke the silence. "Guilt always comes with a death in the family. Always. People dwell on last days and how they could've been different, given a second chance — and, of course, superhuman powers to see into the future. You can't cure them with logic. It's the same when a child goes missing. That's why these parents can't leave this road. They'd be consumed by guilt if they didn't do everything in their power to bring their children home."

"Or die trying."

"I don't think that enters into the equation. I'm sure you noticed that most of these people are single parents. They've lost spouses to divorce, one suicide that I know of. And then there's alcoholism and depression. I know how you picked out the FBI moles so easily. They were playing the part of a happily married couple."

"The moles are doing a crummy job of keeping an eye on the kid."

"Sorry," said Charles. "Sometimes I forget that Mallory's not all that communicative. I thought you knew. The moles aren't watching her at all. The other day, when Dodie disappeared under the table and Peter was screaming her name, the moles turned to look at Magritte. He's their only concern. It makes sense. I'm sure you suspected that the killer was in the doctor's therapy group. Murderers sometimes insinuate themselves into —"

"Oh, shit," said Riker. "That's why Dale pulled that stunt with Joe Finn. He was painting a target on Dodie. He's drawing fire away from his best witness — Magritte."

Witness? Or suspect?

Riker answered his cell phone. It was the moles telling him that they had lost the Pattern Man to an exit ramp, and Dale Berman would not send agents to bring the little man back to the fold. Horace Kayhill was not one of the parents — not their problem.

"So he's expendable? . . . Yeah, *right*. . . . 'I'm sorry' doesn't cut it, kid. . . . No, you tell that idiot in charge —" The line was dead.

Damn moles.

Riker placed his next call to Special Agent Berman's cell phone. "Dale? . . . Yeah, it's about Horace Kayhill. . . . No, Dale, you're gonna send out a posse. . . . Why? Well, if that little guy isn't on your shortlist, you're a moron." After another few moments of listening, he ended the call and folded his phone into his shirt pocket. "They're going after him."

"Nicely played," said Charles. "I know how much you despise Agent Berman, but you always use his first name — like an old friend." He raised his eyebrows and shrugged to say, *Just curious, not prying.*

Dr. Paul Magritte's Lincoln was following the Mercedes when the old man saw Detective Riker turn around, twisting to reach into the back seat. The doctor eased up on the gas pedal to drop behind by one more car length. He took a last look at the blurry photograph of April Waylon. It had been taken while the woman was still losing blood from her slashed throat. This was the face of ongoing terror — not quite dead. He turned his attention back to the car in front of him. Riker was still facing this way.

Perhaps guilt inspired the flight of fancy, the uneasy feeling that the detective's line of vision could travel several car lengths, then bend and dip and turn to dark corners. Though Riker could not possibly know what Dr. Magritte held in his hand, the photograph was hastily concealed inside the folded maps on the dashboard.

13

Riker was so happy to hear Mallory's voice. Apparently, in a lapse of apathy, she had forgotten to turn off her cell phone.

The grasslands of the Texas Panhandle were sliding by his passenger window while he told her the story of the dead wolf and a foiled plot to kill Dale Berman. A breeze ruffled the papers in his hand as he read her snatches of correspondence between the government and George Hastings. "Dale found the kid's body, but he won't release it for burial. So all this time goes by, months and months. Hastings gets tired of begging Dale for Jill's body. He bypasses Dale's field office and writes to Washington. Mallory, I got copies of *everything.* Now, all Hastings got back were form letters, but guess whose office they came from?"

There was silence on the other end. Guessing games annoyed her. He gave her a broad hint. "The Assistant Director of

Criminal Investigations."

"Harry Mars," said Mallory. "He can't be running this circus."

"He's not, and I'll tell you how I know. Mars's office sent a whole slew of these damn form letters. It looks like a stall. I don't think the FBI knows where Dale stashed the bodies of any of those kids. Interesting, huh? But I know he's been digging them up for almost a year."

"All right," said Mallory. "So we're looking for a makeshift morgue somewhere in Dale's comfort zone — near a Texas field office. Not all of the remains are skeletons. He'd want a place with refrigeration. Get the body count from Horace Kayhill's maps."

"I can't," said Riker. "The Pattern Man defected. I've got agents and troopers out looking for the little guy. I even used a news helicopter. No luck. But all this new coverage might scare the freak off till we can find Horace."

"No," said Mallory, "the perp is loving this. Imagine the thrill."

Riker could not, but he deferred to Mallory in all things sociopathic. "Oh, the feds finally ran a check against vehicle registration. One of the parents, Darwinia Sohlo —"

"The name's a fake," said Mallory.

The connection went dead, and it would be no use to call her back. His partner's cell phone worked only one way — at her convenience.

Riker was not inclined to trust the moles with the lives of any more people. He ordered Charles Butler to change lanes and drop back to the end of a parade that stretched out for more than a mile. And now he watched for exit signs and more defections to Route 66, but all the parents seemed content to drive I-40 to their next interview with the reporters.

The radio was tuned to a news station, and the broadcaster was giving a traffic report on the caravan, "— *so travelers should avoid that stretch of the interstate. Our helicopter counts two hundred and seventy-five cars going slower than the legal limit.*"

Understatement.

The speedometer on the Mercedes was showing forty-five miles an hour and falling. The highway was hemorrhaging with the caravan, yet the traffic report had not deterred the local residents. All along the road were groups of people lining the prairie with cars and trucks, picnic baskets and babies in arms, young and old, waving at the cars driving by. Some held up signs of good luck and God love you lettered in bold print that Riker could read without glasses; there was nothing wrong with his long-distance vision, and so he was also able to see the first paper airplane take flight. It was caught by a tall man standing with his family. As the Mercedes rolled by, the airplane was unfolded in the Texan's hands. It was a poster of a missing child.

The news helicopter relayed this sight to the radio broadcaster as more paper planes took flight. Flocks of them sailed out from the windows of the caravan vehicles. The reporter was calling it a swarm — so many of them. Some soared upward, and others were captured by high-reaching hands and the lower reach of chasing children.

Little ships with big hopes.

Mallory's store of coveted cell-phone numbers included one for Harry Mars, and her call went through to voice mail. She planned to trade on a cop's good name — not her name, and so she left the message, "It's Markowitz's daughter."

She felt a pang, and supposed that it was guilt or something like it, and this was not the first time since leaving New York City. Now and again, she felt that she was cheating on the man who had raised her from the age of ten. It was the music that called him to mind, again and again, all along this road.

Music was all her two fathers had in common. Louis Markowitz had never been young — except late in the evening after supper, when the volume on the stereo was cranked up high, and the old man had taught her to dance to rock 'n' roll. His wife, gentle Helen, had called him a dancing fool and took her own turns with him on a floor with a pulled-back rug. Some of Mallory's favorite memories were the dancing nights.

Lou Markowitz had lived to dance.

Peyton Hale had lived to drive. Cassandra had told her that defining detail about her real father, but not much else. Or had she? Mallory had been six going on seven the day her mother died. How many memories had been lost? She had always known her father's name and where her green eyes had come from, though her mother had not kept any photographs, probably wanting no reminder of parting with him and the loss of him.

Before the visit from Savannah Sirus, she had known nothing of her mother's pain. It must have been reborn every morning when young Kathy jumped up and down on her mother's bed, waking Cassandra with Peyton's green eyes.

Another pang.

Her cell phone beeped.

The restaurant's parking lot would not hold all the vehicles. Reporters and FBI agents had arrived first to take up most of the spaces. Riker left the Mercedes to play traffic cop, and Charles Butler watched his friend unwind the mess of backed-up traffic on the road, steering cars onto adjoining land, shouting instructions to form neat rows, yelling, "Fake it! Just pretend you're at the shopping mall!"

In search of his own parking space, Charles was looking out over the herd of media in the parking lot when the cacophony of beeping began. The reporters were all answering cell phones.

Oh, *stampede.*

They were running for their vehicles. He saw the small fleet of news helicopters stirring up dust down the road, rotors whirring, lifting. FBI agents swarmed out of the restaurant, all heading for their vehicles. The sick sound of one fender hitting another could be heard as cars and vans crowded the narrow road leading back to the highway.

Charles now had his choice of prime parking spaces and selected one by the front door. A pleasant surprise awaited him inside — no long line to order food. While he filled a tray for two, Riker had procured a table by the window, and the parents were still filing in the front door — only the parents. Outside in the nearly empty lot, Dr. Magritte was flanked by the FBI moles, the only agents left behind.

Odd.

Well, what could happen here? It was broad daylight. The caravan was perfectly safe. Yet a sense of abandonment pervaded the dining room. All eyes were on the parking lot, though the exodus of FBI and media was over.

Riker held a cell phone to one ear as his fingers drummed the tabletop, the sure sign of a man left on hold. "Still here," he said to the phone, "you bastard."

Ah, the man must be speaking with Kronewald.

Riker jotted down a few lines on a napkin and ended the call.

Charles was looking out the window when he asked, "Where do you suppose they went — the agents and reporters?"

"They're heading down the road about ten miles." The detective dropped the cell phone into his shirt pocket.

Charles set down the tray of fast food, and then turned back to the window. "But I couldn't help noticing that they went off in different directions."

"Yeah." Riker waved one hand toward the east. "According to Kronewald, in that direction, you've got local cops digging up a dirt parking lot. To the west — a grave across the street from a nursing home. Most of the feds will be back soon. The media won't. Digging up little bones makes a better lead on the evening news. Two gravesites, no waiting. So much more entertaining than parents holding up their posters and begging for help."

"This is Mallory's work?"

"No, this time it's Chicago PD. They got a new toy, geographic profiling. They're giving grave locations to local police. Now the feds are playing catch-up with the cops. Police in eight states report directly to Kronewald. That old bastard's just rolling in glory. So he finally won the war — he's running the show. Oh, and he tells me the sun rises and sets on Kathy Mallory. That kid really knows how to stock up the Favor Bank."

Both men were looking at the nearly empty parking lot when one of the FBI vehicles returned. Cadwaller stepped out of the car and pulled his suit jacket from a hanger in the rear seat. He approached the window near Charles and Riker's table and used the glass reflection to smooth down his red hair, not caring that this toilette was being performed only inches from their faces.

"A coat hanger," said Riker, whose own suit jacket was wadded up in his duffel bag. "Not a hook but a hanger." For some reason, this made the detective suspicious. "And check out his car. See the little beads of water on the trunk? Crimes scenes east and west of here, and this guy stops off to get his car washed."

Charles nodded. Perhaps that was excessively tidy. Even *Mallory* had allowed her car to accumulate streaks and dirt, not to mention the bugs on her windshield.

Cadwaller turned around to look over the surrounding ten cars, all that remained in a lot that boasted a hundred parking spaces. The agent watched Mallory's car roll into a parking space, and then, with a moue of distaste for her dirty windshield, he turned back to his own vehicle to get a briefcase from the front seat.

"Ah," said Riker, with great satisfaction. His eyes were fixed on the silver convertible. "The champ of neat freaks has arrived."

Mallory slowly stepped out of the car, her attention already riveted on the FBI agent.

"And now," said Riker, with the flair of a sports announcer, "she's spotted the contender. It's a match made in hell. She just noticed that his car's cleaner than hers."

Cadwaller straightened his perfectly straight tie and headed for the restaurant door, unaware that Mallory was right behind him, her eyes narrowed and fixed on the back of his neck.

Riker smiled at Charles. "She's very competitive."

The FBI man had spotted them and walked up to the table, saying, "I'm looking for Darwinia Sohlo."

"You don't need to talk to her," said Mallory at his back.

The agent jumped and spun around. Riker grinned.

"I've got orders to interview this woman," said Cadwaller.

"Because she's traveling under an alias?" Mallory folded her arms. "She's got nothing to do with this case. If you'd bothered with a background check you'd know that."

Charles scanned the crowd of parents and found Darwinia Sohlo in her customary corner chair. Her eyes were a bit fearful, but she always looked that way. Two parents with trays sat down at her table, and the woman's shoulders rounded as she tried to make herself smaller.

Cadwaller ignored Mallory and turned to Riker, saying, "I'm not planning to shoot Mrs. Sohlo. I just want to talk to her. My orders —"

"Orders from Dale?" Riker shook his head. "You've been had, pal. It's busywork."

In Charles's estimation, this was no surprise to Cadwaller. The agent scanned the crowd and walked off in Dr. Magritte's direction. After a few words were exchanged, the older man pointed him toward the corner table. Now Cadwaller squared off his shoulders and advanced on Darwinia Sohlo with slow, measured steps, clearly regarding her as a criminal.

Mallory turned to her partner. "He's playing a role."

Riker nodded. "Christ, you'd think Darwinia was packing a machine gun."

Cadwaller's words carried a tone of authority, not shouted, but strong. It was the voice of an enforcer. "Miriam Rainard? Come with me." He gestured toward the door.

Charles turned to Riker, who answered his unspoken question. "That's her right name, but I like the fake name better."

The woman, known to all as Darwinia, slowly moved her head from side to side, a gesture of awe and certainly not one of defiance. The man never touched her. No need. Charles could virtually see the strings that had been attached to this woman's psyche long ago. She must have been some other enforcer's property for years and years. She was rising from the table, not even pausing to consider his order. It was an automatic response. Oh, but now the strings had gone slack. Her head moved in another slow side-to-side as she backed up to the wall, and this time she meant no; she was not going anywhere with him.

Charles turned to Mallory. "You know what's going on, don't you?"

She nodded. "Darwinia's cut-rate plastic surgery — that's a repair job."

Of course. The history of a battered woman fitted so well with the camera shyness — a runaway woman hiding from an abusive spouse. "So, all this time," said Charles, "she's been living with the constant fear of discovery?"

"And now," said Riker, "Darwinia can't decide what she wants most — to stay alive or find her kid."

"If she's not a suspect, then maybe you

two could persuade Cadwaller to leave her alone?"

Well, that was a waste of breath.

Mallory pulled out a chair at the table and sat down with Riker to watch the ongoing show. Charles turned in time to see Darwinia's resolve fade and die. The woman was turning toward the door, walking in tandem with the FBI man. Oh, but now she saw Mallory, the boxer's champion, and Darwinia's eyes were begging. It was Riker who rose to the lady's defense. He moved in front of the pair before they could reach the door. Apparently, this detective's intervention was not in Cadwaller's script for the day. The agent stopped short, all authority dissipating — so like an actor with no clue to his next line.

"Cadwaller, she can't help you." Riker waved him toward the window table. "But we can, me and my partner. Sit down, and we'll fill you in." Turning to Darwinia, he said, "Everything's fine. Go finish your meal."

The FBI man joined Charles and the detectives at their table. He sat down and opened a notebook, unaware that he was now the subject of an interrogation. Charles could see it coming as the two detectives smiled in unison and leaned toward the agent.

Lunchtime.

"I get the feeling," said Riker, "that you don't know your boss all that well. How long have you been posted with Dale's field office?"

"Three months."

Mallory leaned in. "But you don't spend much time with him. He keeps you on the road a lot, doesn't he? Away from the younger agents? They're all out at the crime scenes, and here you are — running a fake errand."

Understanding dawned on Cadwaller. His pale skin showed a slight flush of humiliation as he pulled out a pen and looked down at his blank notebook page. "So what've you got for me?"

"Twelve years ago, her kid disappeared," said Riker. "The Wisconsin cops were looking at the father as the prime suspect, and they didn't expect any help from the battered wife. There was a history of domestic disputes. Her jaw was broken twice, but the lady never pressed charges. Two years after her kid goes missing, Darwinia — Miriam, whatever — she disappears, too. And the cops knew they weren't looking for a dead body — not that time. They just wished her luck. But Nahlman could've told you that.

It was her catch, and she gave the whole story to Dale." The detective leaned in closer, as if to impart a secret. "Now, we know you're from the Freak Squad —"

"Behavioral Science Unit," said Mallory, correcting her partner's bad manners and startling Charles. "This isn't Cadwaller's fault." She turned to the agent, giving him her best rendition of sympathy. "The minute you saw that woman, you knew Dale was screwing up again, didn't you? Wasting your time again." And now she had saved a federal agent from looking like a fool.

Not her style.

The FBI man closed his notebook and slapped it on the table. Face saved, the agent raised his grateful eyes to Mallory's. And now it was her turn to lean toward him into that close range of conspiracy, so confidential in her tone. "What if this isn't a screwup?"

"What?" Riker's face was angry when he left his chair and took the one next to his partner. "You're defending that idiot, Dale?"

Charles was confused by this new game of musical chairs and changing alliances.

Mallory's eyes remained fixed on Cadwaller. "What if Dale's playing you?"

The agent turned his face away from hers as he pocketed his notebook and pretended interest in invisible lint on his sleeve. "I guess we're done, here." Cadwaller rose from the table with no word of good-bye and left the restaurant.

Charles turned from one detective to the other. "What did I miss?"

"Not much." Riker changed chairs again to sit before his tray of food. He pushed the laptop computer to Mallory's side of the table, but she would not even look at it. He frowned, seeing this as an ongoing problem, like a failure to eat her vitamins. "I knew Cadwaller wasn't Dale's favorite agent. But if that guy's got something on Dale, he's not planning to share it."

Charles edged closer to Mallory. "So you don't think Agent Berman is just too incompetent to run a task force?"

"No," she said. "Berman's mistakes are really over the top."

"Yeah," said Riker, "very stupid mistakes."

"You're sure about that?" Mallory slung her knapsack over one shoulder. "Think about it, Riker. Dale was smart enough to fool Markowitz once." She picked up her car keys, almost ready to leave. "The way I remember it, he fooled you, too." She leaned close to her partner's ear to deliver a parting salvo. "And he's still doing it."

■ ■ ■ ■

Agent Nahlman had no idea where Barry Allen had gone. She guessed that he had been reassigned to the gravesite west of this one. Dale Berman effected these separations from her partner all too frequently. Today, he had loaned her out to the state police, demoting her to media control. News vehicles had been turned away from the crime scene and into an area where cameras and lights could be set up. Now came the procession of divas, male and female reporters, to take their positions and deliver live feed on a small grave that they would never be allowed to see. Next, she would be called upon to say "No comment" a hundred times, rephrasing it for the more witless interviewers. Wrangling these bottom feeders and their makeup artists — this was the only thing that Dale was truly good at, but he could not be bothered. No, this was a handmaid's job.

Nahlman grabbed a passing rookie agent by his sleeve, promoted him to press liaison, and then walked back to the dig site surrounded by state troopers.

Oh, no.

This corpse had flesh. She had become so

accustomed to bones, but this child had been mummified in arid ground. It was easy to make out a button nose, a delicate chin — a slashed throat.

Agent Nahlman looked down the road, as if she could see all the way to the restaurant where the caravan parents would be waiting for the news — the name of a little girl. Some had children to fit the victim profile. Many other parents were spread out all over the country, and they were no doubt following the broadcasts, never straying far from their television sets, as this body was unearthed, layer by layer of dirt.

Who would win the phone call today?

Unlike Dale Berman, the local authorities were not inclined to keep the parents in ignorance, and this child would have a decent burial. One of the diggers held up an object cupped in one hand. He was a burly local man and probably had children of his own, for his voice was hoarse when he said, "It's a locket. Her name was Karen."

This would not fit any child belonging to a caravan parent. Nahlman knew all their stories now — which missing girl hated asparagus and which one loved baseball more than God. The FBI agent stared at the corpse in the hole.

And whose little girl are you?

A laminated school-bus pass was gently plied from the child's curled fingers. The bus pass held all the information needed to carry her home.

The caravan had been under way for twenty minutes, and Dr. Paul Magritte was at last feeling at ease. He was more centered now, with many cars between himself and the New York detective in the Mercedes. And the FBI moles were driving at the rear.

The doctor had total privacy.

Eyes on the road, he dipped one hand into his nylon knapsack, fishing blind until his fingers closed upon the photograph of dying April Waylon. He crushed it in his fist. Next, he knocked his pipe from the ashtray, replacing it with the wadded picture. He patted his shirt pockets. Oh, where were his matches? No matter. The car's cigarette lighter would do as well. A few moments later, he held its glowing tip to the crumpled image of April.

It caught fire, followed by smoke — so much of it. He had never burned one in the car before, and he had not counted on this. His other small fires had been more ceremonial, and those had been set with the flames of votive candles. He batted the air in front of his face. Smoke was slipping past him to his partially opened window. Eyes filled with stinging tears, he dared to open all the windows until, at last, the smoke had cleared and the picture was burnt to ashes.

His eyes were also clearing, and now, in peripheral vision, he noticed another car in the passing lane had come abreast of him and kept pace with him. Through his side window, Paul Magritte glanced at this other driver.

And Mallory looked back at him.

Her head was sharply turned to one side. She was facing him with no thought of the road ahead, and the young detective held this pose for so long — it unnerved him so badly — his hands tightened on the wheel, knuckles whitening. She stared at him for miles and miles.

14

The campsite was near an abandoned gas station, and one toilet had been promised to be in working condition. However, the owner had not inspected his property in years, and now he renegotiated the amount of money agreed upon one month ago when the trip was first planned. Today's price, the owner said, was "Not one red cent, and God bless you all."

This time, the news media had the affair catered with microwave ovens emitting the smell of reheated pizza to lure the campers and federal agents into the interview zone. But best of all, the most enterprising network crew was unloading Port-O-Potties from a flatbed truck — even better bait that neatly solved the problem of the dysfunctional toilet. As each plastic closet was set upon the ground, a waiting line of parents quickly formed in front of it.

A field reporter stood before a stationary

camera, preparing to say his new opening line one more time. Yesterday, he had reported from the Road of Lost Children, but today he said, "This is John Peechem reporting from the Road of Graves." A cameraman pointed out that he was smiling when he said it that time, too. They did a retake with a more somber expression. And then the lens panned a group of young men and women with the letters *FBI* emblazoned on their jackets. "This hasn't been confirmed yet," the reporter said to his microphone, "but the agents might be looking for body parts."

A less expensive handheld camera pointed at the caravan's only children. Brother and sister stood hand in hand, awaiting their turn at one of the big green closets. Standing behind them, their father carried a roll of toilet paper, tearing off sheets and handing them to Peter and Dodie. A reporter was approaching this trio, fair game in the Port-O-Potty zone, when the little boy put up one hand to ward the woman off, saying, "I bite reporters."

End of interview.

Dodie rocked on her heels and toes, and then she hummed. Louder now. Her father picked her up in his arms and never noticed that his child was pointing to the ground

and the shadow of another man.
Click.

Mallory sat in a folding chair near a car that was not her own, fingers flying across the keyboard of a laptop computer that was not hers, either. Christine Nahlman sat down on a neighboring campstool, not offering any conversation, only keeping quiet company with the detective as she watched some of the younger agents search the caravan vehicles. Others were invading tents.

"It's a waste of time," said Mallory, never taking her eyes from the laptop. "The perp doesn't travel around with little hand bones. He digs them up along the way."

"Well, he's got one hand that we can match up with a fresh corpse."

"Not anymore. He's got no use for it." Mallory looked up at the search in progress. "That's just Berman's idea of busywork, a show for the reporters." She turned her eyes back to the glowing screen in her lap. In sidelong vision, she saw the FBI agent stiffen, and then lean far forward.

There was incredulity in Nahlman's voice when she finally said, "That's *my* laptop."

Mallory nodded as she scanned a state map of graves. "I liked the early pattern you developed in Illinois. It was a good start."

"That's *my* computer."

"Well, you left it on the seat of your car."

"My *locked* car."

Mallory waved one hand to say that these little distinctions were unimportant. "Geographic profiling won't predict a kill site — not in this case. When he kills a parent, it's a crime of opportunity."

"You broke into my car, *stole* my laptop — *government* property."

"*I'm* the criminal?" Mallory was not good at mock innocence. "*You* used a little girl to bait a serial killer." Ah, bombshell. Annihilation was her forte. The agent looked as if she had been kicked in the gut.

"That was never the plan," said Nahlman when she found her voice again.

"Back in Oklahoma, you knew what was going to happen *before* the boxer decked your boss. I saw you arguing with Dale Berman — but you didn't stop him."

"I'm just one agent, not even the —"

"You let him draw a target on Dodie Finn." Mallory leaned close to the woman, the better to cut out her heart. "Fragile, isn't she? I found the psych evaluations — Dodie's FBI file. Federal agents interrogated a little girl who belonged in a hospital. They wouldn't even let her father visit. And why? Because they knew she'd tell them anything — *anything* — if they would only let her go home. But Dodie had nothing to give them. Dodie is crazy."

And now — a little fear.

Mallory only glanced at the lineup of reporters out by the road. "I promised them an interview for the six-o'clock news," she lied, and then opened her pocket watch, though she knew the time to the hour and the minute. "It's almost showtime." The implied threat of ugly disclosure hung in the air between the two women.

"Dale Berman personally guaranteed Dodie's safety," said Nahlman. "Two agents on her all the time. That's why I —"

"He lied. He does that a lot. Berman wanted a serial killer — a *kid* killer — to believe that Dodie could give up something important. Well, she can't." Mallory stared at the screen for a few moments of silence, her best imitation of self-righteous indignation. "Better to sacrifice Dodie than Paul Magritte, right? You'd never risk any damage to your best witness — even though the old man's got it coming."

"Why do you say that?"

"Why does your boss run sloppy background checks? I'm not going to do his job for him. And one more thing. I've seen the

FBI files — *all* of them. You never got any credit for your work. The forensic techs who do your grave digging — they think old Dale's got a crystal ball." Mallory scrolled through the maps and data. "No one but your boss has ever seen this material."

"You do a poor imitation of Agent Berman. That's *his* style," said Nahlman, "pitting people against each other. And he does it better."

"You think I care about your little relationship problems?" Mallory touched the eject button on the agent's laptop computer, and a disk came sliding out. She held it beyond Nahlman's reach, saying, "I only came to steal."

So inattentive were his watchers that Dr. Paul Magritte never feared being missed, though he had driven fifty miles from the campsite to find solitude in this church. Rice grains crunched underfoot as he climbed the short flight of stone stairs. The large wooden doors were unlocked, but, upon entering, he sensed that no one, not even the priest, had remained after the ceremony. A large vase of white blooms graced the altar, and some flower girl had strewn the aisle with rose petals. He pictured a small child in this task, taking slow toddler steps toward the great stained-glass window in advance of the bridal procession. He hoped that this union would be fruitful. If the earth could not restore the lost children, it would at least be replenished.

The psychologist dropped his jacket and his nylon sack on the seat of the first pew. The lightest of burdens were troublesome to an old man with arthritis in every joint, and yet he had come here in search of fresh agony. After climbing three steps to the altar, he lit all the candles and stepped back. Eschewing any comfort of a padded riser, he knelt on the stone floor. This caused great pain to his knees, and he called it atonement.

Mary Egram had been the first to die. It must always begin with the loss of Mary.

The ruby glass beads of his rosary played across his fingers. Each time he performed this ritual, it called up an image of the old Egram house back in Illinois. All those years ago, it had seemed always on the verge of pitching into the front yard. He recalled the interior of the home with the same tension, every wall leaning, and he remembered waiting, moment to moment, for the ceiling to come crashing down.

Next, with hands clasped tightly in prayer, he conjured up the floral patterns of worn upholstery and threadbare scatter rugs. A large television set was the only luxury item, and this would have been chosen by the man of the family, no doubt an avid football fan. In mind's eye, Mr. Egram was seated on the couch and staring at his blank TV screen, feet tapping the floor, measuring time and willing this visit to pass more quickly.

Paul Magritte had played this home movie in his head a thousand times so that he would not forget one detail, not one tap of the other man's foot. Memory also recounted exactly twelve votive candles encircling the photograph of Mary, fair-haired and only five years old. The lost child's shrine had pride of place atop the television set, and this had surely been the mother's work. The parents had been abandoned and their loss forgotten by the media. However, Mrs. Egram had been determined that her husband would never forget, not even for the respite of a ballgame on a Sunday afternoon.

Small plaster saints had abounded in the Egrams' front room. The religious theme had also played out in the dining area and the hallway. Mary Egram's mother had apparently bought out the entire stock of a church gift shop. But that was to be expected, for the woman was a lapsed Catholic who had lately returned to the faith in zealot fashion.

And the father of the missing child? Not a great fan of the Lord.

Sarah Egram had sought to explain her husband's aloofness with the information that he was from Methodist stock. The Protestant truck driver had borne a look of grim tolerance for his wife, who constantly fretted her rosary beads and moved her mouth in silence, seeking help in magical incantations. Her eyes had sometimes strayed to the window, perchance to see if her prayers had worked. Or maybe she had been keeping watch over the child in the yard — the surviving child.

That had been Paul Magritte's second thought on that long-ago afternoon.

His eyes snapped open. Perhaps it was the pain in his knees that had called him out of reverie and back to the cold stone floor of this Texas sanctuary. No, he had *sensed* something — someone. And now the flames of the altar candles flickered and bowed, as if swayed by a body in motion and very close to him. How fragile was he — that a current of air in a drafty old church should have the power to stop his breath — his heart. He feared it still, but never looked behind him, never turned his head. Instead he closed his eyes again, to see the mistakes of his distant past. He escaped into his re-creation of a shabby front room in another time, another place.

Once more, he pictured Mr. Egram seated on the couch beside his wife, reaching out to her with one large hand and gently covering her fingers and beads to end the incessant rattle and movement. The woman's mouth also ceased to move. Out in the yard, their child was approaching the house, and then the ten-year-old stopped halfway up the flagstone path and stood motionless, possibly taking a cue from the mother.

That afternoon, Paul Magritte had waited out the uncomfortable silence, looking about the room and noting the lighter wallpaper that had marked the old outlines of other picture frames, their places usurped by portraits of the Madonna and a court of saints. And, as if a houseful of religious paraphernalia were not imposition enough, poor Methodist Mr. Egram now had a stranger settled into his favorite chair, for his wife had insisted that their visitor must take the most comfortable seat in the house, the one facing the television set.

Their older child had crept up to the front window. Face pressed hard against the glass, the small features were smeared and made monstrous. One eye bulged and one was lost within deep folds of squeezed flesh.

This little horror show had hardly ruffled Paul Magritte that day. He had seen it as a ploy to gain attention, the normal behavior of a child with emotionally distant parents. Despite a missing sibling, the youngster was well adjusted; a psychological evaluation had been done while Social Services still had custody of this ten-year-old — and while the police had been investigating the parents, suspecting them in the disappearance of their little girl.

That day, only the mother's behavior had shocked Dr. Magritte. He had wondered how she could have been averse to his wonderful plan to take her surviving child away from her. Fool that he was in those days, he had assumed that she had been unable to fully grasp it all. "You understand," he had said to her then, "this won't put a financial burden on your family. The surgeon, the hospital and staff — they're donating their services."

For the second time, she had said no to him. "It wouldn't be right." And then, Sarah Egram had elaborated. "You can't make everything all normal that way. Nobody will ever see it coming."

It.

This was how she had referred to her disfigured child.

Memory dissipated like mist, and Paul Magritte's eyes were jolted wide open. The altar flames did not waver now, but he heard a noise behind him, and what was it? A baby rattle? No, and it was not a rosary, either. The rattle of little bones? Lessons of Sarah Egram: He would not see *it* coming. The old man had never known such fear, and he could not move; he could not turn around even to save his life. But he could close his eyes — not to pray, but to carry him away from here, back in time to the Egram house, eyes shut tight.

And now he could see that small misshapen face pressed to the pane of the front window, one eye focused on the mother — center of a child's universe. But Mrs. Egram had been looking elsewhere, and some interior vision had made her tremble. That day Paul Magritte had believed that the poor woman was imagining the fate of her missing five-year-old. Or perhaps the prospect of separation from the older child had unhinged her and made her nonsensical.

"We'd be gone no more than four weeks." That very day, Paul Magritte had planned to personally escort the youngster to Chicago — if the mother would only listen to reason. "This would be the first in a number of operations. Some procedures are best done during the formative years. Later, when the bones are fully matured —"

"You don't understand," the woman had said to him in the slow, mother tones reserved for speaking to young children. "This is not right — not God's will."

The truck driver, roused from lethargy, had nearly smiled. "You say it'll take four weeks? That's fine with me." The man had reached out and snatched the consent forms. Sarah Egram had slumped forward, her eyes downcast, while her husband searched his pockets for something to write with. A pen was found. Defeated, the woman had risen from the couch and left the room.

Pen to paper, the trucker had asked, "One signature? That's enough?"

"It'll do." Magritte's eyes had been focused on Sarah's retreating back. "Your wife needs help."

"I know what she needs." And these had been the truck driver's last words to him.

A metallic sound called Paul Magritte back to the real and solid environs of a Texas church, where he worked his own rosary and incantations, whispering the magic words, not asking forgiveness or relief from pain; he only wanted to stave off his growing fear. He was not alone in this place, and escape was not possible anymore, not by any door in the present or in his past. His skin prickled. He held his breath.

Which one would it be?

"Who are you praying for, old man?"

"For you." This was a true thing, and he said it with awe. His movements were slow and full of pain as he rose to his feet and turned to face Detective Mallory with a smile of *thank God.* It was the first time any prayer of his had been answered, and his new name for this young woman was *Deliverance.* With another sort of smile, a foolish one, he looked down at the rosary in his hands, saying, "Candles, hocus-pocus and magic beads. This must fit your idea of the average witch doctor."

"Oh, but you're more than that, Dr. Magritte." She sat in the first pew, arms folded against him and daring him to tell a lie. "Did they throw you out of the priesthood? Or was it your idea to leave?"

Mallory's leather knapsack sat on the floor at her feet. His own sack of light nylon rested on her lap. The zipper was undone, and that must have been the noise that had frightened him so.

"You look worried, Magritte. You shouldn't be. I don't have a warrant." Mallory reached inside his sack and pulled out an ancient revolver. "So I can't seize this. FBI agents are searching all the cars." She held up the gun. "I don't think this is what they're looking for . . . so that's not why you're hiding out in this church."

"That was my grandfather's revolver," said Paul Magritte. "My inheritance if you like. It's all he left behind. That's why I kept it." Oh, fool, he was making a liar's worst mistake — overanxious to explain in detail, and now he found that he could not stop himself. "I'm afraid I never took proper care of the gun. Rusty, isn't it? I very much doubt that it would work. Just as well. It's not loaded. I wouldn't even know *how* to load it."

Mallory hefted the weight of the weapon, and then examined it more closely. "A twenty-two." This was said with mild derision. And now she held up a small blue pouch that was also his property. "And this? Another souvenir? It wasn't very smart to keep it." She emptied the contents of the pouch into her palm, then closed her fist on the tiny bones of a child's hand.

Struck dumb, he could only stare at her.

"I've got a few possibilities here," said

437

Mallory. "Did you murder all those little girls?" The detective dangled the little blue pouch. "Or did somebody plant this for the feds to find?"

She had actually provided him with a possible way out. Or was it the way into another trap? In the stillness of the church, he could hear the little bones rattle as she slipped them back into the blue velvet pouch.

"Oh, wait," said Mallory. "I've got one more theory. Did this little bag of bones come in the mail with a note? Something like — oh, how does it go?" She produced a slip of paper yellowed with age — another theft from his knapsack, and she read the words, " 'Father, forgive me for I have sinned.' " The detective rose to her feet, holding his gun in her right hand, the blue pouch in her left, and she seemed to be weighing them, one against the other, but her eyes were fixed upon him. He imagined another sort of creature might look at its next meal this way, while the prey still breathed and writhed under one clawed paw.

"You could help me find him," she said. "But that's not going to happen, is it?"

He shook his head.

"The law won't protect you, Magritte. You're not a priest anymore." She waved the yellow paper like a small flag. "And this note wasn't written inside a confessional."

He kept his silence.

"Thank you," said Mallory. "So now I know you've got a long history with this freak." She looked down at the old note and its words of confession, then slipped the small piece of paper into the pouch with the bones. "When the feds see this, they'll take you away. Who's going to look after your parish on wheels?"

You will.

He had such great faith in Detective Mallory even as she planned to bring him down.

"It's too bad Special Agent Berman never saw you as a suspect," she said. "He might've run a better background check. Now me — I suspect everybody. When you were with the Church, I know you treated other priests. Does that narrow down my list? Am I looking for an ex-priest like you?"

He finally understood the intensity of her eyes as she stared at his face: she was looking there for tells and tics and other signs of truth or lies.

"Don't smile at me, Magritte."

He had not meant to do that. "I'm so sorry." He held up his hands in supplication to tell her that he was helpless, as if she did not already know that — on several levels.

And now she seemed to tire of playing with him.

Oh, no — not quite yet.

She raised his grandfather's rusty old gun, aimed at the altar and fired. The air exploded. The vase shattered, water splattered, flower stalks went flying, and — in a special little moment of horror — he fancied that he could hear torn petals softly falling on the stone floor. And then the silence was absolute. All his bones were shaking, legs failing him. He sank to his knees — alone again.

Mallory was gone.

Agent Christine Nahlman was waiting beside the open door as Mallory left the church.

The detective handed her the blue pouch of bones and Magritte's nylon sack. "Satisfied? Now feed him to Dale Berman. They deserve each other."

"Wait," said Nahlman, but Mallory waited for no one, and now the agent followed her down the church stairs, saying, "You know the old man's not guilty."

"Yes, he is." The detective paused on the bottom step and turned around. "He's holding out on me. So arrest him and charge him with obstruction. Keep him in custody till this case is wrapped." Mallory snatched the pouch from the agent's hand and removed the confessor's note. "There," she said, handing back the pouch with only the bones inside. "That should make it easier to hold Magritte for a while. Now you can nail him as a murder suspect. He'll never make bail."

"Mallory, I can't —"

"You can't do anything, can you? If the feds had only cooperated with the Illinois cops, this case would've been wrapped by now. Kronewald's a good detective. But your boss is just a jacked-up PR man — worthless out in the field. And what's your problem, Nahlman? Are you just too damn polite to stomp Dale Berman into the ground?"

"I was assigned to work on —"

"Don't feed me any lines about following orders. I robbed your laptop, remember? I read your personal case notes. One of the Illinois graves was deeper than all the rest — very deep. You knew that one had to be his first kill. Kid stuff. He was so afraid of getting caught — he couldn't bury that little girl deep *enough.* So you know the perp started young — when he lived near that road. With Kronewald's help, you would've had a name for him by now. Fledgling killers have comfort zones — close to home. He was still murdering kids when he moved away from Route 66. And then, when he was old enough to drive, he went back there and replanted those kills on that road. And that's why you found two different types of soil in some of the Illinois graves — the shallow ones."

"You gave all of this to Kronewald?"

"You know I did. He's working the data now. All the missing little girls from Illinois won't be in a federal database. The FBI just can't be bothered with every lost kid. But Kronewald's got access to all of them, decades of missing little girls. Feeling the pressure *now,* Nahlman? Maybe it's time for you to take charge of this mess."

"Mallory, do you know what I see when I look past Dale Berman to the next link in the chain of command?"

"Another incompetent bureaucrat. And you wonder why cops hate feds. Take over. At least, get rid of Berman."

"What do you expect me to do — shoot him?"

"It's a start."

Riker hunkered next to the bedroll of Darwinia Sohlo, alias Miriam Rainard. What passed for her tent was an old canvas tarp anchored to the door handle of her ten-year-old car. The detective took over the chore of making a fire to keep her warm. The wood and the kindling twigs were damp, and the woman was in tears, saying, "It's no use. No fire tonight."

"Just you wait." He held up a road flare he had found in the trunk of the car. "You can set fire to water with one of these." He torched the kindling.

The fire burned bright. The woman smiled.

"I've got some bad news," he said.

One hand flew up to her mouth. "My daughter?"

"Oh, no. I'm sorry, ma'am. It's not about your kid." He settled one more log on the fire. "I was watching the TV coverage. I know you always hide from the cameramen, but one of those bastards got you on film. Your face made national news tonight. If your husband was watching that —"

No need to finish. She was nodding. If the wife beater had seen that news program back in Wisconsin, he would be coming for her soon, coming to collect his runaway property. Riker watched her face by firelight. He had expected fear, but she seemed resigned to this news of a beating in her future. He had come prepared with a six-pack of beer to medicate her jitters, but there was no need for that now. He offered her a bottle more in the spirit of companionship, and, when she was done with it, she told him her story.

"I sent my daughter away with the rescue mission. It's like an underground railroad for women and children."

"I know what they do." Riker was familiar with groups who assisted in the escape from abusive spouses. "But you sent her alone." And that was not normal.

"Yes, I wanted my husband to believe she'd been kidnapped. I stayed with him for two more years — until I was sure he'd given her up for dead. The police always thought she was dead. They watched my husband for a long time. Well, finally it was my turn to run. I didn't even take a purse. I had this idea that I could just go out and meet up with my child. But you had to go from one contact to the next. If one link in the chain was gone, the trail was lost."

"So one of your contacts disappeared?"

She nodded. "I'd waited too long to claim my daughter. So she was really lost — not a lie anymore. It's been twelve years. I'll never find her, will I?"

"It was brave to try," said Riker. "You knew the risks, but you tried."

"But I wasn't brave. The whole purpose of the caravan was publicity — getting attention for our lost kids — lost causes. The most I hoped for was local exposure, a few small-town reporters here and there. I never expected the story to get this big. I was afraid of the cameras, my only chance to find someone who would recognize my little girl. I'm a coward."

"Well, tonight, her picture was on television from coast to coast — yours, too," said Riker. "So now you should be thinking about your next move."

"You mean leave the caravan? Oh, no. I can't do that."

Riker shook his head. "Darwinia, I only wish you *were* a coward. How many times have you left the caravan to paste up your posters?" And, so long as the media was not an option for her, he knew Darwinia would do it again and again. This was the lady's job, going out into the dark, always looking over one shoulder to see if her bone-snapping husband was onto her — him or a serial killer.

Which monster would get to her first?

The elderly psychologist sat in the company of FBI agents. The moles hovered by the door, waiting to see if Nahlman would give them up for failing to keep a close eye on the old man. She had no plans to rat them out; she might find some later use for this leverage if she needed more agents in her own camp.

Special Agent Dale Berman was telling the elderly doctor that he had a lot of explaining to do. The man's voice was more in the range of chastising a child than interrogating a suspect. "What were you thinking, old man — carrying that thing around?"

"You mean the pouch," said Dr. Magritte.

"What pouch?" Berman raised his eyes to stare at Agent Nahlman, who had personally escorted the psychologist and ex-priest to this motel room. The doctor had been her prime exhibit while carefully bringing home the point that the background checks on the caravan were not all that they should be.

Berman prompted her now. "What's he mean, Nahlman? What pouch?"

"I think he means his knapsack," she said. "That's where he kept the gun."

The blue pouch with the tiny bones was locked in the glove compartment of her car. She was the only one to see the astonished look in Paul Magritte's eyes.

Paul Magritte rode back toward the caravan

in Agent Nahlman's automobile. She played the radio, and he replayed his memories of that tumble-down house back in Illinois. For him, it was no longer springtime. Winter was coming. It was not night anymore, but a long-ago day. It was four weeks following his first encounter with the Egrams.

This was no feat of memory anymore. He was reliving it.

Once more he wore a cassock, and again he traveled down a rural segment of Route 66, returning his young charge to the Egram home. The ten-year-old sat beside him as the car rolled down the road of stark winter trees and overcast sky. The child's face was still swollen from surgery.

On this Saturday following Thanksgiving, here and there along the way, men on ladders were stringing up long wires of colored light bulbs to line their rooftops for the next holiday. The priest was in a good humor that afternoon, for he was about to deliver a fine Christmas present indeed. Paul Magritte had lost his smile as he pulled over to the side of the road.

The Egram house had a hollowed-out look. Every curtain was gone from the windows, and blank walls could be seen beyond the glass. The child beside him could not fail to understand what this meant. It was the priest who was in denial.

How could they be gone?

"Stay here. I won't be long." He saw himself leaving the car and walking down the road to the nearest house, and then the next one and the next. No one had seen the couple depart, nor could anyone say where they had gone. The truck driver and his wife had moved by night — and so stealthy. They had not caused one dog to bark. It was only the matter of the dogs that these people found remarkable, not that the Egrams should leave without a word to neighbors of long acquaintance. *That* they could accept.

Had the police been wrong to clear the parents of blame for the little girl who was lost and likely dead? Flight spoke to guilt, and this might explain why the father had been quick to sign the consent forms: traveling with a deformed child would have made the fugitives stand out on any road.

And now little Adrian Egram was standing in the road and staring at the empty house. The priest was reaching out to console the youngster when the swollen face lifted to smile at him, and a small voice said, "Forgive me, father, for I have —" And here the ten-year-old paused to compensate for the lisp of a misshapen mouth, taking great care to pronounce the word, *"— sinned."*

These were ritual words, but this child had not been raised as a Catholic. The mother alone had come back to the faith. Father Paul Magritte looked up to the second-floor window, and there in that upstairs bedroom he envisioned Sarah Egram inadvertently teaching her child these words, this formal prelude to confession — while she packed a small bag for the youngster's trip to a Chicago hospital. In his mind, Paul Magritte could clearly see the woman — even hear her now — repeating the words over and over, though the priest had been waiting downstairs in the front room — unable to hear her confession.

Until that day on the road, when he had found the house empty — the child abandoned.

Young Adrian fed the words back to him like a parrot delivering a long-delayed message, saying once more, "Forgive me, Father, for —"

"No." The priest had gently raised one finger to his own lips, a gesture to silence the child. "No more of that."

So many years had passed. The house was gone now, and even the patch of road they had stood upon that day had fallen into ruin before the rest of Mrs. Egram's message was delivered.

Agent Nahlman checked the rearview mirror. Paul Magritte's watchers were still following them as she drove toward the campground. The old man beside her was lost in his own quiet thoughts.

Christine Nahlman's mind was on the bungled interview. Dale Berman had done his ineffectual little song and dance. Then he had dismissed the idea of any connection that went far beyond a suspected relationship of Internet psychologist and killer. Berman would never admit that his flawed background checks could impede a case. Incredibly, he had even returned the gun to Paul Magritte and demanded that Nahlman apologize to the old man. And she had seen all of this coming her way.

However, now, in the privacy of this car, it was *her* interview. She switched off the car radio as a subtle invitation for Magritte to break his long silence.

The doctor's voice was tentative, testing the air. "Why didn't you tell them about the pouch — the little bones?"

She planned to let him wonder about that for a while. "I have family in Chicago," she said, though all of the people that she had loved best were dead and lying in California ground. "Chicago. That's where you were based when you were a priest — a priest psychologist." That part, according to Detective Mallory, was true. "My mother has the best therapist money can buy. It's a small community, isn't it? Shrinks, I mean. Lots of backbiting and gossip. I didn't know it would be so easy to find out what a third-rate doctor you were." She had run her bluff, and now she caught him in an unconscious nod, her cue that he had not been a financial success in private practice. "So I had to wonder why you left the priesthood. At least the Catholic Church gave you a steady income."

"At one time, I *was* a bad psychologist . . . and a worse priest. How could I stay? Oddly enough, since leaving the Church, I've become a better man."

"I don't think I can buy that," said Nahlman. "You knowingly consorted with a child killer. Did he scare you? Are you scared now? You should be. You're the only one who can identify him." She turned to look at Magritte in sidelong glances, checking her progress, waiting for cracks in composure. "You've known this freak for a *long* time." For punctuation, she slapped the dashboard, hitting the surface hard with the flat of her hand to make the frail old man jump in his skin.

Well, that was a foolish waste of time. Detective Mallory's unique interview style would have inured this man to any more sudden shocks — or loud noises.

Nahlman pressed on. "So your private practice wasn't making any money. Then you started the Internet therapy groups. Anonymity and no expensive malpractice insurance. Not a bad living, either. Now you drive a luxury car, and you don't buy your clothes off the rack, do you? Parents of missing children make the best victims. Shrinks and psychics can really cash in on —"

"I never took a dime from any of them," said Dr. Magritte, defensive now that she had found his sore spot. "I actually made quite a lot of money in private practice. More than enough to retire. And all my work with the parents is free of charge."

This was the long-awaited schism.

"Let's say I believe you," said Nahlman. "Maybe you wanted to atone for shielding a killer of little girls. You saw your chance with the caravan. You wanted to smoke him out. One last shot at grace — but not what I would've expected from a priest or a doctor." She reached out and ripped the knapsack from his lap. With her one free hand, she worked the zipper, then pulled out his old rusted gun. "You were planning to murder the freak."

His silence was all the acknowledgment she needed.

"Cold-blooded, premeditated murder," she said, "that's way more Christian than blowing off the seal of the confessional. But it won't work. He always attacks from behind. I think he's been doing this for decades — lots of practice. You won't hear him coming up behind you till he's close enough to slit your throat." She hefted the weight of the gun in her hand. "But I can kill him for you. Tell me how to find him."

Magritte only stared at the windshield. The glow of the campground was in sight. He was almost free.

But not quite.

Nahlman pulled onto the shoulder of the road and killed the engine. "Mallory tells me you've known this freak since he was a kid." Ah, that startled him. So the New York detective had been right, and the killer had started very young. The skeleton found in the deepest grave might be older than she had imagined. "So tell me this." Nahlman leaned over to open the glove compartment. She pulled out the small blue pouch. "Exactly when did he give this to you? Let me put that another way. How many little girls died while you were walking around with these bones in your pocket? You won't even tell me that much? Well, that's good. Now I can make up a date." She started the engine. "I can tell the parents that you've had these little bones for maybe twenty, thirty years — while their children were being slaughtered like —"

"You're going to tell them?"

A little piece of the truth was laid out in his words. Perhaps it had taken thirty years or more to kill a hundred little girls.

"No, I won't tell them." Nahlman put the car back on the road. "If those people knew what you'd done to them, they'd all want a piece of your hide. . . . So that would be murder."

Silence prevailed until Nahlman drove up to the campsite and parked the car. She placed the old man's gun with the pouch in the glove compartment. The absence of a weapon might make him less brave, less inclined to wander away from the moles.

Dr. Magritte leaned toward her. "Why didn't you give the pouch of bones to Agent Berman?"

"Let me make a confession," said Nahlman. "Forgive me, Father, for I have sinned. I broke the damn rules. My boss is a lazy-ass screwup. If I gave him the bones, he'd lock you up for murder. The investigation would be shut down — and people would die. You can live with pointless death, but I can't."

In the background of the long-distance conversation, Mallory could hear the traffic of a Chicago street. Kronewald excused himself to close the window, and now he came back to the phone.

"I called the FBI lab," he said. "When I asked about Nahlman's soil samples and the bones, they told me they didn't have any results yet. Well, I knew that was crap. They were just playing dumb. And you know what, kid? It's just a gut feeling, but I think this was the first time they were hearing about —"

"Dale Berman never sent in the samples for analysis," said Mallory. "And the lab never got any of the bodies, either. Did you find me a victim who lived near Route 66?"

"Yeah, but I had to go back forty years to find a girl who fit the victim profile — Mary Egram, five years old when she disappeared. Her house was on a state road, an old segment of Route 66."

Kronewald fell silent. Mallory could hear the rustle of paper, and she knew he was paging through a hard-copy version of a police report. Forty-year-old unsolved cases would not show up on his computer screen.

"Okay," he said, "the catching detective on that case was a guy named Rawlins. He's dead now, but I got his old notes. He suspected the father. John Egram was a long-haul trucker — could've dumped the girl's body anywhere. The Egrams had one other kid, a ten-year-old named Adrian. The parents skipped town when Adrian was in the hospital. Nice people, huh? At the time, a priest had temporary guardianship. Not much detail on that. Just a few lines of rough notes. Now here's the kicker. The priest who had guardianship —"

"Paul Magritte. I know," said Mallory. "Anything else?"

"Well, this kid, Adrian, got bounced around from one foster home to another."

"Sounds like a recipe for a serial killer," said Mallory. "Any pictures?"

"Nope, just an old police report from downstate Illinois. When Adrian was fifteen, he stole a car from his foster home and ran away. Works nice with your car-thief angle. But the cops never caught him, so we got no prints in the system. No social security number, either. I figure he stopped being Adrian Egram the day he stole that car."

"But he spent five years in foster care. Not

one picture?"

"Mallory, in your *dreams* Child Welfare has records that go back that far — instead of files rotting in storage boxes. But I got something else you might like. Most of the houses in the Egram neighborhood were torn down or they fell down. We found one of the neighbors in a nursing home. She's got Alzheimer's but her long-term memory is still strong. The old lady says Adrian's mother worked two jobs, so the little boy used to ride with his dad on cross-country hauls. They were probably on the road two hundred days a year. Then Mary was born and it was time for Adrian to start school. No more truck rides with Dad. Now Adrian and his sister didn't get along too well. And here's where it gets strange. Adrian was ten years old — Mary was only five."

"And Adrian was afraid of his little sister," said Mallory.

"Yeah. You were right. Our perp doesn't like being touched. Every time the girl went near her big brother, the boy ran like hell. That was gonna be my big finale. So tell me something, kid — why do you bother to call in for updates?"

Mallory ended the cell-phone call, disinclined to waste words, and it would have taken a long time to describe what she was looking at. The detective could see her cold breath on the air as she walked down the rows of rough wooden pallets, each one the bed of a child. Most were skeletons, but some had been mummified and still held the shape of sleeping girls whose lives had been interrupted on the way to school one day. In the paperwork for this warehouse, twenty miles outside of Amarillo, Texas, the field-office rental fee was itemized under a file name: The Nursery.

A silver-haired man in a dark blue suit walked beside her. He appeared to be trying to make sense of what he was seeing — as if he had no idea that this had been going on. Harry Mars, now based in Washington, was the former head of the New York City Bureau, but he had climbed higher in rank since attending the funeral of Inspector Louis Markowitz. Graveside, he had vouched a favor against a day when the old man's daughter might need one. Half an hour ago, Mars had come through for her, ordering guards to stand down while he stripped the seal from the door of this refrigerated storage facility — *The Nursery.*

"My people count forty-seven dead children," said Harry Mars, who ranked one rung below the deputy director of the FBI. He led her to an open metal coffin. "And here we have the remains of an adult."

"Probably Gerald Linden," said Mallory, "the Chicago victim."

"I just can't believe this incompetence," said Mars. "The case should've gone to our task force for serial killers. I've got no idea how Dale managed to keep all these bodies and bones under wraps."

Mallory understood it too well. A gigantic bureaucracy could never have a handle on what every single field office was up to, not until they heard about it on the evening news. So the Assistant Director of Criminal Investigations was not insulting her intelligence when he told her this utterly believable lie. However, the man was an ally and a friend of the family — and so she would not accuse him of deception — not just yet. Timing was everything.

Harry Mars seemed to be uncomfortable with her silence, and he rushed his words now, so anxious to share.

Yeah, right.

"I can't hold any other agents responsible," he said. "Dale was probably the only one with the total body count. He had different teams working different states. In and out — very fast operation. None of the evidence was ever developed. So it looks like no one but Dale ever had the whole picture."

Oh, no. It was not going to be *that* easy — one sacrificial FBI agent for the media and no harm done to the Bureau.

"Harry, you've known about this case for a while — before you saw it on television." This was not a question, not an invitation to lie to her. "What tipped you off first, the letters from George Hastings? Maybe you'd know him better by his Internet name — Jill's Dad? Or was it Nahlman who got your attention?" Mallory smiled. *Gotcha.*

Assistant Director Mars looked out over the pallets of dead children, stalling for time. Finally, he pulled a sheaf of folded papers from his inside breast pocket. "The lab got these e-mails from Agent Nahlman. She wanted to know what happened to her test results on some soil samples."

"And the lab was clueless, but they didn't want to admit it."

Harry Mars let this comment slide. "Then, the other day, Nahlman made a request to release the body of Jill Hastings. Up till then, I swear I thought George Hastings was a crank." He wadded these papers into a tight ball. "That's when we started looking for this warehouse."

A lie well worded.

Mallory had her own ideas about the

starting date of the FBI's internal investigation. According to Kronewald's sources, Agent Cadwaller had been attached to Dale's field office three months ago, and she took him for a spy from the Assistant Director's office. "Now," she said, "the next question is motive."

"For Dale? He's a bungling screwup."

"No," said Mallory. "That's not it." Her favorite motive would always be money, but there was no market for the bones of little girls.

"I can suspend him pending investigation," said Mars. "But I think you'd rather I took out my gun and shot him."

"Yes, I would." She rewarded Lou Markowitz's old friend with a smile, though she knew this man was still holding out on her. "But you're going to leave him in charge." It was easier to work around Dale Berman. A competent task force would present problems; they might decide to run her case. "I'll tell you how this is going to play out with the Bureau — *my* way."

Harry Mars was appalled as she laid out her list of demands, but he recovered quickly, and then he smiled. "I wish your old man could see you now. All this leverage to embarrass the Bureau. You're even better at it than Lou was. I think he'd be so proud." This was said with no sarcasm whatever.

Riker sat at the boxer's campfire, trading baseball stats with Joe Finn and his son. Dodie lay quiet in the safe cradle of her father's arms. Both children were yawning, and the detective was waiting for them to fall asleep. Then he would talk to the boxer about Kronewald's plan for protective custody. The Finns must leave this road.

The fire had burned low, and Peter dropped his head against his father's shoulder. At this same moment, a teenage girl came walking through the camp with a sleeping baby riding on one hip. Her big brown eyes searched everywhere. She grinned when she looked toward Darwinia Sohlo's fire, and she called out, "Mom!"

Heads turned from neighboring campfires as a stunned Darwinia rose on unsteady feet to embrace the young mother and child. The woman would have fallen to her knees, but a young man rushed to Darwinia's side and caught her up in his arms. He was the same age as the girl, and Riker pegged him as the father of that baby. The youngster was broad in the shoulders and tanned, built like a workingman who did hard labor for his living. This boy was so painfully young that he probably believed he could always keep his family safe; he would not have heard the boxer's story of Ariel. The conversation around Darwinia's distant fire was low and Riker could only watch the smiles, the hugs and imagine the talk of miracles and wonders.

What destroyed the detective in this moment was the look in Joe Finn's eyes. .

And the tears.

If this reunion could happen for Darwinia, why not for him? And now it was clear that the boxer preferred his fantasy that Ariel was alive, for he could not live in a world where she had died. And nothing — not an act of God, not even Mallory — could take him off this road.

Charles Butler waved good-bye as Darwinia Sohlo and her family drove off in separate cars but in the same direction, for the woman had not only found a lost child but also a safe haven — a home.

"Shouldn't they have an FBI escort?"

"No," said Riker. "Those people aren't part of the pattern. The biggest threat to Darwinia was that nutcase husband back in Wisconsin. And *our* freak likes to plan his murders around an isolated victim. Can you see him picking a fight with the son-in-law?"

"Yet Dodie's father's is a professional fighter, and you worry about her."

"You bet I do," said Riker. "Thanks to Dale's little showdown with the boxer, Dodie's a threat to a serial killer. There's a safe house waiting for the Finns in Chicago, but I don't think Joe can get there from here. Not unless I can reach him."

Charles shook his head. "He won't hear you. He's not thinking clearly. Probably lack of sleep. It took him an hour just to assemble that little pup tent."

And now, with his children safely tucked away, Joe Finn was too tired to unroll his sleeping bag. He laid his body down in the grass before the closed tent flap. The man's thick arms were his pillows, and his gaze was fixed upon heaven. The boxer's lips moved, perhaps in an old custom of prayers before sleep.

Good night, sweet prince.

Charles raised his eyes to the stars and also bid goodnight to Ariel.

15

Though Assistant Director Harry Mars had lived most of his life in the east, a Texas drawl was creeping back into his voice as he stood upon the land where he was born. He turned to the young woman beside him. "I won't be going back to Washington just yet. Tomorrow morning I've got a meeting with Kronewald in Chicago. I think that old bastard's holding out on me." Oh, but that was the game they all played. It was an easy guess that Kathy Mallory had not disclosed half of what she knew — and neither had he.

The sun had been up for hours when the two sightseers stood on the old road, just beyond Amarillo, Texas. The FBI man was feeling some wear after a long night in Dale Berman's Nursery. The soil samples had been located, and he planned to ram the tests through the crime lab within the hour. As a final order of business, he had offered a Bureau job to the young detective from New York City, and she had turned him down — much to his relief.

He remembered the year she had joined the NYPD and the toll that had taken on her foster father. "The kid's not a team player," Lou Markowitz used say, "but what a kid."

The old man had proven to be a grand master of understatement. It was a singular cop who could extort the FBI in the upper echelons. Over a morning meal, he had caved in on the last of her demands, only stopping short of giving her a key to the men's room, and he was damned tired. But now Lou's daughter also wanted his promise that, following a speedy examination of the remains, one of the dead schoolgirls would be sent straight home.

"It's a favor to Riker." She handed him a sheet of paper. "This is the undertaker who's going to bury George Hastings' daughter in three days. So Jill's body is your number one priority. When she's in the ground, I'll send you her father's correspondence with Washington — with *you* — all those crummy little form letters you signed — and dated."

It was too late to run a bluff; his jaw had already dropped. Those dates would kill the

Bureau's chance to crucify Dale Berman and then claim clean hands. With this final bit of blackmail, Kathy Mallory was giving up way too much for too little in return — a sack of bones.

After a breakfast of steak and eggs, Harry Mars, native son of the Texas Panhandle and a graceful loser, had offered to play tour guide this morning. "That's it," he said, pointing to a far-off row of falling-down dominoes in a cow pasture. That neat line of slanted shapes in the distance was actually a collection of upscale cars that were partially buried nose-first in the ground. "That's the Cadillac Ranch. I'm not surprised you overshot the field. You were looking for a big sign, right?"

"So that's *it?*"

Could Kathy Mallory be less impressed?

"Well, *I* always liked it," he said. "I remember back when those Caddys were new and the local teenagers hadn't gotten round to the graffiti yet. Damn kids. Sorry, I can see you're disappointed. I guess it's not much to look at from the road, but you can't get any closer. There's a bull out there with the cows." And now, because he had some history with her, he added, "Kathy, it would just be wrong to shoot a man's livestock."

"Mallory," she said, correcting him for the third time this morning.

"Right." Harry Mars watched her check the Cadillac Ranch off her list. He noticed another Texas attraction, the halfway marker for Route 66. "So your next stop is the Mid-Point Café." He waited for some enlightenment, even a simple yes or no, but he did not wait long; he knew her that well. Still staring at her list, he asked, "You plan to tell me how those landmarks figure into this case?"

He had his answer when she closed her notebook, slipped it into the back pocket of her jeans, and said, "Good-bye."

"Kathy — sorry — *Mallory,* I could never see you as a damn tourist." He well remembered their first meeting soon after she had gone to live with Lou and Helen Markowitz. Kathy had been much shorter then, but her eyes had never changed. One look at her, all those years ago, and Harry Mars knew that she had seen it all, whatever the world could find to throw in the path of a child.

The list in her notebook would continue to nag at him. Kathy Mallory would sleep tonight, and he would not. But that was fine by him. He did not care to dream of forty-seven little girls lying upon wooden pallets in a cold warehouse — so young — unfinished when they died.

The detective was ready to leave him now. She sat behind the wheel and revved her engine. There was still one matter that tethered him to her, a question he could never ask; it was a giant rubber band, stretched between them and about to snap as her car rolled away:

Was Dale Berman a major screwup or a very sick man?

Charles Butler parked the car in front of the MidPoint Café in Adrian, Texas. It was as inviting as a private house, small and homey, painted white with black trim. "So is this the way you remember it?"

Riker shrugged. "I was just a kid when I stopped here. And I killed most of my road-trip brain cells with booze. What makes you think Mallory's gonna show?"

"I saw the name listed in her notebook."

Once inside, Charles, who loved every old thing, approved of the place immediately. An early model kitchen appliance served as decoration, and all about the dining room were other artifacts of a bygone era. As he joined Riker, taking a stool at the counter, he averted his eyes from the next room, a gift shop stocked with more modern wares.

The woman who waited on them had a long history with the café and a good memory. By the time they were on a Charles-and-Fran footing, Riker had demolished his pie, and now he was ready for business.

The detective's description only got as far as, "Tall, real pretty, blond hair. She drives a Volkswagen convertible."

And Fran said, "Peyton's kid? You just missed her."

"Peyton," echoed Charles.

The woman nodded. "The minute she walked in the door, I said, 'You've *got* to be related to Peyton Hale! Or maybe I just think that because you've got his strange green eyes and you're driving his car.' "

Charles smiled. His theory was panning out for the author of Savannah's coveted letters, and now he finally had a name for Mallory's father. "I never met Peyton Hale. I gather you knew him quite well. He's from around here?"

"No, he was a California boy the first time he came through. Then he settled in Chicago. Went to school there. But he drove Route 66 every summer for years and years. So he'd stop by twice, coming and going. Always wanted pie. That's all he ever ordered. They're fresh baked every morning."

Riker's voice was blunted, and his smile was gone. "When did you see this man last?"

"It was a long time ago." Fran took a knife to the pie tin. "I'm sure his daughter hadn't been born yet. He would've mentioned that."

"So it's been at least twenty-five years, maybe longer," said Riker. "But you remember her father's eyes? His car? There's gotta be more to it."

"He was a charmer," said Fran. "Charmed me out of twenty dollars once. Gave me an IOU. Peyton was driving west to California that time. Said he'd pay me back on the way home to Chicago. And that was the last time I ever saw him." Fran slipped another wedge of pie onto Riker's plate. "Peyton's daughter was even more suspicious than you are. She wanted to see the IOU. Well, of course, I didn't have it anymore, but she settled up anyway." Fran dipped one hand into an apron pocket and pulled out a hundred-dollar bill. "The girl's a big tipper."

"Yeah, she is." Riker, seduced by the bribe of a second slice of pie, was acting less the policeman now. "Did you find out what happened to Mallory's dad?"

"I never asked." Fran was staring at the window on the road. "I like to think he's still on that road — driving like a maniac. My God, that little car of his could go. Well, like father, like daughter. One second Mallory's car was out there in the lot, and then *voom* — gone."

Another day, another travel plaza.

Finding the caravan was a simple thing; Mallory only had to listen to the parents' radio interviews being conducted on the other side of Adrian, Texas. When she entered the lot, she found it choked with more cars than parking places. She created her own space on a patch of sidewalk that ran around the restaurant. The young FBI agents on guard duty did not object; they even opened the car door for her, celebrity treatment, and they all but saluted as she passed them by and entered the restaurant.

Mallory favored tables near the window, and she picked one out, unconcerned that it was occupied. It was only necessary to hover a moment or two before the agents seated there decided that they had eaten enough for one day. And now she sat down alone, another preference, and opened her notebook of landmarks and murder suspects. In the manner of a schoolgirl at her lessons, she bowed her head over the list and crossed off the MidPoint Café.

She was done with her meal when she saw Charles Butler's Mercedes pull into the lot with Riker at the wheel. He parked it behind her own car on the sidewalk, and FBI agents hurried across the room to hold open the door to the restaurant. This sudden anxiousness to please might be the work of Harry Mars.

Good.

Riker deposited Kronewald's laptop on the table by her knapsack. "You keep walking off without this thing."

Mallory never looked up, and her partner melted away, slouching off in search of a cheeseburger. He passed near a corner table perfect for conspiracy, but failed to catch a word of the conversation between the two FBI agents.

Agent Barry Allen was doing his best to talk his partner back onto the right path following the Bureau's strict chain of command. "You can't cut Dale Berman off at the legs that way."

"I needed those results on my soil samples," said Agent Nahlman. "The bastard never even ordered the tests. I checked with the lab."

"You can work around it."

"No, I can't. It's an oddball element. Two

different kinds of soil in three of those graves — think about it. The perp dug up his kills and reburied them. If I can pinpoint the original burial sites, I can get names and dates — real leads. But Dale Berman doesn't care when we wrap this case. What's one more death to him? He all but offered up Dodie Finn on a plate."

"That's cold."

"And at least a hundred kids are dead. Mallory was right. This case could've been wrapped a long time ago. But people keep dying."

"And that's Dale's fault? So now he's a killer?"

Nahlman sat back in her chair, surprised that this rookie agent was now on a first-name basis with the SAC. "You really like him, don't you?"

"He's a great guy," said Allen. "So promise me this crazy idea just dies right here, right now."

How absurd was this? A baby-faced boy assuming the mantle of wise man and doling out advice *for her own good.*

"All right," she said, lying. "I'm done with it."

Or was this the truth? She was so tired of breaking her fists on all the barriers Berman had placed in her way. And she had yet to answer Agent Allen's question. Did she take Dale Berman for a killer? Oh, yes.

In the neutral territory of a center table, Charles Butler had been waylaid by Agent Cadwaller, and he was doing his best to explain to this man why Joe Finn might want to kill him. "Don't go near the children one more time. Your people have already done too much damage to Dodie." He put up one hand. "Please don't deny that. She was just a little girl, severely traumatized, but she was still talking when she went into FBI custody. Not anymore." Did this come as a surprise to the federal agent?

"The Finns have to leave this road," said Cadwaller.

Well, now that was interesting. This man was the only member of Berman's team to share in that belief. However, he was arguing a case for federal custody.

"You know that little girl needs counseling," said the FBI man. "It would help if I could talk to her. Then I could make arrangements for —"

"No!" Charles had estimated Cadwaller's credentials as something of a joke, and he had tried every polite way to say that a little dangerous knowledge did not a psychologist make. Having failed in that, he decided that good manners were overrated. "Rather than push Dodie into a psychotic break, I suggest you just pull out your gun and blow her little head off. No, really. *Shoot* her. It'll set a good example for the others."

A broadcast reporter and her cameraman passed Cadwaller's table in pursuit of Riker, who warded them off with a New Yorker's one-fingered gesture for love and friendship. And now the detective joined Dr. Magritte, pulling up a chair at the old man's table. He wasted no time with pleasantries.

"Okay, Doc, we're hunting a nutcase and you're leading a parade of 'em. You gotta have a few favorites who aren't covered with doctor-patient confidentiality. You said these people came from a lot of different therapy groups." With a nod, he gestured to the Pattern Man's table. Horace Kayhill was sitting alone with his spread maps. "Horace keeps coming back to the caravan. He likes being close to you, doesn't he? This trip must be nutcase heaven — a doctor who can't get away from his patients."

Dr. Magritte gave up a smile of apology and a wave of the hand to say that Riker would get nothing helpful from him, not even the admission that Horace Kayhill was his patient.

Riker watched the doctor's face, hoping to see something useful there if he should hit upon the right question. "You know who the killer is, don't you? Do you talk to this freak on the phone? Are you Internet pen pals or what?"

And now the doctor, somewhat surprised, said, "You and your partner don't communicate very well. I bet you're wondering how I know that." He smiled. "Your cheeseburger is getting cold, Detective."

Special Agent Dale Berman was basking in camera light and sharing a table with a celebrity anchorwoman. This prime-time personality seemed disappointed in his basic profile for a serial killer. She pulled back the microphone to say, "Isn't that sexist? Why not a woman suspect?"

"It was a man." Dale Berman wore his mask of tragedy today, but only while the camera was on him. "A female serial killer is very rare."

The newswoman extended her microphone to the next table occupied by the wonderfully photogenic cop from New York City. "What do you say, Detective Mallory? Could a female have done all those murders?"

The detective never looked up from her

laptop computer. "Female killers are as common as dust."

Dale Berman's face fell.

"Like that prostitute who killed her customers?" The newswoman's professional smile was waning as she waited for a response. Precious airtime was slipping by. "And then we've got mothers killing their own children." She gave Detective Mallory a smile of encouragement. When was this young cop going to open her damned mouth? The reporter filled in the silence with, "Nurses killing patients? Oh, and the black widows — wives killing husbands for insurance money."

"I like money motives." Detective Mallory looked up, finally hearing something of interest to her, but she was facing Dale Berman, not the camera.

The cameraman stood before Mallory's table, bowing low, hoping for eye contact, and the reporter said, "So, Detective, you think a woman could be —"

"It was a man," said Mallory, who had now engaged Agent Berman in a staring match. "Men are monument builders. That's what the killer's done with this road."

"That's *right!*" And with these words, Dale Berman had recaptured the cameraman's attention and the lens. "The killer believes these murders will make him live forever in the —"

"And what do you think, Detective?" asked the reporter as her cameraman swung around to refocus on the New York City blonde.

"Nobody lives forever," said Mallory to Dale Berman.

At a far remove from Dale Berman and the reporter, Mallory found another empty chair by the window and sat down with the Pattern Man, who promptly spilled his coffee. As she arranged her knapsack and the computer on top of his maps, she had to endure his apologies for clumsiness and listen to the day's figures for the amount of caffeine ingested by way of coffee and cola. He did not seem to mind that she never spoke to him; the little man was more comfortable talking *at* her rather than *to* her. Horace Kayhill unfolded another map so he could describe the new landmarks discovered since his last trip down Route 66. "The road is always changing, you know, just like a living organism."

Mallory slapped one hand down on the coffee-stained map, and now she had the little man's attention. "You're a statistician, right?"

"Yes. I used to work for an insurance company."

"Give me some odds. It's a country of three hundred million people, and only a hundred of them have something in common. What are the odds that they meet?"

He adjusted his glasses, preparing to launch into another lecture. "Perhaps you're referring to a theory of six degrees of separation — that we're all six connections away from everyone else on the planet. Well, that really won't apply here, not if you're looking for a chance meeting. You see, someone has to follow the threads to force the outcome and prove the —"

"I don't believe in chance," said Mallory. "I don't believe in accident or coincidence. You know what I'm talking about."

"Yes. The caravan parents."

"Not all of them, just the ones with little girls buried on Route 66."

"Well, before the advent of computers," said Kayhill, "those people never would've met. But now you have variables that didn't exist in the past. Today, it's possible to cross-index every aspect of your life with the whole earth. If you have an odd tic, a rare disease, or, in my case, migraine auras without the headaches, you can find a chat room for that, a website —"

"Or a therapy group."

"Exactly. I belong to lots of them." He tapped his head to indicate a problem there. "I'm a bit on the compulsive side. But I spend most of my time compiling statistics and information on Route 66. That's how I met the first caravan parent — Gerry Linden. An FBI agent called to tell him his child's body had been found, and this woman gave him the location of the gravesite. But his daughter's remains were never returned to him."

Mallory nodded. Last night, she had seen Gerald Linden's daughter in Dale Berman's Nursery. The remains had been identified by a small gold pin, a distinctive heirloom.

"So," said Mr. Kayhill, "Gerry Linden went to visit the burial site. He told me it was the only place he had to leave his flowers — this bit of road where his child had been found." The Pattern Man leaned forward and smiled. "This is the part where chance comes in."

And perhaps now he recalled that she was not a big believer in chance, for he dropped the smile and spilled more coffee. "Let's call it a forced link for the six-degree theory," he said. "Mr. Linden stayed in the area for a few days — talking to the locals — and he heard a strange story about another grave forty miles down the road. You see, years ago, a man was trying to bury a dog and inadvertently dug up a child. Now that grave was across a state line, and the road was known by a different name, but it was also part of the old highway. So Mr. Linden hooked up with a lot of Route 66 websites. Well, I monitor all of them, and his name cropped up quite a few times. He wanted information on murdered children found along that road."

"He was the one who told you about Dr. Magritte's therapy group?"

"Yes, and I joined it. I collected more data from another one of Dr. Magritte's patients. Now, two such parents with the same psychologist — well, the odds of that happening are just remarkable. That was when I realized that I was onto something huge."

"But you never had a child," said Mallory, as if this might be a defect in him. "Magritte's sessions were only for the parents of missing and murdered children."

"Oh, no. Where did you get that idea? The only criterion was a computer. The doctor never turned anybody away." And now, no doubt feeling the need for immediate therapy, Horace Kayhill packed up his maps and fled.

■ ■ ■ ■

After flopping down in the recently vacated chair at his partner's table, Riker handed her a cell phone. "It's Kronewald. He's got some news." Riker's own conversation with the Chicago detective had been illuminating and disheartening.

She held the cell phone to her ear. "It's Mallory. . . . Right. . . . No, that's all I need." After opening the laptop computer, she flicked the keys until she was looking at a map of the continental United States. A route was marked in a thick red line. "Got it," she said.

Riker could hear Kronewald's rising voice as Mallory depressed the button that would end the call. The old man was shouting toward the end, as if he knew she was going to hang up on him.

Charles Butler was in flight from Cadwaller's table, and seeking sanctuary with the two detectives. He stared at Mallory's computer screen as he pulled up a chair. "That seems a bit different from the other Route 66 maps. What happened to Santa Fe?"

"This is a route from the sixties," said Riker, "after the ends of the Santa Fe loop were connected." The detective gave his partner a disingenuous smile. "I just thought I'd save you the trouble of *sharing* that." Turning back to Charles, he said, "It's a long-haul truck driver's route from Chicago to L.A."

"So," said Charles, "you think the killer is a truck driver."

"No, but his father was." Riker turned to Mallory, still smiling but hardly meaning it. "And you were gonna tell me that, right?" And now he told the story of the trucker and his wife abandoning their son after the disappearance of five-year-old Mary Egram. "That's right, Charles. Our boy didn't start with small furry animals. He killed his own sister. But I'm sure my *partner* was gonna mention that — eventually."

Mallory turned her chair to face away from Riker.

Oh, was his voice getting a little testy? *Well, tough.*

She spoke only to Charles. "I hope you got something useful off that agent."

"You're kidding, right?" Riker was now an invisible man as far as she was concerned. He moved his chair around the table until he was once more in her line of sight. "Cadwaller probably bored poor Charles with his expertise on serial killers. But at least that worthless fed tries to *communicate* with —"

"Cadwaller has no expertise," said Charles. "He's a fraud."

Okay, playtime with Mallory was over. Riker made a rolling motion with one hand to ask the man to continue that thought.

"Perhaps I was harsh," said Charles. "I'd say, at best, he's an expert on bad psychology books written by incompetent hacks for mass consumption. But he's not a profiler."

"Kronewald ran a background check," said Riker. "Cadwaller's got a history with Behavioral Science Unit."

"Sometimes," said Charles, "history gets rewritten. I can only tell you the man is not what he seems."

This information came as no surprise to Mallory, and Riker had to wonder what else the brat had forgotten to share with him.

"Well," said Charles, "at least now you have a name for the killer."

Riker nodded. "For all the good it does. No pictures, no prints, no idea what name the perp's using now. He's good at stealing cars. That's all we know." He shot a glance at his partner as he corrected himself. "That's all *I* know."

Dr. Magritte passed close to their table, and Mallory turned an accusing eye on Riker, asking, *demanding,* "Why isn't that old man in custody?"

"What? Back up," said Riker. "Where does Magritte come in? What did he do? And what the hell did *I* do wrong?"

Mallory stared at him, incredulous. "Doesn't Agent Nahlman tell you *anything?*"

16

They met by chance — or this would be Riker's story. He rehearsed it as he followed Agent Nahlman's car down a side road that led him far south of Route 66. This was a part of the world where people thought nothing of driving fifty or a hundred miles to do a simple errand. In the dark, the two vehicles might be passing through any small American town of windows lighted by the glow of televisions sets.

The FBI agent's black sedan stopped in front of a saloon that would cater only to locals, judging by the license plates at the curb and the distance from the interstate. Riker switched off his headlights and waited in the dark until the door closed behind Christine Nahlman. He parked the Mercedes behind her car and waited a patient twenty minutes before following her inside.

The front door opened onto a wall of smoke and sound. A jukebox wailed

country-music songs of dead dogs and feck-
less women, but that had been expected.
And it was no surprise to see Nahlman
drinking alone at the bar. The lady had a
small but appreciative audience of men with
baseball caps and pool cues, unshaven and
smiling in her direction. They were checking her out and nodding to one another,
seeing her as easy prey.

They had no idea that the lady packed a
gun and more than enough ammo to dis-
patch the pool players and the bartender,
too, if she felt so inclined.

Riker pulled a barstool closer to hers and
sat down.

After the first few minutes of the cop-to-
cop small talk that always began, "Hell of a
day, huh?" Agent Nahlman was reassured
that he was not here to make a play for her,
and that was the truth. He had come to her
as a thief to steal whatever he could.

He was picking up Mallory's worst habits.

The detective was quick to find a common ground with Nahlman: the cop and
the fed both liked the same brand of cheap
Scotch; this was a lie on his part, for he was
a bourbon drinker. But he had hopes that
this bonding ritual would lead to every field
agent's pastime, bitching about bureaucrats
— like the SAC, Dale Berman. Her ability

to hold her liquor was impressive, and it was his fear that she might drink him under the bar before uttering the first disparaging word.

After the third round, he laid on a compliment. "So Mallory tells me you did a great job on the geographic profiling — and Dale took all the credit." Riker shook his head to say, *Ain't life a bitch.*

Nahlman shrugged and slugged back her drink. "In a way — Dale Berman *should* get the credit. He was the one who combed every state database for unsolved homicides."

"He worked cold cases? And they didn't even belong to the feds?"

"He didn't work anything," she said. "He just collected data for dead-end homicides — zero evidence, no clues. He favored skeletons discovered years after death."

Riker had a store of trivia for filling awkward silences. "Did you know that most murder victims are found by drunks stopping to pee by the side of the road?"

"Dale tossed those," she said. "Not enough similarities. He concentrated on buried victims. A year ago, he gave the list to me, hundreds of gravesites all over the country, and he said, 'Make me a pattern.' "

"Not *find* one? *Make* a pattern?"

"That's right." She rattled her ice cubes and spoke to her glass. "He wanted to manufacture a serial killer. It's been done before. A perp confesses to a murder in one state, and cops from all the surrounding states come in with their own unsolved cases. They're hoping this guy can clear the books for them. And sometimes they get lucky. They find an obliging killer who likes the attention." Nahlman turned her calm gray eyes on Riker. "So don't pretend to be shocked, okay? Cops do it, too. Now you promised to tell me how Dale Berman wound up in charge of a field office."

"Oh, yeah," said Riker. That bribe had been offered early on with the first drink, the setup. "It's a real short story. The bastard screwed up a high-profile case in New York. It embarrassed the Bureau. So naturally they promoted him to make the mess stink less."

"Amen," said Nahlman. "Always praise the jerk in trouble."

"But before Dale got the Texas posting, the Bureau buried him in a North Dakota satellite office — in the winter. It *is* a balanced universe." Riker lifted two fingers to the bartender for another round, then turned his most sympathetic smile on Nahlman. "So the bastard fobbed the whole pile off on you. Why am I not surprised?" He was too obvious that time. He could see his mistake in the narrowing of her eyes, a slow wince.

"Riker, you should spend more time listening, and less time manipulating me. I think it's the lack of finesse that pisses me off the most." She lifted her glass to give him a moment to think that over. "I was glad to have the work, even if it landed me in Berman's little dynasty. What a joke — a task force for a killer who didn't exist yet."

He wondered what Nahlman had done to earn this assignment to a disgraced SAC and a limbo of dead-end cases, but he observed the cop's etiquette of not asking how she had screwed up her own career. That would be rude. He wondered if it had something to do with drinking on the job. This was not a criticism. It took an alcoholic to read the signs, and this woman was definitely one of his people — almost family.

She drained her glass — again. "Are you ready to listen?"

"Yes, ma'am." He well understood his own place in this scheme: it was no longer his role to ply her for information — she would never tolerate that; it was Nahlman's plan to feed it to him.

"I mapped out a lot of areas," she said, "every place where a body was dug up over the past twenty years — hundreds and hundreds of them. Then I found the anomaly — bodies buried close to roads. If a killer only wanted to hide the remains, why risk being seen by a passing car? When I recognized the roads as different pieces of old Route 66, I had my signature for a serial killer. Then I knocked out all but eight of the graves on Berman's list. And I had my pattern."

"A pattern for two thousand miles of road?"

"Just listen, okay? Seven years ago, the telephone company dug up a grave in a place where the pavement doesn't even exist anymore, but it used to be Route 66. I called local police for details. The case was so old. Notes got lost — evidence, too. I dug up my own buried skeleton twenty miles down the road, and then I found another one. I checked missing persons reports on neighboring states and found matches on personal items from the graves. Then — big mistake — I contacted the parents to ask them for DNA samples."

"And one of them was Jill's Dad? George Hastings?"

"When Berman found out, he went ballistic. So then he formed the recovery detail."

"The body snatchers."

"Right," she said. "Hit and run, no paperwork with the local cops. Berman had a bona fide serial killer, and he didn't want to lose the case to a task force out of D.C."

"And he had you. You knew where to dig."

"My estimates weren't exact. There were gaping holes in my pattern. So I still have to go out and eyeball the land, looking for likely places — nothing near a town, no homes close by. If there's a house near one of my sites, I have to find out when it was built. And I walk a lot of miles with the cadaver dogs."

"So you've been working the case for a year." According to Kronewald, the war of cops and feds had begun with the graves of three children stolen from Illinois.

"Working it? Yes and no. I spend all my time mapping sites for the body snatchers. I don't know how many of them panned out. And I've got no idea what Dale does with evidence — if he does anything at all." She pushed her glass to the rail of the bar. "I know you don't like my boss, but you always call him by his first name. Why is that?"

In the town of Santa Rosa, New Mexico,

493

Mallory sat in the dark of her parked car and stared at the façade of Club Café. It was closed — forever.

One of the entrance posts was bent, and a neon sign had been taken down and discarded with other trash to one side of the building. In the younger days of Route 66, this place had done a booming business, and she would have known that even without her father's letters. A gravel lot adjoined this paved one to catch the overflow of customers on a Saturday night.

"They finally closed the doors back in ninety-two," said the gray-haired man in the passenger seat. He opened a cold bottle of beer from his grocery sack. Handing it to her, he lifted a second bottle in a toast. "To better times."

The old man had lived in this country for most of his life, but Mallory could hear a trace of Mexico when he spoke of the legendary party that had lasted for years — Club Café.

"But most of all, I miss that man," said Aldo Ramon. He turned to his drinking companion, the young woman who had her father's eyes. "Where has Peyton been all this time?"

"It was my neighbor's fault," said Riker as

he watched Nahlman sign an illegible scrawl on the register for the fleabag motel. "I grew up next door to a man with a dog named Dale."

He had no illusions about this invitation to finish off a bottle in her room. The rest of their conversation simply required more privacy. She paid in cash, no travel vouchers to say that she had wandered away from the other FBI agents — to get tight in a bar.

Outside again, he followed her down a row of doors until she fitted her key in a lock.

"So," said Riker, continuing the saga of why he called Agent Berman by his first name, "the neighbor's dog —"

"A dog named Dale." She seemed dubious about this part as she waved him inside.

"Yeah." Riker plopped himself down in an armchair, lit a cigarette and pulled a bottle from a brown paper sack. "Now, when you meet up with a real mean dog, you show some respect, right? Well, Dale —"

"Your neighbor's dog."

"Yeah, *that* Dale. He wasn't ballsy enough to be vicious — no barking, no warning. He'd come up from behind and sink his teeth into your leg. And then he'd run for cover. I hated that dog — sneaky, nasty mutt."

"You made that up."

"Just the part about the dog," he said. "Your turn, Nahlman. What about Joe Finn's girl? Ariel was a teenager. She never fit your pattern."

"I zeroed in on every odd thing along Route 66. Ariel's body was left on the road, but the dumpsite matched up with a potential grave. I called the Kansas Bureau and found out about the little sister who *did* fit that pattern. That case got stranger by the minute. I found out that Ariel's father wouldn't even look at the body to make the formal ID."

"You suspected him?"

"No, he was in a Kansas City hospital when Ariel was taken. The first time I met Dodie — sweet kid — she said hello and told me the name of her doll."

"So the kid was talking back then. You get anything useful?"

Nahlman shook her head. "I didn't sit in on the interviews when she was in custody. I'm guessing she couldn't describe the man who killed her sister. That would've been a lead that even Dale Berman couldn't ignore."

"He cut you out of the loop, didn't he?"

"Well, I never got any feedback on my leads, but I still had a lot of work to do, lots of overtime. I forget the last night I slept in my own bed." She stretched out on the mattress. Her eyes had gone dark, and they wandered from one corner of the ceiling to another.

She was lost.

"The next time I saw Dodie — at the campsite in Missouri — she was humming that song. I didn't expect her to remember me. But I don't think she even remembers her dolls anymore." Nahlman turned to Riker. "You know that song, right?"

"Yeah, 'Mack the Knife.' "

"That's also the code name Berman used when he opened this case three years ago."

"I don't get it." Riker found it difficult to drink, smoke and do math simultaneously. Or had he missed something here? "Three years ago, he was still posted in North Dakota — no killer, no case. Where's the tie to the song?"

"It's in a bogus case file. The early reports include hearsay testimony of a dead witness, an old woman who tied the song to a murder. But that witness died years before I was assigned to Berman's field office — before I found him a pattern for a serial killer. For some reason, he needed a connection to his early work — collecting random homicides. Do you get it now, Riker?"

"You're telling me that Dale taught that song to Dodie Finn?"

"That's my theory. It's so easy to plant fake memories in a little kid's mind. And by now I'm sure Dodie thinks she heard that song when Ariel died — if Dodie thinks at all. Berman went too far."

"He pushed her over the edge."

"Looks that way," she said.

"Why would he do that to her?"

Nahlman closed her eyes, and Riker assumed that she had passed out, but it was premature to cover the woman with a blanket. She threw it off as she opened her eyes.

"No, Riker, you only think I'm dead drunk. I wish I was. Every damn day, it seems to take more and more liquor so I can sleep at night. A blackout night with no dreams, that's all I want. I'm giving you information because this has to end, and Dale Berman can't or won't wrap this case."

As Riker gently pulled the door shut after him, Agent Nahlman was still staring at the ceiling, entirely too sober. No sleep tonight.

Riker stood at the edge of the campsite, discussing the problems of keeping track of caravan vehicles.

"It's out of control," said Agent Barry

Allen. "At last count, we had two hundred and seventy-five license plates on this list, but eight of the parents are missing tonight, and now I've got close to three hundred vehicles."

Riker scanned the campfires. "I still can't find the Pattern Man, and that little guy's really easy to spot."

"If he's gone again," said Allen, "Agent Berman won't send out another search party. He thinks you were pulling his leg about Mr. Kayhill as a suspect."

"Well, Dale has to start somewhere," said Riker. "Every good cop needs a shortlist, but your boss never developed one solid suspect."

If this agent knew anything to the contrary, it did not show in his face, nor did he offer another lame defense of Dale Berman. The boy had a defeated look about him as he walked away. Maybe the boss's charm was wearing thin among the troops — or, as Riker referred to them, the kiddy cops. Protocol failures were transparent; with the exception of Barry Allen, none of these youngsters had been partnered with a grown-up. Dale had picked them young for good reason: it was harder to con a veteran field agent.

Mallory came up behind Riker and made

him jump when she whispered his name. He blamed her foster father for that heart-stopping habit of hers. Lou Markowitz had taught her this creepy game the year that Kathy had lost interest in baseball. Or maybe she had come to understand why other children never wanted to play with her; she frightened them. But Lou had filled the void as her constant playmate, and the two of them had dreamed up new ways to terrify one another in every room of the old house back in Brooklyn. It had been one of the small joys of Lou's life to come home after a long hard day with murderers — and get scared witless the minute he walked in the door.

"Whatever Dale's up to, Nahlman's got no part in it." Riker recited the highlights of his field report, and then summed it up, saying, "None of Dale's people have more than a piece of this case."

"You trust this woman?"

"Yeah, I do."

Mallory edged a little closer. "Did Nahlman tell you about the little blue pouch?"

Riker shook his head.

"Then you can't trust her."

"Maybe she figured that I'd know what *you* know. Stupid idea, huh, Mallory? You're only my damned partner."

His irritation had no effect on her. Mallory's eyes were tracking Paul Magritte as the doctor slowly crossed the campground. Magritte came to a sudden stop and rifled his knapsack. Now the old man changed direction to head for his car and privacy.

"Why isn't he in jail?" asked Mallory.

Riker would prefer to eat the muzzle of his gun than to ask — one more time — what she meant by that. He walked away from her. He was in no mood for games.

Dr. Paul Magritte held a large, old-model cell phone to his ear and listened to the prelude of every conversation with an old acquaintance, the ritual words, "Forgive me, Father, for I have sinned." The old man sat in the back seat of his car with all the windows rolled up, and still he looked over his shoulder, fearful of what might be coming up behind him.

"No," he said in answer to a question that was also part of their ritual. "I will never betray you." Following the caller's instructions, he opened the glove box and pulled out a new stack of photographs taken with a Polaroid camera. He fanned them out. This time it was not a corpse, but candid pictures of Dodie Finn. A living child was a break with tradition — or was she dead?

501

Paul Magritte's eyes searched the side window for a sign of her.

Dodie, where are you?

One veined hand groped about inside his nylon sack, where, until very recently, he had kept a rusty gun. His hand slowly closed around the hilt of a newly purchased hunting knife. "Dodie Finn is insane," said Magritte to his caller. "What harm could she do to you?"

He heard a low buzz on the phone and words rising to be heard above the noise. He had the ugly sensation of black flies crawling around in his ear.

"Look at her," the caller said. "Look to your left, old man. That's it. You see her now?"

"Yes." The child was sitting on the edge of a folding chair. Her thin legs were drawn up as she perched there, leaning forward and defying gravity as birds do. She began to rock, and the old man feared that she would fall. Ah, but now her father grabbed her up in his arms and held her close. Joe Finn's eyes went everywhere, seeking the cause of this upset.

"There. You see it now," said the voice on the phone. "She rocks, she hums. Dodie's full of little cues and clues."

They debated this for another hour. The

doctor held a perfectly rational conversation with the devil. All the while, Paul Magritte's eyes traveled over the dark windows of caravan vehicles. So many newcomers. The FBI agents could no longer keep track of them. Dodie Finn's stalker had a gift for procuring cars, and there were many here that might harbor him tonight.

"When it's over," said his caller, "I give you permission to hand over my photographs to Detective Mallory."

Of course. Magritte sighed. He should have foreseen this. Now Mallory had been woven into a serial killer's little story of himself — a legend still in the making. It was the young detective who would explain this wondrous design to the world, for Magritte could not be expected to break his silence after all these years. The old man now saw his only role as the archivist — and suddenly he saw the greater value of the photographs, Polaroids with no negatives.

When it's over?

What was meant by those words?

Ah, yes, now the elderly psychologist understood it all too clearly. Every legend must have a dramatic finale. But this quest for fame was pathetic, the ploy of a little boy. It was like a letter written to the parents who had run away from him and gone to ground where he could never find them. He would find them now, and it would not matter if he was alive to see their stricken faces. It went beyond revenge — this maniacal communiqué of the abandoned child. And it was possible for the old man to pity a killer of children — even as he plotted to destroy him. With suicidal ideation in the mix, the murderer would become more reckless. The time was right. Dodie must survive.

Magritte looked down at the knife held tight in his right hand. What a fool he had been to believe that he could save a child this way. His best weapon had always been words. "More pictures to burn," he said to his caller, his torturer.

"What did you say?"

"You didn't think I kept them, did you?" Magritte waited out the silence for an endless crawling minute. "You never made copies, did you? No, of course not. Well, they're gone. I burned them all."

The cell-phone connection was broken, and his usefulness to a psychopath was at an end. He sat bolt upright, the knife clutched in both hands now. Hours passed. The sky was lightening, and every star had been lost when he reached that point where even fear could not keep him awake. His eyes closed, but only for the time it took for the sun to clear the horizon line. The early light was slanting through his windshield when he awoke to the noise of barking dogs. The parents were striking camp and packing vehicles. The caravan would soon be underway. When he turned to the side window, he sucked in his breath. Detective Mallory's face was inches from his own, and she was staring at the knife in his lap.

She ripped open the car door. "You should be under arrest, old man. What kind of a deal did you do with Agent Nahlman?"

17

A new insurrection had begun. Charles Butler stood at the heart of the crowd, yet Riker had found him. The detective carried a plastic sack, the fruits of a beer run to a liquor store. "What's going on?"

"Trouble." Charles pointed to an embedded reporter from a cable news network. The man was standing on the hood of a car, and his voice was amplified by a bullhorn. "He's trying to convince the parents to drive the scenic route to Santa Fe."

"Well, that's not good," said Riker, as he popped the tab on a beer can and took a deep swallow. "The caravan would choke the Santa Fe loop in fifteen minutes."

Now Mallory was visible in the distance as she climbed onto the hood of a pickup truck to stand two heads taller than the newsman. She needed no bullhorn. The crowd was hushed, waiting, and then she said, "Come nightfall, you'll all be strung out as easy pickings in a mile-long traffic jam." She slowly revolved to catch every pair of eyes in this large group of parents, federal agents and media. "And there's no point in taking that route."

"That's not true!" The cable newsman shouted into his bullhorn to regain the crowd's attention. "I can guarantee two solid hours of airtime for every day on the Santa Fe loop!" Raising the ante of his bid, he yelled, "You get the prime-time slot!"

"There were no bodies found on that segment of the old road," said Mallory, and hundreds of heads swiveled to face her again. "None of your children ever went that way."

"If that was true," said the cable reporter, "then the FBI agent in charge wouldn't have approved my route change." He lowered his bullhorn and climbed down from the hood of his car. Now he had to crane his neck to look up at her and smile. In an unamplified voice he said, "The negotiations are over, Detective."

"Wrong," she said.

Charles looked around with the vantage point of the tallest man standing. Dale Berman, the agent in charge, was nowhere to be seen, and Riker had also disappeared. He turned his eyes to Mallory, who still had the high ground atop the truck's hood.

The reporter at her feet raised his bull-horn again. "It's a done deal, Detective. We're going to Santa Fe."

Mallory removed her jacket, the better to display her gun, and now she clipped her gold shield to a belt loop of her jeans. Hands on hips, she addressed the reporter. "I don't want any doubt in your mind that this is a lawful police order. Now shut your mouth!"

Undeterred, the reporter yelled at her. "Freedom of the press, Detective! Ever heard of the Constitution of the —"

"I got it memorized," said Riker, stepping out of the crowd to grab a handful of the reporter's shirt, and now he was dragging the man backward across the campground, his voice trailing off as he loosely para-phrased the reporter's constitutional right to remain silent. "Don't flap your mouth anymore."

And now Mallory owned the crowd. All eyes were on her and every camera lens. The cameras loved her more than the man from the cable news network.

"The Santa Fe loop is part of the old route from the thirties. That's your great-grandfather's idea of Route 66 — not the killer's. He dug his graves along the old trucking route from the sixties. That's *his* Route 66 — and yours."

As she went on to describe all the changes and versions of this shifting historic highway, Charles Butler realized that she had slipped into someone else's words. At times she reminded him of a schoolgirl reciting memorized lines of poems.

The poetry ended. Her hands curled into fists.

"The next stop is Clines Corners," she said. "It's been a landmark on this road for over sixty years. If you take the old Santa Fe loop, you can't get there from here. Your cars won't move. You'll be sitting in the dark — waiting. You think rolling up the windows will protect you?" Mallory pointed at the reporter in Riker's custody. "You think he cares? Hey, fresh blood means a bonus where he comes from. His network turned dead children into a damn TV show, a soap opera. He *wants* to drag this out. That's the only reason for the side trip. And more time on the tube — that's like currency to you. It's all about money. He wants to buy your kids. Dead or alive, same price."

The caravan was under way — Mallory's way. Her final selling point to the crowd had been the fact that long traffic jams were only worth a mention on the evening news. The reporters would desert them for better entertainment — action shots of the police unearthing small bodies on the old trucker's route. And now her silver convertible prowled the shotgun lane of I-40 as she watched for strays up and down the line of vehicles.

Of all the dead who rode with Mallory, she was most compatible with Ariel Finn, perhaps because the teenager never spoke; she could not, for the detective had never heard the sound of the girl's voice. In Mallory's version of this murder victim, the pale skin was without blemish or bruises or gaping wounds, and the girl was made whole again; her severed hand had been restored. Ariel raised it as the small silver car approached Joe Finn's old Chevy. Dodie's face was pressed to the glass of the passenger window when dead Ariel waved to her little sister.

And Dodie — waved — back.

Mallory pushed the gas pedal to the floor and turned up the volume on the radio, blasting Ariel out of the passenger seat, leaving the dead girl and little Dodie far behind. She could not leave them fast enough.

So *this* was fear.

The car went screaming down the road,

her radio blasting the heavy-metal music of Black Sabbath, drums gone wild, all the thrill of a crash without the carnage. But Mallory had the sense of heading into some distant wall and a crash of another kind, one that made no sound at all.

At the landmark travel plaza, where the caravan stopped for food and gas, Riker stood in conversation with the manager, a silver-haired man in a crisp white shirt and black vest. Joe Villanueva had worked at Clines Corners through three generations of owners and renovations.

He had already consoled Detective Riker on the loss of the horseshoe bar, and now he explained the disappearance of the buffalo mural. "It's been gone for a *long* time. We took out that wall to make room for more tables. You're the second customer to ask about the mural." The manager turned to point at Mallory, who was examining a display of straw cowboy hats. "She says she's never been here before, but she even knew the color of the old carpet."

Riker worked his way through the press of people in the gift shop, aiming for the dining room on the other side of the building. Though this place was accustomed to handling large tour groups, the swollen caravan and its media entourage had filled two dining rooms to capacity. Some people jammed the lines of a nearby fast-food counter and carried their meals outside. Others waited for tables to be liberated, and those who were seated waited for menus.

But Charles Butler had managed to secure a table, and it was already laden with food and drink.

As Riker sat down to his customary cheeseburger — and damn the fries were good — he asked how his friend had done this trick, and the answer was "Magic." The detective was left to imagine a sleight-of-hand where Charles had made a fistful of cash appear, or maybe it had been a more tasteful hundred-dollar bill. It was easy to pick out their lucky waitress by the broad smile on the young woman's face.

"You look worried," said Charles.

The detective inhaled the rest of his meal and lit a post-cheeseburger cigarette. "Mallory knows things about this road — about this place — things she never got from a guidebook. And I know she's never been here before."

"Well, the letters might've given her —"

"Her father's letters. Yeah, maybe Peyton Hale has a fixation on this road. You think he might be anything like his kid?" And by that Riker meant to ask if the ruthless streak of a sociopath could run in families.

And so it was predictable that the man who loved Mallory would change the subject. "I hope she turns up before her food gets cold."

"She'll be along," said Riker.

"Mallory? I just saw her in the gift shop," said Dale Berman as he sat down with them uninvited. "She's buying a cowboy hat." His words were aimed at Riker. "It fits, doesn't it? True colors you might say. A cowboy hat for a gunslinger."

Riker exhaled a cloud of blue smoke, and the game was on.

Mallory wore her newly purchased cowboy hat into the parking lot, where she opened the door to a car that was not hers. She had a preference for robbery in broad daylight and in plain sight. And, as she had anticipated, no one had noticed her popping the lock on government property. After ransacking one vehicle, she went on to the next one on her to-do list.

The agents posted outside were running a ragged pace, trying to separate departing tourists and reporters from parents, checking credentials and checking clipboards, and none of them even glanced toward the cluster of FBI cars. The caravan had swelled to ungovernable numbers, and the boys and girls on parking-lot duty were newly minted agents fresh from the academy. Their eyes were glazing over. Because no one had told them their task was impossible, they could only assume they were doing it wrong.

And they were.

Paradoxical Mallory — who despised clutter and knew the names of every cleaning solvent on the planet, Mallory the Neat — thrived on chaos. There was no better cover for breaking and entering. If anyone remembered her in the vicinity of government vehicles, she truly believed that they would only recall the standout detail of the cowboy hat — not the shape of a tall, slender blonde who moved with deep grace, her hair catching sunlight as if it caught fire. And who would remember her unforgettable face? If she did not see these things in her own mirror, then why should anyone else take notice?

When she was done raiding the second car, Mallory dropped the brand-new cowboy hat in the trash on her way back to the restaurant.

Charles Butler was an innocent bystander without the luxury of being able to dive underneath the table as the detective and the FBI agent traded salvos across the dinnerware.

Riker glanced at the window on the parking lot, where another search of caravan vehicles had begun. He took a drag on his cigarette and sent a stream of smoke in Agent Berman's direction. "So I'm guessing you didn't find any baby bones in the first search."

"That's not what I'm looking for." The FBI agent laid an open pocketknife on the table. "This is consistent with the weapon that was used on Gerald Linden's throat. Ask your buddy, Kronewald. It was his pathologist's finding. That was before we —"

"Before your ghouls made off with the body?" Riker smiled so insincerely. "Yeah, those Chicago cops are quick." The detective looked down at the weapon on the table. "You arrested Nahlman yet? Her Swiss Army knife has the same size blade."

Berman's own smile was equally disingenuous. "I'm not looking for a knife anymore. Today, I'm hoping to find a hatchet."

Charles glanced at the window on the parking lot. The trunks of cars yawned open, as did the doors of mobile homes, and tarps had been pulled away from the beds of pickup trucks.

"A hatchet." Riker splayed his hands. "You lost me, Dale. I guess that would only make sense to a fed."

The FBI man leaned toward the detective, and Charles Butler backed up in his chair, as if anticipating splatters from a messy food fight.

"It's really easy," said the agent, "to separate a hand from a little skeleton, but what about the adult kills? Fresh kills — meat and muscle and bone." Dale Berman handed the pocketknife across the table to the detective, and this was perhaps a mistake in Charles's view.

"Look at that blade, Riker. It'll slash a throat easy enough, but do you really think you could chop off a man's hand with that thing?"

"Nothing easier, Dale."

Charles Butler bit down on his lower lip. The detective had a dangerous air of glee about him as he laid the cutting edge of the knife across Dale Berman's wrist. The FBI agent not only allowed this, but the man's smile got inexplicably wider, and he never even glanced at the sharp blade that rested on his bare skin.

Countdown. One second, two seconds.

Never taking his eyes off of Berman, the

detective said, "Charles, do me a favor? Go outside and find me a rock? Not too heavy, just big enough to drive this blade home to the bone."

Enough said.

Now that the FBI man could see how the thing was done, he withdrew his hand from the demonstration. And Riker, the clear winner, dropped the knife in the center of the table.

"If you had the perp's knife," said Riker, "you'd see the damage from the rock coming down on the top edge of the blade. But what are the odds he'll get caught with the murder weapon? He can buy a new pocket-knife in any pit stop on this road."

Dale Berman took this as his cue to leave the table, and when he was gone, Charles turned to Riker. "You really think the killer used a knife to cut off the hands?"

"Naw," said Riker, "it was probably a hatchet, but that was fun." The detective watched the ongoing parking-lot search. Agents had opened the mobile home that dispensed camping equipment to newcomers, and now scores of brand-new hatchets were being laid out on the ground. "What a waste of time. What are the odds of finding a bloody hatchet with a store of new ones for the taking? That trailer's never locked.

Dale's losing more IQ points every day."

"What did that man do to you and Mallory?"

"Nothing. It was what he did to Lou."

Charles smiled — patiently.

Reluctantly, Riker gave up the story of Inspector Louis Markowitz and the FBI. Between puffs of smoke, he described the day when Agent Berman joined the task force — to everyone's surprise. "Dale used to be a public relations man for the Bureau. That means he sat on a lot of barstools with angry cops and nosey reporters. After getting blind drunk with Dale, sometimes I forgot why I hated feds."

"You liked him then," said Charles.

"Well, the drinks were free."

"He used to be your friend. That's why you always use his first name."

"He talked more like a cop in those days," said Riker. "Or maybe that was all for show. He said he always wanted to be a field agent. Well, he wasn't blowing smoke that time. He actually *asked* for a demotion. Lower pay, and no expense account for barstool duty. It made more sense to me later on — after Dale screwed us over. FBI careers are made on big cases — big wins, but the PR guys only come out of the woodwork when things go sour. So it was a good career move for Dale. His first time out with a task force, he talks Lou into taking his help on a kidnapping. A little boy was being held for ransom. Well, normally that's a slam-dunk for NYPD. Hard to make a ransom pickup without getting caught, and the perps who try it are bone stupid. But this case was high profile. The kid came from money — big money, lots of pressure to wrap it fast. So we split the legwork with the feds. Lou had a prime suspect early on, but Dale alibied the guy with a bogus field report, and then he leaked the kidnapping to the press. Now the police phone lines are choked with calls and leads that go nowhere."

"But why would he —"

"It kept us busy while Dale followed up on Lou's suspect."

"The one he alibied."

"Right. So Dale's crew works the case around the cops, and they bungle it. The suspect gets maimed in a high-speed chase across the bridge into Jersey. The kidnapper's comatose. The victim's still out there — God knows where. And Lou Markowitz is so pissed off, he kicks all the feds out of the house. Now the old man puts every dick and uniform on the street to work their snitches. We get the name and address of our guy's favorite whore — and that's where we find the kid."

"Alive?"

"Oh, sure. The NYPD always brings them home. But the FBI? Not such a great record. So the boy was fine. He thought this prostitute was his new nanny. And the kid really liked that whore. She let him stay up late on school nights."

"And that's why you and Mallory hate Dale Berman?"

"No, Charles, that's not what you asked."

"But, the other day, Berman was right when he said no one died."

The detective bowed his head. This was Charles's only clue that someone *had* died. And there would be no more discussion on this matter. It was too hard on Riker.

Mallory appeared beside Charles's chair, and he wondered how long she had been standing there. He smiled, fully realizing that this expression gave him the look of a lunatic in love. "Hello! Sit down. Your lunch is cold. Sorry."

No matter, for she was in the company of a young state trooper, who juggled a plastic bag and a tray with one hand so he could pull out a chair for her at the table. Once she was seated, the officer laid a plate of hot food in front of her.

"I hope it's the way you like it, ma'am." The eager young man in uniform removed his hat before he sat down at the table. As Charles introduced himself and Riker, it was clear that the trooper only had eyes for Mallory, who was making short work of her steak and fries.

Riker explained the trooper's presence to Charles. "I asked the state cops to find the Pattern Man. He defected again."

"Oh, if you mean Mr. Kayhill," said the trooper, "we found him for you, sir. He's dead." The young man continued to smile at Mallory as he relayed this sad news. "Found him in the desert. A helicopter spotted his mobile home a mile from the nearest road."

"Was one of his hands missing?" Mallory bit into a French fry drenched with ketchup.

"Ma'am, I couldn't name three things that *weren't* missing, and there's not much flesh on what was left behind."

"So the buzzards got him," said Riker.

"No, sir, no buzzards. We do have turkey vultures out there, but they didn't make off with his head. I guess every bobcat and coyote for miles around had a turn at the body. We're still looking for arms and legs."

"So tell me," said Riker, "how'd you make the identification?"

"Well, sir, we had a good portion of the torso, so Mr. Kayhill's doctor made the ID over the telephone. The man was born with an extra rib. It's him all right." The trooper handed a black plastic bag across the table. "Some of his things — if you wouldn't mind having a look. Oh, and a Detective Kronewald in Chicago sends his regards." The trooper nodded to the plastic bag. "He said you might want to check that out."

Riker opened the bag for a quick look. Inside was the canvas tote bag with the collection of Route 66 maps. The familiar small crosses in pencil and ink were visible on one. "Good night, Horace." He looked up at the trooper. "It's his stuff all right. So I guess there's no way to tell what killed the little guy."

"A car killed him, sir. We found Mr. Kayhill's shirt. Tread marks all over it."

This could hardly be a traffic accident if the body had been found in the middle of nowhere — no roads. Charles leaned toward the young man, saying, "So Horace was murdered?"

"Yes, sir." Unacquainted with rhetorical questions, the trooper phrased his words ever so politely. "With all that open space, you'd really have to aim a car at a man to hit him. In this case, we got cross tread marks. That means the car hit him more than once. So, yes, sir, we thinks it was real deliberate."

"Well, poor man." Charles was somewhat put off his meal. "This is sad news."

"You don't know the half of it," said Riker with genuine remorse. "I really liked that little guy. He was on my shortlist — right up near the top."

"I always liked him, too." Mallory opened a small notebook and crossed Horace Kayhill's name off her own suspect list. After slinging her knapsack over one shoulder, she picked up the laptop computer and left the table.

The trooper was rising, anxious to follow her, perhaps with the idea that they could be close friends. Riker, with the kindest intention in his smile, placed an avuncular hand on the younger man's shoulder, saying, "No, kid. Only if you *like* pain."

On the pretense of returning Kayhill's bag of maps to the state trooper, Detective Riker carried his cell phone out to the parking lot. He needed privacy for his incoming call. After settling into the front seat of the Mercedes, he resumed his conversation with New York's chief medical examiner. "Hey, Doc, thanks for waiting. So how's it going?"

"Kathy Mallory never answers her phone," said Dr. Slope.

Thank you, God.

"That's okay," said Riker. "I take messages." And before the medical examiner could make contact with his partner, Riker would have to officially notify her that Savannah Sirus was dead. Otherwise, Dr. Slope would find it odd that she had never been told, and the old man might have a few questions.

"Tell her this," said Slope. "I am *not* her personal funeral director. Then tell her the crematorium called. They'd like to know when she plans to pick up Miss Sirus's ashes. . . . Riker? . . . Still there?"

"Yeah, Doc."

"So what should I tell them?"

"Soon — a few more days. So when did you talk to Mallory?"

"She might've called the day after we found the body. I didn't speak to her myself. I assume you were the one who told her about the suicide."

"Yeah," said Riker, in his first lie of the day. In Mallory fashion, he cut off the call with no good-bye.

How had she known that Savannah was dead? Was the woman's suicide so predictable? Had Mallory made the connection between a LoJack tracker on her tail in the state of Illinois and sudden death in New York City? Maybe she had phoned her apartment that night and got no answer from her erstwhile houseguest. Was the morgue her next call?

He did not suspect Mallory of murder. Thanks to Charles Butler, there was no doubt that Savannah had shot herself. What made him close his eyes just now was the possibility that Mallory had stayed to watch.

Dr. Paul Magritte held his cell phone to one ear as he checked the rearview mirror. He was not expecting to see the FBI moles driving behind him. Those two were so preoccupied with one another. He doubted that they would notice his absence for some time yet. He was looking in the mirror for a car that would keep pace with him. He slowed down, and all the traffic went whizzing past his Lincoln.

For the past few miles, he had believed that he was being closely observed as he followed his orders and left the parking lot to ride the interstate. However, now he realized that his caller was not behind him, but up ahead — waiting. The constant phone requests for his exact position could have no other explanation.

He pulled onto the shoulder of the interstate and left the car, removing his jacket as he walked toward an exit sign. He trusted that Mallory, who missed nothing, would remember this article of clothing. Even if she did not recall its color and herringbone pattern, the sight of it waving in the wind — that would be meaningful to her. He devoutly believed that the young detective would be the one to find him.

He laid his plans on faith — in her.

Riker opened the car's trunk and tossed in the black plastic bag with Horace Kayhill's maps.

He heard the shouts before he saw Mallory winding her way through the haphazard lanes of parked cars. Dale Berman called out to her, hurrying now to match steps with her longer legs, and then the man put one hand on her shoulder. Never breaking stride, she turned to give him a look that made him think better of annoying her anymore. Finally the fed gave up and returned to the restaurant.

And Mallory kept coming.

Riker closed the trunk and leaned back against the car. When she joined him, his eyes shifted to the retreating back of Dale Berman. "What was that about?"

She set the laptop on the trunk of the Mercedes and opened it. "I told him I knew he was dragging out this case."

"Well," said Riker, "I guess the longer he drags it out the greater the glory. Some people just like to see their names in the newspaper."

"That's not it. He did everything he could to keep the media away from this case." She powered up the laptop and turned the screen so he could see it. "You thought Dale Berman was just incompetent."

"Well, yeah, but that's true."

She shook her head. "I told you the screwups were over the top — even for Berman. So I followed the money."

Ah, Mallory's all-time favorite. Trust her to find a money motive in the slaughter of little girls. He stared at the glowing screen of number columns. "What am I looking at?"

"Dale Berman's payroll records. He's been reporting fifty hours of overtime every week." She pulled a notebook from her back pocket and pointed to a November date. "That's when Berman takes early retirement from the Bureau. I found the paperwork in his car." She turned back to the laptop screen. "Now look at these figures for earnings with overtime."

Riker whistled in appreciation of the large sum. "Dale's really building up his retirement fund."

"You're close," said Mallory. "This has been going on for years. He started padding his paychecks after the Bureau buried him in North Dakota."

"You see? I told you he was an idiot. That state only has a handful of people and some buffalo. Nobody does overtime."

"And Dale worked in a satellite office — no oversight. That's what triggered this audit." Mallory diddled the keyboard to show him a new set of figures. "Lots of pressure — the auditors are coming. He has to explain the overtime. A federal payroll scam is worth five years in prison. So he makes a bogus file for Mack the Knife, and he backdates it."

Riker shook his head in disbelief. "That's good for another charge — falsifying government documents. More jail time. I told you he was an idiot."

"No," said Mallory, "he was a man with a high-maintenance wife and a field agent's pay grade."

"And he was stuck in a backwater office with no action, no overtime."

"So he gave himself a bigger salary," said Mallory. "That's how it started, and then it snowballed. Berman can't close out a bogus case with no results — not right after an audit. It has to look like an ongoing investigation. Then he gets posted to a Texas field office. He's running it — all those eyes on him every day. More pressure. He can't leave the bogus case with another agent in North Dakota. So he develops a false lead in the Texas jurisdiction. The overtime keeps rolling in, but he's not doing it for the money now. He can't stop. He only has two years to retirement, and he needs a real live serial killer."

"And then he found Nahlman. She saved him."

Dr. Magritte left the car at the junction, and he left his wallet in the middle of the road, the one that led west toward an unknown destination. He was following directions fed to him as he traveled. The knife in his pocket gave him no comfort, but the expectation of being found either dead or alive, this was a joyful prospect. His prayers carried no requests for an angel of deliverance.

Send Mallory.

Mallory closed the laptop. "And now, thanks to Nahlman, he's got a big inventory of bodies and evidence, more than enough to account for his time."

"I got a problem with this," said Riker. "Dale knew that warehouse morgue was gonna be opened some day. If not by Harry Mars then —"

"And the feds would find a hundred cartons of sloppy paperwork — all hard copy with missing files, fake reports, no times and dates for hunting and digging — nothing to match records with human remains. Berman only needed to drag the case out. He never intended to solve it. He would've retired in another six months. The case would get fobbed off on his replacement — along with the keys to the warehouse. The agent who replaced him would put everything down to gross incompetence."

"And Nahlman could back him up on the incompetence," said Riker. "She's Dale's worst critic."

"Of course she is. Berman groomed her for the part." Mallory let that settle in for a moment, and, when the poison had taken hold, she went on. "Even now that the Bureau's onto him, he can still get away with it. Let's say Harry Mars opens an investigation. Nahlman will testify that her boss had no idea what he was doing. If

Harry asks her about the warehouse full of dead kids, she'll tell him that's no surprise, not to her. She'll swear under oath that Dale Berman is just a garden-variety screwup. And he'll still get his pension, even though people died on his watch. He never developed any of Nahlman's leads because he didn't want this case solved — not yet."

"Okay." Riker threw up his hands. "I'm a believer. Dale's not just a screwup. He's a sociopath. The little monster doesn't care who dies. You were right about everything."

Mallory had her half-smile in place, the one that warned him to run while he could; he had seen it before, and he knew she was going to turn on him. Riker braced himself, hands spread flat on the trunk of the car. He had watched her grow up; he had loved her so long and knew her too well.

"And all this time," said Mallory, casually offering him the stolen driver's license of the Illinois LoJack tracker, "even before Savannah Sirus died, you thought *I* was a sociopath — a *monster.*"

Riker was bending over in the manner of a man who has just had his entrails pulled out and held up before his startled eyes.

"Now let's talk about your friend Nahlman." Mallory pulled a small blue velvet pouch from her knapsack and emptied it on the hood of the Mercedes. Tiny bones clattered across the dusty metal. "I found them in Nahlman's glove compartment. Or maybe you think I'm lying?"

Make it stop!

He shook his head. She was telling him that it was time to choose up sides, her side versus the rest of the world. "You're my partner," he said. "I'm with you."

"Good." Mallory scooped up the little bones and put them back into the pouch. "Now it's time to arrest Dr. Magritte."

"What?"

The FBI moles had become engaged behind the travel plaza's garbage dumpster.

One mole gently caressed the face of the other and said, "I love you."

Behind them, startling them, a man's voice said, "How nice. But where's Dr. Magritte?"

The moles spun around to face the detectives from New York City, Riker and Mallory.

"Tell me you didn't lose that old man," said Detective Mallory, "not again."

One of the moles said, "Oh, shit." And the other one was only thinking it.

"Yes, I see it," said Paul Magritte to his

caller. "The turn is just up ahead."

This was a lie. His car was parked, and he was walking back to the juncture of dirt road and hard pavement. He spread an open book on the ground. This might be the most useful thing he had ever done with it. Looking down the unpaved road, he could see for miles and miles, and so could the killer of children. This would be the last time he dared to stop.

Dr. Magritte held the cell phone to his ear and offered more reassurance that he was quite alone. In turn, he received the good news that the kidnapped parent was still alive. And was this story believable? No. Up ahead there was only death on two legs, no heart, no soul. But this time, he would see it coming, and soon — so would every-one else.

He returned to his car and continued to follow the directions of a coldly mechanical voice that conjured up fat black flies inside his ear. He knew his final destination would be some distance away. The man would want privacy for what he planned to do to his old doctor — his former priest.

The moles ran back to the restaurant to make their report. Riker took the old road east, and his partner drove west on the interstate.

Mallory was flying across the highway, taking every exit ramp and doubling back to take the next one. It was slow going even at great speed. Finally, she spotted the jacket tied to an exit sign, and she turned onto a stretch of Route 66, still racing, only slowing when she came to the crossroad and saw the wallet lying on the pavement. She knew it was Magritte's, and she left it there. He was headed west. As she approached another turnoff, her car crawled along in search of other signs.

He recognized the early model car of an impoverished caravan parent.

Paul Magritte knew what he would find even before he had closed the door of his Lincoln. He moved on leaden feet toward the other vehicle. The trunk was open, awaiting his inspection. Inside lay the dead body of a slender man in his middle thirties. This time, the only blood came from the corpse's gaping mouth. The throat had not been slashed, but the cause of death was clear in the tire tread marks made on the clothing. This body had been run over by car, not once, but many times. Magritte had not known this man by name. So many people had joined the caravan in recent days. Yet he grieved for the stranger.

By force of habit, he began the ritual of commending the dead man's soul to God, though they were much estranged these days, himself and the Almighty.

Mallory slammed on the brakes, and stared at the open book lying on the ground, its pages rippling in the wind. She never had to leave her car to know that it was a Bible, an ex-priest's version of the proverbial breadcrumb trail.

She drove over it.

A car was approaching from a distance, coming overland, just a dot on the horizon of mesa and desert brush. He watched it grow — his impending death — and when he could see it clearly, he yelled, "I never betrayed you!" And though vengeance was the province of God, one hand closed on the knife in his pocket.

Soon.

He had anticipated an exchange of words, but that was not to be. The jeep was not slowing down but gathering speed. Impact came with a sickening thud of the metal impacting on flesh and bone. The force knocked the air from the old man's lungs and he was in flight, flying forever it seemed.

He lost consciousness before his body hit the hard ground.

When he opened his eyes again, he tasted blood in his mouth — proof of life.

His assailant — soon to be his murderer — was standing not far away in some new incarnation so different from the misshapen child he had known all those years ago.

Paul Magritte's resting place was a deep and narrow ditch, and now he could understand why he was still alive. It would not be possible to run him down a second time. And so this killer — loath to touch a living body — was helpless. He could only wait for an old man's death rattle.

Wait a little longer.

Paul Magritte suffered much pain. It was agony only to lift one hand — to beckon his murderer — come a little closer.

Mallory looked down at the corpse in the trunk, a clear death by vehicular homicide. Gone were all the trappings of a ritual, a killer's pretense of a twist in the game. Once his monument was finished and all the little girls were laid out in a row, he had simply turned his sights on advertising. But these attacks were different. The old man was a material witness, a loose end. And the dead parent in the trunk of the car? That was bait.

But what was his agenda with the murder of Horace Kayhill?

The detective returned to the ditch and knelt down beside Paul Magritte. The old man had been fading in and out, but now he was conscious again. "The ambulance should be here any minute." She was not looking at him but at the old dirt road, watching for the first sign of an emergency vehicle, listening for a siren.

"Mallory?" Dr. Magritte's voice was weak. He was also staring at the road. "My faith doesn't lie in that direction. . . . It lies with you." And now he turned his eyes to the great prize he had given her.

She looked down at the bloodied knife in her evidence bag. "It was a good try, old man. A good try."

"No . . . a success." His words came out with ragged breath and fresh red bubbles of spittle from his lips.

"Don't talk," she said.

"That blood on my knife . . . not mine . . . significant."

Mallory decided not to tell the old man that it was all for nothing, that this DNA evidence was useful in court but not in the hunt. "It's significant," she said. "He's getting reckless, careless. With any luck at all, he's suicidal, too. That's how it ends sometimes."

"He can't go back . . . to the caravan. . . . I cut him." Magritte's moving finger drew a jagged line on his neck.

"You marked him for me." Mallory smiled with something approaching real affection. "That's why you carried the old revolver. A bullet wound would get some attention, wouldn't it? Did Nahlman take the gun away from you?"

The old man nodded. "Not her fault. . . . She couldn't know."

"So, you decided to knife him instead. That cut was your loophole in the seal of the confessional."

This man had walked into a trap, knowing that he would be murdered. And the knife wound would pass for an act of self-defense — the only act that Paul Magritte's faith had allowed.

"This time . . ." The old man's lips moved in silence. His eyes were closing.

Mallory finished the sentence for him. "I'll see it coming."

18

Paramedics hooked the old man up to portable machines, and then they stabbed him with needles to fill his veins with drugs and plasma. Troopers were standing by for escort duty, and Paul Magritte was nearly stable enough for transport to a hospital.

When Mallory's car reached the paved highway at the end of the dirt road, she was in a quandary. East or west? The New Mexico State Police now owned the manhunt, and the structure of her day had been lost. She could not even guess the time, for the days were getting longer — too long.

She turned east — one decision made. Now for the music. After fiddling with the iPod, she found her old Eagles album. The volume was turned up as high as it would go.

"— take it eeeeasy, take it eeeeeasy —"

On the way back to the caravan, she passed the cars of FBI agents trailed by news vans, all heading off in the direction of the new crime scene — *her* crime scene.

"— don't let the sound of your own wheeeels make you craaazy —"

When the first sign for Clines Corners came into view, Mallory seemed to awaken in the moving car. How much time had passed? How much road? She could not say. The caravan parents were gathered in the parking lot, milling about in disarray like refugees from the end of the world. She parked at the far edge of the lot and watched them for a while. Should she stay or go? There was still time to get back on the road unseen. She could travel westward and rid herself of all these needy people.

Too late.

Agent Nahlman appeared at the side window, bending low to say, "I heard about Dr. Magritte. You knew he was a target, didn't you? Is that why you told me to feed him to Berman?"

"Does it matter anymore?" The detective opened the door and stepped out of the car. "Magritte will be dead by morning." Or he might live a bit longer if she trusted no more federal agents with his life. Back at the crime scene, she had arranged for local police to guard the old man's hospital room.

Nahlman was behind her and talking to

her back as they crossed the parking lot. The agent was almost indignant when she asked, "Why couldn't you let me in on it? I would've turned the bones over to Berman as evidence. Dr. Magritte would've —"

"You *didn't* turn in the bones?" Mallory leaned heavy on a tone of disbelief, though all the while the pouch of bones was resting in her knapsack. Some punishment was called for here.

The FBI woman's understanding came with a look of pain. "If I had, Magritte would've been arrested. He'd be in custody instead of —"

"That was the plan," said Mallory.

Riker stood at the edge of the crowd milling around in the parking lot. He turned to the tall man beside him. "Charles, I need help. The perp's cleaning up his loose ends and Dodie's one of them. The Finns have to go into custody. Kronewald's working out a deal with Harry Mars."

"What about the other parents?"

"As long as they stay on the road, our boy's gonna pick them off one by one. He just loves all this media attention. And the reporters are so excited they're pissing their pants. So, yeah, it's time for the rest of these people to go back where they came from."

"That's a pity," said Charles. "Most of them are better off here than they were at home."

"Oh, sure." Riker nodded, as if this made perfect sense to him. "You mean apart from the fact that they're getting killed?"

"There's dying and there's dying." Charles imagined each one of them sitting around the house with only profound grief for company, knitting socks for grief and spoon-feeding it with melancholy. Here, on this road, these people had a mission. At last, something lay ahead of them, and they could see into the day after tomorrow. The caravan city had nurtured them; it was solace and companionship, and, while the old man had been among them, there had been some order to their daily lives.

All of this came to an end as the ambulance bore their shepherd away.

The emergency vehicle raced past the travel plaza. The parents faced the road in silence, helpless to do anything but watch the distant ambulance spinning its lights, siren screaming, disappearing down the interstate. They revolved in place, turning this way and that, as if they lacked the ballast to withstand the wind of a blown kiss, ultimately deflating, collapsing to sit upon the ground or squat by their cars.

Mallory walked toward them, and, one by one, they turned their eyes to her. Charles understood what was happening. She was law and order to them, a protector of sheep.

Their new shepherd.

They watched as she came closer. Their necks were elongating, eyes widening, bodies all but levitating with expectation.

And Mallory's first pronouncement?

"Go home!"

Well, not the best of beginnings.

The people remained quiet, still hopeful, waiting for the next and perhaps more inspiring words, but Mallory turned her back on them and walked away. They followed her awhile with their sheep's eyes, then nodded to one another, as if agreeing all around, *Excellent choice.*

Riker shook his head. Charles shrugged, then followed after Mallory — an old habit of his.

When the new campsite had been paid for and the vehicles drawn into a circle, Riker sat on the fender of the Mercedes, his eyes turned to open land. The New Mexico mesas were dark purple and the grasslands had turned to gray at nine o'clock.

Charles sipped coffee, and Riker smoked cigarettes while he speculated on the suicide of Savannah Sirus.

"The way I see it," said the detective, "it was all about guilt. Let's say Mallory's mother was pregnant when Peyton left her for the other woman. So Savannah went to New York looking for absolution —" He threw his hands up. "And the lady just picked the wrong confessor."

"A bit simplistic," said Charles. "Back up a bit. First she must've sent Mallory a token letter written by Peyton Hale. Maybe she thought that would end the matter."

"Then Mallory wants the rest of the letters, all of them," said Riker. "She knows she's been cheated. Savannah spent three weeks in Mallory's apartment, more than enough time for a full confession. I've seen the kid break hardcore felons in less than an hour."

"All right," said Charles. "But Mallory was simply behaving like — Mallory. You might as well ask a gun to change its nature. I don't see any intent here, no campaign to drive that woman to suicide."

Their conversation ended with Mallory's approach. And Charles wondered if she could read the guilt in his face. Of course she could — if she wanted to, but Mallory never even looked his way. She sat down on a campstool and settled the computer on her lap. She seemed to want their company, but not their conversation. Her eyes were trained on the glowing screen except for occasional glances at a nearby campfire where a little girl lay asleep on a bedroll.

Joe Finn was struggling to assemble the pup tent without waking his daughter. His son, Peter, was staring at Mallory. The boy was rising now and walking toward her. When Peter came a little closer, Charles could see that his shining young face was at odds with his eyes — the eyes of an old man. The child's walk had purpose in every step he took toward the young detective. He had some serious business with her.

Be careful, boy.

Peter Finn tapped Mallory on the shoulder, but he was unsuccessful in getting her attention away from the computer in her lap.

"What is death?"

"You know what it is," she said, never looking up from the glowing screen.

"But you know more than I do."

Charles closed his eyes. It all made sense. The boy had picked the person least likely to tell a kind lie and most likely to know the truth on this subject.

"Death," said the boy, "tell me about it?"

Eyes still on the screen, she said, "It's the

next thing that happens after life."

"And then?"

Now she did raise her eyes to the boy and gave him a look of mild surprise that asked, *You want more?*

And, no, Charles could see that the boy did not. This life was quite enough, more than enough. Life was hard. The child's idea of heaven was apparently kindred to Mallory's. Simply put: no more of this existence — and nothing more than that.

"My sister Ariel — she's really dead, isn't she?"

"Yes," said Mallory, lover of brevity.

"Well, that's all right then," said the boy. No more of *this* for Ariel. "Will you tell that to my father — so we can go home?"

"You think he'd listen to me?" said Mallory.

Apparently not. His last hope exhausted, the boy turned around and walked away, a hundred years older now.

Charles went after him. "May I talk to you for a moment?"

Peter stopped and turned around, saying, "Please don't tell me that Ariel's in heaven."

Charles knelt down on one knee to be eye level with the boy. "I'll tell you everything I know about heaven. I learned this in Sunday school. Christ said, 'Heaven is all around them and men do not see it.' I think he was onto something there. Personally, I can't imagine anything that can eclipse life. The best part is up ahead, and you don't want to miss that."

He could see that this was cold comfort to a weary child who needed structure and a sense of normalcy if he was to survive. A good start would be something simple like a conventional bed where Peter could lay his head each night. Charles turned to watch the boxer struggle with each rope and stake, trying to work a simple tent into its ultimate shape, all the signs of depression in each failure.

"I'm going to have a talk with your father."

The young fatalist shook his head. "Dad won't listen to you."

As Charles approached Joe Finn, he mentally turned a leaf in the Mallory Book of Hard Truth and Bad Manners. He planned to stab this man in the heart with hard facts. "Ariel is dead, and you know that. She died a long time ago. And your son *wants* to die."

Now that he had all of the boxer's angry attention, Charles turned to look at the man's surviving daughter, awake now, distraught and humming. "And that's gone on much too long. She needs more help than you can give her. I can arrange for a child psychiatrist to work with Dodie. But first you have to go into protective custody in Chicago. It's the police this time, not the FBI."

He sensed the boxer's resistance. The man's closed fists were a clue.

"She's the child most like you," said Charles. "If this pilgrimage doesn't end now, you and Dodie will be rocking side by side, humming in the dark, and your boy will be all alone. And then he'll die. I know you want to do the right thing. That's what this is all about, isn't it? Fathers always go out into the night in search of the lost child. Well, Ariel's *dead.* It's the other two who are lost."

"That's not what the man wants to hear, Charles." Mallory had materialized behind the boxer, making him spin around to face her. She ignored him and spoke only to Charles. "He's not listening to you." She had removed her jacket, and the gun in her shoulder holster was on display. Now she turned to acknowledge Joe Finn, her legs apart, arms slightly bent at her sides. And Charles found this a most interesting moment — a gunslinger squaring off against a pugilist.

"Mr. Finn doesn't want to hear any more crap about denial," said Mallory, eyes on the boxer. "He knows that Ariel's dead, and now he's planning to get even." She glanced at Charles. "If you want to know anything about revenge, you come to me. I've seen it all. I know the signs."

And now it was her turn to go ignored. Joe Finn went back to his chore of planting a tent pole, one of two. Mallory's hand flashed out so fast, he had no time to react before she uprooted the pole and tossed it aside, as if it were merely a toothpick.

"You've got no right —" He shut his mouth when the little girl at his feet began to hum and rock.

"You're stressing her out," said Mallory. "That's the signal, isn't it?" She turned to Charles. "When Dodie hums, there's something going on that she can't handle. A few days ago, Finn noticed it happening more and more — and he was looking around, checking faces for someone to blame. He was looking for the man who killed Ariel."

Mallory circled around the boxer, and he revolved to follow her. She looked down at the child, who was humming softly, rocking slowly. "That's a low-level alert. When Dodie cranks up the sound, that's your cue, Finn. Dodie's your little bird dog. She can't talk, but she can point the way, humming, rocking, scared to death. But what do you care? You're a man on a mission."

"It's not true!"

"Save the lies, okay? You think you can take on a serial killer and win? Well, if you kill the wrong man, maybe you can make a nutcase defense for murder. Maybe Charles was onto something. Plead insanity and you could wind up in Dodie's asylum. Then the two of you can just rock and hum all day."

She turned to Charles. "You wasted your time with him. Dodie won't get any help unless Social Services comes to take her away from her father — if she survives what he's doing to her." Back to the boxer, the target. "This man you're hunting, I'd put good money on him over you. He's a plotter, a stalker, a long-term planner, but you only know how to use your fists."

Charles noticed that Mallory was holding something behind her back, and it was not her gun. The weapon was still resting in its holster.

"I can look after my own," said Joe Finn.

"Ariel gave up her life to save her little sister." Mallory's hidden hand came forward. She held up a photograph of a dead body. It was a teenage girl, dark of hair, blue of eye — Ariel.

"That's not my daughter," said the boxer.

"You know it is," said Mallory. "Look at

her hands, Finn. You *know* how those bruises are made. Your daughter took the first shot. The perp didn't catch Ariel. She attacked him. She was buying the time for Dodie to run."

Mallory put one finger on the crucifix that hung from his neck, pushing it into his skin, as if to brand him. And the boxer seemed powerless to move her hand away.

"Ariel was a hero," said Mallory. "But if you get Dodie killed, then Ariel's death is pointless." She reached for the tent's remaining pole and pulled it up with the mooring stakes, then let it drop to collapse the canvas. The boxer was felled, too, taken down by words and pictures. He turned away from her and called out to his son to come and help with the packing, for they were leaving the caravan.

And the boy came — running, grinning — back to life.

While Riker kept a lookout on the other side of the wall of vehicles, Mallory stood beside Charles, watching the small family pack their belongings into the car. The tent had been discarded, for they would have no more need of it. The little girl stood off to one side, holding a doll, her only valued baggage.

Dale Berman was a very unhappy man. "They'd be better off with the Federal Witness Protection Program."

"Blame it on Kronewald," said Mallory. "He's heard rumors that FBI witnesses are dropping like flies." And the matter was closed. They would proceed with arrangements for the Chicago Police Department's safe house.

Dale Berman rejoined his people, a cluster of agents that included Christine Nahlman and her young partner.

"So you trust them," said Charles, "to get the Finns on the right plane?"

"No," said Mallory, "but the FBI escort isn't my call. It's part of the deal Harry Mars worked out with Kronewald. The case is an official joint venture now — Chicago PD and the feds. Berman's people will deliver the Finns to the airport. That's not negotiable." Mallory glanced at her watch. "Kronewald's plane should be landing soon."

"Well, I don't see how Berman can screw this up — unless he works at it." Charles watched Mallory stroll off with a peculiar, half smile in place and an obvious plan to torture the special agent in charge. And Charles trailed after her — as always.

"So you're riding along," she said to Dale

Berman.

"I'm still in charge." Agent Berman turned back to his clipboard and paperwork. A moment of silence went by, and he realized that she was not quite done with him yet. "Look, Mallory, I've got eight guns, and that's not counting the state trooper. As far as cover goes, this is overkill. Nothing can happen to the Finns."

And still the detective remained silent, letting the agent's imagination do all the work for her. Finally, Dale Berman seemed to grasp the fact that if something *should* happen to that little family, something worse would happen to him. Charles wondered if the hand holding the man's clipboard was slowly descending to the testicles in a subconscious gesture.

If Charles accurately read Mallory's face as she turned away from Berman, she did not trust the man to do this simple thing without damaging a child. Apparently, this was also obvious to Agent Nahlman, who caught up with her some distance away.

"Look," said Nahlman, "my daughter was Dodie's age. I knew the name of her favorite doll. I could even name the doll's boyfriends. I know how to take care of a little girl."

"I know all about your daughter," said

Mallory. "She's dead."

Nahlman bent forward slightly, as if she had taken a blow. Regaining her poise, she said, "I'll be driving the Finns. She'll never be out of my sight. You've got my word. I just want to keep Dodie safe." The agent turned and strode off to her car.

Mallory showed no signs of trust, but neither did she shoot out the tires to prevent the FBI agents from carrying the small family away.

Riker appeared behind Mallory, tapping her shoulder. "What was that business about her kid?"

"Her daughter was shot to death," said Mallory. "The shooter was a neighbor's boy the same age, six years old. They were playing with Nahlman's gun. That's when she started drinking alone — and drinking a lot. She's been in therapy for years."

"You got that from her personnel file?"

"No," she said, "I got that off Dale Berman's personal computer. It was a memo he sent to every agent on this detail — except her. Berman was explaining to the troops why they had to make allowances for Nahlman's little episodes. I'm guessing he meant the times when she stood up to him. Maybe she challenged his orders." Mallory was staring at the group of young agents surrounding Christine Nahlman. "They won't want to work with her again. They don't trust her now. But I do."

Agent Nahlman had just ended a call when Riker reached through the open car window. He took her hand, the one with the cell phone.

"I'm not making a pass at you," he said.

She was still holding the cell phone as the detective pressed the buttons to enter his own number into her electronic address book.

"In case you haven't got it memorized," he said. "You can never have enough backup." Done with this little chore, he did not release her hand. "Now listen carefully, Nahlman, 'cause this happens to be one of my favorite song lyrics, okay?" He gently closed her fingers over the cell phone. "Just call, and I'll be there."

He whistled the tune that went with those words as he moseyed away from the car. And, though she understood that he only wanted to keep her alive, it was her most romantic moment since that old song was new.

19

State troopers had displaced the remaining
FBI agents. By foot and flashlight, they
patrolled the perimeter of the caravan city,
and, courtesy of a local appliance store,
three hundred civilians were watching small
television sets powered by batteries, car
chargers and mobile home outlets.

The camping experience had begun to
wear on Charles Butler. There was no
escape from the constant din of changing
channels, and the glow of TV screens out-
shone the firelights and lanterns. The parents watched the New Mexico manhunt
play out across the state as if this were not
their own story but someone else's drama
— possibly because so much of it was fiction. The news broadcasters aimed to enter-
tain, undeterred by an absence of facts. The
caravan's field reporters had long since
departed, following the night's big story,
and the two detectives from New York City

sat before an open fire and finished the last of their reports to the local authorities.

Charles was somewhat leery of Riker's latest experiment, though he approved the use of an old-fashioned pot. After mingling the water and the grounds, the detective brought the whole mess to a boil and then added cold water.

"It settles the coffee grounds," said Riker, handing a steaming cup to their guest from the state police. "It's called cowboy coffee. Ever tasted it?"

"You bet I have. Finest kind," said the New Mexico investigator with a smile of appreciation for this campfire brew. The two of them alternately sipped hot liquid and picked coffee grounds from their teeth. Charles and Mallory abstained.

And now their guest informed them that Paul Magritte had never regained consciousness after surgery. "Sorry, folks. He's dead," said the local man. "But it was good of the doctor to mark that bastard for us." He turned to Mallory as he traced a line on his neck. "That's how the old man described the cut?"

"Yeah," said Riker, answering for his partner.

Mallory was distracted and perhaps tired of repeating herself in interviews with state and local police. Her face was lifted to the sky. Charles doubted that she was stargazing, for heaven could not compete with the surrounding illumination of fires and flashlights, lanterns and scores of glowing television screens. Their own campfire was bright enough to light up Magritte's blood on Mallory's blue jeans and her shoes, but more alarming than that, one of the laces on her running shoes had come undone and gone unnoticed. And there were other breaks with her compulsive neatness. She was wearing yesterday's clothes, and some of her fingernails were broken and ragged.

For a short time, Charles had forgotten that he loved her, and he saw her with a clinical eye. She caught him in the act of taking mental notes, and he turned his eyes elsewhere to keep her from reading his every thought — his fears. He stared at her untied shoelace.

The state's investigator was leafing through his notebook, and now he found a page he liked. "We got the make of the vehicle from the tire treads at the crime scene. So you can leave the rest to us. We'll get him." He looked out over the great circle of television screens. "At least he won't be picking off any more of these folks."

"Don't count on him keeping that jeep

for long," said Riker, surprising the man who had not shared the vehicle model. "He's an experienced car thief."

"I'll bear that in mind." And it was clear by the tone of voice that this investigator did not care to hear any more helpful tips from the New York contingent of the law. "Our boy made a real good choice for off-road driving, so I expect he'll keep it awhile, and we won't find him on the interstate. You should get some rest tonight. A manhunt's best left to people who know the terrain."

The two detectives, manhunters extraordinaire, appeared to be too tired to find any humor in this.

Done with his coffee, the New Mexico man bid a hasty good night and left them.

A cell phone beeped, and Riker said, "It's not mine."

"It's Magritte's." Mallory went digging in her knapsack.

Charles could not recall any mention of her pocketing the doctor's cell phone, not while the state investigator was making note of all her other details. Until this moment, he had no idea that Paul Magritte had owned one of these devices.

Mallory pulled out a phone that was so large, even Charles could recognize it as an antique by the standards of modern technology. "Analog," she said with distaste. Extending an antenna, more proof of antiquity, she said, "Hello?" After listening for a moment, she lowered the antenna. "Another hang up."

"No caller ID?" asked Riker.

"Nothing that fancy." She turned the phone over in her hand, examining it as if it were an interesting artifact from an old-world culture. "No voice mail either. I'm surprised it works at all."

Charles stared at her chipped red nail polish, regarding each fingernail as an independent wound. "The calls might be from Dr. Magritte's patients. They hear a woman's voice and think it's a wrong number."

"Maybe." Mallory returned the phone to her knapsack. "I've got Kronewald's people working the cell-phone records." She picked up her knapsack, rose to her feet and walked away from them.

"Wait!" Charles called out to her, making long strides to catch up with her, because Mallory waited for nobody. Circling round the young detective, he blocked her way and held her by the shoulders, forcing her to stand still. And now he released her to kneel down in the dirt at her feet. He tied her loose shoelace, so afraid that she might trip and fall. It was the sort of service one did for a child, yet she allowed it.

He was still kneeling there, head bowed, when she moved on.

"Very classy." Riker appeared at his side, leaning down to offer a hand up. "I gotta remember that move."

On his feet again, Charles watched Mallory drive away. "Where could she be going at this hour?"

"My guess? A five-star hotel," said the detective. "Camping really isn't her style."

Nearby, the few remaining FBI agents and the two disgraced moles were seated around a single portable television set. They were all so young.

"So who's in charge here?"

Riker clapped a hand on his friend's shoulder, saying, "Me and thee."

Agent Christine Nahlman passed the first sign for the Albuquerque International Airport. Before she could use the turn signal, another agent's car swung into the lane alongside her, matching her speed. She was going to miss the exit for the airport road. Hand signals were useless, and the agent in the other car would not respond to her horn. Mannequinlike, he stared at the road ahead. And now they rolled past the exit and continued west on Interstate 40.

What in hell was going on?

Calling the SAC for an explanation was not an option. Dale Berman had forbidden cell-phone contact, no incoming or outgoing calls. And that troubled her, too. She could think of no scenario where that made any sense, but she had long ago ceased to hunt for logic in command decisions.

She turned to her partner. Barry Allen's face was placid, though he must have seen her boxed into this lane; the boy was green but not blind. Damn him. He had known that they would miss the airport road. That was the plan. Her partner, a good little soldier, had yet to question a single order from Dale Berman. However, this was hardly a good time to accuse Agent Allen of conspiring against her.

Nahlman watched Joe Finn's reflection in her rearview mirror. Apparently, the boxer had seen nothing amiss. He was wholly concentrated on his children — reading to them from a book of fairy tales that they were much too old for. Yet they listened to his every word, loving this attention from him. Dodie seemed like any normal child, like Peter, enraptured by the sound of her father's voice, eyes on the big man's face, unable to get enough of him.

The construction zone ahead was a divided highway. Opposing traffic was separated by high retaining walls. Two lanes of westbound vehicles moved through the narrow canyon of concrete, and Nahlman was reminded of a cattle chute in a slaughterhouse. It went on for miles before she could see ahead to a break in the wall. And then she heard the words that she had been waiting for, counting on.

"I have to pee," said the little boy in the back seat. "Dodie does, too. See? She's squirmy. Can we stop?"

"Yes, we can," said Nahlman. The timing was perfect. She had already spotted the sign for the next gas station, and it carried a warning: the turnoff beyond the construction zone would be a sharp one.

"Call in the toilet stop."

"We're not supposed to use the cells," Agent Allen reminded her. "Dale said —"

"Agent — *Barry,* you know you can't use the car radio. Too many private police scanners on the road. So use your cell phone and blame it on me." Her eyes were on the car driving alongside her, herding her, locking her into a lane with no turns. The exit sign was in view when she leaned toward her partner and raised her voice. "That's an *order!*"

A cell phone was quickly pressed to Barry Allen's ear. "No answer," he said. "Dale's going to be pissed off about — What're you *doing?*"

Nahlman moved into the occupied lane, forcing the other vehicle into the retaining wall. The other agent's car was dropping back as sparks went flying in the scrape of metal on concrete. And now the lane was hers alone.

Agent Allen's mouth hung open and his eyes bugged out.

Nahlman glanced at the rearview mirror. The boxer was still reading, turning pages of the storybook, but young Peter, eyes on the passenger window, whispered, "Cool."

Mallory was a hundred miles short of Gallup, New Mexico. The top was down, the night was fine, and I-40 was light on traffic. The construction zone was like an arcade game, zinging through curves bound by concrete barriers. On the other side of the zone, out on the open road again, there was no sign of the Finns' FBI escort.

Good.

Evidently Dale Berman had ceased to play the fool long enough to find his way to the airport road.

She drove faster until the speedometer's

needle could be pushed no farther, and she was pleasantly surprised. Back in Kansas, Ray Adler had given her more than a roll bar. He must have tweaked the factory settings on her Porsche engine. The hump of the Volkswagen ragtop had previously cut her speed to one-eighty, but now she was doing two hundred and ten miles an hour.

Thank you, Ray.

This was truly a race, for she was bone tired. Before sleep could overtake her, there was one more landmark to see, and, once there, she could close her eyes to doze and dream, though dreams exhausted her.

Waking or sleeping she was always driving this road.

The Chicago detective's traveling companion was high on the FBI food chain, the Assistant Director of Criminal Investigations, and the airplane seats were first class — courtesy of taxpayers everywhere. Between the Illinois airport and their current holding pattern over New Mexico, the only useful information Kronewald had obtained from this man was a telling protest.

"I haven't memorized the name of every damned field agent," said Harry Mars. "Sorry, I can't recall an Agent Cadwaller."

Detective Kronewald took this denial as

confirmation that Cadwaller was Washington's spy in Dale Berman's field office. "Well, the guy's supposed to have a background in profiling. Does that help any?"

In a further evasion, Harry Mars launched into another Lou Markowitz story that began with "That wonderful old bastard" and ended with "So what do you think of Lou's kid?"

"Ah, Mallory." Kronewald forced a smile. His irritation was growing. He knew that Mallory must have done some dirty backroom deal with the fed beside him. But something big was definitely going down — that much was clear. The Bureau's assistant directors did not run errands; Harry Mars was here to take over and run his own game.

Detective Kronewald had grown weary of being sidetracked and *handled.* Leaning toward his window, he looked down on the landing lights of Albuquerque International and began the prelude to his best shot. "So, you think Dale Berman can do this one little thing without screwing it up?"

The man from Washington checked his watch. "He'll be waiting with the Finns when we land."

"Only if you're sure Dale doesn't know what you've got planned for him."

Gold!

The AD's composure had been fractured, and Kronewald knew he was on to something. In the past hour, Harry Mars had racked up four failed attempts to make a cell-phone connection, and the Chicago detective did not buy the story that this bureaucrat was calling his wife. So Mars had lost contact with his people on the ground.

The plane touched down on the runway with a bump and then another in a not-so-smooth landing.

An omen?

Joe Finn was waiting by the door to the ladies' room when Nahlman emerged hand-in-hand with Dodie. The boxer had only been parted from his daughter because neither child could wait. Now he scooped Dodie up in his arms and carried her off to the aisle of chewing gum, a staple of every child's road-trip diet.

A state trooper had been watching Nahlman's back during the potty detail, and now the man faced the convenience store window. "That boss of yours is a real piece of work."

She followed the track of the officer's eyes. Dale Berman was outside in the parking lot, casually leaning back against his show-and-tell exhibit, a car missing paint on the side where she had forced an agent to drive it into a concrete barrier.

The state trooper stood beside her, and his voice was low, confidential. "Just for the record, ma'am, that was a real fine piece of driving tonight. I'd bail out of this detail, too, if I could." He nodded toward the window on the parking lot and her boss. "You should talk to that asshole about using the radio." Before she could ask what he meant by that, the trooper turned smartly on his heel, saying over one shoulder, "While you take care of that, I'll get these folks back to the car." He walked toward the small family standing by the cash register.

When Nahlman stepped out of the convenience store, Berman pointed to the damaged area of the other agent's vehicle, saying to her so calmly, "Nobody has to pee that bad."

Agent Allen had a worried look about him as he hovered at the edge of this conversation. Nahlman smiled. She could not trust her partner; he was Berman's creature now, but she could appreciate Barry Allen's concern for her. She turned her eyes to Special Agent Berman, saying, "If we don't turn around right now and head back to the airport road, we'll miss the plane to Chicago."

"We're not going to Albuquerque International. Our destination is an airport on the other side of Gallup."

This seemed to reassure her partner, but not Nahlman. "That's an air force base."

"And a more secure location," said Special Agent Berman. "Excuse me if I don't share every damn detail with you. Your only job tonight was to follow the car ahead of you, and you botched that. Oh, and don't let me catch you using a cell phone one more time." He turned around to glare at Agent Allen. "Got that, son?"

"Yes, sir." Barry Allen stood at attention, holding up his phone to show his boss that it was not turned on.

"Now yours," said Berman.

Nahlman pulled out her cell phone and depressed the button to turn it off.

Dale Berman turned to Barry Allen, saying, "Thanks to your partner, I'm missing two cars that couldn't make that hairpin turn. That's four agents, four guns." Whipping around to face Nahlman, he said, "If anything goes wrong tonight, it's on your head." He walked to the nearby state police cruiser. The trooper was keeping his eye on the Finns when the agent in charge leaned down to his window, pointed at the radio and asked, "You mind?"

The trooper nodded and passed the radio handset to Berman, stringing its cord through the window. The officer then turned his eyes to Nahlman and gave her a shrug that said, *I told you so.*

Dale Berman had made contact with his lost agents, and now he was directing them to fuel up their cars at the nearest gas station. "Then pull over and wait. Our next rendezvous has no gas pumps. It's a few hours down the road, a highway rest stop just past Exit 96."

Nahlman shook her head, incredulous, but kept the edge out of her voice. She was long accustomed to Berman's style of baiting. Normally, she was not inclined to state the obvious; she said this for her partner's benefit. "So all the other car radios are tuned to the trooper's frequency?"

"Well, we've got a trooper in the party, don't we?" Berman thanked the officer and returned the handset.

"Police scanners are as common as dirt on —"

"Shut up, Nahlman." The man's back was turned on her partner, and he could not see the younger agent's well-scrubbed face coming to terms with this advertisement of their position. Barry Allen's perfect world was cracking, and Dale Berman's great-guy status was now in some doubt.

A small win.

Berman grabbed the keys from her hand and tossed them to her partner. "Barry, you've got the wheel from now on." He turned back to Nahlman, saying, oh so casually, "No more hysterics in front of your passengers, okay?"

The manager of the El Rancho Hotel had never before been interrogated by a detective. It was difficult to take his eyes off the gun in her shoulder holster. And he still could not fathom his crime.

All the other guests *liked* their rooms.

"No," he said in answer to her accusation about renovations, "it was a *restoration*. Quite a difference, you see. Everything is the same." His sweeping gesture took in the spacious lobby with its elegant appointments and a southwest flavor of the nineteen forties. The upper gallery was lined with photographs of famous actors from a more glamorous era of black-and-white movies. Indeed, every day when he came to work, he felt as though he had stepped into just such a film, staring up at the grand staircase and waiting for the stars to come down.

"And the autographs are authentic, too. They all stayed here while they were filming on location —"

"What about my *room?*" The young detective glared at him with strange green eyes that called him a liar. "The furniture is *new.*"

"Oh, the *rooms* were renovated. The furniture was replaced with —"

"It's all different now."

He gave up. "You're right." When a hotel guest carried a gun, this enhanced the meaning of his motto: The guest is always right. "Everything changes." And, by that, he meant life, the universe — everything outside of his *restored* lobby. "Nothing stays the same." He saw the disappointment flicker in her eyes and forgot to be afraid of her. "I'm so sorry."

Riker stretched out on Joe Finn's abandoned sleeping bag. The fire was dying, and Charles Butler was keeping him awake — by thinking. "Okay, I give up. What's bothering you?"

"It's the cell phone," said Charles. "I didn't even know that Dr. Magritte had one until Mallory pulled it out of that knapsack. One thing the doctor and I had in common was an avid dislike for those things. He said it was like a sword hanging over your head. You can't get away from the world if you carry a cell phone. But now it turns out that he actually owned one."

"Well, the old man had patients calling him."

"No, that's not it. You said that phone was what? Six, seven years old? Dr. Magritte left his regular practice twelve years ago. His Internet groups meet online. The patients might have e-mailed him, but they never telephoned. Now, if he bought one just for the road trip, it would be a new phone, wouldn't it?"

"Maybe he borrowed it from a friend," said Riker. "They do come in handy on the road."

"Is there any way to verify that?"

"Sure thing." The tired detective pulled out his own cell. "Kronewald should know everything about that damn phone by now."

Click.
The camera flash had taken Pearl by surprise.

And the man with the camera had also looked damned surprised to see her step out of the tow truck.

Well, most of her customers had that same reaction. Pearl Walters was a robust woman and a first-rate mechanic. She had thirty years of experience in every automotive problem that could make a car break down on the road.

She did not offer to shake hands with the man. That put most people off. Though her hands were clean, her fingernails were not quite up to par. Grit and oil went deep where a cleaning rag could not follow. Pearl's coveralls were greasy and her boots were showing some fresh spots. Her bright orange vest was stained with years of motor-oil adventures under the carriage of one car or another, but it still came in handy on a dark night. Oncoming traffic could spot the reflective orange a mile away. Parking lots were her favorite place to do business. Yes, this was a good safe spot to work on a car without dodging damn fools asleep at the wheel.

Tonight's customer was not a talkative man, but then his problem required no explanation. That front tire was just as flat as could be.

"No jack," was all he said to her.

"No problem," said Pearl, coming right back at him. "I'll have you on the road in no time at all." She knelt down to set up her jack and never felt the pain as a knife slid across her throat. It was more a feeling of wonder.

What the hell?

Hands from behind her pulled open the snaps of her orange vest before she could splatter it with her blood.

Click.

Dale Berman turned to the young agent at the wheel. "See any likely comers yet?"

"No, sir," said the rookie, glancing at his rearview mirror. "Nobody's following us. You really think he'd try to kill that little girl with all these agents around?"

"You bet I do. I invited him to the party." Berman lit a cigar, leaned back and smiled. "I'll tell you how we usually catch these bastards. They get too damn cocky. After a while they do something really stupid."

"But, sir, this killer's been active for thirty or forty years."

"Where'd you hear that? From Nahlman?" Her name was said with derision. He continued his monologue on the serial killer, a rare species he had never encountered in all his years with the Bureau. "This guy's at the end of his run. His little rituals are falling apart. No more throat slashing. He's running people down with a damn car. Panic kills. So all his careful detailing — that's gone to hell. This is his last shot at the kid. He won't come at us with a plan this time. He'll just come running, and we'll see him a mile off."

The driver kept silent. Perhaps the boy had a contrary theory of his own, or maybe he objected to child-size bait.

In Dale Berman's view, it was bad for morale when the kids did their own thinking. "Now, our guy was getting reckless even before I put the pressure on." He had allowed all of his agents to assume that transporting the Finns tonight had been his own idea and not the direct order of Harry Mars. "The perp's really frantic now." As if Dodie Finn could ever give him away. Crazy Dodie. Dale closed his eyes, saying to his driver, "Wake me the second we pick up another car on our tail."

Special Agent Berman feigned the sleep that angst would not allow. It was an all-or-nothing kind of night.

Assistant Director Harry Mars had taken to making his futile phone calls outside of Kronewald's hearing. And now he connected to yet another field agent's voice mail. In his last hope for a rational explanation, he turned to the man beside him, the liaison from the New Mexico State Police. "Is there any chance that my people could be driving through a zone where their cells won't work?"

"No, sir, not between the campsite and the airport. This ain't the Bermuda Triangle." The New Mexico man pulled out his own cell phone. "We got a trooper riding point. I can ask his barracks commander to raise him on the radio if you like. It's your call, sir. Me, I wouldn't want to broadcast anything covert on that frequency. Too public."

A few yards away, the detective from Chicago was taking a call of his own, raising his voice to be heard above the static of airport traffic. "Riker!" yelled Kronewald. "My plane landed twenty minutes ago. Where's the feds and the Finns?" Apparently, Riker's answer was unsatisfactory. Kronewald jammed his phone in his coat pocket.

Harry Mars tried one more number and had no luck reaching Mallory, but then she never answered to anyone.

Christine Nahlman turned her head to look at the passengers in the back seat. The children were sleeping in Joe Finn's arms. The boxer's eyes were also closed, but she had seen him go from deep sleep to full alert. Was he only dozing?

Ah, snoring, a sign that Joe Finn was finally beginning to trust her.

Agent Barry Allen drove with his eyes on the road, but his mind was obviously elsewhere. After the incident with the trooper's radio, he was probably questioning everything he had ever been told from kindergarten on. When he did look her way, Nahlman saw the face of a puppy that had made a mess on the carpet.

Finally, she had won his soul back from Dale Berman.

Riker hunkered down by the agents' campfire. In the manner of a parent on a school night, he turned off their portable television set. Five pairs of very young eyes turned to him.

"I'm making a run to the airport." The detective handed a slip of paper to the oldest agent, the only one who was sporting a day's growth of beard. "That's my cell. You got any trouble, call me right away."

"I can't," said the agent. "No cell-phone contact."

Riker smiled at the boy for a moment, not quite believing what he was hearing. "What? Are you nuts?"

"Dale Berman's orders, sir. No incoming or outgoing calls."

Riker held out his hand, palm up. "Give me your cell phone."

The rookie agent, so accustomed to following orders without question, handed it over. The detective turned it on, then pressed the menu buttons and held the phone to his ear. After listening a moment, he said, "You're stacking up voice mail from Assistant Director Harry Mars." He returned the phone to the startled agent. "Does that make you nervous, kid? It should." And now they were all turning on their phones. As he walked away from them, he heard the beeps of their incoming calls.

It took three seconds for the import to settle in — Dale, that son of a bitch — and Riker traveled from a mosey to a dead run across the campground. Opening the door of the waiting Mercedes, he told his friend to move over. "No, offense, Charles, but I need some speed." The siren was wailing, wheels churning up dust, and they were off.

Nahlman fixed the layout in her mind as Allen pulled up to the walkway and cut the engine. This was the long parking lot of an ersatz comfort stop for interstate travelers. Two outlying buildings of cinderblock housed toilets, and the center structure was an open arcade of maps and locked vending machines. A separate lot for trucks and motor homes held three big rigs, but there was no sign of the drivers; they were probably napping in the back of their cabs. In the slots reserved for smaller vehicles, a tow truck was parked a few spaces away from an SUV. On the far side of the picnic tables was another parking lot for cars. A man in workman's coveralls and a bright orange vest was pulling bags from the large trash receptacles.

Government vehicles rolled into the slots on either side of her car. Doors slammed and flashlights came out though the lot was well lit.

In the back seat, Peter was wide awake and antsy, ready for another toilet call. Joe Finn roused his daughter and asked if she wanted to use the little girls' room. It was a revelation to Nahlman when the child responded to her father's voice with a nod. And now came a moment when the girl's eyes fluttered open and the vacant look was gone. She seemed so normal in that second, fully cognizant of her surroundings. Was the girl truly insane or very sanely hiding out from the greater adult world? Nahlman's last thought was that she was merely tired and reading too much into the simple nod of a little girl. But suspicion was a lingering thing. Perhaps Dodie Finn could teach her father something about the extremes of distrust.

Nahlman had one hand on the door when she said to her partner, "Wait till another agent clears the men's room. And before you go in, make sure you've got somebody watching your back."

Allen nodded, taking no offense that she repeated these simple rules to him for the second time in one night. He was looking about him, utterly focused, remembering what she had taught him about burning the landscape into his brain. At last, she was confident that he would not be taken by surprise, not tonight.

"There you are," said Dale Berman, upon finding one of his rookies entering the ladies' room. "Start checking those rigs in the parking lot."

"I've haven't cleared the restroom, sir."

"I'm on it," he said with a smile for his prettiest and greenest agent. He entered the ladies' room with his gun drawn and checked all the stalls. When he came out again, he was met by a park attendant in coveralls and an orange vest. The man was carrying a green plastic trash receptacle on one shoulder.

"Make it fast," said Dale Berman, standing to one side so the man could pass into the ladies' room. And now he saw another rookie standing around with his hands in his pockets. What the hell was this idiot called? Ah, he had it now. He clapped a hand on the young man's shoulder. "Hey, Bobby. I need you to help the trooper." He pointed to the parking lot on the other side of the building. "He's checking the perimeter."

"Who the hell is Agent Cadwaller?" Harry Mars broke off this phone conversation with one of the field agents left behind at the campsite. He was watching the action beyond the lineup of waiting cabs. He recognized the detective, though he had never seen the man move so fast in the old days. Riker sprinted across the lanes of moving traffic. Brakes squealed. Horns honked. And now the New York cop came to a dead stop at the glass doors where Kronewald was standing, and he grabbed the older man by one arm.

Oh, what fresh crap is this?

With a new sense of urgency, Harry Mars turned back to his conversation with a rookie agent. He cut short the youngster's report on the mysterious and now unaccounted for Agent Cadwaller. "Get on the fucking road, *all* of you! The troopers can guard the parents." And they would probably do a better job of it. "I don't give a shit about Dale Berman's orders, and I don't care about the speed limit, either. Get *moving!*"

He turned to see Detective Kronewald piling into the back seat of a Mercedes. A portable siren was slapped on the roof of the car, and now it was screaming through the airport complex.

The boy read the sign for the ladies' room and shook his head. No, he was not going in there. Though Peter was doing that little dance of legs pressed together, he was determined to pee standing up beside his father in the men's room. Joe Finn was loath to let go of his daughter until the last moment. Still distrustful, he gave up Dodie's small hand to Agent Nahlman.

Dale Berman sauntered over to the opening in the wall and the short corridor that led to the ladies' room. "Get on with it, Nahlman. The kid's gotta go." Dale smiled at the father in apology for his agent's slowness, and Joe Finn did not knock the man cold, though both his hands were tight fists.

Dubious, Nahlman turned to the opening. "The room is clear?"

"You had to ask?" Berman shrugged in Agent Allen's direction, code to say, *You see what I have to put up with?* "Yes! I checked it myself." In fact, he had checked it twice, unable to account for the park attendant's departure. And now he was certain. "It's clear."

Barry Allen turned around, moving stiffly as he led Joe Finn and his son toward the men's room on the other side of the building. The agent was only a few steps away when he heard Dale Berman say, "What are you waiting for, Nahlman? I got your back."

With these last words, Agent Allen made a small stumble.

Charles handed the cell phone back to Riker. "Sorry. Agent Nahlman's not taking calls. Her messages are going to voice mail."

Riker nodded, pocketing his phone and pressing his foot on the gas pedal. "You remember what time the Finns left the campsite? I don't think the FBI escort is in a big hurry right now. So figure the speed limit and —"

"Got it," said Charles, anticipating Riker's request, computing figures and reviewing the maps in his mind. "If you can maintain a hundred miles an hour, you'll catch up to them in about forty minutes."

"He's a genius," said the Chicago detective, not realizing that this was actually true. Kronewald reached over the front seat to slap Charles on the shoulder. "I love this guy. So back to your problem with Magritte's cell phone. Well, the doctor's not listed with any wireless outfit. He's not paying the bills either."

"Spit it out, you bastard," said Riker. "What've you got?"

"It wasn't Magritte's phone. The doctor's got credit cards out the wazoo and a nice healthy bank balance, but the phone bills get paid a year in advance by money order. Interesting, huh? It gets better. I sent a guy out to the address where the statements go. It's a graveyard. That phone's gotta belong to our killer. He dropped it at the scene after he killed the old man."

"No," said Charles. "I think it belonged to Dr. Magritte."

"Why?"

"Because it's *old.*"

Kronewald answered the beep of his own cell phone, listened for a moment, and then said, "Good job." He leaned over the seat. "That was Harry Mars. There's a state trooper riding with the feds. But he's not responding to the radio. Now that might mean something. Or maybe the guy's just taking a leak by the side of the road."

The state trooper was looking down at the asphalt. More interesting than the pool of blood was the fact that someone had attempted to hide it with a thin sprinkling of soil. He followed a trail of red drops to the locked SUV. With his flashlight pressed against the window, he could make out black plastic trash bags blanketing the bulky shape on the back seat. After breaking the window and unlocking the vehicle, he opened the door to pull back the covering plastic. Now he stared into the wide eyes of a middle-aged woman dressed only in her underwear and work boots — a dead woman.

He turned to the young agent beside him. "You might wanna go get your boss."

Oh, how that young girl could run.

While he waited for her to return with Special Agent Berman, the trooper took a close look at the Medic Alert tag that announced Pearl Walters' allergy to penicillin. Next, he opened the glove compartment. It was not her name on the vehicle registration.

Christine Nahlman was about to lean down and flush the toilet for Dodie, but this time the child smiled shyly and flushed it herself.

Was there another noise riding below the sound of the rushing water?

Agent Nahlman turned her back to the child before she pulled out her gun. Walking around the open stall door, she checked the room's common area. The lid of the green garbage pail was now on the floor.

And the pail was empty.

Someone had come in and emptied the trash on Berman's watch. Well, great — just great. *Son of a bitch.*

Dodie was humming.

The child was coming up behind her.

No, not Dodie — someone else.

The wound did not register at first. Nahlman never saw the knife as it slashed her throat. She watched it happen in the mirror, light sparking on metal, the red spreading from ear to ear. In that first second of shock, even a little girl could have taken her gun away. After it was knocked from her hand, she heard it skittering across the floor when he kicked it. Nahlman spun around and slipped in her own blood. Her head hit the tiled wall, and she was going down, leaving a slick red trail as she slid to the floor.

Dale Berman stared at the dead stranger in the back seat of the SUV. "Well, the missing clothes — that's new, but the slashed throat — yeah, our guy did this. He's here." Berman turned to the gathering of agents. "Okay, people," he said, clapping his hands. "We're gonna make another sweep of the area, all the buildings, the grounds and those rigs in the lot."

The trooper was standing by his cruiser, the radio receiver in one hand, as he called out, "Her name's Pearl Walters and she drives a —"

"Yeah, yeah — good to know," said Berman, losing patience with this plodding state cop. He turned to the road leading back onto the highway. "Why isn't somebody watching that exit?" He looked down at the rookie who had fetched him to this new crime scene. "That's pretty basic. I shouldn't have to spell out every little thing. Get on it. Now! Nobody leaves." He looked up at the trooper as the man joined them. "I need you to find that park attendant. Get him to help with the —"

"*Listen* to me!" said the trooper, who did not care what the special agent in charge wanted. Apparently he did not find Dale Berman all that special. "There are *no* park attendants this time of night. And Pearl Walters drives a tow truck." He pointed to the other side of the grounds and the second lot. "There was one over there, and now it's gone."

Christine Nahlman put her hand to the wound that spanned her throat, as if she could close the long gash that way. Her second thought was to fire her weapon to summon help. She had heard the gun fall, but could not see it anywhere.

Blood flooded down the front of her blouse to pool in her lap. Vocal cords cut, only gurgles came from her mouth. Shock was a hammer. Thought was slow. She pulled the cell phone from her pocket. Wasted effort. Who would answer? No one here would even have a cell phone turned on.

She worked the buttons for the named entries and found Riker. As she depressed the button to call him, she was dying — and she knew it.

But what of Dodie?

Speech was impossible. One chance only. Riker's phone would be turned on. It would print out the name of his silent caller. Yes, now they were connected. She could hear his voice.

"Nahlman? You okay?"

Oh, no. She was draining of blood and life.

"Talk to me," he said to her, begged of her.

Sorry, so sorry.

She heard the sound of other conversations, asides to other people, Riker saying, "Something's wrong."

Her eyes closed, her heart slowed.

"I'm on the way," he said to her.

The cell phone clattered to the floor, and she was no longer there to hear him say, "Nahlman, hold on."

She could not wait. She was dead. She was gone.

20

Peter Finn stood beside the urinal and watched Agent Allen frowning, puzzling over a cell phone with a dark screen. Was it broken? No, for now the FBI man decided to turn it on. The small device in his hand came to life and beeped. The agent raised the phone to his ear, saying, "Allen here. . . . Riker?"

The FBI agent left the men's room on the run, and Peter had his father all to himself, though Joe Finn was behind the closed door of a stall.

Better that way.

The boy had been waiting for this moment for so long. "Dad?" He pressed his forehead to the cool metal of the stall door and asked, "Do you hate me — because I lived — and Ariel died?"

There was a moment of silence, and then he heard his father crying.

■ ■ ■ ■

Barry Allen ran past the startled agent guarding the entrance to the men's room. He was heading for the other facility. All that Riker had said was, "Get to Nahlman now!"

As he rounded the side of the building, he saw Dale Berman in the far-off parking lot. Who was watching Nahlman's back?

No one, fool.

The young agent entered the ladies' room at a dead run and went flying, skidding on the slick floor — falling and landing on Nahlman's body — his face pressed to hers. He screamed, but not out of fear. It was a high keen of anguish that brought other agents running into the tiled room. Shoes were all around him now, and above him were voices all taking at once. "Jesus Christ," said one. And another agent, the son of a doctor, knelt beside the body. This young man never tried to find a pulse; he was informed by the gaping wound that had opened Nahlman's throat; the blood had ceased to flow — no living heart to pump it. He shook his head — no beat, no life, no use. "I'm sorry, Barry."

A voice was yelling from Barry Allen's cell

phone. Another agent picked it up from the floor and made her short report to Detective Riker. "She's gone, sir."

The state trooper concluded his radio request for backup and roadblocks at exits east and west of the rest stop. He was behind the wheel of his cruiser when he leaned out the window with a few final words for Special Agent Berman. "Don't *touch* anything. There's a crime-scene unit on the way. I'm going after that tow truck."

"I'm in charge of this investigation," said Berman, raising his voice to be heard above the revving of the other man's engine.

"Yeah, sure you are," yelled the trooper as he peeled out of the parking lot, siren screaming.

Berman turned to see a gang of agents converging upon him. "Spread out!" he yelled. "I want this whole place —"

Oh, shit!

Joe Finn was muscling the others aside, and the man's eyes were crazed.

Agent Allen was younger and faster than Finn, running, flying, aiming himself like a cannonball. In the next second, Berman was flat on his back with the younger man on top him. Allen, handicapped by eyes full of tears, only got in two good punches to the face before he was pulled off. As he was being dragged back by other agents, Barry Allen screamed, "You stupid, incompetent son of a bitch!"

No man or woman in his company had any disagreement with this assessment of the special agent in charge. Cell phones were appearing in every pair of hands.

Dale Berman looked up at the sky, listening to beeps of incoming calls drowned out by the boxer's screams of "Dodie! My baby!"

They were close to the reststop where Agent Christine Nahlman had died.

"I'm sorry about your friend," said Charles Butler. "I'll drive if you like. I think I've got the hang of speeding now."

Riker shook his head, only glancing at the exit sign in passing. He would deal with Nahlman's death tomorrow. A child was missing. Seconds counted. Yet miles farther on, he left the interstate for a segment of the older, slower road.

"Good thinking," said Kronewald after fifteen miles of dark highway. "That's gotta be it." He was staring at the abandoned tow truck parked on a side road. "I knew he wouldn't keep it long." The Chicago detective scrambled out of the car to train a light on the dirt road that joined the paved one. "Yeah, he had a car stashed here." The beam of his flashlight followed the other route. "Looks like our man's heading north."

"Not for long," said Riker. "This was just too easy, but get the troopers on it. We're going back on the interstate. We're going west."

"What the hell for?"

"That's the way Mallory went," said Charles Butler, and when this did not enlighten the man from Chicago, he added, "It's about the old phone."

"I wanted the Alan Ladd room," wrote Peyton Hale. *"He was the star of my favorite western. But tonight, the William Bendix room was the only one they had left."*

All that remained of his stay in this place was the window view of a backstreet in Gallup, New Mexico. Mallory sat on the hotel bed amid her father's scattered letters, looking for more clues to the man, but all she found was a dated love affair with his road. The pages of creased paper fell from her hands as she wrapped herself in her own arms for comfort.

Time — how much time had passed before she began to rock back and forth — just like Dodie Finn?

Crazy Dodie.

Is this how it ends?

Mallory sat very still — hyper alert. Dr Magritte's cell phone was beeping. She plunged one hand into the knapsack, wrenched out the phone and raised its antenna, saying, "It's you, isn't it?"

"You're sure about this?" asked Riker.

"Absolutely," said Charles. "The El Rancho Hotel was on her list of landmarks." And now he had made a connection via an information operator. He spoke to a man on the hotel's night desk, then concluded his call. "She's there. They've gotten to know her quite well. But she's not taking any calls."

"What else is new," said Kronewald.

"And," said Charles, "they don't plan to push any notes under her door, nothing like that."

"Dodie's running out of time," said Riker.

"What?" Kronewald leaned over the front seat to grip the other detective's shoulder. "You know that little girl's dead, right? That's a big part of this perp's signature. He kills 'em quick."

An old pickup truck drove west on the interstate, heading toward the Arizona border, and the driver was abiding by the posted speed limit.

In the bed of the truck, sat a large green plastic trashcan with a lid battened down by rope. It rocked. It hummed.

"Yeah, that's right." Kronewald sounded less than enthusiastic as he spoke on the cell phone to the liaison from the state police. "This guy's a great car thief."

"He only takes junkers," said Riker, interrupting. "Tell them that. No alarms, no Lo-Jack."

Kronewald relayed this to the liaison, adding, "That should narrow it down." He covered the phone as he called out to Riker in the front seat. "You're dead sure about the direction?" With the nod of the other man's head, he said to the liaison, "We figure the perp stole a car with Arizona plates. He'll wanna blend in when he crosses the state line." Kronewald pocketed his phone. "They're checking stolen car reports from Arizona."

Riker sent his passengers lurching forward when he slammed on the brakes in the parking lot of the El Rancho Hotel. "There she is." The detective left the Mercedes and ran toward her.

Charles was watching at the side window

when Mallory flung a duffel bag into the back seat of her convertible. Her silver car was in motion before Riker reached it. He gripped the edge of a door, running alongside her. And now he dived into the front seat. The man's right leg could be seen hanging out in the wind as Mallory sped away with her uninvited passenger.

Click.

After the mooring ropes were untied, the green plastic trashcan was unloaded from the back of the old pickup truck. Once he had the receptacle on the ground, he tipped it over on its side, removed the lid and stood back quickly. The child huddled inside showed no signs of wanting to come out. She was silent, no humming, no rocking, and her eyes had the vacant look of no one home.

"Come out," he said. When she made no response, he lifted the can at one end and spilled her out on the ground. She lay motionless in the dirt. "Stand up," he commanded.

Their eyes connected for a second, and then hers drifted away. He wondered if she somehow knew that he could not bear to touch her. Maybe she had guessed as much when he had used the lid to herd her inside the trashcan. There had been a moment then when their skins had touched, and he had drawn back from her with revulsion. And fear — had she seen that, too?

Did she understand the power she had over him?

Tonight, there was a touch of dark respect for Dodie Finn, and he had no plans to lay one hand upon her; he would sooner jump into a sea of wriggling cockroaches.

It was his way to carefully consider every possibility, and children, particularly little girls, were not to be underestimated. His sister, Mary, had terrorized him every day toward the end of her very short life, and one outstretched hand had been her only weapon. His father had called him a sissy boy — until Mary disappeared. That day, he had only to smile at his father, and the big man knew — but never asked — where his little girl had gone. *Revelation.* That great burly truck-driving man had been afraid of a ten-year-old boy — locking the bedroom door at night, never coming near his son, nor asking any questions. Then, finally, Dad had run off in the night with his psalm-singing wife, leaving a son to fend for himself and a daughter to rot in the ground.

Reverie ended. Another child was waiting.

The rest of his gear was pulled from the cab of the stolen pickup truck. He knew a toddler harness was too small for a six-year-old, but the dog harness would be a perfect fit, or so said the pet-shop clerk when he had given the woman Dodie Finn's estimated weight. However, now he must fasten it to the child — without touching her. Dodie must stand very still and lift her arms high. If she could wipe her face with a napkin when her father asked her to, then she could raise her arms on command. But would she? He had not counted on passive resistance from a child. Upon returning to the back end of the truck, he found the little girl still lying in the dirt.

"Stand up." He knelt on the ground a few feet away, holding out the harness so he could explain what must happen next.

Dodie reached out for him. It was only a threat; she was not within touching distance, and yet he fell backward, toppled by shock.

The child knew. She *knew.*

He scrambled to his feet and watched her rise from the ground; it was mesmerizing. As she walked toward him, her eyes still had that vacant look, but her small feet had perfect direction. One pale hand was reaching out to him. His chest constricted — hard to breathe — and his feet would not obey him. He pulled out his knife, but the child's crazy eyes did not see it. She was so close to him now.

"Do as I say!" he yelled, or thought he did. It was more of a squeak, and the girl was still coming, walking slowly. "Do as I say!" His voice was hoarse; his throat was closing; it was a fight to get out the words, "I'll kill your brother."

The girl stopped.

He breathed more easily. "And I'll kill your daddy, too." He brandished the knife. "I'll go back there right now and slit his throat. Is that what you want?"

Dodie's head moved from side to side. No, that was not what she wanted.

"Raise your hands high."

The child did as she was told.

21

By the time Charles Butler had climbed into the driver's seat of the Mercedes, Mallory and Riker were long gone.

His sole passenger, Detective Kronewald, ended another cell-phone call. "That was Riker. He says the perp talked to Mallory. I told you guys that phone belonged to the killer."

"Oh, I'm sure he's the one who bought it." Charles left the old road and turned onto I-40. "But the phone belonged to Dr. Magritte. Call it a present, so he could stay in touch with his doctor — his priest. Mallory found the cell phone in the old man's knapsack. There's no reason for the killer to plant it there."

"He might — if he wanted an open line to the cops. Or maybe he just wanted to know if we'd found that body yet. Can't you go any faster?"

Charles ran the portable siren as he drove

down the road at one hundred miles an hour. "I think he recognized Mallory's voice when he called. That's why he hung up. It startled him. He doesn't like surprises."

"Okay, let's run with that idea," said Kronewald. "If he recognized Mallory's voice, then it's somebody she knows. He was riding with the caravan."

"Right," said Charles, minding the speedometer. "And he would've seen Mallory chatting up his doctor a few times."

"Interrogating him, you mean. Yeah, I know the kid's style. But Dr. Magritte was an ex-priest, for Christ's sake. The seal of the confessional still holds up in court. Even Mallory couldn't break that old man."

"Back to the phone," said Charles. "Originally, I believe it only had one purpose. Dr. Magritte was a serial killer's confessor."

"You're right. Okay, I buy that part. An ex-priest *and* a shrink — the perfect audience for a serial killer. These freaks just love their bragging rights. But Dr. Magritte could never rat him out — so why kill the old guy?"

"Perhaps, toward the end, this killer had more faith in Mallory. And now *she's* got the phone."

At his partner's request, Riker fastened his

seat belt. That was his only clue that he was in for one hell of a ride. "You wanna tell me where we're going?"

"The Painted Desert," said Mallory. "Call the park rangers. If the road in is gated, I want it opened up before we get there. I'm not ripping up this car going overland."

"Wait a minute. This freak told you he was there? In a national park?"

"No. He only told me he was in a dark place, waiting. He knows this car. He'll blink his lights twice if I get it right. If he sees any cops or feds, he'll just kill Dodie Finn and dump her out on the road."

"Are you sure the kid's still alive?"

"I could hear Dodie humming."

"That desert is huge, Mallory."

"But it's only got a few segments of the old road running through it. They don't show up in maps or guidebooks. I think he'd know where they are, but no one else would. Even the buffs on the Internet wouldn't know where to look. It's perfect."

"I'm sorry," said Charles to his passenger. "I can't match speed with Mallory's car, and I can't predict an outcome for you."

Too late he had come to understand that his function on this road had nothing to do with the capture of a serial killer. He fixed his eyes upon a highway sign to reassure himself that he had not left the earth for the moon; but he was drawn back to the strange dark landscape framed in his side window. The prairie was so beautiful, though not hospitable to humanity, not welcoming nor forgiving, and it held not one whit of sentiment for the living or the dead. This was his only view into Mallory's mind. One could easily get lost in such a place.

"You gotta gimme *something*," said Kronewald, "any damn thing."

"Well, it would appear that the killer feels some connection to Mallory — since he invited her to chase him down tonight."

"Gimme more," said Kronewald, slipping into the interrogation tone.

"I can string together a line of logic for you. Best guess?"

"Anything."

"He definitely plans to kill the child — that's hardly guesswork. The plan will be well thought out. Dodie Finn's death will cap off his monument, and he's planning something spectacular. That's the most logical reason for keeping that little girl alive this long."

"So he's got a thing for Mallory?"

"She probably fascinates him, but it's nothing sexual, no fantasizing in that direction. This man is repulsed by the whole idea of physical contact with a living person."

"But the guy takes big risks. He's not afraid she'll catch him after he kills this kid?"

"I think he's counting on it. Mallory thought he got sloppy with the murder of Dr. Magritte — when he left the old man's bloody knife behind. It was the killer's blood, *his* DNA. What if that was deliberate?"

Kronewald nodded. "He wants credit."

"Right. Now, if he wants us to know who he is — then he'll escalate his personal risk for the grand finale. He won't care if he lives through this night."

"Back in Chicago," said Kronewald, "we call that suicide by cop. So he's planning to take that little kid with him?"

Charles nodded. "But not Mallory." His eyes were on the road, searching for a familiar pair of taillights. "He called her out because he needs an audience tonight — someone who can appreciate his work."

And what would that do to Mallory, who did not take well to failure?

Some people had reoccurring flying dreams. Charles had the toppling dream. An object would be about to fall, and he would startle himself awake by physically reaching out for it. Lately, he dreamed not of objects but a toppling woman, and it was always Mallory he reached for. And now he truly understood why Riker had brought him along. The police did not require his help to catch a serial killer. His job was to catch Mallory — when she fell.

The two detectives had found the first abandoned segment of Route 66 inside the national park and just beyond the ranger station. It had gone to ruin, crumbles only — fruitless and disappointing.

And now Riker had the ride of his life, a dizzy run of turns and curves for miles and miles of dark road.

Mallory said, "Watch for a sign. We're looking for Lacy Point."

Riker shouted, "There!"

The car stopped on the park road, and Mallory stepped out, flashlight in hand, to show him a sight he would never forget.

"I had no idea this was here." Riker stood beside her and, disbelieving, head shaking, stared at a road that was not there. It had vanished long ago. Ghosty telephone poles, all stripped of their wires, trailed off into the desert and disappeared in the dark of night beyond the flashlight's beam. Nature had reclaimed every bit of land and replanted it with scrub. There was no sign of pavement anymore, nothing left to say that millions of cars had gone this way. All that remained was a straight march of tall wooden poles — grave markers all of them — to show him where an old highway had died.

Mallory blinked her flashlight twice. They waited in the dark, counting off the passing minutes, time enough for despair to settle in. They would not find Dodie out here.

"I guessed wrong," said Mallory.

"Kid, it was a world-class guess," said Riker. "Your knapsack is beeping."

Mallory's caller wanted to voice a complaint. He was still waiting in the dark, and he would not wait for long.

So much time had been lost on the park road through the Painted Desert, and the silver convertible was making up for it in speed, flying westward again on the interstate.

"He says he can see for miles and miles," said Mallory. "So I know he's not sitting in the pine trees around Flagstaff. He'll be near the old road. No lights, lots of open ground. He's laying out a murder scene with maneuvering room. He wants me to see him kill Dodie, but he doesn't want me to get close enough to stop it." She waited for feedback, but her partner evidently had no better theory. Riker would always defer to her in all things sociopathic and monstrous. Mallory gripped the wheel a little tighter.

"Did you hear the kid this time?"

"No." During that last call, she had not heard Dodie humming in the background.

Riker pulled a beeping phone from his shirt pocket and pressed it to one ear. He turned to her, saying, "The Arizona cops turned up a report on a missing pickup truck, the only old junker stolen all day." The detective continued to listen and relay what he was told. "Good news and bad news, kid. There's no airbag on the passenger side. The guy who owns it has an elderly mother — brittle bones — so he had the thing taken out."

"And a kid Dodie's size might get killed by an airbag," said Mallory. "So that must be the good news."

"There's a loaded rifle in the roof rack," said Riker, cupping one hand over his cell. "And it's no squirrel gun. I've got the owner on the phone. He says it's a damned good gun. He can shoot a flea off the head of an eagle a mile up and in the dark. Infrared. Now that fits. With a rifle sight like that, the perp can see us coming, just like he said. In a car, on foot — no difference. And he can pick us off."

"If he even knows how to fire a rifle," said Mallory. "Most people can't shoot worth a damn. Find out if the sight is accurate."

After a moment on the phone, Riker said, "It's not. This owner has to shoot low and to the left."

Dodie Finn was motionless and dead quiet. The wind was blowing cold, but she did not complain. Her eyes were open, and she saw nothing, only darkness all around. The leash to her harness was loosely wrapped on a piece of rusted chrome, and she could so easily undo it — but she did not. Something small was crawling up her arm, a thing with many legs, and she did not brush it off, nor even glance down at it. Dodie played the children's game of statue, and all that betrayed her imitation of stone was the prickling of her skin, every downy hair standing on end.

She was on best behavior tonight so that her father and brother would not be hurt like Ariel, who had disappeared, leaving only her blood behind — so much blood.

The many-legged insect was crawling on Dodie's face, but she continued to look straight ahead, staring at the world through unfocussed doll's eyes. Inside her head, where she truly lived, she flitted from one side of her brain to the other, screaming, "Daddy! Daddy!" Her thin arms flapping like white wings in the dark. But outwardly, Dodie so loved her family — she never moved at all.

Charles Butler was running the portable siren as he changed lanes, proposing to take the Crookton Road, Exit 93, heading north toward Seligman, Arizona.

"No, not that way." Kronewald waved him over to the side of the road, and obediently, the Mercedes came to a stop.

The Chicago detective put his phone away, giving up on Riker's busy signal. "We're not gonna find them up there." Kronewald had his personal map of dead children spread on his lap. "I got an inventory from Harry Mars. Berman's crews dug up all the graves in Arizona months ago. That road's just like the Santa Fe loop. No bodies were ever found north of I-40."

"Then the FBI missed a few, or perhaps they never looked for them there." Charles nodded to the guidebooks piling up on the floor mat at the detective's feet. "My favorite is the Route 66 trivia lovers' guide. The Seligman loop is not quite the same as the Santa Fe segment. You're sure the killer's father was a truck driver, right?"

"Yeah, and the kid used to ride with his old man."

"And Mallory believes that he's following his father's route. Well, Route 40 connects the two ends of the Seligman loop, but it wasn't finished until the nineteen eighties. When your killer was a child, his father would've driven the old road north and around the Seligman loop. Now consider this. Those undiscovered graves might be the reason he picked that area. He wants full credit for *all* of his kills — or his work won't be complete."

"Why couldn't he just phone in the grave locations?"

"Maybe he did."

"While Dale Berman was in charge of the case. That incompetent prick." Frustrated, Kronewald turned his face to the passenger window. "Okay, I see the problem."

"And there are other good reasons," said Charles. "It's a dark segment. No lights from the interstate, very little traffic this time of night —"

"Hey, look!" Kronewald pointed to the road as Mallory's car sped past them and then changed lanes for the exit that would

612

lead her to the northern loop of Route 66.

"So," said Charles, "on toward Seligman?"

Up ahead was the Black Cat bar, one of Riker's fond memories of the road through Seligman. He could not recall the cattle ranges that Mallory spoke of. In his teenage days, grazing land had not been on his mind so much as booze and girls and good times that could not be had in the company of cows. The old saloon slid past his window, and he looked out on the scattered lights of small buildings near and far.

"Look behind us." Mallory was staring at the rearview mirror, and she was not wearing her happy face. "It's the Mercedes — Charles."

"Get used to it, kid," said Riker. "Every time you turn around, he'll be there. I think sometimes he forgets that you're the one with the gun." Riker reached for his cell phone. "I'll get ahold of Kronewald."

"Get them off this road. If the perp spots a tail —"

"Even if he's seen Charles's car, he won't know one Mercedes from another. The perp's looking out for cop cars, not tourists."

Past Seligman, the land opened up. It was dotted with the occasional lights of houses and then nothing but darkness — until he saw the black cow in the headlights, and yelled, "Oh, God — they're all over the road."

The brakes were screeching, smoking, dust clouds rising all around them. Mallory swerved to graze one animal, rocking the car onto two wheels. It slammed back to earth on all four tires, and she cut a hard right to miss the next cow. Riker was lurching the other way, and now back again toward Mallory, rolling as the car rolled over. The air bags imploded, massing up in an instant and blinding him with white; it felt like a punch from a giant fist large enough to pound his chest and his gut with one mighty shot. Just as quickly, the bag deflated, and the last thing Riker saw was a fence pole coming through the windshield, missing Mallory and snapping his arm bone. A second pole hit his head.

Good night, all.

And the car rolled on.

22

Charles Butler was the first out of the Mercedes. The Volkswagen convertible had flipped over and the passengers hung upside down, held in place by seat belts. The ragtop was badly damaged, but the roll bar had held. Mallory and Riker still had their heads. As Charles wrenched a door open, Kronewald's hands were reaching inside to undo Riker's seatbelt, and the unconscious man was eased out in Charles's arms and then laid upon the ground.

Running to Mallory's side of the car, Charles heard Kronewald sing out, "Riker's still breathing, but his arm's broken and he's out cold."

Mallory's door hung open, and she was working her own belt loose as Charles reached inside to cradle her body and keep her from falling head first. When she was on her feet again, she looked around at the cows milling about on the road. Kronewald was doing traffic control, his arms spinning, his screams full of obscenities to move the animals away from Riker's prone body.

"Somebody opened a gate," she said.

"It would seem so." Charles was staring at the damage her convertible had done to the barbwire fence that lined the road. "Or maybe another car had a mishap." He returned to the road, where Riker lay motionless and wheezing with one arm bent at an unnatural angle. "I think his ribs are broken, too." When Charles looked up again, he saw Mallory wandering off, preceded by the beam of her flashlight.

Kronewald held up his cell phone, saying, "The ambulance is on the way from Kingman, but there's a wreck on the interstate, and it might take a while." He turned to see the back of Mallory. "Where does she think she's going?"

"You might keep an eye on her — in case she's in shock."

"Got it."

A few minutes later, the Chicago detective returned. "Mallory sent me back. Says our perp's got an infrared sight on his rifle. He won't wanna see her with company." The old man held up one hand. "Hold on, Charles. He's not gonna shoot her. You know he didn't drag Mallory all the way out here for that." The detective paced near a ditch on the other side of the road. "There's some rusty metal piled up here. Same stuff the fence posts are made of. She needs that car back on the road." The detective climbed down into the ditch and lifted a length of pipe, yelling, "Give me a hand!"

A short way up the road, Mallory found the source of the wandering cows. She stood before an open gate and faced a dirt road leading off across flat open land in the direction of distant foothills. It was the gate that held her interest. Two strong metal poles supported a high crossbar that displayed the name of the ranch and its brand. But was the crossbar welded on? She looked down at the ground, wondering if the supporting poles were footed in cement. Her flashlight picked out loose lengths of well casing piled up on the other side of the gate, but these were obviously meant for mending fences. She turned back to the gate posts. No shorter section of pipe would do. Back down the road, she had tools for this job — and Charles Butler was one of them.

She turned her eyes upward to consider the problem of a welded crossbar, and the flashlight dropped from her hand. So surprised was she to see her father's million stars in the sky above — just as he had promised and right where he had left them, his *"— brilliant stars and lesser ones, millions beyond counting, beautiful — mesmerizing."*

A child was waiting.

Mallory picked up her flashlight.

Down the rancher's road far past the gate, twin points of light blinked twice. The cell phone in her knapsack was beeping, but she had no intention of answering it. That would surprise her adversary. She was in control now — not him. And he would learn that soon enough; nothing would happen as *he* had planned. She ran down the road. The grade was dropping, and soon she would be out of his rifle sights.

Another surprise.

And he could do nothing about it but wait for her return. All his threats to the contrary, Mallory knew that he could not start without her.

Charles Butler counted to three, then put all his muscle into pushing the metal lever upward in order to roll the small car. Kronewald's contribution was more puffing and wheezing than muscling his own section of the long pipe.

Mallory came up behind them, asking, "Where did you get that well casing?"

"Is that what it's called?" Charles nodded toward the ditch on the far side of the road. "Over there."

She crossed the pavement, pausing only a moment to look down at the unconscious Riker. She could hear his breathing; it was ragged — but air was life. The beam of her flashlight played over the selection of long pipes in the ditch. She had a good eye for measurements and estimated the longest section at twenty-five feet. Long enough. She would not need to tear down the rancher's gate after all.

Kronewald stood in the middle of the road, watching for the ambulance with one hand pressed to his aching back. Charles had finished the job of righting the car by himself, and now he leaned on the frame of the battered and torn ragtop. "I understand this killer is armed with a rifle?"

"Not a problem." She raised the hood, and pulled out a tool kit.

"Equipped with an infrared sight," added Charles, "the better to shoot people in the dark."

While rummaging through her duffel bag, she said, "It isn't his rifle, and he doesn't know the sight is off. You can't hit a moving target with another man's gun. He's just using the rifle sight like binoculars." She held up a pair of opera glasses. "Remember these?"

Yes, he did. He had given them to her one Christmas, and he was gratified to see that she had found a use for them — since she missed that performance of the opera, and every one since.

Charles was still grappling with the idea of the rifle. "But he *could* shoot if he —"

"No reason for it." She turned her key in the ignition and the engine purred to life. The automatic control of the roof would not function, and she tried to force it back manually, but it would not budge. "I won't have a clear target behind the truck's headlights. I've only got one chance to take him down."

Charles held up one hand. "Allow me." And now he pushed the convertible's tattered top back into the boot. "So, obviously, you have a plan."

She held up a cutting tool from her kit. "I'll get the wire we need. You load the pipe."

While she cut through sections of barbed wire, he picked up the one she liked the best, the longest one, and carried it to the car. "I gather you're not planning to shoot out his headlights, anything like that?"

"No, Charles, not with a handgun." She

laid three sections of wire on the hood. "But even if I could make those shots, it only takes a second to slit a little girl's throat. So I don't plan to give him that much warning time."

A beeping sound came from her knapsack. "That's him now, isn't it?"

"Pretend you don't hear it, Charles."

Following her direction, he jammed one end of the pipe into the steel skeleton of rolled-back ragtop. Then he tore his hands on pieces of wire to secure it. The rest of the pipe was angled across the center of the roll bar, and Mallory lashed it down on top of the windshield frame, twisting the barbed wire to make it tight. And now there was blood on her hands, too. The twenty-five feet of pipe remained straight, no sag, no bowing, though at least two thirds of its length was unsupported, stretching far beyond the nose of the car — and aiming upward.

Charles stood back from their handiwork to see what they had done, and it chilled him. The upward angle of the pipe fit so well with the higher windshield of a pickup truck met head on. Mallory had designed a lance for a one-sided joust. For a fraction of a second, the pipe might be visible in her opponent's headlights, but it would appear to him as a small round dot — and then —

"That's right," said Mallory, reading all of this in his face. "I plan to kill him. I'll take his head off if I can."

Kronewald was down the road, herding cows and clearing the way for the ambulance. He came back to them, cell phone in hand. "It'll be a few more minutes."

"Did you tell them it was an officer down?" she asked.

"Hell, no. They would've sent cops."

"Good job." Mallory got behind the wheel. "You two stay with Riker."

"Not so fast." Charles climbed over the dented passenger door to settle in beside her. And they were off. She tested her high-beams then killed the lights, rolling, creeping forward in the dark.

Charles's eyes were on her face when he said, "If you crash into that truck —"

"No crash," said Mallory. "His pickup truck is sitting still. Nobody can judge the speed of an oncoming car, and he has no idea what this one can do."

"But there's a child in that truck."

"A tap, Charles. That's all it'll take to send this pipe through his window — and his face. I can kill him without even setting off his air bag."

■ ■ ■ ■

Mallory positioned her car just beyond the gate and facing down the rancher's road. She blinked her lights twice, and, in the distance, another set of headlights turned on. "Check out the window on the driver's side. You see the rifle?"

"No," said Charles Butler, holding the opera glasses to his eyes.

"Then he's not using the infrared scope. There's not enough room inside that —"

"You have another problem." Charles handed her the opera glasses. "Better take a look."

She fixed the lenses on the pickup truck, where Dodie Finn was harnessed and tethered to the grille between the headlights.

"Sorry," said Charles. "You weren't counting on that. So what's next?"

"Same plan."

"You're mad."

"I don't have a lot of options here," she said. "He'll sit tight until I get closer. He wants me to watch when he kills Dodie."

Charles was more than mildly disturbed. Mallory found it too easy to slip inside the mind of a serial killer. "You can't go ahead with this," he said. "Not with Dodie standing in front of the truck."

She cut her lights and backed out of the ranch road, then reversed down the paved highway below the rise. "That'll make him nuts for a few minutes. If this is going to work, I'll need a slight adjustment in the pipe."

"I'm sure you've done the math." Charles climbed out of the car and began to undo the wires that bound the pipe to the frame of the broken windshield. "Speed and distance, that sort of thing." Of course she had. Mathematics was her gift. At the risk of annoying her by stating the obvious, he said, "So you realize that if we go full out, you won't have time to brake before we crash. Even you can't alter the laws of physics." He was close to smiling, though he shredded his fingers on the barbed wire, winding it, changing the angle to suit her and saying, "Well, this should give us more clearance on the left side of the truck." Almost done. "I gather we're going to miss the truck altogether."

"Something like that."

It was the tone of her voice that set off all his internal alarms, but nothing could have prepared him for the sight of Mallory pointing her gun at him. And his crime? He was holding onto the pipe, holding on tight, for this was his only means of preventing her from going anywhere without him.

"Time to let go, Charles. You're not coming along."

Though he loved his life, he shook his head, badly frightened now, for he was staring at her seat belt and it was undone.

She raised her gun a little higher, aiming for his face. "I think you know I like you well enough to shoot you."

He understood at once, and he believed her, but he would not let go.

She dropped the gun and threw her knapsack at his head. Reflex made him release the pipe to catch the sack, and — that quickly — she was gone.

His heart was banging on the run as he reached the rise in time to see her car poised once again on the rancher's road, her headlights flashing twice, then steady. Charles ran faster, legs churning, chest burning. He was so close. Mallory revved her engine to a roar. The car lurched forward. In seconds only, she had closed the distance, and in the duel of clashing headlights, horizontal stalks of brilliant light blended into fusion — with the breaking of glass and the crash of metal on metal. Each vehicle was blinded by one lost headlight and married together by Mallory's lance.

The running man stumbled when he saw her body in silent flight, shooting upward in an arc that ended behind the obstacle of the ruined silver car.

Dodie, unharmed, was still standing in front of the pickup truck. Her harness leash had come loose, and yet she was slow to move away from the one unshattered headlight. Charles ran past her, past the wreckage where Mallory's right fender was joined to one side of the truck's twisted grille. Following the beam of her surviving headlight, he found her body broken on the ground.

Mallory had counted on Newton's first law: the pickup truck, the vehicle at rest, had remained at rest, despite the impact of her car. She had stayed on course long enough to send her lance through the other windshield, and she had turned hard left, but one bumper had crashed into the truck. The swerve had saved Dodie, but there had been no time for Mallory to save herself.

No need to look inside the cab of the pickup truck. Surely there was a headless corpse behind the wheel. Charles was busy staunching the blood flow from Mallory's wounds to the tune of a musical fragment, eight notes hummed in a child's voice. Dodie Finn was lost in the dark of some interior landscape with no moon or stars or ken of pain.

The strangled sound of crying . . . that came from Charles.

23

No more reporters ran wild in the streets of Kingman, Arizona. The media was long gone — off to Chicago, following a trail of breadcrumbs left by Detective Kronewald.

A celebrity patient in the Kingman hospital was awake and making good use of his recovery time. Mallory's knapsack lay on the bed beside Riker; it was unzipped, violated, and the detective was reading the words of Peyton Hale. Caught in this act of trespass, he smiled at his visitor. "Hey, Charles." He held up one page of lines penned in faded blue ink. "Well, you wouldn't read them. Somebody had to. It's a character flaw — I always want the whole story."

Apparently Charles Butler also liked to know the beginning, middle and end to things, and he was an admirable upside-down reader, but the man showed no interest in the letters scattered on the bed in plain sight. Instead, he picked up the type-written pages half buried by sheets. "So this is the official police report on the wreck."

"Check out the line about the seat belt on the driver's side." Against the law and hospital rules, Riker lit up a cigarette.

Looking up from his reading, the psychologist met the detective's sorry eyes. "You have to get past this business of her accident."

"Is that what we're calling it?"

Charles, the most loyal of conspirators, opened a window to lose the smoke before the head nurse, a woman with the nose of a cadaver dog, could rush in to confiscate the detective's last pack of cigarettes.

"It was a matter of bad timing," said Charles. "I was there, remember?"

"I didn't have to see the wreck," said Riker. "I watched Kathy Mallory grow up. I've seen her take falls from bicycles and playground swings. When she was thirteen, she *borrowed* a cop's motorcycle. It was parked right in front of the damn station-house. Well, it was a learn-as-you-go kind of thing. The kid popped the clutch and did this amazing wheelie. God, I'll never forget that — she must've ridden thirty feet on the back wheel — and then she went flying. So I'm the expert here, okay? The kid always landed like a cat. And she should've walked away from that wreck."

"I'm sure she intended to." Charles laid the accident report on the bed sheet and turned away to look out the window — to hide a face that could not hide a lie. "Mallory tried to steer clear of the truck after she sent that pipe through the windshield."

"No, she didn't," said Riker. "Mallory only steered clear of the kid. She always knew she'd have to hit that truck's front end. Even a dead man's foot on the gas pedal would've killed Dodie Finn." The detective picked up the report and waved it like a flag. "You read this, Charles. You know her seat belt was functional. But Mallory — didn't — buckle — up." He wadded the document into a tight ball. "Even though she knew the crash was coming." Riker held up his next piece of evidence, letters from Peyton Hale that were once the property of Savannah Sirus. "And I know who to blame . . . for all the good it does me."

Upon entering the hospital room, Charles Butler was surprised to see the bedside chair usurped by a friendly bear of a man, who introduced himself as Ray Adler from Kansas. "I'm a friend of the family." And now the Kansan turned back to the unconscious Kathy Mallory and resumed his earnest lecture on the terrible importance of seat belts.

When Ray Adler left Arizona, he had the wreckage of the silver convertible in tow. And he had left Charles Butler with a better understanding of Mallory's simple quest: All she had wanted was this one small thing — to drive her father's road through his life and times.

The New York detective with the fewest broken bones and sutures was the first to be released from the hospital. Riker donned dark glasses to shade his eyes from the Arizona sun as he walked past the first bright window. He turned to the large man beside him, who had just won the luggage war and carried the detective's bag down the corridor. "So, you read her father's letters? Would you say that guy was obsessed with Route 66?"

"I didn't read them." Charles Butler set down the duffel bag and depressed a button to bring the elevator. "But when I gave her the letters, she accused me of reading them anyway."

"Well, a little hostile paranoia is a good sign. More like my old Kathy."

"Really? She seems to have lost all interest in this case. Does that sound normal to you?"

"Sure it does." Riker fished in his pockets for a pack of cigarettes so that he would be ready to light up just the moment that he escaped from the hospital. "If I was back in New York right now, I'd have a new case on my desk before I could get blind drunk and wonder what the last one was all about. So, yeah, this is normal. It's over."

"No, it isn't." The elevator doors opened, and Charles stepped in.

Riker limped in, and they descended through the floors. Above the mechanical sound of the gears, the detective could hear the tumblers working in the other man's brain. "Okay, what's your problem with this case?"

"The killer has no name."

"Well, he doesn't need one anymore. He's dead."

"Then why didn't Kronewald release the name of that suspect from Illinois?"

"Egram? That's never gonna happen, Charles. Kronewald can't find any relatives for a DNA link to the corpse. At a time like this, the only thing that draws relatives out of the woodwork is a nice fat lawsuit. Kronewald's gonna bury the Egram file. Count on it." Riker watched the descending floor numbers, clicking his lighter in anticipation.

"Well, he had another name," said Charles. "The reporters think the killer was posing as one of the caravan parents. And what about Agent Cadwaller? The last time I —"

"Oh, yeah," said Riker. "That guy sent me a get-well card and a witness subpoena. You were right about him. He wasn't a profiler. Cadwaller's a forensic accountant from another agency. He's building a case against Dale for padding overtime and falsifying government documents. And New Mexico has a charge for endangering the welfare of a child. Did I tell you Dale's wife left him? Oh, and his lawyers — they own his house, they're driving his car." The detective lightly punched Charles on the arm, grinning, saying, "Hey, is this a great country or what?"

The elevator doors opened, and upon exiting, Riker limped at a faster pace, following the exit signs to freedom and his first smoke of the day.

"All right," said Charles, "so the killer was posing as someone on the caravan."

"Hey, works for me."

"Well, one of those people is dead. Doesn't that help you narrow it down a bit?"

"Yeah, yeah." The front door was in sight;

the cigarette and lighter were in hand. "You'd have to start with a picture to find a match. Between the parents and the news crews, it's not like we got a tight list of everybody in that caravan." Riker pushed through the doors, and now he stood outside at last. "I saw the autopsy pictures. Mallory really did a number on the perp's face. Damn she's good." The air was clean and unpolluted, but he had a remedy for that; he lit a cigarette and inhaled deeply.

"What about a forensic reconstruction of the skull? They might be able to —"

"Nobody's gonna spend that kind of money on a dead cockroach, Charles. There was no ID found on the body. No picture — no match. Sorry, pal."

Charles set the duffel bag on the ground and raised one hand to alert a teenager standing near the door, and the boy ran off to fetch the Mercedes. Apparently, the concept of valet parking had been recently introduced to Kingman, Arizona. When the car pulled to curb, Charles tipped the youngster and turned back to the detective, saying, "There must be some clue to the man's identity — *something*. . . . Well, surely you at least know the color of his eyes?"

"Naw," said Riker, as he opened the trunk of the Mercedes. "The eyeballs probably went out the back of his head in a stew of brains and blood. Or they could be in the glop that was jammed up inside the pipe when it —"

"A simple *no* would've sufficed." Charles tossed the duffel bag into the trunk.

"But you didn't ask me a simple question, did you?" Riker dropped the cigarette and crushed it under his heel. "You wanted to know if a serial killer had Mallory's green eyes. You just asked me if the kid killed her own father that night." The detective smiled. "But, hey, we never had this conversation, okay? Who cares what the freak looked like?"

Obviously, Charles cared, but the man was looking at his shoes, a sure sign of guilt, and he asked no more questions.

Riker stared at the open trunk. Almost time to say good-bye. "Mallory killed the right man that night. That's a fact. But she can never be sure *who* he was. Nobody can, and maybe it's better that way. Less . . . personal."

Charles only nodded in agreement, and both men knew they would never talk about this again.

The detective looked down at the keys in his hand. "You're sure about this?"

"Oh, yes. Please take the car. The last thing I need is another road trip."

And Mallory's driving had not produced a cure for Riker's fear of flying.

"When she's discharged," said Charles. "I'll take her back on a plane."

"Ray Adler's busting his butt to get her car fixed in time."

Charles shrugged. "I'll have him ship it directly to New York."

"No," said Riker. "I got a better idea." He reached into the trunk and pulled out a black plastic bag. "Here, a present, a souvenir. You'll remember this." He opened the bag and pulled out a coffee-stained canvas tote that bulged with maps.

"Horace Kayhill's collection?"

"Yeah." Riker slammed the trunk. "But the state line is a straight shot from Kingman, so all you need is the map for California. Take her down Route 66 all the way to the coast. Mallory deserves to finish this trip. God knows she's paid enough for the privilege." The detective climbed in behind the wheel of the Mercedes and rolled down the window to say, "So take her to the end of the road, and *then* see the lady home."

Ray Adler had made good on his promise, delivering Mallory's car, dent-free, on the day of her discharge in the month of June. "Good as new," said the man from Kansas, "and maybe a little better."

Charles Butler went up to Mallory's hospital room to fetch down the bags. The door was ajar, and he hung back in the hallway to watch, or, more accurately and clinically, to *observe.* She was packing clothes, moving slowly, as if she did this chore underwater. The bruises, casts and bandages were gone. The curls of her hair hid the savage scalp wound that had cost her so much blood, and her other suture scars were covered with a T-shirt and jeans. By outward appearances, she was healed, or nearly so — or so it seemed.

She was not wearing her weapon. It lay wrapped in the straps of her shoulder holster on the bedside table, and this worried Charles. Some people kept their identities in their wallets; hers was in the gun. One by one, she was losing every quality that defined her. And he was also changed. Now he was the one who kept up her ledger for all the cheats of her young life, everything lost or stolen from her. She was numbed to all of these injuries. Charles felt the pain for her; he was reeling with it.

He stepped into the room. "Did Kronewald call? Are you going to testify at Dale Berman's trial?"

She shook her head as she opened a

drawer in the bedside table. "Riker won the coin toss."

Bad news. This could only mean that she no longer cared about revenge, and he might applaud that as a sign of growth in anyone else of his acquaintance — but not in her unique case. He sat down on the bed to watch her fold T-shirts. "Kathy," he said. And she did not shoot him. "I know why you hated Dale Berman so much. It's all about Louis's wife, isn't it? Helen . . . and the way she died."

The young detective idly perused the contents of a nightstand drawer. "Helen Markowitz died of cancer."

"Yes, right after a high-profile case was solved." Charles had anesthetized Riker with contraband beer while the man was still on his sickbed in order to extract a few painful facts. "The police in New York had just found a kidnapped boy."

"The old man found the boy," she said, crediting her foster father in a listless monotone.

"And his wife died the next day," said Charles. "Louis was supposed to be on family leave that week. But when that child was kidnapped, all the leaves were canceled."

Mallory nodded as she collected small items from the drawer, filling her hand with

638

a toothbrush, a comb, a pen, saying, "I walked off the job."

"To be with Helen — but Louis couldn't do that, could he?"

"No." She slammed the bedside drawer. "He had to stay and find that kid. There were feds in the house. He thought they might get the boy killed."

"I remember the day of Helen's funeral," said Charles. "Louis ran into me on the street — literally. He ran his car into mine. That's how we met. Well, of course, he apologized profusely. Said he couldn't see the traffic for the tears. 'I put my wife in the ground this morning,' he said. 'My kid's locked in her room. And me? I'm driving around in circles. Everybody's gotta be somewhere, right?' And then he smiled."

Louis Markowitz's smile made him the most charming man on the planet, even though he had also been crying on this particular occasion. Charles had taken the policeman home to keep him off the street and out of further trouble. He had cooked dinner for the man and stayed up all night listening to favorite stories about the remarkable Helen Markowitz. "We were friends for years, but Louis never told me about the FBI agent who lied to him and led him down false trails . . . and cost him all the days he had left with his wife."

No, Louis had let go of that baggage early on, a wise choice, but not suitable for the likes of Kathy Mallory, who so loved revenge. Charles planned to help her savor what she had won. "Louis told me he only had a few hours with Helen before they wheeled her into the operating room. Poor man, he was expecting a surgical cure."

"That's what all the doctors told him." Mallory dropped a tube of toothpaste into her duffel bag. "That's why the old man didn't walk away from the kidnapping case."

Charles nodded. "That last day, Louis still believed that he was going to grow old with Helen."

"And then she died on the operating table." Mallory stared at the items laid out on the bed, as if the order in which she packed them might need all of her attention.

"And you blamed Dale Berman for dragging out that old case, for deceiving Louis and stealing all his precious time with Helen."

Mallory carefully folded another T-shirt, as if she had never loved Helen beyond all reason, as if she had never felt the loss of this good and gentle woman who had fostered her and loved her back.

No reaction at all — not from her.

It was Charles who balled his hands into fists, Charles who hated Dale Berman — hate enough for two, himself and Mallory. He turned his tell-all face away from her and made a show of searching the room for overlooked items that she might want.

The flowers were gone. Once, this room had smelled like a florist shop — or a mortuary. She had also thrown away her press clippings collected for her by Detective Kronewald. And gone were all the cards sent by high-ranking politicians and police officials. The only one she had saved was a card handmade by Dodie Finn, and this was added to the duffel bag — Mallory's only trophy.

"I love that one." Charles looked down at the card in the open bag. He smiled at the childish rendering of the Finns' farmhouse and the happy-face stick figures of a small family. "The drawing is perfectly awful. Shows no artistic talent whatever — so utterly normal."

According to the companion letter from Joe Finn, his daughter had ceased to hum, and now she talked to him, and he could not shut her up. This had been followed with a phrase that came awkwardly to the boxer: He had wished Mallory the same wondrous recovery.

A bit optimistic in Charles's view.

The great injury done to Mallory had no single cause, nor was there a cure. In the best foreseeable outcome, her malady could only be survived. And, in the best of all possible worlds, she would have no name for the man she had killed that night on the Seligman loop.

The packet of old letters fell from the bed. The enclosing ribbon came undone, and the pages scattered across the floor. Mallory continued to fold her clothes, failing to care. She was letting go of the evidence for Peyton's betrayal of her mother, Cassandra — these love letters written to another woman. He knelt at Mallory's feet to retrieve them, handling them carefully. And now, for the first time, he saw the puzzling salutation and read it aloud. " 'For O.B.' Well, that's odd." All the letters in his hand began in this same way. "Is it some sort of pet name for Savannah Sirus?"

At the mention of her late houseguest, Mallory looked down at him, only mildly distracted from the packing. "Why would my father write letters to *her?*"

Oh, bloody hell.

24

Ray Adler entered the hospital room and ended the conversation. He never noticed the odd expression on the face of Charles Butler, a man left wondering how many times his head could be twisted round before he lost it.

An hour later, smiling and waving good-bye, the man from Kansas was a reflection in the rearview mirror. The silver convertible's top was down, and the warmth of the summer sun lulled Mallory to sleep in the passenger seat. Charles, a lapsed Luddite, had worked out the mechanics of her iPod and its connection to the radio, but he found no music to fit well with fear.

If the letters had not been written to Savannah Sirus, what else might he have gotten wrong?

He was still pondering his failings as he drove across the state line of Arizona, leaving the grasslands behind. The California terrain was sandy and spotted with clumps of green. No mountain peaks or mesas, only long tedious tracts of desert stretched out before them. Finally, Mallory awakened, and he leaned toward her, prompting her with the puzzle that began each letter from Peyton Hale. "For O.B.?"

But she closed her eyes again and left him clueless for all the miles to Barstow, California, where they sat in the parking lot of a landmark hotel that had gone to seed. He watched her cross this place off her list of roadside attractions. Other tourists, no doubt following guidebooks, also stopped here for the length of time it took them to turn around and run. Charles put the car in gear and followed suit.

"On to Los Angeles?" He took her silence for yes and handed her the California map. "Care to play navigator?"

She unfolded it and stared at the familiar markings, Horace Kayhill's arcs and lines to define a serial killer's territory and the crosses that stood for graves. "What are you doing with this?" Unmistakable was her implication that he had stolen it.

"Riker *gave* it to me — the whole collection. He thought the California map might come in handy. And I must say it's superior to the average —"

Mallory was not listening to him. She was foraging in the back seat, and now she retrieved the small canvas tote bag with the rest of the Route 66 maps. She pulled one out and spread it across the dashboard. "How did Riker get this away from the New Mexico cops?"

"Well, a state trooper gave it to him. I was there." And for that matter, Mallory had also been present at the table on the day when it was handed over. Ah, but she had only seen the covering plastic bag. And, as he recalled, Riker had made a cursory inspection, just a glance inside to identify the contents as belongings of the little Pattern Man — poor Horace.

"Why didn't he turn the bag over to Kronewald?"

"Why would he?" asked Charles.

"And why is Kronewald calling his serial killer a John Doe?"

Apparently, she *had* been reading the daily newspapers he had brought to her hospital room. This continuing interest of hers promised upsides and down. "There's a lack of physical evidence," he said. "No solid tie to Adrian Egram, and I doubt that he's used that name since he stole his first car. I suppose we'll never know what persona he adopted." Charles had intended this as reassurance, a kind of promise.

"Riker knows," she said.

"Well, he might have a *theory.*" Was she looking at him now? Did she catch a give-away blush? Could he afford to play a game with her that involved deceit on any level? "There's certainly no way to prove it — no DNA link, no fingerprints or pictures on file, nothing to —"

"Riker's not working a theory," said Mallory. "He knows."

Her eyes closed.

Though California's desert landscape was rather dull, tedious in fact, Charles Butler was in dangerous country within and without. The subject of a serial killer's identity was off limits to him now. She made that clear. Mallory might be sleeping or feigning it. Either way, she was hiding out, a time-out from her life. And Peyton Hale's letters were all he had left, the only materials with which to build a bridge to Mallory. However, when she awakened, every word on the matter of Savannah Sirus and the letters was met with cold silence.

They stopped for the night. In the hotel restaurant, he asked if she would mind just one more question. "How did Savannah get the letters?" He fell silent as a waitress dropped the menus on their table, and then Mallory told him that the letters had been mailed to Cassandra in Chicago.

"But she never saw them. My mother was working insane hours at the hospital. So her roommate, Savannah, was the only one home when the mail came . . . when the telephone rang. Peyton called every night. She never knew that, either."

"When did you discover this?"

"When I found Savannah Sirus."

Their salad was served and eaten in silence. They were well into the main course when he learned that, after many phone calls from Mallory, Savannah had mailed her one token letter, claiming that she had found it stuffed in an old chair. And thereafter, the woman had ceased to answer the telephone.

"I knew she was lying," said Mallory. "That first letter promised the whole road. So there had to be more of them." The telephone assaults had escalated to ringing the woman's doorbell in Chicago, sometimes for hours with no response. "But I wore her down." And a compromise had been arrived at. "I told her she could keep the letters. I just wanted to read them." And Savannah, only wanting the harassment to end, had accepted Mallory's invitation to

New York City. "I sent her airline tickets and theater tickets. I sent her menus for the best restaurants in town. She thought I was planning a nice friendly visit. I wasn't."

Charles wondered how far into that visit Mallory's houseguest had discovered the merits of full confession. He could not get the image out of his mind — Savannah and her interrogator — the story hour from hell.

"Toward the end, Savannah *wanted* to confess." Mallory chased the roast beef with long draughts of wine. "After Peyton left on his road trip, my mother told her about the pregnancy . . . and the wedding plans."

And then?

Charles waited — and waited. Patience fraying, then lost, and he said, "So . . . stolen letters, diverted phone calls. Cassandra never heard from Peyton when he was on the road?"

Mallory shook her head. "She was worried. She thought he might've wrecked the car. Peyton didn't have any family, so my mother called some of his old friends along the road. That's how she knew he was still traveling. And then she had to wonder why he never called or wrote to her. Months went by, but she never did find out. Then she gave up."

"Cassandra never heard from him again?"

"No. After a long time, she decided that he'd just abandoned us. I always thought so, too . . . until I found Savannah Sirus's phone number."

"You knew this woman when you were a child?"

"I never met her. When I was little, Savannah sent Christmas cards, but I couldn't remember where they were from. I couldn't even remember the woman's name." Before Mallory had finished her wine, she gave up the story behind the wall of numbers in her New York apartment. "When she was dying, my mother wrote a phone number on my hand. She said, 'You call that woman, and she'll come get you.' " All but four numerals had been smudged away. A child's tears would do that. Mallory tossed back the rest of the wine and poured another glass. "It took a long time to find the rest of that number."

"So your father never went back to Chicago?"

"He had no reason to come back," said Mallory. "And that was more of Savannah's work."

Charles knew this theme of obsessive love; he had heard that tune playing inside his own head several times a day for all the years he had known Mallory. "Well, now I understand why you despised that woman."

"No, you don't. Not yet."

Maddeningly, she left the table, swinging her room key as she walked away.

On the road again the next morning, Charles made his first error of the day by begging an explanation for the initials O.B. Mallory dodged all conversation with sleep until late afternoon, when they were driving into more congested traffic.

In the area of Los Angeles, Californians had apparently not grasped the concept of passing lanes and turn signals, but this was merely harrowing. The last leg of the trip was the most grueling. Only a few miles along Santa Monica Boulevard, traffic was at a bumper-to-bumper standstill. He might have saved them from this ordeal. Six news bulletins had tried to warn him off, but he had been determined to drive this historic route to the end.

Mallory, however, assured him that it was a better fate to be shot in the head than to die of old age on this twelve-mile-long parking lot of detours and road construction. "Pull into that gas station," she said, nodding toward a nearby escape path. "This is the end of the road."

"Oh, no," he said, hardly believing that he

was suggesting this, "we have another ten miles to go before we reach Ocean Boulevard. That's the official finish to Route 66." And then, at the end of this road, if he still had his wits, he planned to drive the car into the sea so that they could fly back home to New York.

"No," she said. "Stop the car. This is where my father's road trip ended." She kept her silence until he had pulled into the lot and parked the car some distance from the gasoline pumps and a line of customer vehicles.

Charles was somber now, for he believed that he knew what was coming next, and it gave him hope and despair in equal amounts. According to Mallory, the last letter for O.B. had been mailed from Barstow far behind them. This tale could have only one logical end.

Mallory was staring at the gas station. "There used to be a bar on this lot, and there was a phone booth on the corner. He stopped here to call Chicago one last time. Savannah told him that my mother died in a fire."

"But that's madness. Savannah must've known she'd be found out."

"It helps if you think like a cop. That was when I knew she'd planned to kill my mother." Mallory said this with no animosity. It was a simple statement of fact. "It took a long time to break that woman, but I did it. Finally, she told me about starting a fire outside of Mom's bedroom. My mother could've died that night, and I would've died inside of her. While Savannah was talking to Peyton on the phone, the apartment was filling up with smoke. If she hadn't stopped to answer the phone, she could've gotten out in time. But she was an amateur arsonist. And she was afraid the ringing would wake up my mother. It did. By then the smoke was everywhere, and Savannah couldn't find the door. She was disoriented, almost unconscious when my mother dragged her out of there."

"Your mother saved Savannah's life."

"And she never knew her best friend tried to burn her to death."

Mallory left the car and walked toward the corner. She moved slowly, perhaps using the time to rebuild a long-gone telephone booth so that she could watch Peyton Hale make his last call. "He believed my mother was dead when he hung up the phone and walked into the bar." She turned to face the gas station, where that saloon had once stood. She rose up on the balls of her feet, chin lifting, anticipating, waiting for her father to finally put down his last glass and come back outside.

"I found the old police report. He drained half a bottle of Jack Daniel's before he got behind the wheel again. He backed up the car to the end of the parking lot, then aimed it at the brick wall."

She closed her eyes, as if she had just heard the impact of man and machine smashed across a wall that was no longer there. "He went through the windshield, no airbags then, no seat belt. They found most of the blood high up on the bricks where he cracked open his skull." She raised her eyes the better to see the blood that she had only heard about and read about. "And they found his body on the crushed hood of the car."

When she had returned to the convertible, Charles started up the engine, feeling the imperative to get her away from this place. "We'll finish it for him, all right? We'll go to the end of the road."

There was no protest on her part, but he knew better than to take this for consent. She simply did not care — about anything. Portrait of a woman on the unwind.

But one thing was a certainty on this road where paradox was the everyday thing: this sad news was reason for rejoicing: her father had died before she was born, and Mallory had not committed patricide on a dark road in Arizona.

They rolled on in silence and finally reached the official end of Route 66. Turning left on Ocean Boulevard, he drove on to the famous pier mentioned in every guidebook. It looked rather like a circus in progress. Electing something more tranquil, he chose the beachfront parking lot, then led her across the wide expanse of sand to the water's edge. "Later," he said, "after you were born, Cassandra never tried to contact your father?"

Mallory shook her head. "My mother waited a long time. She was eight months pregnant with me before she gave up on him and went home to Louisiana, where I was born. And after a while, my father just forgot about her — and me."

Oh, wait! Back up!

"After *a while?* You mean *after* you were born? Peyton didn't die in the crash?"

An hour had passed before Mallory would speak to him again, and then he learned that Peyton Hale had been badly mangled. One leg had been smashed into twenty-six pieces, and his skull had also been broken, yet he had survived.

A much calmer Charles Butler was revived by the salt-sea air, and he was experiencing his first corndog on the boardwalk of the Santa Monica Pier. He sat on a bench, listening to the music of a carousel and the rest of the story.

"Savannah told me he went through years of physical therapy." Mallory discarded her own corndog in a trashcan. "She was still obsessed with him. She tried to visit him in the hospital, but he wouldn't see her, and every letter she wrote to him came back unopened."

"Understandable," said Charles. "If Peyton believed that Cassandra was dead, he might not want any confrontation with reminders of her." And for all these years, Savannah had remained in love with Peyton Hale. Else she would not have kept the stolen letters. "And now," he said, "if you don't mind — could we go back to the part where your father just forgot about your mother? Did Savannah tell you that?"

This time, Mallory's selective deafness was not a problem. He could answer his own question. She would never believe this from a liar, a monster like her mother's best friend. "Mallory, you tracked him down, didn't you? You've met Peyton Hale."

"We never spoke."

And what did that mean? How should he put this so as not to sound too harsh, not too anxious to pressure her? He yelled, "You never *spoke!* What the *hell* does that mean?"

He sat beside her in the shade of the car, watching the ocean. She told him a tale that jibed with Louis Markowitz's version of a child's lost weekend. This was the episode that had driven Louis mad with worry over his foster daughter.

"I was only fourteen years old," said Mallory. "The Markowitzes thought I was at computer camp for those three days. It was a school award for good grades."

Charles recalled Louis's rendition: *"Helen was so happy when she signed the school's permission slip. Finally, Kathy wanted a normal childhood experience. I was less trusting. I put the kid on the bus and stayed until it pulled out of the schoolyard."*

Mallory's side of the story filled in a few gaps that Louis had not mentioned, or never knew: In her after-school hours, she had used a police department computer and traced Peyton Hale to a remote town in northern California. She had used the same computer to purchase her airplane tickets, charging them to the NYPD. However, arranging for a limousine to meet her upon arrival had proven too problematic. And so the child had hitchhiked north from the San Francisco airport. Young Kathy had slept on the beach that first night, not expecting to meet her father there, for his home was miles from town. The next morning, she had been surprised to see him coming toward her. "I knew who he was the minute I saw him. His eyes — *my* eyes." He was so close to her, almost within touching distance. In passing, he had turned to her with a curt nod, a greeting to a stranger, and then he had passed her by. "He didn't know me."

"That's *it?* You never spoke to him? You just walked away?"

"What was the point? He didn't *know* me." She splayed her hands to ask why she must repeat herself. And now she laid it all out for him — again, though it annoyed her to do it. "I look just like my mother. I have *her* face, *his* green eyes, and he had no idea who I was. He just forgot about her . . . and me."

"He thought you were both dead."

Evidently this was not an acceptable excuse in Mallory's ruthless accounting of what was owed to her. "But *I* didn't know that," she said, as if this might point out a defect in Charles's logic. When she spoke again, her tone of voice warned him not to side with Peyton Hale. "It was like my mother and I never existed."

More accurately, in Charles's opinion, it was like her father had punched her in the gut — and she would have had no defenses at that young age — only pain. And so Charles thought to change the subject before she could shut down again and lock him out with another prolonged silence. "Did you talk to Louis about this — when you got back home?"

"He didn't wait that long. He knew I was missing when he called the computer camp the next day — just to see if I was playing nicely with the other kids — that was his story. Then the old man tracked me down to the San Francisco airport. He was waiting at the gate when I showed up with my return ticket. We flew home together."

"I suppose he was very upset." In Louis's version, the man had been badly frightened in every passing minute until he had found his lost child.

"No. The old man just asked if I was okay. He never mentioned it again, and he didn't rat me out to Helen. He said Helen liked the computer-camp story, so we'd let her go on believing in that one. After a while it was like somebody else took that trip to

California, not me. And I didn't care about my father anymore."

Charles very much doubted that, but knew better than to accuse her of human frailty. At least, Mallory had found the best part of her father, the young man who would always be in love with Cassandra, the Peyton Hale she had rediscovered on Route 66.

And what now — what next?

She had no plan beyond this moment. She could not see one day into the future, and this worried Charles. Those who could not see a day ahead might not have another day to live.

He picked up the canvas bag of maps and pulled out the one for California. As he plotted a therapeutic drive up the coast, she was staring at him. No — she was staring at the map with its arcs, circles and little crosses.

"Why would Riker give you a bag full of evidence?"

"Personal effects," said Charles, correcting her. Oh, that was a mistake. She never took criticism well. And now his attention was diverted to other items at the bottom of the bag, things he had overlooked before. He pulled out a pair of dark glasses, distinctive for their great expense and style — Mallory's sunglasses? Yes, for next he found her gold pen, a gift he had given her years ago. He stared at these items for the longest time. "Some of your things," he said, holding them out to her. "They got mixed up with Horace's effects."

She shook her head. No, he was mistaken about that, though these items most certainly belonged to her. "The killer stole them. They belong with the rest of the evidence."

And now, as Mallory would say, they had a game.

Charles carried their bags into the Santa Barbara Hotel, prime beachfront property and room service; his world was complete. All the people in the lobby were dressed to the nines, and, though blue jeans and denim shirts were acceptable attire among wealthy travelers, he made the error of laying the car keys on the reception desk. The Volkswagen emblem branded him as scurvy middle class in the eyes of the hotel clerk. The young woman said nothing in response to his request for two of her best rooms. Instead, she wrote down a price, and he fancied that her frosty little nose actually tilted up as she pushed the slip of paper across the desk. She was no doubt certain that this would send him on his way to some lesser establishment and a room without a view.

Hardly.

But it was Mallory who snatched up the paper, read the price and found it not nearly exorbitant enough, saying, "You must have better rooms than these." Her hand was on one hip, the denim jacket incidentally drawn back, the gun exposed, the clerk surprised, and now it seemed that deluxe suites were available.

When they stood alone on the balcony overlooking the sea, Charles took this romantic moment to say, "I know it wasn't Horace Kayhill." Was she even listening to him? No. She was inspecting the label on a complimentary wine bottle. He tried a different tact. "I wonder why the killer left your sunglasses and pen with Horace's body."

Mallory took her own time pouring the wine. She sipped from a glass and seemed to be considering the taste. "So Riker never told you who the killer was. That's interesting." She scrutinized his face, looking there for signs of lies.

This test — this torture was proof enough that she was back in form. This was a cause for celebration, and he wanted to throttle her. "Who was he?" If she did not tell him now, his head might explode.

"You met him, Charles." She sipped her wine *slowly.* "I think you even liked him."

"So he *was* with the caravan."

She nodded. "He was the Pattern Man."

All right. That was interesting, though it could not possibly be true. It would be a grave error to question her logic. She hated that — and he could do miles better. He poured himself a glass of wine and courted a more hostile response, saying, "You're wrong. The Pattern Man — Mr. Kayhill died in *New Mexico.* His bones were picked clean by wild animals." Failing to get a rise out of her, he added, "Horace was *quite* dead." He slugged back the wine in one swallow and said, "*Extremely* dead."

Mallory's voice had no inflection when she volleyed. "That's right, but you can't tell the time of death from skeletal remains. Horace Kayhill died before you met the Pattern Man back in *Missouri.*"

Well, good solution — cleaving her prime suspect in two. So simple. He poured another glass of wine. "It's a bit of a stretch," he said, somewhat charitably. "That little man —"

"They always turn out to be little men."

She seemed to take no offense that he still doubted her. Or was she setting him up for a pratfall? It was so hard to tell with her — just like old times.

"Only the maps belonged to the Pattern Man," she said. "He was driving Kayhill's mobile home when he wasn't stealing cars. But then he had to get rid of it. Now that was Riker's doing when he organized a search for Kayhill. The Pattern Man would've picked that up on his police scanner. He thought Riker was on to him. Panic time. He couldn't risk a photograph of the real Kayhill showing up on the evening news. The body — what was left of it — had to be found. So he ditched the mobile home at the crime scene — a beacon for the searchers. Good plan. The feds had no interest in Horace Kayhill, and the local police never met the Pattern Man." She retrieved the canvas tote bag from a chair by the door. "When Riker saw this, I know it only took him six seconds to figure it out. But he gave the evidence to you. Why?"

Charles now regarded the bag as a dangerous thing, and he shook his head in denial. Fortunately, in Mallory's eyes, this passed for confusion instead of a challenge. He could never tell her that her partner's only suspect had been Peyton Hale — that Riker believed she had killed her own father. Lies were not his forte, and so he countered with the truth. "I'm not sure that he ever looked that closely at the bag when —"

"Riker's no screwup," said Mallory, insistent. "He *saw* the evidence. Hard evidence." She pulled two maps from the bag. "But he could've worked it out if all he had were these. While I was in the hospital, the state police found the graves on the Seligman loop." She spread the Arizona map on the bed.

Had Riker done more than glance at the folded maps? Doubtful.

"Look," said Mallory. "See the little crosses on that segment?"

"Yes . . . because the children were buried on the old trucker's route."

"Right. Now the Pattern Man claimed to be a Route 66 buff. But look at this." She unfolded the map for New Mexico and handed it to him. "All the hardcore fanatics take the road north to Santa Fe."

Charles stared at the Santa Fe loop — no graves. But this was not evidence of an alias, not proof enough to split one man in two. "Kayhill could've worked it out. He was one of Dr. Magritte's patients."

"No, Magritte's patient was the Pattern Man. That was his Internet name. Kayhill was just some poor tourist he met up with on the road."

Mallory upended the canvas tote bag, spilling the remaining contents on the bedspread in a pile of maps, credit-card receipts and sundry items. She picked up a driver's license and placed it in his hand. "That's what the real Kayhill looked like."

Charles stared at the license photo. It was a face he had never seen before. It resembled the man he had known as Horace Kayhill only in the broadest sense of hair color, height and weight. "Well, license photos are always bad. The killer probably showed this to lots of people, agents, troopers, and no one noticed that it wasn't him."

"But you noticed right away," she said, as if she had caught him in a lie. "I promise you, Riker would never miss a thing like that."

Oh, but he had. Riker had only glanced inside the trooper's plastic sack, just a quick look to see a familiar canvas bag and the markings on a wadded map. The detective's own theory of Mallory's father as a serial murderer was proof that the man had indeed overlooked this driver's license.

"Think carefully, Charles. You said you were there when the cops gave it to Riker. Did you see him sign a receipt? Any paperwork at all?"

Charles shook his head, hardly paying attention.

"Good," she said. "Then it never happened. Are we clear on that?"

He was staring at the damning canvas bag. So much had happened on the day when Riker had received it, but Charles could see no way that his friend would ever recover from this — oversight.

Then Mallory showed him the way.

"We don't have to turn it over to Kronewald," she said. Anticipating him, she added, "So the freak is never identified — so what? It's better this way." She snatched the license from his hand and then gathered up the maps and bits of paper on the bed. "The reporters probably have film of the fake Kayhill. They'd splash his face all over the tube." She jammed the contents back into the bag. "They'd turn up leads and backtrack his life all the way to Illinois. Then there'd be the books and movies — TV specials — all for a child killer." She seemed indignant over these events that had not happened yet. "And the public — they just *love* their killers. They wouldn't be able to get enough of this one. And all those murdered kids. Can you see the media chewing on their bones?" She dropped the tote bag into a metal wastebasket. "You think that's why Riker ditched the evidence?"

What?

Not waiting for an answer, she carried the wastebasket out to the balcony. "It fits. I've never heard Riker use a child killer's name. He always calls them cockroaches." She turned to the neighboring balcony, leaning over the rail for a better look at the windows of the next room.

Checking for eavesdroppers — witnesses?

She looked down at the contents of the wastebasket. "If the chain of possession ever led back to Riker, he'd lose his badge. But he couldn't destroy evidence — he just couldn't go that far." She came back inside and walked up to Charles. "So he gave it to you. But you're not the type to collect souvenirs from a murder."

What now? Was she accusing him of something?

"I told you," he said, "Riker thought the California map might be useful."

"He knew you'd throw away the rest of it."

What rubbish. However, in a twisted way, he looked upon this rationale of hers as a sign of healing; Mallory was more herself, for only a truly paranoid personality could come up with a contrivance as tortured and far-flung as this one.

No — that was unfair.

Her bedrock for this cracked idea was her absolute faith in her partner. She would never come up with any scenario where that man could make an error as careless and costly as this one. She must believe the bag had been given to Riker after the case was closed. Or did she?

"What if the New Mexico police come looking for their evidence?"

"The chance is pretty slim." She took his arm and led him through the open door to the balcony. "Kronewald helped them close out Kayhill's murder, and they pinned it on the right man. No harm done. Odds are, they think one of their own guys lost the bag. And they'd be right about that. No receipt — that's really sloppy police work." Mallory looked down and nudged the wastebasket with her shoe. "I'm a cop. I can't destroy evidence."

However, Charles apparently could, for now she handed him a book of matches.

"Up to you," she said. "If you burn it, Riker can never know about this. Nobody can. You understand that, right?"

Indeed.

Mallory would continue to believe the worst of her partner and trust him less because of that — if Charles could only keep his silence and commit a crime to obfuscate Riker's innocence.

She walked back inside, closing the glass door behind her, and now the drapes were also closing. No need to watch — to witness. She had every confidence that he would break the law for her.

Left alone on the balcony, he looked down at the metal wastebasket — and the evidence. After railing against Dale Berman's incompetence, Riker would be destroyed by this oversight of his own — a detail missed, a life lost. Armed with the identity of a serial killer, a man known on sight, the Finns' FBI escort would have been searching faces instead of shadows, and they would have detected the fugitive in their midst. If not for Riker's failure to inspect a small bag — Christine Nahlman would not have died.

Was Mallory convinced that her partner had committed the crime of concealing evidence? Or did she guess the truth in that moment when she handed over the driver's license with its damning photograph? Had she detected a flicker of horror on Charles's face — his tell-all face? He could never risk posing the question to her, and she knew it. Or did she? He would never know. But this was a knot worthy of Mallory, tied with threads of truth and lies and loyalty, and it could not be undone.

Everyone was tainted except for Charles Butler, the last one standing with clean hands — until he struck the match.

EPILOGUE

They continued on a northern route up the coast highway, fairylands of woods breaking into dazzling vistas of rock cliffs and crashing ocean waves. Charles was beginning to enjoy the road. The scary, hairy turns made it more like a carnival ride with a view. When he gave the wheel over to Mallory, her malaise seemed to brighten, and he picked this lighter moment to ask about her father's eyeglasses.

No, she did not remember if he had been wearing glasses when she saw him all those years ago. "Probably not. Ray Adler said he never wore them."

And now Charles had her permission to ransack her knapsack for the old photographs and the letters. He sifted through the pictures of young Peyton Hale, studying them by the poor light of the dashboard. In every snapshot, a pair of wire-rimmed spectacles rested in the man's shirt pocket.

"He always kept them close — the glasses."

But he never wore them. Neither did Riker. Did Peyton Hale also have the flaw of vanity? That would explain so much.

Mallory's concentration was elsewhere. Her eyes were on the twisty road, the ride. She simply did not care why Peyton Hale had passed her by on that faraway beach in her childhood. Charles might as well be talking to himself when he said, "He's very young in these photos. His prescription for glasses would've been much stronger by the time you met him. You could be mistaken about —"

Oh, no. She was listening that time, and how dare he challenge her? She turned to glare at him while completing a sharp turn with the precision of a missile guidance system, no sign of human fear for the inch-away trees and rocks in the headlights. "He *saw* me, Charles. He was as close as you are now. He looked right at me. But he didn't recognize my face, my *mother's* face."

Well — Mallory the Machine was back.

Charles sensed more progress in these moments when he irritated her the most. She was rebuilding herself, taking back all the flyaway pieces, the paranoia, the suspicion and her cold calculation for debit columns of cheats and losses. Cold as stone, but such a lovely face — unforgettable. In the old black-and-white photographs, it might well be Mallory standing beside Peyton Hale, so alike were mother and daughter.

With the aid of her penlight, Charles read the letters written for O.B. They had been authored by a deeply romantic man, though there was nothing to say that Peyton had ever taken a lover and not one word about Cassandra's coming child. The letters were all about Route 66, the man's only passion. In one context, they comprised a book of rules on how to live in a world of constant motion, where the road could suddenly shift beneath the traveler's wheels or vanish from sight. Every line was polished prose and suitable for publication.

And the opening — for O.B.? A book title perhaps, or the initials of an editor.

Mallory must have been so disappointed in these pages, for her theory was vindicated here: When the letters were all one had to go by, it seemed that she and her mother had never existed.

The silver convertible drove on in a winding fashion, climbing, climbing, and then came a sensation approaching freefall as they dropped down the roller-coaster road in the dark, kissing mountainside then leafy branches. They were heading toward that far patch of coastline once visited by fourteen-year-old Kathy Mallory. He could see her as she was then, a girl poised on a beach at the edge of the world — so young to have no safety net — so full of hope for this meeting of father and child. Then came the moment. And the child had walked away alone.

It was a rare road that had three endings and one resolution.

They had arrived in this small coastal community at an unnatural hour for visiting. And so it was morning when the silver car pulled away from the hotel on Main Street and rolled through the fog that shrouded Mendocino, California. The sun had risen hours ago; Charles took this on faith since he could not see it.

Not an auspicious beginning for the day.

The road climbed up through cloudland, and the car broke into bright sunlight and lush green forest thick with fern and flowering plants. There were no houses visible from the road, only lot numbers to tell him that the more reclusive citizens of Mendocino were in there somewhere. These outlying rural householders seemed to like their privacy. The car approached a small dirt road that could only be a private driveway, and here Charles slowed a bit for there was no number to be read on the mailbox — in fact no mailbox, only a broken post. Half of it protruded from the ground, and the rest of it lay on the grass, having fallen victim to wood rot.

Through breaks in the foliage, he could see a man walking down the driveway and carrying a mailbox attached to a sound new post. His hair had silvered in middle age, but Peyton Hale was not an altogether different creature. The boy of the photographs remained in his lined and sun-brown face. His shape was much the same and still clad in blue jeans and a T-shirt. The cords of his arms stood out in bold relief as he pulled the remains of the rotted post from the ground.

Charles rolled onto the side of the road and cut off the engine.

The broken wood was cradled in one arm when the man looked up, as people will do when a stranger comes calling. The vehicle surprised him, and his smile was wide.

Nostalgia?

Most likely, for this car was the image of Peyton's own silver Volkswagen convertible, and he must have found it worthy of closer scrutiny. With his free hand, he reached into a breast pocket and pulled out a pair of wire-rimmed spectacles with thick lenses. He donned them in the moment that Mallory stepped out of the car to face him down on this road.

Her shoulders rolled back, and her feet were planted slightly apart in pugilist fashion. She would give him one more opportunity — only one — to know her by her mother's face and his own green eyes staring back at him.

Charles remained behind the wheel. His heart ached for her; she had set the bar far too high. He whispered a litany, "Last chance . . . last chance . . ."

An answered prayer — Peyton Hale was turned to stone.

It was easy to follow the workings of the mind behind those bespectacled eyes so magnified and shocked wide — then shattered. Charles could virtually see Peyton's brain crashing with the overload of irony in memory and possibility — the hammer fall of Savannah's lies. Here before him was the living evidence that Cassandra had not died with his child still inside her.

Peyton's mouth contorted in pain, as if his daughter had stabbed him in the heart — and, in a very Mallory way, she had. Now her father had no bones, legs failing him, arms dangling and helpless. The old mailbox post dropped to the earth, and Charles feared the man would also fall. Peyton's eyes were fixed upon his daughter's face, the image of her mother, and Charles Butler well understood the man's new expression. He called it *epiphany,* the hallelujah of a father who has beheld his child for the first time — his perfect child. Still unsteady on his feet, he reached out for her, as if she could save him. "Our baby," he said.

Charles closed his eyes. Of course — *our baby.* Peyton's child had not yet been named when the man had begun his final road trip. The letters for O.B. had been written to Mallory before she was ever born. Her father's passion for a vanishing highway was his present to welcome her into the world. He had wanted to give her his road before it was gone.

Upon opening his eyes again, Charles saw that it was Mallory who had fallen. She was on her knees, her face full of tears. Her head was thrown back, and she was laughing, *laughing.*

Charles was awed by this evidence that all her possibilities were intact, and he had no more fears for her. Joy augured well for a life worth living.

Not wanting to play the voyeur at this

reunion of the lost father and the lost child, he turned the car around, steering it toward the hotel in town, and the silver convertible descended below the fog line. Charles Butler had completed his assignment per Riker's request, though not in the anticipated order of things, not the specified destination or even the proper route; but he had seen the lady home.

And Mallory's road was run.

ABOUT THE AUTHOR

Carol O'Connell is the author of nine Mallory novels, including the national best-seller *Winter House,* and of *Judas Child.* She lives in New York City.

The employees of Thorndike Press hope you have enjoyed this Large Print book. All our Thorndike and Wheeler Large Print titles are designed for easy reading, and all our books are made to last. Other Thorndike Press Large Print books are available at your library, through selected bookstores, or directly from us.

For information about titles, please call:
(800) 223-1244

or visit our Web site at:
www.gale.com/thorndike
www.gale.com/wheeler

To share your comments, please write:
Publisher
Thorndike Press
295 Kennedy Memorial Drive
Waterville, ME 04901